Sharing Hamilton

Sharing Hamilton

The Reynolds Affair, The Nation's First
Sex Scandal

Diana Rubino and Brian L. Porter

Dedicated to the memory of Enid Ann Porter, 1913 –
2004
Always in my thoughts

Introduction

Romance, deceit, blackmail, betrayal and murder are very much to the fore as historical novelist Diana Rubino and bestselling thriller author Brian L. Porter join forces to present a stunning fictional account of the U.S.A.'s first acknowledged sex-scandal, The Reynolds Affair. Ms. Rubino has taken the historical facts of the well-documented affair and added her own fictional twist, with Mr. Porter adding his unique touch, introducing a serial killer stalking the dark night-time streets of Philadelphia.

As Alexander Hamilton and Maria Reynolds conduct their nefarious relationship, behind closed doors, a supposed madman is on the streets attacking and killing the young innocent servants of the wealthy. British-born 'doctor of women's medicine,' Dr. Severus Black, newly arrived from Paris, quickly becomes a close confidante of Hamilton's wife Elizabeth, but could the debonair doctor also be hiding a closely guarded secret?

Together, U.S. award-winning author Diana Rubino and British award-winning author Brian L. Porter have created a tour de force that shouldn't be missed. Without further delay, we present, for your edification and entertainment, SHARING HAMILTON.

Chapter One

Maria Reynolds

Home of Congressman Jonathan Dayton, New York, December 20, 1790

Where is he? On tiptoe, craning my neck, I searched the crowded room for Alexander Hamilton. I never forgot our first meeting ... our gazes locked...time stood still. Oh, for a glimpse of those violet eyes.

"Maria!"

I jumped. My husband's eyes blazed as h e draped my cloak over my shoulders. "We're leaving." He steered me toward the door.

"James, what are you—" We dashed into the frosty evening to our fancy carriage—hired for tonight. I slid inside, shivering.

"Home, post haste," he ordered the coachman and climbed in next to me.

I caught my breath. "James, what happened in there?"

He cleared his throat, his jaw grinding. It chilled me more than the cold seat seeping through my skirts. "We're leaving town and not coming back. When we get home, start packing."

Fear clutched my heart. "What have you done now? Cease your nattering and tell me what happened," I demanded, past politeness. "Why must we flee this time?" My voice rose to a desperate shriek.

He drew a deep breath but still wouldn't look me in the eye. "Jon and I were discussing our business venture—"

"Which business venture? Keeping track of your schemes makes my head spin." I flattened my palms to my throbbing temples.

"The land parcels in Ohio. Our words got heated. I questioned his honesty in handling my half of the investment." His voice faltered. "Before I could blink, he challenged me to a duel."

I fell back against the cushion as if struck.

"I have no intention of dueling him," he declared. "Ah'm too young to die on a field of honor. Hence, we are leaving town."

"James, you—" I wished I could spew forth 'coward' or 'weasel' but I never spoke to my husband in this manner. "You cannot run from a challenge. He will find you, surely."

"Not if we reach the Pine Barrens of New Jersey by tomorrow nightfall. We have three days to abscond," he mumbled, gazing through the window. "I need re-

4

turn this vehicle, purchase a cheap one and a decent draft horse—"

I interrupted, "And do you plan for us to hide in the Pine Barrens indefinitely?"

His shoulders relaxed and he tugged at his lace collar. The rise and fall of his chest slowed as he settled into the seat. "Of course not." He shook his head. "We're going to Philadelphia."

"By God, that is over two hundred miles away!" My fingers curled into fists.

"And a fine place to thrive, as say all the folk I know there." He turned to face me. "My crony Sam Bass discovered abundant opportunity for advancement. Charles Olton reported the class barriers are not so high. There's hope of hurdling them." He waved a hand as if this move were across the road. "Hence, I shall flourish there." He returned his gaze to the darkness outside.

I leant forward and grasped his sleeve. "And Jon won't find you hurdling over all these class barriers?" I challenged.

He glanced my way, brow cocked. "He'll not follow me there. He'll die in the bed he was birthed in. But for us, we shall explore the new frontier. Then mayhap later on, we kin move west."

He'd plotted all this between shirking on a duel and dashing into this carriage. Exasperation planted a fiery ball in my stomach. Although we'd moved four times in three years, for economic reasons—nonpayment of rent, joblessness—never had we fled two hundred miles. Fighting my anguish, I wondered … *hmm, this move could add a spark to my life.*

I didn't realize until late that night what that spark was.

Philadelphia, the Nation's Capital…

…the new Treasury Secretary, Alexander Hamilton, lived there.

Eliza Hamilton

Mon., December 20, 1790

I preened like a fairy princess draped in my new crimson gown of brocade adorned with Brussels lace and pointed bodice. Specks of powder dusted my rolled hairpiece, my cheeks rouged like cherries on alabaster. My flash fawney, a string of pearls and ear-bobs, completed the ensemble. Posing at the looking glass, I twirled. The skirt whooshed as it swirled round me. After spending all day chasing tots, I became a debutante again.

I looked forward to this holiday soirée at the home of Jon Dayton, one of Alex's friends from the Congress. Our coach pulled up to his door as a man and woman dashed into the coach in front of us, far grander than ours. The man looked like James Reynolds. *Is that his wife or one of his doxies?* I wondered as it rumbled away.

A servant ushered us into Dayton's parlour. As we mingled, the delightful strains of a string quartet floated through the air. "There he is." I gestured to Alex as I spotted Jon wandering the room alone. Hunched over, he puffed on a cheroot.

"There you are, my good man." Alex halted the congressman.

Jon gave us a shaky smile. "Good eve, Alex, Eliza." He bowed first to Alex, then to me.

"You appear distraught." My husband placed a hand on Jon's shoulder in almost motherly concern.

Jon's darting eyes and fidgety hands warned me. *Uh-oh, something is amiss.* He took a deep breath, wiping sweat from his brow. "Sorry. My mind is elsewhere. I must tell you, as my most trusted friends—" He released a sigh. "I've challenged a man to a duel."

I lifted my fan to hide my gaping mouth. "Saints above, Jon, who?" Alex asked him.

"J—Jimmy Reynolds," he stuttered getting the name out, as if he could not believe it himself.

"Reynolds?" Alex shook his head. "I just saw him leave. Why, you're closer than most brothers. What brought this on?"

"You know Jimmy and his Scots temper—sorry, no offense—we entered an argument, it grew hostile, and we're to meet at the Weehawken riverbank Friday next. Alex, I must ask you—will you be my second?"

Raw panic shook me. Dear God, why couldn't Jon ask Aaron Burr? He was everybody's second. I glanced about but didn't see Burr among the guests. "Alex—" I clutched my husband's sleeve, tracing finger marks in the velvet. "I want you nowhere near that dreadful place."

7

"I shall be honored, Jon." He faced me, his eyes stating, *silence, little wife.* Anger drew my lips tight.

After Jon excused himself, I turned to Alex. "Oh, poor Maria. I wish I could console her." I still seethed with anger at my husband, but at least he wouldn't be the one dueling. "She's a bright girl from a respectable family Why did she settle for the likes of James Reynolds?"

"Who knows what attracts one to another?" He shook his head. "Since James lost his bid for the Continental Congress, he's been branded a loser in our circles. Let's hope he loses the duel, too."

Maria

Phila., Wednesday, August 3, 1791

"Hell's bells, Maria, ye think I'm made o'gold?" James thundered as I entered our parlour laden with packages: a bottle of Madeira, a satin bonnet to match my new pelisse, and kid gloves, having left my old pair at the White Rose Coffeehouse.

"These are hardly extravagances. After all, you boasted you made three hundred dollars last month." I relished reliving the moment when he showered coins and notes all over our bed, foretelling how I was "coming into money."

I dumped the packages onto our new Rococo settee. "Do you want your wife looking like a slattern?" I flicked his gold watch fob, which he'd bought because "Hugh Dugan has a new one."

"Nay, but you ain't Mrs. James Monroe, either, so dinna try puttin' on airs like her."

"Mrs. Monroe couldn't get a rise out of you if you downed three scores of oysters. She's frigid—so I hear." I smirked, slapping his thigh with my new gloves.

"At least she reads all the books she owns. Did you ever read any of these flub-dubs?" He swiped at my row of leather-bound books, knocking Volume I of Shakespeare to the floor.

"Of course I've read them. Twicet and thricet." I picked up my well-worn Bard tome and replaced it on the shelf. "I read the Bard's plays over and over. But I never discuss England with strangers. Too dangerous these days."

"You know more about Macbeth than about me," James scoffed. He stood the new Madeira bottle on our table and uncorked it with the screw he wore on his key chain.

"All *you* read are those tittle-tattle sheets," I accused, and rightly. He paraded his brotherhood with the scandal mongering Thom Callender, whose weekly tabloid tarnished many a sterling reputation, from senators down to their stable boys.

"Aye, and mayhap our names will appear in them someday." He poured wine into his pewter tankard he'd named Douglas. Hard-swilling males named their tankards *and* their members. James bestowed "Canute the Great" upon his member—but I hadn't the heart to tell him it was less than accurate.

"I keep our private life private. So don't blabber to Callender about what a tigress I am," I teased as he poured me a goblet of wine.

"Nay, I shan't. But ah'm glad you brought it up. Sit down, Maria, we need to talk." He clasped my fingers and walked me to one of our matching Chippendale chairs—his last splurge from a profitable venture—and pushed down on my shoulders till I sat.

"Brought what up? Talk about what?" I trembled. I never knew from one day to the next what—or who—James would bring home.

"Have you more 'golden geese'? I hope so. We can use some more plate and furniture." We moved "up" thrice since settling here. We now dwelt in a three-story brick townhome on Pine Street with one outbuilding. We always rented. "Or can we finally buy a house of our own?" I fixed my gaze upon my husband of seven years. Our passion and lust matured into love and devotion, but the desire lingered on.

He'd been an apprentice and journeyman goldsmith until the Revolution, but he hadn't the capital nor the patience to rise to master. He made a gold chamber pot for his most famous client, Thomas "all men are created equal" Jefferson, and his reputation grew from there. But goldsmithing wasn't enough for James. He lived by his wits and one scheme after another. He groomed and dressed as a dandy, but when he opened his mouth, he made it obvious he hailed from a Glasgow slum.

I harbored mixed feelings about it—I admired his shrewdness, yet he courted disaster, speculating in land deals and currency. With my urging, he ran for the Continental Congress but lost to his friend Dayton. No hard feelings. James didn't want the job. Too much traveling. As I gazed at his muscular figure 'neath his tight britches, a familiar surge of desire warmed me. With his swarthy good looks and persuasive charm, he made a fitting match for politics.

With his political run over, he served a brief sentence for counterfeiting. He posted bail, but our landlord evicted us. I stayed by his side as we trawled the streets of New York in the dead of winter, scrounging for lodgings.

"No golden geese this time, my pet. Not yet, anyways." He took a sip.

Disappointment crushed me. "I fear this announcement more than all your other schemes. What is it?" I gulped the fruity wine, hoping to be tipsy for this.

He scraped his chair back and sat, fingering his watch. Whenever he fiddled with his watch or rings from Ben Franklin's estate auction, I knew something vexed him.

"Maria..." His eyes pierced mine. My heart sank farther. "We were well on our way to being gentry till this morn. I lost it all on a land deal." His eyes dropped. "For the now, we stand on the line between hard up and impoverished."

My ire heated me head to toe. "What about the two thousand you invested?" I struggled to steady my voice. "The shares in the Bank of the United States?" Alexander Hamilton created the bank earlier this year, although James didn't like the Treasury Secretary. He called him a snob to his face. "How could you be so irresponsible?" I grabbed the nearest object, a brass candlestick, but he snatched it away afore I could fling it.

"It looked like a sure thing...but ah'll make more." Another of his promises. "Til then, we're one hunk of bread, these wine bottles, and a dram of whisky from malnourishment. And five days from eviction. The rent comes due Monday."

I shook with fear. "There you go, pulling it out from under us, as you do time and time again! When will you learn, James?" I had some coin hidden. But after that—what? Too distraught to even look at him, I swept away tears of exasperation with my clenched fist.

"Money slips through your fingers like shucked oysters." My voice shook. My entire body shook. "I know not how much more of this I can take. What's next, the almshouse?"

As he stroked my cheek, my rage yielded to pity. He'd become poor in an endless quest to be rich. "No, we'll never resort to the almshouse. Before we met, I lived in a stable whilst seeking work, too proud to apply to the almshouse as a pauper."

I released a deep breath. "Oh, James, I love you so, but I feel trapped, with nowhere to go but up and down with you." Desperate for a solution, I began spewing forth ideas about what I could do: "I can take in laundry. Or work as a cook. Or a whitewasher. Or a soap maker." I paced the floorboards, wringing my hands. Then a much better source of income struck me. "I can give violin instruction to those toffynoses in the court end of town!"

He cleared his throat and shook his head. "Bah to all that. Listen. I know a brilliant way to make money—a lot more money—in a shorter time than ever before. And it involves Alexander Hamilton, Mr. Treasury himself."

At the sound of his name, I heated up. That recurring memory made me tingle all over: the first time I'd met Mr. Hamilton, his violet eyes nestled on my décolletage, his russet hair glinted in the candlelight, his lips kissed my hand—my heart surged just thinking about it.

"What about Al—him?"

"I dinna know the chap intimately, but I do know his weakness: beautiful women. Adams once said 'Hamilton's ambitions have their source in a superabundance of secretions he could not find whores enough to draw off.' " He clucked, as if in disapproval. "Tis not idle gossip. If a curmudgeon like Adams knows about it, tis true. Secondly—" He refilled Douglas to the rim. "Hamilton recently got embroiled in a payoff scheme, being seen with a trull. He favors paying hush money, rather than harm his reputation. Hence—we can chip away at that weak spot and wear it down farther."

I shook my head. "Already I do not like this. Underneath the bad metaphors, you are saying you can bilk Al—Secretary Hamilton out of some money."

"Tis not bilking, dear wife. He shall git something much more valuable in return."

I paused. "I'm afraid to ask, but ... such as?"

He cracked a smile and winked. "You."

Chapter Two

Eliza

"Indeed my Dear Betsey you do not write to me often enough. I ought at least to hear from you by every post and yer last letter is as old as the middle of Sept. I have written you twice since my return from Hartford." – Early Love Letter from Alexander Hamilton to Elizabeth Schuyler

Albany, NY, Fryday, August 12, 1791

Tis ever so hot and I am heavy with child. Thursday last, Alex insisted the children and I retreat to Albany. Hence the six of us came, with two maidservants and a nurse. I took ill in the carriage and used Philip's lap as a pillow. He's ever so manly at nine and a half. Albany is equally hot, though a breeze stirs here under the willow tree.

I miss Alex and wrote him thrice already. Whilst courting, he wrote frequent letters, but mine were rare. I had no confidence with my grammar to pen a clever letter. I convinced Angelica to write him in my stead. The most educated of us girls, she attended the nation's finest girls' school. Her first letter to Alex and his immediate reply blossomed into a regular correspondence, which they continue to this day. Tis obvious she is smitten with him. Her letters to him resemble that of an ardent lover rather than a married woman to her brother-in-law. As the most beautiful of us three, she eloped first, claiming to love John Church. But I am the lucky one who won—and kept—the gold. I swell with pride as women swoon over Alex. Yet he always shuns them. Tis his nature to labor on his financial programs and law practice rather than chase coquettes.

After ten years of marriage, I am still his bride. If one examines the Schuylers, one will see that some of us married "down," that is, for love. I fell in love with Alex the minute I set my eyes upon his. I hounded Papa to introduce us. At first he refused—"Hamilton is a cad!"

"Not true," I'd corrected Papa, "But so what he courts Kitty and Susan Livingston at the same time?"

Then Papa directly quoted John Adams: "He's the bastard brat of a Scots pedlar who left his mother."

"True enough, Papa," I conceded. "His father didn't marry his mother and abandoned them, but is that Alex's fault?"

"He is a foreigner," he further accused.

"Wrong there, Papa," I informed him. "He was born on Nevis and grew up on St. Croix, but now he's as American as President Washington."

"He may have Negro blood."

"Entirely not true!" I protested. "His bloodline is of Scottish nobility, strewn with royal titles including viscounts, barons and dukes."

Then came more reasons—Alex's elitism, believing the aristocracy should rule. Why would Papa object to that? We came from tough pioneer stock, but had a mansion in Albany, a summer estate in Saratoga, silver, carriages and servants. My father was a Continental Congressman, a Major General of the Continental Army, and a U.S. Senator.

That led to his most important concern of all— "He is marrying you for money and advancement."

Alas, I could not disprove this. "But even if that were true," I defended Alex, "he still loves me."

I was so in love with Alex, I'd live in a garret with him. I sought him out behind my father's back. Our destinies met at my Aunt Gertrude's soirée in Morristown. We met in secret, our rendezvous thrilling and forbidden. I climbed out the same window both my sisters had eloped from, just for a stolen hour with Alex.

But he entered Papa's good graces the night he refused to hide any longer. He strode into the drawing room, greeted Papa with all the charm and bearing of the lieutenant he was, and asked for my hand in marriage. Papa gushed, "Why, yes, Secretary Hamilton, I would be honored to have you as a son-in-law." I think Papa was just relieved I wouldn't leap out the window to elope. Then Alex turned to me and with a flourish, took from his waistcoat pocket a small box. Opening it, I gasped. Two entwined gold bands glinted up at me. Through tears of joy, I read the sentiments engraved on each ring:

Alexander and Eliza.

Coupled for eternity.

"Oh, yes, Alex." I clutched the harpsichord to steady myself. "Nothing—or nobody—will ever come between us."

But many things—and many bodies—have come between us.

This summer President Washington is keeping Alex busy running the Treasury Department, the Customs, and starting up the Bank of United States. Far too complicated for me, he modeled it after the Bank of England to create credit. I did understand that Thomas Jefferson considered it unconstitutional. He and Alex always rowed over it.

Alex was the son Washington never had, and Alex told me that the president held harmony in his "official family" highly.

From what Alex explained to me, he envisioned a central bank for the new nation, instead of separate ones for each colony, with so many different kinds of money. After Alex's enemies tried to stop its creation, Congress chartered the bank this year. Alex headquartered it near our Philadelphia home, and it sold 25,000 shares in the initial offering. I remember him telling me the bank would have $10 million when they all sold. I almost fainted. I didn't think there was $10 million in the whole world! But he invested what we had, assuring me "we're sitting on a gold mine."

The Bank of the United States soared in popularity, shares in high demand. We may be sitting on a gold mine, but I still have to dig deep to pay the bills.

Alex is also beginning the third of his great state papers, his Report on Manufactures. I don't understand it all, but gentleman farmers such as Jefferson oppose it. Alex wants to secure our independence by manufacturing, disallowing imported goods, and encouraging inventions. Personally, I agree with Jefferson on this—I believe this would greatly decrease the number of farmers and landowners. But what do I know?

If Alex is not busy enough, his "pastime" is battling Jefferson in the press, attacking him in scathing articles under the pseudonym "H. Bent" for "Hell Bent." He also maintains his law practice. All this leaves scant time for socializing—and for us.

At that moment I decided to go home for an unexpected visit. Ah, will he be surprised!

She must be young, handsome (I lay most stress upon a good shape) sensible (a little learning will do), well bred (but she must have an aversion to the word ton), chaste and tender (I am enthusiast in my notions of fidelity and fondness), of some good nature, a great deal of generosity (she must neither love money nor scolding, for I dislike a termagant and an economist). She must believe in God and hate a saint. But as to fortune, the larger stock of that the better. - Alexander Hamilton on finding a wife, 1779.

Maria

I sat stunned. My mouth gaped wide enough for hornets to nest. The wine soured in my stomach. I dared not ask James to repeat his words. "This is the most preposterous scheme you've ever hatched. It even tops your last invention." That was a microscope he claimed magnified a louse to twelve feet long. Many gullible souls paid three shillings for this spectacle, netting James a tidy sum.

"First, you'll invite Hamilton here for a tryst," he continued as if deciding where to play marbles, "and when you've rendered him helpless under yur feminine spell, preferably with his britches round his ankles, I burst in and demand compensation for eclipsing my wife's honor. That will net us a few hundred. I shall request a hundred up front, and knowing his generous nature, he'll up it to two hundred."

A shiver rattled my bones. "James, this outlandish plot is naught short of prostitution! I refuse to seduce a man I hardly know."

I could almost hear his wheels grinding. His eyes fixed on a knot in the table's wood. His foot tapped a beat on the floorboard. "Git him to return for another bit o'honey," he thought out loud, ignoring my refusal, "and I shall request a larger sum, in exchange for my silence. We'll collect thousands from the upstanding secretary! And he'd never breathe a word of it to his cronies, 'specially that knobdobber Burr. With a wife and six pups, Hamilton's reputation and entire career would come crashing down." He slapped his palm on the table, rattling the silver tea service. "We'll milk him dry!"

"*We*? Do you intend to seduce him as well? No, James, this is not going to happen." I held up my hands, shaking my head, teeth clenched.

"Look, Maria, you are my wife, and you will do as I say. Now go fetch some o' that coin you got layin' round—" He waved his hand airily. "And buy yurself some perfume or rouge or—whatever it is you ladies smear on to lure us out of our senses. And fetch us some supper as well."

I shot him my sourest scowl. "Did you not hear a word I said? I shan't seduce Alexander Hamilton!" The thought of it made my palms sweat. I wiped them on my skirt.

"Maria, there are worse men than he. He's cleanly. He has all his teeth. Tis not like ah'm foisting you upon John Adams."

"No matter who it is, this is naught short of pimping me," I declared.

He splayed his fingers. "I thought you'd be pleased I think highly enough of you to choose someone of his caliber. I've seen men fob their wives off to the lowliest curs, for much less than Hamilton is capable of providing."

I narrowed my eyes and stood my ground. "Nay, James, I shan't do it. And I cannot remain your wife if you think so little of me, my body, our vows, as to sell me." Not granting him a last word, I grabbed the Chaucer book containing my hoarded stash and leapt up the steps to pack a bag.

I had to leave him.

I stuffed my carpet bag to bursting with a dress and undergarments. I dashed down the stairs and swept past him.

He glanced at me, fingers circled round his tankard. "Ah, gonna fetch supper? Git me half a capon and a pickled egg."

"Fetch your own supper," I called over my shoulder. "I am leaving you. I shall send for the remainder of my possessions. Unless you sell them first."

I threw the door open. He shouted, "Come back here, Maria!"

"Take your pickled eggs and stuff them wide end first!" I slammed the door behind me. My rapid steps broke into a run. Before turning the corner, I peered over my shoulder. He hadn't followed. I heaved a relieved sigh. Catching my breath, I asked myself: *Where to now?*

I knew of many boardinghouses in Southwark, an area occupied by the lower sort. It was all I could afford. Scurrying south, I prayed for a vacant room. Else it was sleep on the street. My money would not last but a few days. I cooked up a few ways to stave off starvation.

The first boardinghouse was full. Dejected, I dragged myself farther down Christian Street. Two more landlords turned me away. I trudged east toward the river. Trembling in fear, I approached Hell

Town, packed with bawdy taverns and "disorderly houses." But with nowhere else to go, I headed in that direction. Mayhap Mary Norris had room in her lodging house on Drinker's Alley, one block south of "Three Jolly Irishmen," Philadelphia's toughest tavern.

I approached the shabby wood-framed row house and knocked. The door squealed on its rusty hinges as it swung open. There stood a splatter-aproned Mrs. Norris puffing on a pipe.

"Why, Miss—eh—" She scratched her head under her mob cap as she looked me up and down as if to say she knew me, but not from where.

"I'm not a Miss. I'm Mrs. Reynolds. I need a room for a few days." *Please don't ask why,* I silently begged, and mercifully, she did not.

"All I've got's the garret room, luv. Two dolls fifty cents in advance, and one doll fifty a day."

More than I could afford, but either that or the street. I opened my purse and handed her the money. I climbed three flights of stairs to the sweltering back room, threw the window open to the sultry night and collapsed on the rickety cot.

Chapter Three

Eliza

"May I only be as successful in pleasing you, and may you be as happy as I shall ever wish to make you!" – Love Letter from Alexander Hamilton to Elizabeth Schuyler

Feminine instinct told me that Alex suffered terrible loneliness without me. In my third letter this week, I expressed my desire to come home, to alleviate his tension. "My angel," he replied two weeks later, "Let me know beforehand your determination that I may meet you at New York."

How sweet of my darling Alex, interrupting his work to journey to New York and travel home together. But I shan't have it.

I shall make the journey alone and surprise him! I shall arrive at our house in the dead of night, tiptoe up the steps and into our bedroom, where my beloved sleeps, whisper words of love, my lips upon his.

That night at dinner, I told the family, "I plan to surprise Alex in Philadelphia, then I'll return to finish the summer in clean air and your familial affection."

They all stared, stricken, as if I'd told them I planned to paddle a canoe across the ocean.

"But, Mother, your journey here was so difficult," Philip reminded me, the caretaker, wise beyond his years. His mathematical calculations looked Greek to me.

"I shall be fine." I dismissed the harrowing two-hundred-thirty mile journey, relishing the moment I'd touch my husband's lips with mine, and the bliss that would follow. "He needs me, I know it in my heart," I added, to assure myself that it was no whim. "I know what he is thinking, and especially what he's feeling. Our love transcends great distances."

"Then," said Papa, "I must insist that you at least consult with Dr. Black before embarking on such a journey. If he assures us all is well and you are strong enough to undertake such a trial, then you may go with our blessing."

Ah, the mention of that name evoked tingly sensations inside me. I'd first encountered Dr. Severus Black at one of Alex's soirées to raise funds for his political crony Jon Dayton. By the doors to the garden, a gaggle of adoring females, young and old, surrounded the handsome figure. How he sensed my interest I do not know, but when I blinked, his cobalt blue eyes seemed to burn into mine. Even from that distance, his eyes stood out. With his gaze fixed on me, he excused himself from his harem of admirers.

He strode straight up to me and halted within embracing distance.

"Mrs. Hamilton, our hostess, I presume?" His deep voice greeted me with resonance...and a sensuous English accent.

"You have me at a disadvantage, sir." My knees wobbled.

"Forgive me." He bent slightly forward and took my hand, raised it to his lips and kissed it as a gentlemen should. "Dr. Severus Black at your service. Your husband intended to introduce us, but it appears I have beaten him to the pleasure."

He towered over me, his hair and his clothes black, his boots polished to a mirror-like finish. But much as he smiled when speaking, that smile somehow failed to touch his eyes, which bored into me, as though reaching through to my soul. I failed to suppress an involuntary shiver.

He noticed it. "Are you cold, madam?"

"No, no, just a sudden chill from the open window, I think." I shivered and sweated at the same time.

My husband appeared as if by magic, full of apology. "Ah, you two have met, I see. I'm sorry for not being here to introduce you to my wife, Severus, but I see I now have no need."

The next few minutes passed in a blur as Alex informed me that Dr. Black was newly arrived from England, via Paris, France of all places. "He's a specialist in 'women's matters', Alex went on, then added, "Doctor, I wish you to examine Mrs. Hamilton to ensure all is well with her state of health."

Stunned as if stung, I said, "Alex, I'm in no need of a physician right now."

But as I was clearly great with child, our third, the doctor assured me, "Mrs. Hamilton, I shall care for you far better than any American physician, if you'll give me the chance. Our training in England is far more intense than what the quacks get here." Once again that smile curved his lips, but his eyes stayed as steely as if he'd witnessed a murder.

Of course Alex's wishes prevailed. The following week I attended the first of a number of pre-natal consultations with the well-trained doctor.

As I approached my confinement, Dr. Black behaved with impeccable propriety towards me, yet I felt a certain antipathy towards him. Why, I couldn't say, and made it my business to keep our appointments as short as possible. I didn't linger for small talk or scrutiny of my other body parts. But those eyes—they amazed and enthralled me. I couldn't stop myself from peering into them at each appointment. This always elicited a smile that never reached his eyes.

Returning to the here and now, I realized I had little choice but to accede to Papa's request. "Very well, I'll send for Dr. Black."

He arrived within the week, and thankfully, in a short examination, pronounced me fit to travel. "Shall we travel back to New York City together?" The doctor gestured at his fancy coach and matched grays gracing Papa's gravel drive.

I refused. "Oh, no, Dr. Black. I'm not sure when I'm departing. And you need return to your practice." I showed him the door. A three-day journey alone with him? I trembled at the thought.

Why I experienced these feelings when in close proximity to the doctor I couldn't say, for he always treated me with courtesy and respect. Still, as his coach's wheels crunched over the drive and clattered into the distance, I released a sigh of relief. I downed the sleeping draft he'd left for me and slept like the dead.

At daybreak, servants loaded my trunks onto the carriage. I kissed my children goodbye—for now. Papa helped me into the carriage and handed me a basket of provisions.

In three days I'd be locked in my husband's arms.

I'd never surprised Alex before, with anything. Even when expecting our babies, he seemed to know before I did. So this would be the greatest surprise I'd ever bestow upon him.

Maria

In three days, I still hadn't found work. I offered violin instruction to rich families. But looking as disheveled as I did, and with no violin in hand, the matrons looked down their imperial noses at me. I gave up.

I then went to Mary Allen's shop which I patron-
ized weekly. But she had nothing. I slunk away, burning with shame and humiliation. I begged storekeep-
ers—and I do emphasize begged—for employment.
Alas, no one else had any use for a shop girl, clothes
washer, potato digger, maid or latrine scrubber.

After three days with no prospects, I held up my
purse and shook it. The few remaining coins clinked.
After tomorrow, I would be out on the street.

Oh, if only I'd banked some of that money James
had given me instead of frittering it away on flub-
dubs. I'd followed every step of Alexander's creation
of the First Bank as it appeared in the newspapers,
and so admired his fiscal genius. Now, instead of being one of his bank's first depositors, I wandered the
streets destitute.

That eve, I lay on the thin mattress in the stuffy
garret room and closed my eyes. A vision of Alexander entered my mind and I grew warm inside. I let
my mind journey to the first night we met: January
of 1786, at Aaron Burr's home. Aaron had asked me
to bring my violin and perform. I willingly accepted.

The group gathered round me in a whoosh of
rustling taffeta and fluttering fans.

I looked up to see Alexander, his gaze fixed on
mine. As he smiled, a hot surge ripped through me.
The chandelier candles heated my skin like the blazing sun. Returning his smile, I forced my eyes off him,
nestled the violin under my chin and gave a lively
performance of Mozart's Turkish March. I finished
to a burst of applause and cheering.

Still aware of him watching me, his eyes slipping to my décolletage, I dipped a curtsey. "You play as exquisitely as you look." He caressed my violin like a beloved pet. Then he clasped his fingers round mine, raised my hand to his lips and kissed it. "I want to hear more from your violin, but much more from you, Maria."

His nearness enthralled me. I knew he was a flirter. But I was a married lady. And he a married man. With wads of children.

The reverie over, I opened my eyes to my shabby surroundings and oppressive confinement.

Knowing what I must do, I pushed myself off the cot, dashed down the stairs, out the door and to the nearest stationer's. I purchased a paquet of elegant writing paper, with barely enough coin left for breakfast.

Returning to the house, I borrowed a pen and ink from Mrs. Norris's desk and composed the most important, and I admit, pitiful letter I'd ever written.

Desperate, hungry and bereft of dignity, I begged Alexander Hamilton to help me.

I put nib to paper and with great care, penned my woeful entreaty to the Treasury Secretary. My trembling hand spattered drops of ink across the page. So he would not regard me a common beggar, I wrote: *I am the sister of Colonel Lewis DuBois, who led the Fifth New York Regiment during the Revolution. He is now brigadier general of the Dutchess County militia. My sister Susannah is married to distinguished attorney Gilbert Livingston of the powerful New York Liv-*

ingston family. My husband James has treated me cru-elly, leaving me for another woman. alone and desti-tute, I embellished. *I need immediate assistance and appeal to your sense of generosity to come to my aid.*

I recited the missive aloud, blotted the paper and addressed the envelope to Secretary A. Hamilton as personal and confidential. I had the post deliver it to his residence, a walk I could have made myself, but heaven forbid he should espy me on his doorstep.

Next morn, I gave the last of my coin to a scrap of a boy in rags on the street. With no money for breakfast, I found a stale hunk of bread on the kitchen cutting board and choked it down with ale from a cracked jug.

By suppertime my stomach clenched from hunger. I offered to do Mrs. Norris's laundry and beat her rugs in exchange for a meal.

I spent the following morn pressed against the window, waiting for the post carriage to rumble down the street. My empty stomach growled. Aside from some stale coffee and a hard roll, not a morsel remained in the kitchen. "Come on, postman, come on!" I twisted my hankie, tapped my feet on the threadbare rug. Finally, the old carriage ambled up to the house. I burst out the door, swiping the post from the old man's hands before he even alighted. "Ta, my good man!"

I strode back inside, stumbling on cobblestones, rifling through the letters with trembling fingers. Naught from Mr. Hamilton. I let out a heavy sigh. Did he even get the letter?

Pacing the corridor, I shook my head in despair, my heart heavy, for I'd prayed he would at least reply, or offer to visit with a small loan. Even a rejection would have been welcome, rather than this waiting, wondering, longing.

Frightful images haunted me—begging in the streets, weak with hunger, crouching all night in alleys. Placing my hand over my racing heart, I knew what I must do. I needed go see him in person. I pictured the ladies about town staring me down, murmuring "harlot." But my hunger and desperation drove me. I now believed Alexander Hamilton was part of my destiny.

I rehearsed my speech before the hall looking glass. "We met at Colonel Burr's soirée, do you remember that?" I shook my head. "My husband James has treated me cruelly—he deserted me and I am destitute—" No, too self-pitying. "I am alone and appeal to your sense of generosity..."

I memorized my plea.

By eight that eve, a breeze whispered in the twilight. I washed in the courtyard's communal basin with water from the public pump and a sliver of lye soap from the kitchen. I washed my hair and pinned it up with no powder, for I hadn't any. Having no shawl, I draped a fringed throw from a chair about my shoulders. Shoring up my courage, I began the walk to his house, too nervous to take a coach even if I had the coin. Walking helped calm my pounding heart and my rapid breaths. Leaving the stench of the open sewers and grunting hogs behind, I en-

tered an elegant neighborhood. I passed stately brick
Georgian-style houses. Rows of buttonwood, willow
and poplar trees lined the pebble-paved streets. Yet I
trembled as I walked.

Everyone round town knew that Mrs. Hamilton
and the children summered in Albany. But as the
Mrs. carried her sixth child, could Alexander spare
any funds for a poor woman he barely knew?

A Paul Revere lantern glowed in an upstairs window of 79 South Street. The downstairs windows
gaped open, lace curtains fluttering in the breeze.
I knocked on the door. Footsteps grew louder. I
held my breath. The latch rattled. The door opened.
Knowing I'd see Alexander's violet eyes brought a
dreamy smile to my lips. I squared my shoulders and
raised my hand to be kissed. The door opened—and
revealed what I'd never expected. I stumbled back,
stunned.

"Yes? Oh, good evening, Mrs. Reynolds."

There stood Mrs. Elizabeth Hamilton.

Chapter Four

"M—M—Mrs. Hamilton—" I'd been so expecting Alexander, I stammered out her name, as nothing else could come out. I gulped.

She rescued me—in a way. "Please, do come in." She held the door open. I entered, my tongue so dry, it stuck to the roof of my mouth. "What can we do for you?"

"I—that is, my husband—" My eyes darted round the entry hall and up the stairs. The house sat in dark silence, the only light from a candle she held in a brass holder. I wondered if she'd been asleep. Shadows of fatigue surrounded her eyes. Her belly protruded. "I hope I didn't disturb your rest. My husband wanted me to speak with Mr. Hamilton about—about investing in some land out west—he's busy, so he sent me. But if now is a bad time—" Looking into the eyes of Alexander's pregnant wife, I no longer considered this a rational idea. But at least I'd conjured up a halfway believable excuse. Relief flooded me.

"Mr. Hamilton is not at home at the moment but should return shortly. Would you care to wait?" She glanced at the doorway to her left.

"Uh—no," I stammered, my legs so weak, I nearly collapsed. No, I couldn't face him now. Not with his wife at home! "No, I can have James call—would tomorrow be convenient?" I backed out, my hands groping behind me for the door. I couldn't get out of there fast enough.

"Certainly. I shall tell my husband to expect yours." She smiled so sincerely, it crushed me.

Out of curiosity more than an attempt to be cordial, I asked, "Do you plan to visit your family in Albany this summer?" After all, the papers said she was already there.

"I was, but returned for a short visit. I could not bear being apart from my husband. Something told me to come home to him." She tapped the side of her head. "Tis a woman feeling. Do you know, in your heart, when your husband needs you?"

No, mine did not. A pang rippled through me. But I nodded.

"Thank you, Mrs. Hamilton. I'm sorry I disturbed you." I pulled the door closed—and ran smack into Alexander.

Stunned, I leapt back, my hands fluttering.

Mrs. Hamilton said, "Mrs. Reynolds came to see you, Alex, on behalf of James."

He nodded. "Ah, yes, James. How can I be of assistance, Mrs. Reynolds?" His calm tone soothed me. I caught my breath—almost. The sight of him melted me.

"Well, he—" If I was tongue-tied with his wife, I was dumbfounded now. "James asked me—"

Sensing my discomfort, he clasped my elbow and led me back into the hall. "Betsey, give me a minute with Mrs. Reynolds."

"As you wish, sir," she obeyed, bobbed a curtsey, turned and vanished. I was surprised she didn't back out.

Alexander and I stood almost eye to eye, which unnerved me even more. His hand still held my elbow as he led me into a parlour. He gestured to an overstuffed sofa as he pushed up his sleeves. "Saints alive, I am hot." He pushed a side window open.

You're hot, all right! I bit back the words as I sweltered, gazing at him.

He sat across from me in a wing chair, our knees nearly touching. "How may I help you?"

I tried to remember what I'd written in my letters, but only fragments came to me. Knowing I'd be out of here within minutes, I tried to regain calmness. I recited word for word, "Mr. Hamilton, I am from Dutchess County. My husband James treated me cruelly and left me for another woman. I am in so dire a condition that I have not the means to return to New York. I appeal to your humanity. Will you, sir, assist a woman in despair?"

He nodded even before I finished speaking. "Your situation is interesting, Mrs. Reynolds. I am disposed to help you. Unfortunately, tis not convenient at the moment to provide any assistance. I have no money readily available. Could I send some money to you at your place of residence?"

Drowning in relief, I released a deep breath. Thank God this mortifying episode was nearly over. "Why, of course. I'd be ever so grateful."

Then, with a smile, he said what I'd been dreading and longing for at the same time. "I shall deliver a bank note personally later this evening."

I stood too quickly. Without a decent meal in days, I lost my footing and grabbed the sofa. My head spun. He clutched my arms, steadying me. "Shall I fetch you a glass of water? Or wine?"

"No, I am fine, I'll be on my way—" I escaped his grasp and darted for the door. "Thank you again, sir, and I'll expect your visit. I currently reside at Number Two Drinker's Alley, between Second and Front Streets." I omitted any reference to its proximity to the Three Jolly Irishmen. I was sure even *he* knew it sat dangerously close to Hell Town. "Good evening, sir."

I gulped sweet air and fled down the street as if chased. *He's coming to visit later tonight!* Pondering James's nefarious scheme, I shuddered. Flirtatious as Alexander was, I now understood the meaning of his overture that first night we'd met. Offering him my body made me quail with shame, yet enraptured me. Now, the enraptured part blossomed.

What will happen tonight? I wondered. I harbored a strong premonition that tonight my life would change forever.

Chapter Five

Eliza

"You will laugh at me for consulting you about such a trifle; but I want to know, whether you would prefer my receiving the nuptial benediction in my uniform or in a different habit. It will be just as you please; so consult your whim and what you think most consistent with propriety. If you mean to follow our plan of being secretly married, the scruple ought to appear entirely your own and you should begin to give hints of it." – Love Letter from Alexander Hamilton to Elizabeth Schuyler

Alex dismissed me. I obeyed and went to bed. Poor Mrs. Reynolds. Her husband's shady dealings plunged them into financial ruin. But I hoped Alex would have the sense to keep his money in his britches and not hand it over to that cad. Alex wasn't one to gamble on land speculation anyway. His Scottish background prevailed when it came to finances, as frugal with our funds as with the country's.

"The debt of the United States is the price of liberty," he told everyone who visited. No matter where the topic started, it always ended with the debt. "A centralized government needs to be created," he told me time and again, determined to be the one to create it.

But now I agonized for Alex, working so hard, too tired to relish our short visit. My plans to surprise him in bed vanished when I'd entered the house late Wednesday last and found him laboring over a stack of papers in his study. He'd turned to look at me and gaped as if I were a ghost. When I assured him it was I, alive and well, he swept me into his arms and carried me to our bed. But he didn't join me. "I'm buried under work," he explained away as he returned to his study.

He paid me fleeting visits to our bed during the course of the day, and at night fell into his place next to me, snoring within the minute. Hardly a romantic interlude!

A few eves later, the stairs creaked as he approached. He opened the bedroom door and peeked in. "Betsey?"

"Yes?" I struggled to sit up, hoping we could have perhaps an hour together, to kiss and hug, if naught else. "Come to me, let us spend the rest of the evening together."

"I cannot, I must go to Mrs. Reynolds. She needs my assistance." He turned to leave.

My jaw dropped. "Wait! At this hour? Can she not survive till morning?"

"She's desperate. James left her for another woman. I need to deliver her a bank note to hold her over." He held up the note as if to prove the visit wasn't frivolous.

I fell back down onto the pillow. "She'd told me it was to discuss a land deal of her husband's, but it seems she was too embarrassed to tell me the real reason. Of course, go to her. I shall be fine. I have Winifred if I need anything."

"I shan't be long." He quit the room so fast, I got not another glimpse of him. I lay on my side, cradling my belly, my ears perked for his return. But I fell asleep, did not wake till morn, and he was already gone.

Dr. Severus Black

Late that night as the city slumbered, I crouched in the shadows, stock still, watching the house, peering into the lighted windows—why, I couldn't rightly say. Hidden behind the sturdy trunk of a well established oak tree that stood sentinel beside the street, I remembered the previous eve. Alexander Hamilton passed no more then two arm's lengths away as he hurried down the street. I'd seen another lady enter the house not long before that, tarrying a short time before departing again. Hmm—intrigue, mayhap? Was the upstanding Treasury Secretary involved in some tryst with the lady? She'd looked vaguely familiar, but in the darkness of night, I couldn't make out her features in order to identify her. Had she come to confront her lover and been sent packing by Mrs. Hamilton, Alex scurrying away the next eve to make amends to his scorned harlot?

This was conjecture on my part, naught more. And why was my mind so beset by thoughts of the fair Elizabeth? Twas not romantic love that brought me to this point, for I'd never loved that way and never would. The emotion was as foreign to me as pity.

Craving fresh air and an impromptu promenade, I ended up here without thought as to route or destination. I felt some duty of care towards the lady of the house. Truly, she'd shown me naught but kindness on the occasions I'd called on her.

Among this jumble of thoughts, of one fact I was certain: the thought of Alexander involved with the familiar but unknown lady aroused a stirring I hadn't felt since my days in Paris—or London before that. I stood, brushed off my trousers, and took a step away from my shadowy lair to trail Alexander. Then I rejected the idea. I could stalk him anytime. He'd soon sneak out to another tryst, surely.

I headed in the other direction and prowled one lonely street after another. I found it disappointing how desolate these city streets became after dark, unlike the throbbing, darkly alluring paths and alleyways of London and Paris.

As I despaired that my needs would remain by force unfulfilled, the unmistakable sound of a female in distress reached out to me in the darkness. A small passageway lay some ten yards or so ahead. I needed no compass to discern it was from there that the sobs emanated. Sure enough, as I turned into the dark alley I spotted her. She looked young, no more than twenty at most. Her attire gave me a clue to her status. The white blouse and long black skirts—she was a servant, mayhap a maid in one of the area's grand houses.

She crouched on the bare cobbles that made up the surface of the alley, where merchants and deliverymen daily traversed.

I ambled up to her. "And what besets you so, child?" My most accommodating, gentle inflection floated through the air.

She jumped, startled, and looked up at me. "Oh, sir, I'm sorry. I had no thoughts of disturbing anyone."

"What disturbs me is seeing you in such a state." I crept closer. "Surely things are not so unbearable that you cannot tell me what troubles you so, that you sit here in the dark so late at night. At least tell me your name." I trained my eyes on her, confident they possessed their usual hypnotic properties.

"Rose, sir." Her fear dissolved and she smiled, meeting my gaze.

I strained to hear her quiet voice. "Ah, a pretty name, Rose. Now, tell me what troubles you. You can trust me. I'm a doctor, I can help you. My name is Dr. Black. There, now you know who I am. Come, let me help you up." I bent over and reached for her hand.

Rose clasped my splayed fingers and stood, those innocent trusting eyes fixed on mine.

"Now, what is wrong?" I inched closer. Our toes nearly touched.

Rose took a deep breath and cleared her throat. "I suppose I can trust you. The son of my employer, sir, he took advantage of me in my room one night and now I fear I am with child."

The sobs erupted again. I reached into my pocket and removed a kerchief, pressing it into her palm. She dabbed at her tears.

"I see, Rose." I forced a warm smile upon her, baring my teeth. "And have you informed your employer of this state of affairs? For surely his son is at fault in the matter."

With a gasp she shook her head. "Oh, no, sir, for he would surely dismiss me from his employment. He would never believe I did not encourage his son, though I give you my word I did not."

"I believe you, child." I placed my hand on her bare arm and squeezed. It was so thin, I could feel the bone beneath her skin. "You must let me help you. Come with me, Rose, and I will take this fear away for you."

"You will?" A spark of hope raised her pitch.

I bestowed another smile upon her. "Of course, have I not said so?"

I trailed my fingers along her arm. Her muscles relaxed.

"Despite the warmth tonight, you're very cold, Rose." I unwound my scarf and draped it around her neck. I looped it once, then twice. "There, that helps."

I glanced around, making sure no others prowled the vicinity.

"Where are we going, sir?" Her voice still carried that spark of hope. "Can you bring me to a place where they can take away the pregnancy? I've heard such things could be done."

"Going? We are going nowhere, Rose." I enfolded her in my arms, as if to embrace her. "Such a sweet name and such a little harlot." In an instant I grabbed both ends of the scarf, pulling them tightly around her neck. My breaths increased. I began panting, my tongue protruding like a wild beast. As my excitement mounted, my second self, the cold-blooded predator, emerged and now controlled my actions.

A minute later I picked up her limp body and placed it on the cobbles where I'd first seen her. As I checked again that all was quiet and deserted in the vicinity, I knelt beside my latest victim, placed my fingers on her neck to confirm the end of life, and then, my arousal complete, I slowly raised her skirts.

Chapter Six

Eliza

Next eve whilst we slept, safe against the dark of night, another was not so lucky. With Alex gone to work, I reclined in my parlour chair for a few moments' peace. The newspaper's front page headline stunned me. I read the article, bile rising in my throat.

A terrible and dastardly crime took place last night—a murder barely a mile from our own home. We would not learn of the gruesome details until after the investigation. All we could discern was that the victim had been a young woman. I pictured every young woman in Philadelphia cringing in fear. All we could do was share in the horror. The worst had touched the respectability of our privileged existence—cold-blooded murder.

I plowed through the boardinghouse door, fetched a pail, filled it at the pump and scrubbed till my skin glowed. I washed away the perspiration of fear and heat. I donned one of the two garments I'd brought, a plain brown linen dress with elbow-length sleeves and a modest neckline. I also changed my petticoat.

Thoughts of my upcoming meeting with Alexander swirled around in my head. *He intimidates me, he paralyzes me, he renders me tongue-tied!* Next to him, I was no one. But now that he'd agreed to see me and hadn't dismissed me like a street beggar, my hands stilled and my heart calmed. My confidence return'd. I straightened my back, needing carry myself with the utmost poise and sophistication.

At the looking glass, I pinched my cheeks and smoothed stray hairs from my forehead. I wandered into the parlour, picked up a piece of newspaper and tried to read, but the print blurred before my eyes. After endless glances at the hall clock and out the window, the door knocker finally sounded.

I stood, adjusted my bosoms and dashed to the door before anyone else could.

There he stood, glowing in the streetlamp's light, his burnished copper hair pulled back into a queue. I stood back to let him in.

"Mrs. Reynolds." He took my hand and kissed it. I melted. Alone with him, no spouses in the way or embarrassing questions to be asked, I wanted him with a desire that turned me to liquid fire. I flushed with shame.

"Secretary Hamilton. Please come in." My body shook more than my voice. "My room is upstairs, we shall have more privacy there." He followed me up the stairs, commenting on the recent thunderstorms, the heat rising with each step. The third floor seemed a mile away. I reached the top step and opened my door. As he stepped inside, he took a bank note from his pocket and handed it to me.

"Thank you so much. You know not what this means to me." I struggled to steady my voice. I unfolded it to see that it was worth $30. Relief drained me. "Oh, this is so generous. This will keep starvation at bay and buy several weeks' shelter. I shall pay you back soon, I promise."

He waved a dismissive hand. "No need. Not right away, I mean. It requires a heart harder than mine to refuse it to beauty in distress."

His calm tone kept me from quivering. But my heart hammered too hard for my brain to work properly. "Please have a seat." I offered him the room's only chair.

He sat in the ladder-backed chair as I sat upon the cot. "I regret I have no refreshments to offer you. I have literally nothing left."

He patted his middle. "I imbibed sufficient at dinner."

I folded my hands to hide their trembling. "I was hoping you'd help out a kindred soul—another New Yorker, that is."

"Yes, you did mention in your letter that you're related to the Livingstons."

So he *had* read it! I resisted blurting out, "Then why didn't you reply?"

"By marriage only," I said. "My sister Susannah is married to Gilbert Livingston. She married 'up and out' as Mother would say." I clasped my hands even tighter. "Gilbert interested me in British history and politics. He urged me to read your Federalist articles every time they appeared in the papers. Somehow he knew the pen name Publius was you. He knows people who know James Madison, so the connection must have been there."

"I didn't write them alone." He sat back and crossed his legs. "Madison and John Jay helped me out. Jay fell ill and wrote only five, but they were coherent. I must say, Madison's collaboration made the papers achieve greatness."

I glowed with admiration for his gracious crediting of others, when everyone knew he was the genius behind the entire project. "I learnt a great deal from those articles about the Constitution, preparing for war, and our need for a navy."

"Did you not find the reading tedious at times?" He flashed a quizzical eye, mayhap because the articles were not popular reading among members of my sex.

"I had to read some more than once, but had no problem comprehending them. You and I can hold a lively debate—if there were aught to disagree about." I gave him a coy smile. By inviting debate, I was inviting further discussion—and inviting him—on future visits.

"I was the butt of much criticism as you know." His gaze wandered. "The most scathing came from Louis Otto. He said I missed my mark, the work was of no use to educated men and too long for the ignorant. Otto spoke this before he knew I'd been the primary author. But, seeing the frigate *Hamilton* being pulled down Broadway in the parade must have convinced him."

"Who is Louis Otto?" I didn't want to sound ignorant, but he was obviously someone Alex disliked as much as he did Jefferson, or he wouldn't have mentioned him.

"A Jefferson sycophant. French." He smoothed his britches over his knees. "The worst kind."

"I would not put any stock in critics. Tis because of your Federalist articles I'm a staunch Federalist. And a proud one." I held my head high, because I *was* proud.

He nodded his approval. "I'm happy you know what's best for our nation, Maria."

I relished the intimate sound of my name on his lips. "It wasn't much of a leap. Our entire family are exceeding patriotic." My muscles relaxed as we eased into the tête-à-tête. My hands unclenched. "The Lewises left England in 1685. My father served in Colonel Frear's Third New York Regiment. John Lewis, maybe you've heard of him."

"Can't say I have." He shook his head. "But I could have met him. During the war I met so many soldiers, seeing their fighting spirit. Is it any wonder we won?"

We shared a smile. "It was my brother-in-law Gilbert who introduced me to my husband James. James and his father also served—not on the battlefield, but in the Commissary Department."

"Yes." He nodded. "James's father is David, is he not?"

I didn't want to talk about James or his father. I'd conveyed my patriotism—and Federalist allegiance. But I felt it my duty to tell him my family supported him—with our beliefs *and* our money.

"My father bought the two bound Federalist books when they were first published. I bought another two hardcovers for myself. But it was Gilbert who sat me down one day when I was reading *Julius Caesar*," I hastened to add, so he'd know that I read Shakespeare.

I went on as he sat forward with interest, "I remember this, because he told me to stop reading about foreigners and urged me to read something American—'and imperative' he'd said. He handed me the first installment of Federalist Papers, from the New York Journal, and said 'I don't wish to sway you either way, but this is brilliant.' I read every one of them and discussed them with Gilbert. Then my sister Susannah and brother Asa joined in. Next thing I knew, Father was no longer a Democratic Republican, and condemned Jefferson for his womanish attachment to France, and drinking too much of the French philosophy, as Gilbert put it."

"Actually that was I, as quoted by Gilbert," he corrected with a half-smirk.

I flushed, emitting a feminine snicker. "Oh. Sorry. He must have found that compelling. Tis his favorite cocktail party line. I shall right him on that."

"No need." He waved the notion away. "Imitation is the sincerest form of flattery. Quoting is even sincerer than that."

My nerves now surprisingly calm, I voiced my feelings. "I feel I've known you for years." I warmed with delight at this chat. "I started reading the broadsheets more carefully after that discussion. Gilbert, Asa and I would sit round the table and discuss the events. They let me speak my mind and respected my opinions without pushing theirs on me. It made me feel so—so independent, so worthy, so American. 'Remember,' Asa told me more than once, 'we're allowed to speak our mind here in America.' From then on, I was never afraid to speak my mind, knowing I wouldn't be dragged to the guillotine for it."

"A woman who speaks her mind. That would take some getting used to." He brandished a rakish grin.

Was this something he'd welcome? I wondered. I knew how often Mrs. Adams spoke her mind. But how about Mrs. Hamilton? I daren't ask. I forced myself to take this slowly. If he was to respect me, I wanted him to esteem my mind first. I thanked the Almighty I was a Federalist. As much as I enjoyed arguing politics, the last man I wanted to be on opposing sides with was Alexander Hamilton—because of attraction as well as fear. So I continued, becoming more settled on our common ground, and our common nemesis, Thomas Jefferson.

"Gilbert and Susannah actually met Secretary Jefferson at a dinner party." I anticipated a lively exchange now. "Susannah began speaking to him in French. Jefferson took her for one of his toadies and began an intricate political discussion in French, so she spilled wine on him and fled in embarrassment." I laughed at the scene: demure Susannah splashing purple liquid on the imposing Jefferson's Holland cloth britches, watching it run down his legs. "But she was hardly embarrassed, because it was hardly an accident!"

Alexander's hearty laughter brought a smile to my lips. "Oh, I relish those stories about Jefferson's mishaps. He fancies himself such a wag, yet makes a right prat out of himself at the worst times."

Elation skipping through me, I met his smiling eyes. "I regret I have no more Jefferson anecdotes. But I can tell you that he commissioned James to make a solid gold chamber pot for him. And paid a dear price."

Alexander let out the sincerest laugh I'd heard from him yet. "Naught but gold is good enough to collect his piddle. And he calls *me* an arrogant snob."

"Right," I added, "and all men are created equal, according to the slave owner."

"Do not provoke me on that." He held up a hand. "We can discuss the slavery issue another time."

Another time? My blood warmed. I began to hope—as I hoped he didn't see my heart beating beneath my blouse. "Well, I am against it," I had to say.

"Tell your sister for future reference the biggest mistake to make with Jeff is to start speaking French. Why, he often plays the bon vivant, even affects a French accent at times."

"You speak fluent French, do you not?" I asked. "I'd heard it is another of your many talents." I fought to keep the ardent admiration—and flirtation—out of my voice.

"*Oui, mais seulement quand approprié.*" He translated, "Yes, but only when appropriate."

"Oh, how I wish I understood French. I could listen to your French all night, sweet as music." I cringed as those words passed my lips. Did I say 'all night'?

To my relief, he continued, "But with Jeff, tis all smoke and mirrors—meant to make him look like French royalty. At the same time, he accuses me of making my fellow bankers an American aristocracy and myself king, emperor or dictator. He had the culls to accuse me of plotting to commandeer the government after President Washington departs. He says we conceal a thirst for power. Well, he does naught to conceal *his*!" He pointed in the air, an effective lawyerly gesture.

"Ah, yes, I know how oblique Jefferson is." A soft chuckle spilled from my lips. "That is laughable. You have no kingly aspirations, I can tell." From everything I'd read about Alexander, and now speaking with him on such intimate terms as he smoothed back his hair—his own, not a wig, and unpowdered—I knew in my heart that this man was everything good our Republic stood for. "Does Mrs. Hamilton want to be queen?" I joked.

His brows drew together. "I sometimes wonder. The Schuylers are good people, but a bit haughty at times, being to the manor born. With many of the same pretentions as Monsieur Jeffer-*son*." He affected a French accent at the end. We shared a laugh.

"They'd be over the moon if Jefferson got his way and aligned the United States with France." He glanced at his fingernails. "Mr. Schuyler disagrees with my fiscal programs. He's not in favor of a central bank. He thinks the Federal government should stay out of the states' business. But I told him in a diplomatic way to butt out of my business, which *is* the Federal government."

My eyes widened in surprise—and respect. "And what was his reply to that?"

"He bought fifty shares in the bank. Gave me the money right then and there, out of a safe. But not without adding the comment, 'I wouldn't be doing this if I couldn't afford to lose it.' So I let him have the last word. Why not?" He chuckled with a haughty grin. "I had his money."

"My my, we do think alike." I respected this brilliant man. His mind attracted me more than his body—for now. "James bought shares as well, but nowhere near fifty. Still, that depleted our coffers at the time. He sold our horses and our landau—at a loss, but decided we didn't need the luxury, and investing in the bank was more prudent—and patriotic. He calls himself a Federalist, but being Scottish, he has a European mindset. He looks up to the monarchy and enjoyed being a subject of the crown ... but not enough to stay there," I added.

"I look up to the British monarchy, too," he agreed, "and their government, the only proper one for such an extensive country as ours." He raised his hands, palms up. "Monarchy in America would be impossible, but my first wish was for the next best thing—an elective monarchy."

I leant closer, intrigued. "You mean electing a king?"

"Washington cared not to be called king, so we settled on president. But I hoped for an aristocratic centralized union. I modeled our bank after the Bank of England. I think we would do well if our president and senators served for life. But by an electoral process, not by birthright."

I nodded. "Yes, I've read all about the British bloodlines—some family trees don't fork. It makes me glad our next president won't be related to Mr. Washington."

"Let us hope he won't be Jefferson either." He knitted his brows.

"Him as president? Perish the thought."

He gave a mock shudder. "Yes, Adams would be bad enough."

We shared another smile. Then our eyes locked. We connected on a deep and meaningful level.

I'd never been alone with any man other than my husband, and here I sat with one of the most prominent figures in the nation! We seemed to have exhausted politics for the time being. As he studied me, his lips parted and he asked a more personal question. "What happened with James?"

I stiffened my spine and looked him in the eye. "He mistreated me, not physically, but he left me for another woman," I repeated what I'd written in the letter, but cringed with guilt over that lie. The kind-hearted Alexander kept me from starving; I owed him the truth. My cheeks and chest flushed. "That is—I assume it was another woman. I never know with James." Before I knew what I'd said, I divulged my most intimate feelings: "I still love him, but my life with him is too unstable. I feel abandoned half the time, even when he *is* home." I dropped my gaze, embarrassed to bare my soul like this.

Something struck a chord within him, because he poured his heart out to me, telling me things I doubted he'd ever shared with Mrs. Hamilton.

I'd never known he was born on Nevis and grew up on St. Croix, or that his parents were not married, or that his father left them when Alexander was ten, and his mother died, leaving him orphaned. His saving grace was an article he wrote for a St. Croix newspaper, which impressed the community so much, they formed a subscription fund to educate him here in the Colonies.

He went on, "I confess this to you—my anger at my father's abandonment drove me to complete my education and earn the entire nation's respect by becoming central to its growth. Wherever my father is, and I would not rule out hell, I want to make him sorry he never married my mother and deserted us." His voice gathered volume. "And as sure as I sit here, I know he will regret his actions for all eternity." His eyes narrowed and he shook his head as if to chase away the anger. "Conversely, I want my mother to be proud of the son she left behind at age thirteen, a boy who made his way here to make her proud. If only she'd lived to see all this." He gestured out the open window at the tiny patch of dirt that contained the privy, but I knew exactly what he meant—that dirt belonged to his colonies, now the Union he was helping to thrive.

"I am proud of my Scottish lineage that includes royal titles. I have viscounts, barons and dukes among my forebears, and will not let the good fortune of my father's birth diminish that."

I looked into his eyes, my heart heavy. "I am at a loss for words, Secretary Hamilton. My plight is naught compared to what you suffered as a boy, ten years younger than I am now. Yet I'm an abandoned wife, as James proved unfitting as a husband."

Confidence and strength blossomed inside me during this heartfelt talk; if Alexander could begin a new life at thirteen, I certainly could do the same at twenty-three. At that moment, I vowed to better myself, to stand up as Maria Lewis Reynolds, rather than "et ux."

My future, bright and with promise, awaited me. I gazed into those smoldering eyes and longed for his embrace. How badly I wanted to share my future with my new-found kindred soul!

As if he'd read my thoughts, he reached forward, grasped my hand and said what I'd never dreamt in my fleeting fantasies, "I believe I have found my equal in every way, Maria." The next thing I knew, we both stood. He met my lips with his. My arms slipped round him as our kiss deepened. He embraced me, pulling me to him so our bodies met and melded.

His growing arousal pressed against me as fireworks exploded behind my closed eyes. He ended the kiss and pulled away, running his fingers over my cheek. "I want you, Maria." I knew the husky sound of desire, and his voice conveyed it.

If not now, then never. "What about your wife?" I whispered before I knew it was out of my mouth.

"We hardly see much of each other. We have next to naught in common to begin with. A mutual respect. A household. And five young ones."

Then how did you sire those five young ones and the expected sixth? I thought, but dared not say another word. I ached for his touch.

He closed and locked the door behind us. He clasped his fingers round mine and beckoned me toward the bed. I glanced at the open window as if his wife could peek in on us. The breeze cooled my heated body.

"Are you agreeable to this?" he asked.

I nodded. After tonight, my life would never be the same. Without another word, he slid my dress from my shoulders and it spilt to the floor. I stood before him in my chemise and petticoat.

His nimble fingers unbuttoned his linen shirt and he shucked it off. He was now half naked. "Hotter in here than at my house, is it not?" he whispered into my ear.

I forced a light laugh. "I am sweating buckets if you must know the truth, Secretary Hamilton."

He smiled, slipping out of his shoes. "Let us dispense with the formalities. Those close to me call me Sandy. Or Alex if you prefer."

"Oh, Alex sounds much more..." I sighed as he trailed kisses along my most receptive spots: the tips of my earlobes, the hollow of my neck. "...majestic." I lost my senses and let his exquisite lovemaking carry me away.

Afterwards, we lay in each other's arms, our mingled breaths slowing, calming. "Alex, how did you learn all this? You know just what to do." I gave him a lazy smile.

"Here and there." He wiped his brow. "Trial and error."

"I was a virgin when I married James," I confessed, my nervousness easing into the comfort shared by lovers. I'd wanted someone like Alex all my life, and now that he was here in my arms, I never wanted to let him go. James faded into a vague entity, although come morn, I knew not where to go next. "I've never been loved this way."

"Such a sweet, beautiful lady deserves it." He gazed at me as if I were the only woman he'd ever loved.

"I've always admired you and believed you a visionary, Alex, as well as a strikingly handsome man. And I'm sure you don't remember, but the first time we met was five years ago. I played violin at Aaron Burr's soirée," I prattled on, but needed him to know I wasn't simply soliciting sex for money, and the most important truth—I had feelings for him before I ever saw his naked body tonight.

"Of course I remember. Except for a single sentence, all our exchanges were with our eyes." He gazed at me that same way.

"I hope you don't think I'm that kind of woman," I blurted.

"What kind of woman?"

"A not respectable one." What did he think I meant?

"Not at all." Then he said what I didn't dare voice out loud. "You and I both know there's an attraction that couldn't be denied any longer. Now that we've had a chance to share our common beliefs, our wounds and our feelings, I hope it will be much more."

"So this isn't—this won't end with tonight?" His wife and my husband forgotten, I wanted to know one thing: "When will I see you again—and how often?"

"I shall find time for you, I promise." He traced my arm with his fingertips. My entire body tingled.

After that, I floated down the stairs to see him out. I dropped to my knees, bowed my head and clasped my hands. "Almighty Lord, thank you for bringing Alex into my life." My eyes slid shut. "I vow to become a significant part of his."

"Some conversation ensued from which it was quickly apparent that other than pecuniary consolation would be acceptable." –Alexander Hamilton on 'The Reynolds Affair'

A stiff prick has no conscience. – Benjamin Franklin

Chapter Seven

Eliza

Thurs. Eve, Half Ten

"Alex," I approached my husband sitting at his desk. "I'm sorry to interrupt."

He peered at me over his specs. "What is it, Betsey? I have loads of work to do."

"That's what I have to tell you." I stood in the doorway, never entering until invited. No invite was forthcoming, so I plowed on. "I know you're far too busy for me. But I am too ailing for you. I do not belong here now. At such a crucial time in our nation's growth, I am simply in the way. Your talents are in too much demand for me to expect your affection. President Washington and the nation need you more than I do. Besides, the children are still at Albany, and I miss them."

Pen still poised over the paper he'd been writing on, he nodded. "'Tis probably best. I haven't time for much else besides work."

Still standing in the doorway, I added, "I instructed the servants to feed you three nourishing meals a day and a light repast before bedtime. I shall leave in the morn."

Next morn, I couldn't bear to turn and gaze at him as the carriage pulled away. We exchanged a brief wave and parted.

As the carriage jostled over the bumpy road out of town, I gazed out the window at the passing landscape, already missing Alex. A slender young woman came out of a shop. Maria Reynolds? I brought my hand up to wave, but stopped when the carriage drew near. It wasn't she. But I now wondered how she'd fared. I hoped Alex was able to help her. From what I knew about her shifty husband, she was well rid of him. I'd never heard much good about him besides his losing bid for the congressional seat Dayton now held, but we didn't need his kind in our government. I did know that he earned and lost money as if playing a game, and his poor wife suffered his failings with him. Perchance Alex and I could invite Maria to our home and cheer her up with a good meal and some lively discussion. I trust Alex wouldn't mind—no doubt he'd leave us ladies to our own devices anyway. I doubted someone as young as Maria could hold his interest.

As we traveled the placid countryside, the blue sky streaked with clouds, the green and rolling Catskill

Mountains to our left, I looked ahead to the birth of our next child. All I'd wanted were six children, but if Alex wanted more, I'd gladly oblige him. I lived to do his bidding.

Maria

With coin jingling in my purse, I walked on air. After a hearty breakfast in the Old London Coffeehouse, I rummaged through the Chestnut Street bookstore for more books to discuss with Alex. As we reclined in love's afterglow last eve, he told me he was an omnivorous—a new word I learnt—reader, ranging from the classics to novels. He especially enjoyed Shakespearean plays. Entwined in each other's arms, we'd discussed Shakespeare and the books we'd read. I was proud to sustain my end of the conversation, and my knowledge of these books and plays seemed to greatly impress him.

He was mighty eager to discuss Winn's *History of America* and *The Letters of Socrates.* I'd read Socrates as a young girl. It made me love Greeks and their history. He'd raved about Hume's *Essays*, which I looked for now. I couldn't find it, but purchased Adam Smith's *Wealth of Nations*, one of Alex's favorites. I hesitated before splurging. The book was over 1100 pages and heavy as a brick, but well worth the investment.

I walked down Chestnut Street, a mere two blocks from where Alex lived, looking for a house with rooms to let, but dwellers in this neighborhood did not need to let rooms. Discouraged from this paradox, I took a left turn and went into Nathan Shepard's tavern for my midday meal. Women weren't allowed in taverns unescorted. We had to use the "snug," the women's section in back.

As I pushed open the snug's door, a hand clamped down on my shoulder. Startled, I turned to face my husband.

"Maria, where in hell were you the last four days?" His tone was more pleading than demanding. His eyes betrayed gratitude rather than anger.

"I found a room. I've been on my own and surviving quite nicely," I informed him. My tone reflected my confidence. Yet I fought the urge to tell him how pleased I was to see him. Now that the initial rage of the insult had time to fade, I was almost—but not quite ready—to entertain his plea for forgiveness—if any was forthcoming.

"Maria, come home. This has gone on long enough." His hand slid down my arm to clasp my fingers. I clasped back, cementing an unsaid bond between us as a husband and wife of seven years.

"Do you still consider me your prostitute?" I challenged, wanting him to beg, to plead, to grovel.

"Nay, I ne'er did. Twas only a way to make money. But we needn't pursue it. I realized I canna live without you. I procured employment as Josiah Bank's assistant. He even advanced me a week's wages." He added a smug grin to that.

"The largest goldsmith in town? How did you convince him you are worthy of employment—and to advance you money? You must have sweet-talked the very britches off the man." I tilted my head with a saucy smile.

"Remember that gold chamber pot Tom Jefferson commissioned? That he said was so exquisite, he couldna even piddle in? Well, Mr. Bank paid a visit to Monticello, and he spotted the pot in his guest bedroom. Seems Bank also thought it too fine for piddling into, and begged Jefferson for the craftsman's name. Bank called on me to make a matching set for him and his wife." He sported a satisfied smirk. "I told him I'd be obliged if he'd provide steady employment. He took my offer on the spot. Imagine—all this from a piss pot!"

"I am happy for you, James. You must thank Mr. Jefferson—perhaps make him a gold cuspidor." I itched to tell him what I'd accomplished. That the great Alexander Hamilton had become my kindred soul, and declared me his equal—and not because of any scheme of James's. But I kept quiet—for now.

"Now will you come home?" He squeezed my hand, pleading in his eyes.

"Very well, James, I shall go home with you." *For now*, I added silently as I linked my arm through his.

Together we walked to Mrs. Norris's, where I gathered my few belongings. Heading back home with James, I knew I could accomplish anything, I still loved my husband—but did not need him.

When he pushed open our door and stood aside to let me enter the house, a strange mix of comfort and detachment washed over me. Being alone and pennies away from starvation changed me. I gazed at my familiar surroundings: my sagging sofa, my cozy throw, my beloved violin lying atop a stack of music. I breathed in the aroma of coffee and baked bread. Yet something was missing.

He poured each of us a goblet of wine and we settled on the sofa.

"I could not deny that I still love you, James." I enveloped his free hand in mine.

"Don't vanish inna thin air like that again, Maria," he said over a weary sigh. "You scared the shite outta me if you want to know the truth."

My eyes downcast, I promised, "I won't. But we do have some things to iron out."

He moved closer and brushed my lips with his. These teasing feathery kisses of his always made me tingle. "We kin iron later." He embraced me. My ardor for him came rushing back as his nimble hands unlaced my blouse. We lay back on the cushions and made languid, comfortable love. But I sensed a detachment.

We lay together in a familiar embrace, my head resting upon his chest. After a long silence, he inquired. "What is it, Maria? It seemed you were elsewhere."

So I told him. I told him everything that had ensued in the last four days. Including my entreaty to Alex, and his visit with financial assistance. But I ended the story at that exact spot.

James blanched, as if I should have negotiated more out of him. "Thirty dolls? That's all he could spit up?"

"That's all he had available. I wasn't about to force his hand. Your problem, James, is that you know not how to be subtle," I chided. "I'm sure you'd succeed at many more ventures if you knew how to cultivate people. One of Franklin's sayings 'a spoonful of honey will catch more flies than a gallon of vinegar' is true, and believe me…" I tossed my head. "…if Alexander Hamilton were a fly, he would have drowned in my honey." I let the double entendre hang in the air. But James didn't so much as give a 'hmmph.'

"When will he make his next appearance?" was all he wanted to know.

"I have no plans to see him again." Which was the truth. He hadn't given me an exact date. I could only hope that I'd be part of his life from now on.

"It was generous of him to offer you assistance without expecting aught in return," James commented. "In fact, ah'm quite surprised. After what I've heard of him and his romps outside of his marriage—and outside of his britches."

"He expected naught in return." Which was also the truth. Our attraction that culminated in a frenzy of passion had nothing to do with the $30 he'd given me to keep starvation at bay. If Alex never gave me another penny, I would still cherish his company.

James grabbed his britches off the floor and stepped into them. "Ah'm off to a card game over at

Congressman Wynkoop's house. I believe Madison is attending, and you can rest assured ah'll walk out with moore than Hamilton sputtered up last night. Ah'm always able to lighten Madison's wallet." He shrugged into his shirt and buttoned it. "He may as well hand it to me on a silver salver when he challenges me. That will earn me enough to pay back some debt with a bit left over for flub-dubs, along with my advance from Josiah Bank until I begin this new employment."

"Bring some more Madeira home. I plan to read my new book tonight, so I shall be busy." Donning my wrap, I followed him down the stairs and into the parlour.

"What in bloody hell is this?" He lifted my *Wealth of Nations* book, glanced at the cover and dropped it as if it'd grown horns. "I'd have to smoke a poond of opium to get throo a single page. Are you sure you can sustain interest in this codswallop for more than three seconds?"

I bounced on the balls of my feet and cocked a brow. "Unlike the drivel you read, tis on a level higher than that of a six-year-old. This is a book Alexander recommended. It seems I've appealed to him as his intellectual equal. Something he lamented he does not get from the missus."

"Nay, he only got six wee ones from the missus." He smoothed his wavy hair down with water from the basin and adjusted his queue ribbon. "Dinna believe everything a married man whispers in yur ear. Specially if he's shaggin' you."

I had an inkling James knew what took place last night after all the talk about politics and books. I ignored his remark and opened to page one of *Wealth of Nations*. It would take me a while to finish this thick tome. But I'd always wanted to learn more about economics and capitalism. The more I read, the more I agreed with Adam Smith—and grew excited knowing Alex and I would have many engrossing discussions about it. I became so absorbed in the book, I didn't hear James leave.

I took a break from reading. My mind wandered to last eve and seeing Alex again. Knowing I was far too hasty, I fetched paper and pen and wrote him a letter, telling him I'd returned home, but I longed to see him again. With his wife out of town, I knew he'd be lonely. Busy as he was, the nights still dragged, minute by painful minute.

I slipt the letter through his the mail slot after midnight. I wondered if he was inside, poring over papers, or at a tavern in discussions with other statesmen. Was I surprised when I returned home and found James lounging on our sofa, barefoot, smoking his pipe, sipping wine. I nearly fell backward when he told me whom he'd unmercifully beat at bid whist!

"Ah, the sweet smell of success." He stood and fanned bank notes over the table like playing cards. "The cards may as well have been marked, and none other but yur illustrious Hamilton was there—and this, my lass, come from his very pockets!"

It looked like hundreds. Alex—a gambler? I'd never heard this of him. All I'd heard was that when it came to money, Alex was tighter than—what had John Adams said a few years back? "Tighter than a crab's bum, and that's waterproof."

"What was Alexander doing there?" He could have been spreading *me* instead of a hand of cards!

"Grew lonely for male company, I reckon." James shot me a sly look, yet it gleamed with amusement. "Ye canna expect a chap to dally with the fair sex every night, now. He kin only do so much. Then he needs re-fuel."

Not wanting to believe Alex dallied with anyone but me, I fought an ugly pang of jealousy.

"He didna want in on the game at first, but Wynkoop talked him into it. Hamilton's as pathetic at cards as he is brilliant at banking. I coulda beat him blindfolded with both hands on me willie," James gloated, counting the money over and over again.

"Did he say anything to you about—me?" I had to know.

He shook his head. "Nary a word. Those cards, he played close to his vest. Sneaky bugger."

"He's not sneaky, just discreet." I breathed a sigh of relief. But my heart tripped in delight. Alex was mine—for the time being! I'd have to warn him not to play cards with James, but I knew he was too sensible to fall into that trap again. The other trap James had planned to set for him—extorting money in a much more devious way than at cards—I was doubly glad we both hadn't fallen into that one.

Chapter Eight

Eliza

"*I meet you in every dream.*" Love Letter from Alexander Hamilton to Elizabeth Schuyler, 1780

Thursday, September the First

I am enjoying our summer back here in Albany. The children have rosy cheeks, Angelica's hair is sun streaked, and James grew chubby from all the pies Gran baked for us. I grow larger every day. We plan to return home Friday next.

I received a letter from Alex this morn. I read the romantic bits over and over: *I am myself in good health but I cannot be happy without you. Yet I must not advise you to urge your return. The confirmation of your health is essential to our happiness that I am willing to make as long a sacrifice as the season and your patience will permit. Adieu my precious. My best love to all the family. Yrs ever & entirely, A Hamilton.*

No, I could not stay away any longer than planned. Although his letters convinced me how much he missed me, they also contained snippets about his work. But when I asked questions, he always explained in simple terms the meaning behind his efforts and how his enemies tried to thwart him. In his last letter, he told me he'd met with President Washington about the Bank and toiled eighteen hours that day. His wobbly penmanship betrayed his fatigue. I shall take the matter up with President Washington, as to why he works his surrogate son so hard.

Now our new capitol stands on the Potomac, as was Alex's wish, built on a swamp called Foggy Bottom. They named it Washington City, but since Alex was instrumental in deciding its location, I believed it deserved to be called Hamilton City. Perchance another town would be named after him someday.

I read his letter again and kissed his name at the bottom. "I shall relieve your burdens, my darling," I whispered.

Not until after I'd read Alex's letter thrice did I notice another letter addressed to me. It bore a Philadelphia postmark, but I recognized neither the penmanship nor the seal. After reading it, I was inclined to dispose of it, but better judgment told me to keep it and bring it home. Alex must see this. It was signed 'Anon.' and went on for the entire page about a rumor. A rumor about my husband and Mrs. Maria Reynolds, seen together late Thursday eve.

James Reynolds was also seen entering his house after word got round that he'd left his wife. What was going on? I knew that he'd once tried to persuade Alex to invest in some speculation. When Mrs. Reynolds called that August eve, she claimed that as her reason for the visit. But she'd told Alex her husband had left her. I loathed confronting Alex with this. He had so much on his mind. But now it festered on *my* mind. Who would write this, not having the strength of character to sign his (or her) name? Swindlers always tried to take advantage of Alex's good nature, but this time I would not let it happen.

Maria

A courier delivered a letter to me the next morn, whilst James was still abed. It was from Alex, on his engraved stationery. My heart surged as I tore into it, his first letter to me. I memorized every word, every loop of every 'y', every slanted cross of every 't'. I kissed his name at the bottom of the page, again and again. I vowed to keep it till my dying day. He wished to come back to me after finishing his work. I began counting the hours till his arrival though I knew not what time he'd call.

James woke and broke his fast with the usual whisky and water with a hunk of bread and pungent cheese. He smacked his lips and belched. "I've a full day's work for Josiah Bank, then a business meeting at The Grog. But dinna hold yur breath, the deal may not go throo. Later, there's a card game at Jonathan Trumbull's, and it may be an all-nighter. Ah'll be too bevvied to make my way home, so ah'll kip there."

I never held my breath over any of his deals. If I did, I'd have suffocated a hundred times.

"Cheers, lass." He strode out the door.

By nightfall, in anticipation of Alex's touch, I'd reached a level of arousal I'd never felt before. As the eve's shadows crept up the bedroom walls, I leant out the window, the ledge pressed against my ribs, craning my neck to see down the street. After two hours of waiting, Alex's lean figure emerged from the darkness and he rapped on the door. I shivered in delight and ran down the stairs. I flung open the door and pulled him inside. My heart tripped.

I offered him a drink but hoped he'd refuse. I wanted him in my arms, ravishing me. Thankfully, he declined. "Later, Maria. We have plenty of time for imbibing and discourse. Let us quench our most urgent desires first."

"You read my mind, Alex." We drew closer, my lips ready for his. He kissed me deeply, taking my breath away. I ended the kiss, gulped air and guided him upstairs to the bedroom next to James's and mine.

We removed each other's clothing, top to bottom. I was no longer a bit shy with him. We were lovers now, intimate as any man and wife. He walked around me in circles, drinking me in slowly and deliberately, up and down, naked longing in his eyes. Drowning in desire, I lost my senses, unable to think.

"You're a work of art, Maria." His voice rumbled. "A glorious sculpture in marble. Like Venus DeMilo."

"She has no head. And no arms!" I laughed.

"Well, nobody's perfect. But you—you are perfect. A work of art beyond human." He stood back and stared some more.

He finally approached me and began working his magic with those fingers that penned all those brilliant essays, caressing my bare body with light strokes, like I was a statue in the making. "Your skin is ever so soft," he whispered.

"I use creams in abundance." I wanted him to know I took extra pains to care for myself.

"Do you bathe in milk like Cleopatra?" His hands slid down my arms.

"No." I smiled. "Bathing in milk would be far too dear."

His fingers played over me. I blazed, on fire. "Do you crack walnuts with these thighs?"

"I never tried." I sighed.

"Such a ravishing body." Then he stepped back and caressed me with his eyes.

"Alex," I groaned, "take me now."

He smiled and brought me to the bed. "Very well, come here."

The universe exploded around us. I'd never felt so feral, and yet so connected, my spirit and his.

Afterward, I poured us each a goblet of claret from the carafe on the bedside table, glad I'd put clean glasses out today. He sipped as I asked, "Now, Alex, how was your day?"

"You truly care to know?" His voice carried both surprise and pleasure.

"Of course." From the way he'd asked, it seemed he had no one to share mundane anecdotes or major triumphs. Did his wife never want to hear how his day had gone? "I want you to share your everyday asides as well as major events—if you'd received any orders from President Washington or read another scathing letter in the papers by Jefferson, if you'd made more headway in running the treasury. I want to share it all with you, Alex."

He didn't hesitate a moment. "I actually did accomplish something today." His tone brightened with pride.

"Tell me. What was it?" I propped myself up on an elbow and brushed his hair from his eyes, ran my finger over his brow, down his cheek, over the contour of his strong jaw line.

"I formed a private state-chartered corporation called The Society for Establishing Useful Manufacture. Five directors and I plan to utilize a river to supply waterpower by diverting its water through a raceway system, and use it as a power source for gristmills. Actually it is the brainchild of my Assistant Treasury Secretary Tench Coxe. He told me of his idea for the creation of a manufacturing town and won my full support."

"What will you—the corporation—be making there? This sounds as visionary as your creation of the First Bank. Tis centuries ahead of Jefferson and his gentleman farmer ways and means." I beamed at him, adoring him.

"Starting with the most important would be linen, cotton, and wool to make hose worn by all ranks of people. Our increased population and wealth have greatly increased the consumption of those articles. Things folk need—" He counted on his fingers, "table linen, bedticks, fustians and jeenes for men, and white dimity for the ladies. Then we need paper, shoes, pottery and earthen ware—" he took a breath and continued, "carpets, blankets, brass, iron wire, wool, steel—any goods that need to be manufactured. Eventually, the mills can manufacture every kind of apparel—shoes, boots, gloves." He finished his wine, set down the goblet, sat back and clasped his hands behind his head. "The sky is the limit. Not only the wealth, but the independence and security of a country appear to be connected with the prosperity of manufactures."

"Where is this town?" I hoped it was close by. My selfish side didn't want him traveling great distances.

"We haven't chosen one yet. These plans are still on paper." He yawned and rubbed his eyes. "But I would like to use a river as a source for mechanical power. We can discuss the details another time." He stretched his legs and his eyes closed. "My days have been longer than my nights. And as of now my mind is feeling it."

"Is it turning to mush?" I teased, massaged his scalp, and smoothed his hair over the pillow.

"After such a long day, tis as useless as my—" He glanced downward and turned onto his side, facing me. "I hope you weren't planning on an encore performance."

"Not at all. I'm still enthralled by the first act," I spoke the truth.

He pulled me into the warmth of his embrace and I drifted off to the beat of his heart.

He nudged me awake. I opened my eyes to see him standing by the bed pulling on his britches. "I need to return home, Maria. I have some more work to do this eve and an early appointment in the morn."

I did not pressure him. That would surely drive him away.

He shrugged into his shirt and I tied my déshabillé about my waist as we descended the steps. What a sight we must have been. It made me laugh and shiver with delight at the same time. We basked in the afterglow of lovemaking and certainly looked it.

At the bottom of the stairs, he turned to me and I stepped into his open arms. "Til we meet again, my darling."

Our lips met. My rapture shared an urgent need to fuse with this man. At the same time, I wanted to know—besides his sad, lonely childhood, political beliefs and drive for success—his fears, his philosophy on life and death, his religion. I hadn't yet delved that deeply into his mind, his life.

"When will that be?" I persisted after we ended our kiss. As he began to speak, the lock rattled and the door swung open. We froze, still locked in each other's arms, as James stumbled in. For a long agonizing moment, we all stood, stunned.

James broke the silence. "Ah. I see you two are now beyond Shakespeare comedies and Mozart ditties." Well into his cups but plainly coherent, he tossed his keys on the table and observed us—his half-dressed wife, and now obviously my lover, shirt open, locked in an embrace, our hair disheveled, our lips inflamed from kissing, our faces blotchy with sexual flush.

"I—I—" I stammered, numb with embarrassment.

James poured himself a shot of whisky and held the glass up to Alex in the gesture of a toast. "Here's lookin' up yur kilt." He downed the shot. "Care to partake in some aqua vitae, Hammy? You look like you kin use a refill."

"Jim, listen—" Alex broke our embrace and approached my husband, now sitting in his chair, tilting it back on two legs as he smacked his lips.

"No need to elucidate, Ham. Ah'm no dumb shite, I see what went on here. But I hope you know this'll cost you more than thirty bucks here on in." He winked at Alex and belched. "Scuse me, ah've bin dippin' in a cookie jar of another sort this eve." He stood and looked at me. "I shall leave the candle lit for you, when you care to join me in our conjugal bed, if you've hadn't enough already. Good eve, dear wife. Cheers, Hambone." He gave Alex a mock bow, brushed by us and vanished up the stairs.

I quaked, too mortified to speak.

"So now he knows." Alex saved the moment and put me at a semblance of ease. "And he hardly seems to care. It actually makes things easier for us. As long as he maintains his affable apathy, we have no problem."

"I suppose," was all I could choke out. "But did you hear James's insinuation? It sounds as if he plans to blackmail you."

"I shall deal with that when the time comes. Nevertheless, I must keep this under wraps. Not just for my wife. For the entire country. I trust you understand why." His tone harshened. His eyes focused on me and narrowed.

"Of course, Alex. I know your reputation is far too revered for a scandal such as this to leak out." Inwardly I cringed. I didn't want to be part of a scandal. I wanted the world to know how much I loved Alex.

I followed him to the door, loathe to let him go. I cupped his cheek and drew him close, my breath hovering over his lips. "Please, Alex, one more kiss. One more embrace."

He moaned. "Oh, why can I not disentangle myself from you…" His arms enveloped me and he kissed me deeply. As I grew dizzy with pleasure, he pulled away. "I must go. Spend tomorrow on yourself. Shop for dresses, pamper yourself. Here." He handed me a fistful of bank notes. I couldn't see their values in the dark. "Good eve, my love."

He vanished into the night. I unfolded the bank notes by the light of the wall candle and saw that they totaled $50. I sobbed with gratitude. Oh, that big-hearted, kind, generous soul!

I nearly floated up the stairs, repeating, in quiet whispery tones, "He called me *love!*"

James was sawing logs when I got to bed. I hoped our appalling encounter would be forgotten next morn. I did not want him to blackmail Alex, but at the same time, I heaved a sigh of relief that James wasn't the sort to go through with a duel. I knew Alex was far too sensible to ever duel anyone. So they were both safe on that count.

Chapter Nine

Eliza

Philadelphia, September 4, 1791

My Beloved Betsey

*I hoped with the strongest assurance to have met you
at Eliz Town; but this change of weather has brought
upon me an attack of the complaint in my kindreys
[sic] to which you know I have been sometimes subject
in the fall. So that I could not with safety commit myself to so rude a vehicle as the stage for so long a journey, I have therefore prevailed upon my clerk Mr. Meyer
to go to Elizabeth Town to meet you in my place. I am
not ill though I might make myself so by the jolting of
the carriage were I to undertake the journey. If I can get
a proper machine I shall make use of a warm bath to
which I am advised and from which I am persuaded I
shall receive benefit.*

Fryday, September the Ninth, Midnight.

We arrived home from Albany at mid-day. "Where is Father?" my three younger ones asked in unison.

"Working." As they knew. But in their minds, he should have been home to greet them, even though he hadn't been expecting us today. He stole in late that eve after they were fed and abed. We embraced and whispered our familiar endearments. I did not ask him where he'd been, and he didn't tell me. We were too tired to make love, but before falling asleep, I had to tell him what had troubled me, the reason I'd come home a week early. I got out of bed to fetch the anonymous letter.

He re-lit a candle and gave the letter no more than a glance. "When did you get this?" In the public eye so long, he ignored rumors.

"The day before I left Albany. Who would write this?" I gestured at the hateful item.

He tossed it onto the nightstand. It missed and floated to the floor. He didn't bother picking it up. "Who knows? Mayhap Jefferson or one of his ilk, in retaliation for those letters I've been sending the newspaper about him. He had the sense to figure out twas I. I shan't get into a war with him over that."

"Then why write to me?" My ire rose, quickening my pulse. "Why get me involved?"

"To get to me. Do not believe it, Betsey. Tis a lie." He yawned and stretched his legs.

"But what were you doing with Mrs. Reynolds late at night?" I persisted, determined to find out something other than simply "Tis a lie."

"It was *Mr.* Reynolds," he corrected me. "He wanted me to invest in some land."

"And you begged off, I trust." My voice gained volume.

"I made him a small loan," he said what I'd dreaded hearing. "Not for land, but because they're destitute. Worry not, my dear, you'll hear no more about Mr. or Mrs. Reynolds."

The conversation over, he turned away and began snoring. I needn't ask more. I trusted him.

Maria

Early next morn, I headed to my dressmaker. Mrs. Joseph Graisbury lived on Water Street among several tailors clustered between Walnut and High Streets. Mr. Graisbury, a master tailor, outfitted the city's richest men, who'd made him nearly as affluent. He fitted James with the latest fashions, when we had funds to fritter on fashions. Now, once again, we did. I ordered from Mrs. Graisbury two brocade dresses, one in gold and one in silver. The skirts would open in front to display their satin underskirts, with daring décolletages and lace-trimmed sleeves. The panniers would puff out at my hips and shrink my waist so Alex could circle it with his hands.

"Planning on attending some posh events, Mrs. Reynolds?" Mrs. Graisbury measured my bust and hips.

"Possibly. I cannot be seen in the same habiliments all the time." I feared Alex would think he'd given me too much money. A destitute woman would not wear this quality of dress. "My present wardrobe is hardly adequate," I admitted, but didn't tell Mrs. Graisbury that I was now in competition with Mrs. Hamilton—as well as other women who caught Alex's fancy. If he tired of me, he'd drop me like a rock. With this in mind, I purchased *The Letters of Pliny* at the old bookstore, more hair powder... and more perfume.

I returned home to James writing at his desk, an empty whisky bottle and half-eaten chicken leg at his elbow. Not my place to ask of his business, I helped myself to his leavings of bread and cheese from the sideboard and fetched the newspaper.

Quill scratched across paper as he penned his signature with a flourish, blotted the page and waved it through the air to dry.

I glimpsed the salutation and stiffened when my eye caught the "Secretary Hamilton."

"Pray what are you writing to him, James?"

He seemed proud to oblige me as he puffed out his chest. "Ah'm requesting a meeting with the king of the Feds."

"What do you expect to accomplish with a meeting?" I steadied my voice.

"Now that Secretary Hamilton is my wife's uh—liaison—he's capable of using his vast connections to assist me." He smacked his lips.

Holding up his missive, he continued, "I informed him that I know some facts he may find interesting, personally as well as in his favor as Treasury Secretary. He knows I engage in speculation occasionally—"

"Occasionally?" I cut in. "If only!"

He ignored my remark. "And I believe I could give information about the conduct of some speculators in the department which he would find useful."

"What speculators?" I placed my fists on my hips. "Who are you slanderizing now?"

"Tis no slander when true, and these persons' reputations are in the privy already," he explained in a matter-of-fact tone. "I divulged no names in the letter. I shall reveal names to Hamilton when we meet. What I know about these scoundrels' high jinks can prove helpful to him, if he can return the favor."

"What favor?" I sneered. "You want to sleep with *his* wife?"

"Nay, she doon't give me a rise," he replied, perfectly serious. "I hope to secure a position in the Treasury Department."

I blinked in surprise. "You in the Treasury Department? You've never had a real job in your life."

"But now ah'm in the position to bargain for one. Besides," he added, "tis easier than hustling." It sounded like an afterthought.

"But hustling is in your blood, James. You wouldn't last two minutes in a government job." I brandished my most scornful smirk.

"And how many more minutes do you plan to last in his bed?" He sealed the letter and trotted out the door.

Weak with relief that he hadn't resorted to his blackmail scheme, I hoped this would render James a respectable citizen—as when he ran for the Continental Congress. Alex knew that James had worked in the Commissary Department with his father during the Revolution, supplying the army. Then last year, desperate for work, James hired himself out to Benjamin Chaffin, a New York merchant. They achieved national notoriety as speculators, raking the countryside to buy unwary veterans' back-pay certificates at deflated prices. James was brought up on criminal charges, but no convictions followed. I reckoned James must have information—more likely, *dirt*—that Alex could use on those speculators.

That night a knock sounded at the back door. Busy reading *Wealth of Nations*, what I now called "our" book, I dismissed it, but when it loudened to rapping, I went to investigate. No one used the back door but our servants, when we could afford them. I opened it and blinked in shock. A weary and disheveled Alex stood there, dark circles under his eyes, hair uncombed, coatless, shirtsleeves pushed past his elbows.

"Alex! Why the back door? Oh, I wish you'd warned me of this visit. I'd have washed, donned décolletage, and changed the sheets." With a titter of delight I stepped back to let him in. "I—wasn't expecting you." Giddy with joy, aroused already, I restrained myself from leaping into his arms.

"I need to speak with you, Maria." His tone didn't sound inviting or romantic.

No! I wanted to cry out loud. My heart plummeted. *Please don't end it!* "Is that teasing letter of James's at the bottom of this?"

Oh, did I gulp in panic when he pulled it out and unfolded it before me!

He gave me a knowing smile. "I trust you're happily reconciled with James."

"Not quite happily," I shot back. "I doubt we'll stay together, now that he knows—"

He held up a hand. "You need not divulge the details. I received this letter from him, called for him this afternoon, and he arrived promptly."

"I know he was anxious to see you, but I have not seen him since this morn. I've been reading our book." Clutching his hand, I beckoned him inside and he followed. "I apologize if he was too forward in the letter. James can be brusque at times. Did your meeting accomplish aught?"

"Besides telling me that he and you had reconciled—and he knows of our liaison, and has no objections, but didn't mention another word on that subject—he offered me some information in exchange for a clerkship in the Treasury Department. He would work on the books and accounts of impost and tonnage and excise accounts. For five hundred a year. I agreed to his bargain." He rubbed his eyes. "Because he and his father served in the Commissary during the war, I trust the credibility of James's insider information. And—because of you." He tucked a tendril of hair behind my ear. I tingled but didn't dare invite him upstairs yet.

"Me?"

He opened his arms and I stepped into his embrace. "He was insane to leave you for another woman—or for any reason. But I shan't presume to state that you're better off without him." He planted kisses on my cheeks and lips. "You make it extremely difficult to disentangle myself," he murmured.

"Then please don't." My breaths increased. "I want you in my bed upstairs."

But he broke our embrace. "Tonight I must return home. But let me know when James will not be in residence, and I shall return."

"Now with a government position dangling before him, I can tell James not to come home and he'll gladly oblige me. Come back tomorrow eve, Alex. James has another engagement."

"Tomorrow night it shall be. Until then, adieu." He kissed my hand, and I mustered every ounce of restraint not to throw my arms round his neck and press my lips to his, to lure him upstairs for a few stolen moments.

"Alex, will you stay, only for a drink?" I tugged on his arm. "We needn't discuss your work or politics. We can chit-chat about books or music, your pleasure."

"No, my dear, I must do more paperwork before retiring." He backed away.

"But you look so tired already!" I smoothed stray strands of hair that had escaped his queue.

"I know." He stifled a yawn. "Sometimes I feel the weight of the world on my shoulders. But it will make our leisure time all the sweeter. Bonsoir."

My hand lingered in his as he stepped out the door, our gazes hard pressed to part. But he broke away and vanished. Oh, how I wanted him to unburden his weight on me! I shut the door and leant against it, catching my breath, counting the hours till we'd next meet.

I hope Mrs. Hamilton has returned to you with restored health & with the most sincere affection –Letter from Henry Lee to Alexander Hamilton, October 18th. 1791

Chapter Ten

Eliza

I entered Alex's study at teatime to see if he cared for a repast, but whom did I see sitting across from him, sipping sherry like an honored guest? James Reynolds. In true gentlemanly fashion, he stood and bowed with a flourish. I bade him good day, turned and closed the door. I prayed Alex wouldn't squander any money on a shady scheme. I knew how Reynolds's notorious ups and downs wore down his wife. But now I wondered—was Mrs. Reynolds mixed up in this? She seemed innocent and unassuming enough, but James was a master at persuasion. Perhaps she'd bent under his influence. I considered paying her a visit but kept my wariness to myself for the time being. If Mr. Reynolds became a regular caller here, I'd bring this to the forefront. Meanwhile, I had five children to raise and another to birth.

Alex arrived next eve after I'd given up on him. I forced myself not to pull him through the doorway as I had that first time.

"Good eve." He brushed his lips against mine as a husband greets a wife after a day's work. It saddened me that I wasn't this wife who knew he'd always come home to me, even after a tryst.

He crooked his elbow and I slid my hand through his arm. He escorted me into the parlour. "And how went your day, my dear?" played on my lips, but I bit my tongue. I cared not to sound that much like a wife! "I missed you, Alex," I said instead, unashamed to admit it.

"And I did you." We sat and I poured us each a glass of wine. He sipped, but I gulped mine. Being four hours since supper, it shot straight to my head.

He shifted his body so that our thighs touched. Of course I wanted him in my bed, but I preferred to talk first. Halfway through "our" book, I was eager to show him how well I'd absorbed the subject matter. If we tarried, I knew he'd be too tired, especially at this late hour.

Tonight I intended to show him I wasn't a wanton. As our lips met, I regained my senses and pulled away. "Alex..." I found it physically painful to break that kiss. How I longed to succumb to my desires and let him escort me up to the bedroom. But this needed build up slowly. "Let us start the evening with conversation." I placed my fingertips on his chest and gave him a nudge, but built of solid muscle, he didn't back away. He only came closer.

"Why wait? You make it difficult for me to hold back, if you want to know the truth." His voice rumbled. His lips brushed my ear, his hot breath sending a shiver of anticipation through me. Liquid fire surged to the core of my femininity. Since we'd become lovers, I longed for his hard body pressed against mine, to lie back on the pillows, to throw back my head and cry out in ecstasy.

But I did not want to surrender so quickly—I needed to show some willpower. I backed away, giving us some breathing room.

"Why do some women prolong the agony?" He lowered his head to nibble at my neck. I buried my face in his hair.

Oh, I ached for him. My mind fought to control my body's desires. A moan rumbled in my throat as I pushed him away, disentangling our arms—and in a moment what would have been our legs. "Alex, I don't want it to be like—" came out in a breathless whisper that sounded like I was begging him to take me.

But I cleared my throat, intoxicated from closeness, unable to regain my senses. With him fully aroused and panting after me, my body won out over my brain. I'd plan more carefully next time. And not sit so close. "Very well, next time we shall take it more slowly. Now take me."

"Of course," he said. "We can discuss anything you want. Later. But now—pleasure before business."

I shuddered in delight. Instinct told me it was now or never. Tonight I'd make him want to stay, to beg for more.

He eased me away, studying me in the glow of the candle in the wall sconce. His eyes, sparkling like rare gems, gazed at me. "Do you still prefer coupling here on the sofa?"

"Yes, right here," I whispered, trying to keep the urgency out of my voice. "It will take too long to go upstairs." We coupled on the sofa.

In the aftermath of release, we caught our breaths and rested on the plush cushions.

"Now can we talk, Alex?" With my ear against his chest, the steady thump of his heart soothed me. He twined his fingers through my hair and chuckled.

"Why do you ladies always need talk after a bit of fun? Are you not spent enough? I can barely remember my name, much less engage in chit chat."

I lifted myself up and faced him, eye to eye. "A bit of fun is it? To me, our souls fused as one in a rapturous conjoining, akin to the bursting of fireworks all around us. And to you tis a bit of fun. That spends you so?"

"A bit of fun, my dear, is an Old English expression, dating back to the Middle Ages if not longer. But I stand corrected. It was a superfluity of fun." He placed his hand on my bare thigh and brought it to rest atop his leg. A spark of desire awakened in me. But knowing how "spent" he was, I reined it in.

"Then I am pleased I spent you so well." I planted kisses on his lips that grew into a mingling of our tongues, something I had never done with James. Alex's leisurely technique made lights burst beneath my closed lids as we came up for air. I felt his arousal stirring again. But not enough to repeat the act and have another "bit of fun."

I reached over and poured a glass of wine, gulping in thirst. He drained his glass.

"Now my senses have returned." He pushed the hair off my forehead. "My name is Alex. I think."

"You just remember that because I shouted it out in the throes of ecstasy." I felt so natural with him. I wished to tell him so, but held back. We had plenty of time to talk about us. I still needed to appeal to him intellectually. Thus I began with, "I want to talk about what I read today in *Wealth of Nations*. Tis slow reading—not exactly leisurely."

"Ah, yes." He settled back and stretched. "I've read it twicet. Up in the garret as not to be disturbed. I can only guess that Smith wrote it that way, too. What did you want to talk about? Laissez-faire? Divisions of labor?"

"No. Asses," I stated.

His eyes grew wide and he blinked. "Asses?"

"Yes, he wasn't trying to be humorous, but he tickled my funny bone."

"I must have missed that part." His eyes slid shut as he smiled.

"The Romans had only copper money until 270 B.C., according to Smith," I explained. "Then they began to coin silver."

"That is correct, copper was their measure of value." He nodded. "Now I know what you're talking about. The 'As' was the denomination of a copper coin."

"Yes, and the plural of 'As' was 'Asses.' So they traded 'Asses' for goods all day." Wanting to go beyond tipsy to silly, I reached over and poured another glass. It spilled over, onto his bare chest. "Oops!" Squealing with delight, I lapped it up as a kitten with a bowl of cream.

He moaned with pleasure. "So what was it about copper Asses you found so intriguing?" he asked me.

"Just picturing Romans exchanging Asses all day, it struck me as funny, among all that pedantry." I smoothed his hair back.

"And a bit of it was a piece of Ass," he cracked.

I laughed at that.

As he emptied the wine bottle into my glass, he said, "A man meets an acquaintance and says, 'I was told you were dead.' He replies, 'Well, you can see I am still alive.' But the first man disputes this on the grounds that 'the man who told me you were dead is much more reliable than you.'"

That made me smile. "Clever," I said. "Where did you hear that? John Adams?"

"Close," Alex replied. "'Tis from Ancient Rome. Apparently they told jokes whilst exchanging Asses. And during and after coupling, I assure you."

I kissed the length of his body, swimming in delightful lightheadedness from the wine, the aftermath of our loving, and him. "I shall finish the book by week's end. And I shall quiz you on it."

"Fair enough." He fell asleep, his breathing slow and steady. I didn't want to wake him, yet I craved his company—and wanted to talk more, about every subject from politics to music to birds. I nudged him and he jolted awake, apologizing. "What is the time?" he asked.

"I care not." I petted him, unable to keep my hands off him. "James isn't coming home. I want you with me right here on the sofa, at least until daybreak."

But he began to sit up. I grabbed my petticoat off the floor and covered my lower half.

He stood, pulling on his stockings.

"Where are you going?" My voice cracked, shattered with disappointment. *Don't leave me now*, I wanted to beg, but that wouldn't make him stay.

"I've a long day ahead of me. I must go. But we'll be together again soon. By the bye—do you need any more money?" he tossed out the offer as he buttoned his shirt and searched for his shoes.

"No, I do not." I resented the offer this time. "Alex, I do not care to appear a courtesan, taking money after every tryst."

Slipping into his shoes, he looked down at me, brows raised. "I do not see you that way at all, dear. I just want to help, until James starts the treasury position."

"I do not need additional funds," I informed him. "But thank you for your generosity. James wangled—er, procured employment with Josiah Bank, the goldsmith. He's busy with commissions. But this treasury position would be his salvation, I pray."

"I know you want to save him." He pulled on his frock coat. "And he may not be beyond redemption. Only time will tell." Buttoning his coat, he cast a liquorish look at my breasts, bared and vulnerable.

Seeing me flushed from the ecstasy we'd shared, why hadn't he begged for more? But his face hardened into a mask of seriousness. "Maria, you will be careful if venturing out after dark, you must promise me this."

"I am a woman, Alex." I crossed my arms over my chest. "It is in my nature to be careful if I am out and about alone in the dark."

"But I cannot stress the importance of extra vigilance at present. You must have heard of the recent murders." He buttoned his coat.

A chill struck me cold. "I know. Word of those gruesome murders has been spreading like plague, and not just close to where they happened. There cannot be a living soul who hasn't heard of them."

"Then I implore you to be extra vigilant if you must leave the house alone at night. Only today I spoke with the commissioner. Extra constables are being assigned to the streets at night in an attempt to capture the fiend who is terrorizing our women."

"Surely," I said, "the killer will be deterred by these additional officers of the law."

"Mayhap, and mayhap not. The commissioner informed me of some of the more debauched aspects of the murders in the course of our discussion. I should

not want to disturb your mind by going into details."
He headed for the door.

For the first time, I realized he was seriously worried. After the murder of Rose Webster, which had been horrific enough, word soon spread of a second killing, another young girl, not yet twenty years of age, slain in an apparently identical manner.

"You are really worried about this matter, are you not, Alex?" His words of concern alarmed me. Aware of the open window, I closed it—and latched it.

"Very worried, Maria, for, after speaking with the commissioner, I had the good fortune of a chance encounter in the street with Dr. Black, with whom I also discussed the murders."

I followed him to the door. "Dr. Black?" I queried. "I haven't had the pleasure of making the gentleman's acquaintance."

"Yes, Severus Black. I'm sure you've seen him at one or more of the fetes you and James have attended round town. Tall, very handsome..." he paused, "so my wife says, always dressed immaculately, all in black and with penetrating eyes, not an easy man to ignore."

I tried to conjure up an image of him in my mind. When his haunting visage appeared before my eyes, my flesh crawled. "Oh, yes, now that you mention the eyes. But I didn't know his name before now. I've seen him at various venues, though we've never been introduced, nor had I occasion to speak with him. His eyes—" I paused, now trying to purge his image from my mind. "You're right, they look right through you. You spoke with him about the murders?"

"Yes, indeed." He nodded. "Since arriving from Paris, he's looked in on my wife—in a professional capacity," he hastened to add. "He is a specialist in women's matters and has been of some comfort to her during her pregnancy. His bedside manner, like his appearance and standards of personal grooming, is always impeccable."

"What did you and the doctor talk about?" Morbid curiosity made me ask.

"I mentioned to Severus my conversation with the commissioner. Severus postulated that the killer may be an escaped lunatic, or someone with a pathological hatred of women. He stated clearly to me that whomsoever the killer is, he must be a man of great strength, as to strangle another human being, even a woman, takes a great deal of strength and perseverance."

"Perseverance?" I asked, puzzled.

"My question also." Alex nodded. "He replied that the victim of a strangulation must surely be fighting for her life, and therefore it follows she would be struggling, trying to scream and so forth. The killer must therefore possess enough personal strength to overcome her and then hold her firm as he tightens the instrument of strangulation about her neck."

I shuddered at that graphic description. "He did not use his bare hands, then?"

"It appears not. The commissioner told me about evidence of some form of ligature having been used on both women, a scarf, or a belt mayhap. Anyway, I pointed out to Severus that we would know if a lunatic had escaped from a nearby asylum. But he was at pains to point out that such a man may easily have escaped from a Bedlam in another town and made his way here in order to evade capture. It appears also that the women were both…well…" He lowered his eyes—and his voice. "They were sexually violated, Maria. I shall say no more of that side of the crime. We only talked for a short time and then parted, he going one way and I the other. So please, now you must promise me you will avoid venturing out at night." He took my hands and I clung to him.

"I don't want to let go. I'm scared." In fact, I shook. "I don't want to be left here alone."

"There's naught to be scared of. He doesn't break into houses. He strictly does his work—er, commits his crimes on the street," he attempted to assure me.

Still clinging to him, I said, "Well, of course to venture out alone after dark is indeed foolhardy. I shall be vigilant to the point of obsession if it will make you happy. But, oh, how I wish you could stay with me."

He disengaged himself from my clutches, but gave me one final kiss. "You're safe here. Just lock up. Adieu, my dear."

I sensed regret in those last words as he stood on the threshold. "Alex, when will you—" I stopped myself from saying those final words and was glad I had. I realized that the way to keep him was to know when to let him go.

Chapter Eleven

Severus

My brief encounter with Alexander Hamilton made me tingle with delight. To hear my friend espousing the useless drivel of law enforcement, that ineffective and inefficient band of legal riff-raff, curled my lips with mirth. After my short dalliance with the unfortunate Rose, I'd returned to my lodgings, spent but not entirely satisfied. My mind drifted back to my Paris days. All went well until that scourge of the criminal classes, Detective Remy Le Clerc, became obsessed with me after a witness reported seeing a man with penetrating blue eyes close to the scene of a young parlour maid's murder. With no other evidence and no proof to support his suspicions, Le Clerc had nonetheless made my life a misery from then onwards, shadowing my every move, preventing me from furthering my murderous intent. Finally, frustrated beyond belief, my life in England also soured by a close call with the law, I gained passage to the New World.

Now I basked in the smugness of safety, having spent time building up my reputation. Respected by those with whom I mixed on a social level, I at last felt free to pursue my other needs. As I began to gain invitations to balls and other social functions, I cultivated the rich and famous, those in positions to afford me with greater credibility and substance.

Since I started specialising in the doctoring of women's matters I found that those wealthy men's wives and daughters readily approached me and confided in me of their ills, seeking my help and advice. But never once did I consider satisfying my lusts with any of those women. No, that would point too much attention in my direction. Better that I focus my needs on those ladies' maids and servants. There were plenty to choose from, most young, pretty and easy prey for such a *gentleman* as I.

The night following Rose's demise, my urges niggled at me, needing further satisfaction. I took to the streets once more. I knew of a ball taking place three blocks from the home of Secretary and Mrs. Hamilton, and though not invited, I dressed as though I were, crouched behind a tree and watched their servants' comings and goings. Many of them took time out from their duties for a short break, when permitted, away from the noise and bustle of the kitchen, the pantry, or the ballroom itself.

A young lady now leant against a fence at the rear of the house, a short walk from the entrance to a wide portico through which deliverymen approached the house during the day.

After ensuring no one else lurked about, I approached the girl. "Oh, Miss, thank heaven. Please, can you help me?" I rushed my words, appearing breathless. "My wife has fallen on the street and she is with child. Please help me get her to her feet as she is in a dead faint and not herself at all!"

"Of course, sir!" She agreed to my entreaty.

I rushed towards the street, to allay any thoughts she might have that something was amiss. At the street I turned to the left. She followed in my wake until I turned into the gates of a small park opposite the grand homes.

"Uh... sir?" Pangs of doubt crept into her voice.

"Don't panic," I warned her, keeping my voice soft and soothing. "My wife is within the park. We were taking the air after leaving the house when she collapsed. I made sure she was comfortably lying on the grass before seeking help."

"But sir, would it not have been quicker to return to the house to get help, instead of walking all the way round to the back?" She cast furtive glances around as she began to shake.

I stopped in my tracks and turned to face her. "Of course it would, but then, I should not have met you, should I? And speaking of which, what is your name, young lady?"

"Anne Denton, sir." Her eyes met mine, widened in a mixture of fear and wonder. She backed away.

I took two steps forward. "And where do you come from, with that charming accent?"

"Cardiff, Wales, sir. I'm fortunate to find employment so soon. With my parents' blessing, I accepted the position and moved into my employer's garret." She backed away again as she blathered on, her voice high-pitched and quivering with fear. With each step backward, I took a step forward. "The work is hard, the hours long, but my employer is considerate and fair, and lets me spend a half-day each week with my family." Out of breath and now out of room to flee, she backed into the gatepost. We now stood toe to toe. She trembled, her teeth chattering.

"Oh, dear God, look!" I pointed down, at the base of a small shrub. "My dear wife! Oh, please, no."

Anne stepped sideways and crouched to peer under the bush. It was enough. My second self emerged, controlling my actions. I whipped the scarf from around my neck and tightly wrapped it round the girl's throat. She kicked out at me with her heels to no avail. I grunted with satisfaction as I felt her body go slack. Her final breath passed her lips with an audible gasp.

I hurriedly dragged her limp body to the rear of the shrub, unseen from the pathway upon which we'd walked, and took a moment to gather myself as my arousal soared.

Ready at last, I knelt beside the girl and raised her skirts. At the sight of the pure fresh flesh of her young legs, and with my arousal at bursting point, I took my latest lover.

Chapter Twelve

Maria

The next morn as I rinsed undergarments in our wash basin, James greeted me with an expectant smile. "Top o'the mornin' to you, my bonny lass."

"No money changed hands, James." I got it over with.

"Dinna he offer any?" He poured honey on a biscuit and shoved it into his mouth.

"Yes, but I refused it." I wrung out a pair of petticoats.

He snickered. "What else of his did you refuse?"

I knew it was a rhetorical question. He was hardly interested in what went on between me and Alex. "He fell asleep." That was all James needed to know. And it was the naked truth.

"That useless, eh?" He shook his head, still chewing. "He's gettin' old, I reckon." Licking honey from his fingers, he poured himself a glass of ale.

"You were born two months apart. If he's getting old, you're getting old," I retorted.

"Not at the same rate, obviously." He sprawled out on the sofa with his ale, leaning his head on the cushion Alex and I made love on. I looked away, reliving last eve in my mind—how he held me, how I clung to him. I longed for his touch, even now, my hands wet and raw from washing.

After hanging petticoats out on the line, I started reading Shakespeare's *Richard III*, which Alex recommended, but found it hard to believe this king was as sinister as the Bard made him out to be. Mr. Shakespeare did tend to "take license" at times; he put a clock in *Julius Caesar* which chimed thrice, and had Cleopatra playing tennis!

Neither of us mentioned Alex's name all week. I kept my feelings to myself. James stayed busy with his gold smithing commissions, pubbing, dice and card games. I combed through the newspapers, but tried not to seek out Alex's name. Still, thoughts of him filled every waking moment. Anticipation kept my heart aflutter. I took special care with my hair, my teeth, my overall cleanliness. I made extra soap and bathed every day now. "You'll drain the Delaware dry afore long," James commented. "Sheesh, who needs wash every day?"

Next Friday morn, James tossed me *National Gazette*. "Yur paramour made the news again. This time he wants to tax the poor farmers on their bloody whisky."

The headline, CONGRESS APPROVES WHISKY TAX AT SECRETARY HAMILTON'S URGING, shouted at me to read the article. I didn't miss a word. Now I knew why Alex was too busy to write or call on me.

According to the article, Alex convinced the Federal government to approve taxes on 'ardent spirits,' a luxury according to him, to pay down the national debt. The Fed, in assuming the states' debt from the war, amassed a huge debt. The tax is "more as a measure of social discipline than as a source of revenue," The paper quoted Alex as saying. "I want the tax imposed to advance and secure the power of the new Federal government."

The tax levy, placed upon imported liquors and domestic distilled, would raise about $800,000.

Smaller distillers would pay nine cents a gallon, and larger distillers would pay a flat fee. President Washington's consent surprised me. He was the largest whisky distiller in America!

I read aloud his reasons for the taxation, to make sure I understood them. "When a manufacture is in its infancy, it is impolitic to tax it. The tax would be unproductive and add to the difficulties which impede attempts to establish it. But when a manufacture, as in distilled spirits, is arrived at maturity, it is as fit an article of taxation as any other."

I agreed with Alex wholeheartedly. "What do you think?" I asked James as he slurped coffee and chomped on a piece of my apple tansey.

"I think he's daft." He finished chewing and wiped his mouth. "And so's the entire bloody government. This will spur a revolt." His voice rose. "Another storming of the Bastille. And I need no crystal ball to tell you that." He gave a resolute nod.

"For nine cents a gallon?" I re-read the article, my eyes lingering on Alex's name.

"Do you know how long it takes a farmer to earn nine poxy cents, Maria? Bloody hell, spirits are no luxury, they're a necessity. Those folk in the west haven't got a clue what luxury is." He stood and flung his serviette onto the table. "They needs break their backs to trundle their grain to market on the treacherous roads as it is." A vein bulged in his neck. "They first need distill it into spirits they can transport. These wee producers will suffer much worse than the immense ones." He paced in a circle and halted before me, staring me down. "If I were Hamilton, I wouldna leave the house. The mad rabble are itchin' to tar and feather his plutocratic hide."

I panicked. Sweat moistened my palms. "Would a mob of backwoodsmen storm the Capital and seize the lawmakers, creating another French Revolution, because of a nine-cent tax on their whisky?" My voice shook.

"Just watch," came his eerie reply.

No, it couldn't happen. But James's portent stayed on my mind till he left for work.

I devoured the rest of the newspaper.

KILLER STALKS THE STREETS blasted the headline on page 2. The article went on to report the two murders committed, *so far*, it said, intimating that mayhap there could be more in future and criticizing the authorities for what the reporter described as *the laxity of investigative success from the authorities and the paucity of resources being applied to the case.* It was evident that at the time of writing, the reporter, one Silas Blunt, had not been privy to the commissioner's intent to add to the number of constables patrolling the streets at night. I shuddered. Seeing the case described in black and white did cause me trepidation and a resolve to do as Alex had asked. I vowed to restrict my movements after dark. Just to be sure, I checked the doors and windows again.

To stay busy, I wrote Alex a letter.

I read about the whisky tax and I support it—and you. We need pay our nation's debt. I also saw the piece about the murders. Fear not, for I shall take great care as you asked of me.

I added nothing intimate, desperate or longing.

The week dragged on. I received no reply from Alex, but James's prediction had come true—as if he had a crystal ball.

Next day's headlines barked about how unjust western farmers considered the tax on whisky, and their bitterness about it. In their protest meetings, they cried discrimination, as they always converted their extra grain into whisky. Alex's solution for the frontiersman was simple: drink less. "*It depends on themselves to diminish consumption,*" he was quoted as telling Congress.

James crumpled the paper in disgust. "That supercilious two-faced pillock," he grumbled, imbibing his own ardent spirits. "Drink is but all those men have. Aye, let them abstain from their *vice*. When he bloody well abstains from his *vice*." He wiped his mouth and refilled his glass with the whisky he'd purchased yesterday—a dozen bottles of it, "to help the poor farmers," he'd said.

Unwilling to add one word to this conversation about Alex abstaining from his "vice," I shut my mouth on the subject. It mattered not; a tax, however burdensome, wouldn't separate James from his *aqua vitae*.

But it didn't stop me from reading about it. I hadn't yet heard from Alex and still worried about his safety. Would those farmers travel here from the frontier in their wobbly ox carts or on foot, brandishing canes and blunderbusses? Was Alex worried? I longed to speak to him, about this if naught else.

A character called Tom the Tinker now appeared in every daily paper. I knew not if he was a real person or a fictional embodiment of all the angry farmers, who called themselves Tinker's Men.

Tom the Tinker had a fiendish way with words: "You might find a note posted on a tree outside your house, requiring you to publish in the *Gazette* hatred of the whisky tax and your commitment to the cause; otherwise, the note promised, your still would be mended," James read aloud from the *Gazette*.

"*Mended*," he explained to me, "means shot full of holes."

I shuddered.

To my relief, during the Whisky Rebellion, Tom the Tinker and his men kept their protests out of the Capitol. Some Pennsylvania farmers threatened to declare their independence, but didn't tar and feather any tax collectors. Not yet. I wrote Alex again, asking if he was safe enough. Still no answer. But every morn when I combed the papers and read no news about any assassinations. I went limp with relief. James insisted this would lead to a revolt, forcing President Washington to send out the militia. I thought it strange that the papers reported no more about the murders, but mayhap the lack of further press reports would herald an end to the horrific crimes. Or the next article would report this lunatic's capture. I was wrong, of course.

James heard naught about the Treasury Department position, either. But his friend Ephraim Heald began a clerkship there paying $500 a year. "Why had I bin passed over? I got sacked before I even got the job," James groused at least thrice a day.

"I wish I knew." I dragged myself about, with no interest in anything except receiving a letter or a surprise late-night visit from my lover. *He's swamped with work*, I convinced myself.

James now wrote Alex another letter, kindly asking for the job again, to no avail.

After two weeks, unable to sleep or eat. I suffered profound loss as if Alex had abandoned me. I lost my temper over the slightest mishap, my fists clenched and my chest tightened more often. Had he been using me? After all we'd shared? I pushed that thought away. He still cared, he had to!

I also felt sorry for James. Although the gold smithing commissions brought in a steady income, he coveted this treasury position.

Early next morn as I brewed coffee, James ushered in a thin redheaded woman wearing a wrinkled linen dress and carrying a battered satchel. "This is Miss Maggie McKivan, my wife Mrs. Reynolds," he introduced us.

As she curtseyed and greeted me with her Irish brogue, I knew he'd hired her as a servant. She held the kitchen chairs out for us, sat us down and began cracking the eggs I'd bought at market. We chit-chatted about the weather as she set the table and poured our coffee.

"How did you find her?" I asked James as Maggie bustled about, lit the fire in the wood stove and scoured the fry pan.

"Maggs sailed here from Belfast on the *Friendship*, the same ship Patrick Bevin came over on, another goldsmith I work with. In fact, he paid her passage, and tis he from where we inherited her."

"Inherited her? He died and left her in his will?" I kept my voice low.

"Nay, not quite so dramatic. Yestermorn she finished her seven years of indentured servitude to him. She came up for hire, so I hired her. We kin well afford it."

I hoped her employment would be long-term, not subject to James's rising and falling fortunes. This morn, she served us omelettes using nearly my entire dozen eggs, and scrubbed up till the kitchen sparkled. She then asked, "What else can do, ma'am? I'll do anything." I gave her some ironing and stockings to mend, not needing anything else.

As she worked and I read on the sofa, James settled at his desk and busied himself writing. This letter took him two hours whilst he used up all his ink and most of his whisky. I'd never seen him put so much effort into anything. "Shall I read it to you," came out like a statement rather than a question, as if I'd dare say no.

He cleared his throat and began: "Sir, you have deprived me of everything that's near and dear to me. You took the advantage of a poor broken-hearted woman, instead of being a friend, you have acted the part of the most cruelest man in existence. You have made a whole family miserable. She sees there is no other man that she cares for in this world, now, sir, you have been the cause of cooling her affections for me, but now I am determined to have satisfaction. It shan't be only one family that's miserable, for I am robbed of all happiness in this world."

He paused for effect. "Now, sir, if I can't see you at your house, call and see me, for there is no person that knows aught as yet. And I am determined to see you, by some means or other, for you have made me an unhappy man forever. Put it to your own case and reflect one moment, that you should know such a thing of your wife, would you not have satisfaction? And so will I before one day passes me more."

He finished reading and looked at me as if expecting me to applaud. "Well?"

I sat there at a loss for a response. I disliked the letter, but I was just as upset with Alex. James was not a patient man. He wanted this job, and to be fair, he had given Alex useful information.

I shook my head and turned towards the kitchen, needing some strong coffee. "Sending that letter won't make him act any faster, James. Rein in your spur."

But he posted it anyway.

Two days later, a letter from Alex arrived. My heart slammed my ribs. I gasped for breath. But it was addressed to James. As he opened it, I peered over his shoulder, desperate to read it. It stated that no job was available, but he wanted to meet with James at his earliest convenience.

"Now is early enough." He tossed the letter aside, grabbed his new velvet cloak and loped out the door.

I awaited his return with frayed nerves. I went for a walk, played my violin and tried to read because I couldn't eat. James finally came home near six of the eve. I wanted to drag the words out of him. "What did he say?" I nearly screeched.

"The department has no immediate openings, but he referred me over to Congressman George Clymer, who might need an assistant clerk. I told him I can procure some more damning evidence about—"

I held up my hand. "Spare me your deals till later. What did he say about me?"

116

He shrugged. "Naught at first. But I encouraged him to continue to see you. Then he said since his wife's return, he needed to step back from…yur assignations."

"So that is why I hadn't heard anything…" Dejection crushed my spirit. "What did he say when you suggested…encouraged…" I gestured with fluttering hands.

"He'll be back." James flipped his hand as if swatting a fly. "The bit about the missus was an excuse, I take it. I should'a known. He ain't the devoted family man all the folk think he is. He may be peltin' some doxy this very minute."

"No one ever said he was a saint." But the thought of him "peltin' some doxy" tore me apart. I swiped at tears with my balled fist.

"Just keep yurself prepared." Exactly what James meant by that, I knew not. Prepared for Alex's amorous attention? Or for a shattering rejection should he never return? But James had heard it first hand, and Alex didn't lie. I knew in my heart I'd see him again. But I continued hoping James wouldn't resort to that diabolical blackmail scheme of his. After this lapse of time, I reckoned he'd forgotten about it.

Next day I received a letter from Alex. I tore it open with fervor bordering on lust, read it over and over, kissed his signature, hugged it to my breast. "He wants to see me again!"

"Immense." James nodded. "Now for the second order of business."

"Which is?" I feared he was about to extort more money from Alex.

"Never mind." He headed for the door. "Ah'm off to the stationer's. We're out o'paper."

Alex came to me that night. Tingling in anticipation, I ached to leap into his arms. But I restrained myself, unlike our last meeting. His genius intrigued me, and knowing that I in turn intrigued him made me feel his equal. I longed to be his wife, but his equal would have to do for now.

He stepped inside and kissed my hand. I didn't fight the shiver of delight that thrilled me. Neither did I throw myself at him. "Alex, why did you not write or call on me? I was ever so worried about you, after that whisky tax passed," I rambled, taking rapid breaths. "I read about the mad farmers, and so feared they'd storm the Capitol. Please do not ignore my letters when I implore you to reply. Let me know you're safe. I was so... I was afraid you'd..." I cut myself off when I realized I was begging. I forced myself to calm down, finding it painful.

"I am sorry, Maria. No one stormed the Capitol. We are all safe for now." He gave my hand a reassuring squeeze. "I did not reply because I am working night and day, non-stop. I had time for naught else. Don't take it as an affront."

Something made me believe him. I couldn't bear to disbelieve him. It was then I noticed his hands, stained with blue ink. He'd been writing all day. Every time I saw him, every inch of him was impeccably washed. This affirmed my belief. Relief lightened my heart. I breathed calmer now.

"What have you been writing, Alex?" He followed me inside and sat on the sofa. "Your memoirs? I believe you're a bit young for that yet." I poured us each a goblet of claret from a crystal decanter I'd put out for this eve... with matching goblets.

"Would that I'd play cowtow to my whimsy. No, I've been working on my Report on Manufactures. I hope to present it to Congress by the end of the year. I've been writing so long, my fingers are still curled, albeit round an invisible pen." He sipped his wine. "This is why I did not write or call here. This has taken every waking moment. I skipped meals to write this. I wrote in the privy. I skipped Sunday services. It literally consumed me."

"You poor dear. I'll fix your fingers." Taking the goblet from his hand, I leant over and straightened his fingers one by one. As he flexed them, I kissed their tips and knuckles. "Why do you not dictate to a secretary?"

He gave a dismissive wave. "I cannot express myself orally as well as with my hands."

"Oh, I can argue that," I teased.

I knew he spoke the truth. This report was consuming him. He sat hunched forward, his gaze fixed on the floor.

"Alex, tell me about it. I want to be here for you and hear everything about your work, and you. Share with me. Ask me for opinions, ideas. Anything at all."

He looked pensive, a crease between his drawn brows. He took a sharp breath and nodded. "Actually, you can help me with this. Remember when I told you about the corporation I formed, the Society for Establishing Useful Manufactures? We call it S.U.M. now. I met with my board today, and we discussed possible locations for grist mills. But none seemed suitable to me. Of course it has to be on a river, as I told you. We need to utilize its power. One of the men suggested the Mississippi. He was laughed out of the room. We want to power a town, not the entire nation." His eyes brightened as if hit with a brilliant idea. "In your travels, have you seen a good site for some mills?"

He'd never asked me such an important question. An opinion was one thing, but where to base mills for his manufacturing corporation? If he accepted my suggestion, I could be instrumental in shaping the nation.

"How about along the Delaware or Hudson River?" I suggested.

His eyes focused on the floor. "Somewhere less prominent. Where the land is cheaper. We need to lease the land to other mill ventures. Not everyone is wealthy. It needs to be affordable."

"I traveled through New Jersey with James when he fled his duel with Jon Dayton. We went through a town with lovely waterfalls...wait." I squeezed my eyes shut to recall. "I believe we crossed the Passaic River at one point. Yes, the Passaic." I nodded. "There were some waterfalls. That can serve the purpose better than a river."

He released his gaze from the floor and regarded me with such pleased surprise, his eyes glittered in the candlelight. "Now that is clever, my dear."

My heart danced at his praise.

"The Passaic River and the waterfall. I was there once. In seventy-nine as I recall, with then-General Washington, the Marquis de Lafayette and his aide-de-camp James McHenry. En route to Paramus, we stopped there. It was called—" He tapped the side of his head. "What was it? Oh, yes, the Totowa Falls. We picnicked there, and I commented to the other men about the natural beauty and power of the falls. Somehow I always knew I'd return."

His eyes focused on a faraway point, as if he relived a fond memory. He went on, "A charming gentleman, Colonel Theunis Dey, commanded the Bergen County militia." He stood and paced back and forth. "Our troops bivouacked on the property sur-rounding his house, and some of us stayed in the house itself. Colonel Dey gave me a lovely upstairs bedroom to myself. His house is a stone's throw from the falls."

His gaze locked on mine. "Oh, Maria, thank you so much for reminding me! It would be ideal for mills to be built there." He inspected his ink-stained hands, as if just realizing he hadn't washed them. He began stammering an apology.

I refilled his goblet. "Good heavens, Alex, you're growing the nation by leaps and bounds, and worrying about blue hands? Never mind. You can wash them later. Now I want to hear about your manufacturing report." I added, "Of course, being from New York, my family believes the economy of the merchant North far superior to the agricultural South. We all supported your creation of the Bank. But you're far ahead of what my father or brother had ever discussed. Forming a corporation, building mills and leasing them? You're not merely a visionary, but an entrepreneurial genius as well!" My curiosity piqued, I blurted out, "Alex, you must let me read this report."

"In time." He gave me a confident nod and sipped his wine. "As you're reading in *Wealth of Nations,* I praise the many-sided benefits of the division of labor. There is naught of greater moment in the nation's economy than the proper division of labor. Manufacturing will also attract immigrants. Jefferson's belief that the cultivation of the earth as the most reliable endeavor is outmoded. At least by a century and a half." He swirled the wine in the goblet and took another sip.

"Then you're saying farmers should abandon their farms and begin producing textiles, nails and shovels?" I leant forward.

"No, not all farmers. But in order to ensure our independence from foreign countries and be competitive, we need to manufacture our own goods, many more than we're producing now. Ever since the first settlers began engaging in commerce, our economy has navigated itself with adequate velocity. And it will remain stagnant as long as people are governed by habit."

He stared into the goblet. "They will fail to imagine the simplest improvements and innovations. Workers will stick to their ordinary occupations and routines unless some are moved by curiosity and daring. Who can provide this stimulus? Our government, of course. We need inventors. There is at present a fermentation of mind and enterprise. If left to itself, 'tis vulnerable to destructive effects." He took three rapid gulps, draining the goblet.

I sipped my wine. He continued, "Yes, farming is rewarding, but not everyone can or should farm. I come from a long line of merchants. But with a few mills—the sky is the limit as to what they can produce. Jefferson and Madison are missing the boat. Jefferson finally admitted my plan would make the nation wealthier, but couldn't resist arguing that republicanism and democracy would suffer if the nation succumbed to corrupt industrialists."

"And he believes all industrialists are corrupt?" I asked. "That's very democratic."

He snickered. "Jefferson emphatically pointed out to me that the Revolutionary War had been won by farmers who fought for their freedom. But he is dead wrong. At least in New York and New England, many of the continental and militia soldiers were mechanics, artisans and urban laborers, not just farmers. And my propositions are unconstitutional, as he is opposed to government financing private enterprise."

"If he wants the nation to remain a nation of farmers, we'll be stuck in the Middle Ages, with naught but agriculture to sustain the entire economy." I stated the obvious. "A schoolchild would know this."

He beamed at me. "My point exactly. Imagine an industrialized nation." His eyes grew wide. Again he paced, as if preparing to present a case to a packed courtroom. He twirled on a heel and faced me. "Factories, plants, mills humming with activity, turning out yards of silk, wool, linen, hundreds of saddles, shoes, boots, gloves, sheathes of paper, shovels and nails, as you are correct, the sky is the limit."

I could almost hear Yankee Doodle on a fife accompanying his speech. He took a deep breath and sat.

"But this idea, brilliant as it is, may not go over with the anti-Federalists. Will it?" I had to ask.

He shook his head. "No. Not right away. This may take an entire generation to accomplish. But I would like to see some progress in my lifetime. And be the one to begin it."

My mind whirred. Alex was serious about this waterfall on the Passaic River. "This is too lofty for James to consider jumping into, but my cousin George Lewis, my brother-in-law Gilbert, or even James's friend Jacob Clingman, another visionary, and with ample funds, will back you a hundred percent on this. They'll invest in your corporation when the board secures the location."

"The more the merrier." He smiled and emptied the wine bottle into his goblet. "Oh, sorry, do you want some more?"

"No, thanks. I couldn't think of drinking more. Have you sought out any investors yet? I'm more interested in this than getting your report through Congress. I'm sure Jefferson and his cronies will dismiss it out of hand. But our idea, rather, this idea, is something worth exploring. Together," I added, thrilled at this venture, Alex's and mine.

"I'll seek them out when I'm sure of the location. But siting it on the Passaic River at the great waterfalls, my dear, that is a stroke of genius. I must outright give you several shares just for thinking of that." He clasped my hand.

Warmth enveloped me, and it wasn't from the wine. "Oh, there's no need. I can buy some. Besides, you'd been there only a few years ago. You would have remembered the site without my help, surely."

It hit me like lightning—little Maria Reynolds planning our nation's future with the great Alexander Hamilton!

But I was too overcome with the idea and its prospects to realize how visionary it was. "My brother-in-law Gilbert wants to open a textile factory someday," I told him. "He's tiring of his law practice. He wants to see tangible things produced, not just sell services. He thinks it's more honorable, too."

"Of course." Alex nodded, eyes atwinkle. "And it puts more people to work. Entire families can be gainfully employed."

"Families?" Ah, yes. He meant children. "That is one thing I'm against, child labor. Alex, why are you in favor of putting children to work?"

"Why should they not work? They shouldn't grow up spoilt." His tone bordered on chiding. "I started work myself, clerking at age nine. Why cannot American children do the same? Working them in cotton mills cannot be worse than working them on farms."

I shook my head in despair. "Both are equally repugnant. Will you make your own children work in this mill? Or any other?"

He waved a dismissive hand. "This is to keep the poor from starving. My children do not need to work."

Vexation niggled at me. I swallowed it down. But I had to make my point. "I would never make my children work. I want them to be educated. So they can do whatever they please, be it lawyering or running a saw mill. But working? No. I've seen child labor. I do not want to see any more."

"Now you are the visionary." He chuckled. "Maybe your great-great-grandson can do something about that. Look, Maria, we're rushing way ahead of ourselves here. Let me further explore the waterfall idea. I can arrange a visit there within the week and inform you of what I find."

I felt a bit hurt he hadn't invited me along. After all, it had been my idea. "May I accompany you?" I asked brashly.

He nodded, obviously not having given it the slightest thought. "If you wish."

"What will you tell Mrs. Hamilton?" I dreaded the answer. I didn't want to hear that she'd be accompanying us.

"That I'm traveling on business. She never questions my travels, before or after."

I turned my head so he wouldn't hear my relieved sigh.

He continued, "She wouldn't be the least bit interested in this anyway. She's against manufacturing. She likes Jefferson's idea of agriculture, being close to nature, tilling the soil."

"But that won't grow our nation and create rapid prosperity and make us competitive," I maintained. "I care not to challenge Mrs. Hamilton, but I feel the complete opposite."

He pointed his finger at me, like a pistol. "Bang. You hit the nail on the head. Birthing and raising six children won't create our nation's prosperity, either, but that is what she wanted."

I dared not voice any further opinion on this. I shared no common traits with Mrs. Hamilton. If I did, her husband wouldn't be here sharing his visions of the nation's growth, asking me for my contributions, and sharing my bed.

I wanted to strut the room in smug superiority. But I didn't dare show it. I simply reveled in it... silently.

"Let me know when we can journey to the river, and I shall pack a lovely lunch. We can make a day of it." The words rushed out of me in my haste to be a part of this.

"It will be more than a day, Maria." He sat back. "'Tis at least a hundred miles from here. Two days to get there, at least half a day to survey the area, two days back." He focused on me, desire in his eyes, whether for me or for his grand plan, I couldn't tell. "Will you be able to travel this length of time?"

My body responded before my brain. A week alone with him, all to myself! "Yes, of course. Maggie, our servant, is here to run the household."

"I mean what will you tell James?" He leant forward. "We must keep this under wraps, of course. Perhaps even travel separately, or in disguise."

In my excitement, I hadn't thought of James. But I'd disguise myself as a gargoyle for time alone with Alex. "No need to worry. I shall tell him the truth." While on the subject of James, I thought of something else. "Alex, how long have you been playing bid whist?"

He looked away and fidgeted with his cuffs. "I don't play often. Sometimes a friend drops by and invites me to a game of cards for a diversion because they all know I work too hard. But I..." He gave a one-shoulder shrug, "...I win my share of games."

"James told me of your late-night losing streak. He gloated over his winnings, from your pocket."

He tried to suppress a smile. "Yes, James is a skillful player. He had me there. At any rate, did you finish the book yet?"

"Why are you avoiding the subject?" Ah, of course! "Alex, did you let him win the other night?"

He tried to show surprise in his eyes, but truth be told, he was a terrible actor. "Now what gave you that idea?"

"Because he cannot even beat *me* at whist," I informed him. "He's terrible at cards."

We sat in silence for a heartbeat, and then he nodded. "Very well, I wanted to help him out."

"But, Alex, he's a swindler by nature. If you give him that government appointment, he'll ballocks it all up. I know the position would greatly elevate our status, but don't put your reputation on the line by helping him this way. Next thing you know, he'll be selling your secrets to the British."

His brows shot up. "He's been known to spy?"

"No, but he'd sell our fourteen states to France and ship them there if he got a good enough offer. He still rambles on about how much he admired Benedict Arnold. He said, and pardon my Anglo-Saxon, General Arnold had 'the codlings of an ox,' an old Scottish expression."

The amusement on his curved lips told me he'd heard that expression before. "The colonies were crawling with would-be spies. They believed it glamorous and exciting. All the more so because Arnold, when he got word that his treachery had been exposed, absconded into the British army's open arms. James obviously knows naught about Arnold's British contact, Major André, who was tried and convicted as a spy."

Alex breathed a sad, thoughtful sigh. "Myself and several other sympathetic aides begged Washington to let him die by firing squad, as befits a soldier, but he would not hear of it. The poor lad met his demise at the end of a rope. Washington carried out the sentence with tears in his eyes. Tis the only time I'd seen the great man cry." He paused, a pained look darkening his eyes. "Fret not. James won't be privy to any clandestine operations. He'll be at such a low level, he won't be near anyone important. Not that I'm important..." He cast his gaze away.

He and the whole world knew how important he was, but I thought it sweet and endearing how he always tried to humble himself. I no longer wanted to discuss James. I was doubly sure he cared not to discuss Mrs. Hamilton, so I changed the subject to music. "I wish Mr. Mozart would visit us."

"Word has it that he's very ill, and not yet thirty-six years of age. He'll never make a voyage across the sea for us to witness his brilliant playing or conducting. But we'll always have his music," Alex said.

"What a loss for the world—and his poor widow and children. I'll be sure to keep his memory alive by playing his music. Mayhap I can find a violin instructor to further advance my technique." I glanced at my violin on the shelf. "I need to play it more often."

"Will you play your violin for me?" he asked.

I loved to perform, but I was still rather nervous around him. Playing for my audience of one made my palms even moister. "I'll play a short ditty." I fetched the instrument, tuned the strings to my trained ear, and performed a minuet. "This is one of the first pieces I learnt as a child." I was too nervous to attempt anything more complicated. He tapped his foot and clapped at the end. At the finale, I heaved a relieved sigh.

"Keep playing," he urged, and rose to stand behind me. I chose a medieval tune as his hands slid up my waist, stopping to cup my breasts. By now I was distracted enough to play a few wrong notes. I lifted the bow from the strings. "Please," he breathed into my ear. "Keep going." He slid his hands under my skirt and unbuttoned it. It slid to the floor. "Don't stop," he whispered, panting more heavily now.

He removed my clothes as I continued drawing bow over strings. Now greatly distracted, I didn't even hear the music, it was a jumble of noise to me. He fondled me under my blouse and chemise. His growing arousal hardened against my flesh as he embraced me. He kissed my neck as he played his magic with his hands. Finally I could stand it no longer. I relinquished my grip on the bow and dropped it on the rug. He took the violin from my other hand as he guided me to the sofa. He shed his clothes, clasped my wrist and brought me down beside him. "Now let us make some real music. Who needs a string quartet in the background?" he purred. "Tonight our music will be sweeter than anything Mozart ever wrote."

He leaned over and kissed me. Yes, he certainly had bathed. And he wore spicy cologne. The sensual scent aroused even my taste buds.

Our arms wound around each other in a tight, clinging embrace. I'd never wanted to hold anyone this close, to consume him with all my energy, to drink him in and quench my yearning thirst. He molded me to the contours of his body and made me his own.

Between feathery kisses over my neck and earlobes, he whispered words I recognized from our favorite Shakespeare play: Antony's words. Not letting his mounting passion interrupt one word, he said, "Come, my queen. Last night you did desire it."

I came up with a line of my own. "Last night I did desire it. But tonight I ache for it."

He stroked me, fondled me, put me to music. Our bodies harmonized in an exquisite blend as we exploded into crashing chords. I shouted out as my passion came to a crescendo. "Alex! Oh, Alex!"

He transported me to some otherworld. Shouting his name felt so natural to me now, as he was truly mine.

Spent, he lay beside me, winding his fingers through my hair. Locked together with the ebb of our pulsating bodies, we lay side by side on the cushions, our breaths slowing, calming.

"Alex, what is it about us? Why did fate keep us apart until we'd wed others, only to sneak stolen moments? We share so many interests, beliefs, and I feel like I am out of my body when we..." I pulled the chenille cover from the sofa and draped it over our bodies.

He laughed. "Of course. What is closer to immortality?"

I had to agree with him. We were ever so compatible, as if destined to live here and now. "I know you belong to someone else, and in most ways, I still belong to James. But when we're together, no one else exists, just us and the sweet strains of Mozart in my head." I kissed his lips. "And what is that intoxicating fragrance you're wearing?" I asked. "Because I want you to wear it every time we meet. It drives me wild."

"Tricorn. President Washington's favorite."

"I can picture Lady Washington breathing in this scent, going wild with desire for the General." I couldn't help laughing.

When he left me that night, I felt fulfilled enough to give him as much time as he needed till our next meeting. I wouldn't bother him with letters. I'd keep busy reading "our" books, studying newspapers so we could talk about daily events, practice the violin and make him look forward to coming back to me. Of course this also meant leaving his home, wife and children behind. I had a very difficult job.

Chapter Thirteen

Eliza

Sabbath Day, September 18th, 11 of clock

While sleep eluded me, I went down to see if Alex would take a break from his endless workload and join me in brewing some tea. He was not there. Disappointed, I glanced at his private possessions—his reading specs, his favorite tankard, his waistcoat thrown over the chair back. His scent of Tricorn cologne lingered in the air. I longed for his company.

"Alex, where are you?" I asked his powerful presence. The clock ticked in the corner and chimed eleven times. I peered out the window into a black void. Raindrops splattered the windowpane, came in and wet the table. I shut the window.

I glanced at his desk, strewn with papers, pens and inkwells. I couldn't imagine the president's desk more cluttered. I did not want to know what he was working on, it was all so intricate and complicated to me—the Report on Manufactures, the banking system, interest rates. He could recite all this in his sleep. Most of our conversation of late was about our strongest bond, the children.

He had companions to share his ideas, discuss politics and policies, his Shakespeare plays, his Voltaire, his Greek myths. Alas, I had not the necessary level of interest in this subject matter. I wasn't even musical enough to go to an opera or a symphony. So he attended with others.

At the only opera I accompanied him to, *The Magic Flute,* I fell asleep before Act Two. He escorted me out uncomplaining. But its purpose eluded me, dancers prancing around in bird costumes. He'd explained it contained Masonic symbolism. Alex wasn't a Freemason, as were the president and most of his cronies, but he knew about their rituals and customs. These were just a few things we couldn't discuss because I belonged not in that realm. My realm was feeding, dressing, chiding and chasing after children. We did not have enough servants to keep up. I could not be the perfect mother *and* the perfect wife. Which meant, unfortunately, he had to settle for less than perfect.

Earlier in the day my maid had led an unexpected caller into the parlour.

"I of course have a personal interest in your well being and called purely on a whim," Dr. Severus Black explained. "And how goes your health?"

"I'm hale and hearty," I assured him as I gestured to the wing chair across from me. "Stay and take tea with me."

This he did, and we engaged in pleasant conversation for some twenty or thirty minutes. He then stood to take his leave. "I have another pressing matter to attend to. I'll see myself out."

Dr. Black was something of an enigma. Most physicians of my acquaintance had premises from which to conduct their practice, but Dr. Black appeared to specialize in calling upon his patients within their own homes. How he made a profit in such a way I could not fathom. Still, he was charming and personable, and his finances were of course not my concern, so I reined in my inquisitiveness and enjoyed his company. Those cobalt eyes enthralled me, sparkling as a sun-kissed ocean, yet lacking in the warmth that should come from within.

Before leaving the parlour, I bent over to pick up a sheet of paper that had fallen to the floor. I glanced at it before placing it on the table next to Alex's favorite chair. It bore a signature I'd seen before—*Anon*. The same penmanship as in the letter I'd received in Albany, the same stationery. The salutation read "Dear Mrs. Hamilton—" and as I continued, I wished I'd never seen it. It informed me that my husband was seen again entering Mrs. Reynolds's house and not leaving till late at night—more than once. Someone was spying on him to destroy his reputation, and possibly our marriage. But when I guessed at motive, politics came to mind. I ran down the list of his political rivals—Jefferson first, Adams second, Burr a distant third. But would they stoop to such a tawdry tactic?

I resented my husband opening my post and leaving it lying there. But I resolved to find out the truth by paying a visit to Mrs. Reynolds.

Chapter Fourteen

Maria

By the glow of a candle, I dressed in James's britches, his linen shirt belted at my waist and laced up the front, his woolen hat low over my forehead. At the stroke of midnight, I pranced down our porch steps and slid into the carriage next to Alex. Giddy with delight, I squealed like a naughty schoolgirl. Plopping my satchel down, I clasped my lover's hands, leant over and planted a hungry kiss on his lips. My entire body throbbed with excitement.

"Good eve, Mr. Reynolds," he greeted me. "Restrain yourself, sir, I do not kiss men," Alex joked as the carriage lurched into motion.

We laughed and I gave him a squeeze. "Have you ever made love in a moving carriage?" I walked my fingers up his thigh, but he steered my wandering hand away.

"No, I reckon it would be rather painful. We will share pleasure in pleasurable surroundings. I obtained the name of an inn in Paterson, but we must enter and exit separately. And I trust you did bring more changes of men's attire?" He gestured to the burlap sack at my feet.

The carriage picked up speed as the driver led it out of town. "James gave me these articles of clothing with his blessing."

"Would that I had an understanding spouse." He turned to look into the blackness of night.

"Not so much understanding as uncaring," I corrected him. "Why should he disapprove of what we do at this point? I told James everything about this journey, and he even gave me a bottle of whisky to bring along. He applauded my idea of siting a mill on the waterfall. He also told me his brother would be interested in investing in a mill, when the time came. But to him, tis a bit too speculative. That made me laugh." I snickered. "One quality about James—he does make me laugh. Intentionally or unintentionally."

Alex faced me again and clasped my hand. "I am proud of you also."

I returned his smile in the shadows. "Oh, how I wish this magical feeling would stay with me forever." But of course we'd need return to the real world in a week or so.

At first too excited to sleep, we talked about Henry VIII and his wives until my eyelids grew heavy. I snuggled against his chest as the horse's steady gait lulled me into slumber.

When Alex woke me, weak daylight filled the carriage interior. I stretched my stiffened limbs and licked my lips, my mouth dry and stale. "Are we there?" I dug the whisky bottle out of the satchel and took a sip.

"Almost halfway." He stretched and opened his door. "Tis nearly daybreak, but we're stopping at this inn for a few hours' rest."

I peered out the window. "All I see is a ramshackle farmhouse. What inn?"

"This one, *Mister* Reynolds. Stay put." He and his driver entered the weather-beaten clapboard house. Alex came back out. "Go to the room at the top of the stairs—alone," he ordered.

I gathered my satchel and entered the old house, my face hidden beneath James's hat. I gave the sleepy innkeeper a nod and clomped up the stairs to the small frigid room. Too tired to think, I collapsed on the narrow cot and let an exhausted sleep overtake me.

After a few hours, we grabbed some bread and butter with cups of lukewarm coffee and departed. The low hanging clouds cast a gray pall over the day. A bone-shivering chill seeped into the carriage. My teeth chattered. What I'd hoped would be a romantic interlude became an exhausting push to reach Paterson as soon as possible. Too tired to discuss any complex topics, we bantered about Italian food.

"Ah, for a whiff of a succulent red tomato sauce garnished with sweet basil and doused with garlic." He pressed his fingertips together and kissed them in the Italian style. "And the tang of Parmesan cheese."

"Garlic?" I wrinkled my nose. "That is medicine. My aunt uses it for a purge."

"Yes, tis medicinal," he agreed. "But tis also a delight to the pallet when consuming strictly for pleasure."

He surprised me when he said our elder statesmen, including Ben Franklin, were Italian cuisine aficionados. "Jefferson even had a few dozen Tuscans living and working at Monticello as gardeners. He never passed up the chance to brag about his Italian garden, all his olives and grapes and melons." He rubbed his middle. "Now I've made myself hungry. And a hunger for an Italian meal is a hunger like no other."

"We had figs once," I recalled, "and I've made potpourri with basil, parsley and marjoram. Alex, we must share an Italian meal sometime," I urged. *Preferably in Italy*, I added silently.

Our tête-à-tête drifted to Shakespeare. "The Bard didn't write any of those great works," he said. "As the son of a yeoman he couldn't have been privy to royalty's private lives and court intrigue."

"Mayhap Queen Elizabeth let him live at court to soak up the culture," I suggested over a yawn. "His acting company, the Lord Chamberlain's Men, performed his plays at court. But I must believe he wrote all those plays—and those beautiful sonnets and words of love. 'My heart is ever at your service,'

I quoted the Bard, but saying it to Alex, it came from my own heart.

"How fancifully romantic," he replied. "Too romantic for a breeder ever to have written."

"A breeder?"

He nodded. "Yes, a man who breeds with women, as opposed to a molly, who engages in—you know—" He gave his wrist an effeminate flick. "—buggery. He had to be a molly to write like that. And anyone who cavorts with a band called The Lord Chamberlain's Men—" He rolled his eyes.

I playfully slapped his arm, nestled against him and dozed.

When I woke, I overcame my embarrassment and asked the driver to pull over so I could relieve myself in a clump of bushes. My shoes covered in mud, I finished James's whisky and didn't eat another morsel nor drink another drop till we reached the skirts of Paterson. By then, in the dead of the moonless night, my stomach growled with hunger. We filled Alex's flask and James's bottle with water from a well, our only sustenance.

"Oh, Alex," I lamented as the carriage jolted and lurched onward. "When will we enjoy these pleasurable surroundings you told me about?"

"When we get to the falls. That will be our pleasurable surroundings. Be happy we have the luxury of the carriage. If I'd taken this journey alone, I'd be on horseback."

The thought of making love next to the roaring falls gave me a surge of energy and excitement. But once again, fatigue overtook me, and I fell into a dreamless sleep amid the jolting and jouncing.

He nudged me awake and I drew a tired breath.

"Look." He pointed out the window. "There it is." The carriage lurched to a halt. I nearly fell off the seat, rubbed my eyes and looked out. Before me stood the falls as I remembered, a foamy rush of roaring water cascading off towering cliffs into a rocky gorge. "Beautiful, is it not?" He draped his arm round my shoulders. "It will soon be ours."

I laughed. "Ours? Are we going to buy it?"

He opened the carriage door and stepped out. I shielded my eyes from the light, although the sky was a dull gray like tarnished pewter, laden with clouds. "No, but I'm impressed with this site to the point of decision." He pointed to a spot on the opposite bank of the river. "This is where The Society for Establishing Useful Manufacture will build its first mill. In which you shall own fifty shares."

"Fifty shares!" My jaw dropped. "I'll be wealthy beyond my wildest dreams if this mill becomes profitable. And James thought this too speculative? I need to lecture him on what's speculative and what's a sound investment."

We strolled along the river arm in arm, the wind whipping my hair into my face and chilling me under James's overlarge clothing.

"These are the pleasurable surroundings you told me about, Alex? Mayhap in June, but not now. I am freezing." My teeth chattered.

143

"We shall return and couple under that clump of trees, then," he assured me. "After our first mill is built."

I kept my head down against the wind. My shivers from the cold overpowered my shivers of delight. I nudged him toward the carriage, but his feet seemed rooted to the ground. He wanted to stay. "One day a great city will rise on the west bank of the Hudson River." He gazed into the distance, his eyes narrowed in concentration.

"Right here? Our city?" I already felt we'd created what could be an empire.

"May well be, mayhap not."

"It may well be Jersey City then," I joked, huddling closer to him.

"Stranger things have happened." He led me back to the carriage. We climbed in and I burrowed into his warmth. "Oh, I wish for a bearskin rug before a crackling fire! Alex, let us go to Greenwich Village, rent a cozy brownstone and live in splendor for a few days," I suggested. "What's a few more days? We never had time alone together, with no need to hurry or listen for approaching footsteps."

"I wish I could, but I must hurry back. I've much work to do. Mayhap another time." But I'd nearly drifted off. This was the most tiring trip I'd ever taken. And the least romantic.

He looked around a bit more and took notes whilst I huddled in the carriage. During the tiring return trip we stopped at another dilapidated farmhouse at the roadside. We entered and exited separately between four hours of sleep on lumpy cots. No time for romance or anything close to it. But at least we'd spent this time alone—almost.

When I arrived home, I slept nearly round the clock. When I awoke, darkness shrouded the bedchamber. I slid across the bed and peered at the clock on James's nightstand. Half past eight. James was not home, but he'd left a note. "*Gon to work, then to bisnuss meeting. You had a visiter, she requests that you visit her.*" He'd drawn an arrow pointing to a calling card next to his note.

As I saw the sender's name, Mrs. Hamilton, a stab of fear sliced through me. Had she found out I'd snuck away in disguise with her husband? But we were so discreet, now coming and going by the back door. Still, I convinced myself she'd learnt of our excursion.

I couldn't honor her request. Not yet. I needed to rehearse what to say, how to comport myself.

There was still no word from Alex about the treasury clerkship either. Over the next few days, James grew irritable and testy. He did go to the congressman Alex had suggested, but he had no openings. Ergo, James slid back to square one.

I did not hear from Alex, either, but knew he was busy. I did not try to contact him.

The next day, James sat down and without a drop of alcohol in his system, cautioned me not to disturb him. "Ah'm composing a most important letter," he stated.

This scared me. "I hope you're not considering blackmail or blabbing to your notorious cohort Callender. James, be civil," I begged.

Without a word, he scratched pen over paper.

I picked up the newspaper and skimmed the front page headlines. Naught had happened to fret about since yesterday. Page two displayed a headline about The Society for Establishing Useful Manufacture. The article reported the plans to build a mill on the Passaic River. I smiled with satisfaction, knowing it was all because of me...rather, us.

On an internal page I spied a short piece. It quoted the commissioner as saying he believed the murders of young women had ceased due to extra vigilance by constables. The hunt for the killer continued, but he may have moved on to another town.

As I read about a local performance of *The Magic Flute,* James fanned his letter to dry.

"I hope you didn't threaten him," I warned James. If he had, I could do naught about it, but I could not live without Alex. These had become the happiest days of my life. We needed the money, but I feared my lecturing James about the art of diplomacy hadn't sunk in.

"That isna my way, you know that." He stood, as if ready to give a speech to Congress, and read: "Certainly you did not show the man of honor," he recited in a chiding tone, "in taking the advantage of the afflicted, when calling on you as a protector in the time of distress. Your answer I shall expect this evening or in the morning early, as I am determined to wait no longer. I know my lot. I shall abandon my wife for good, in return for a cash payment of one thousand dollars."

I staggered backward and knocked a pitcher to the floor. "A thousand dollars! Are you daft?"

He folded the letter. "I offered to let him pay me in installments, interest free."

I couldn't even look at him. Alex had told me he would face this when the time came. Now the time had come. Would he abandon me—or pay James that exorbitant sum?

Chapter Fifteen

Severus

I awoke, drenched in sweat, my nightshirt stuck to my skin. The nightmares had returned, those awful dreams that so defined who I was, and what I'd been. Only when they persisted did I feel the need to satisfy my darker urges. Now they recurred with greater intensity.

My mind drifted as I remembered that time and place so long ago, when my life changed forever.

I worshipped my father. The tall lean strong-willed God-fearing scholar and magistrate Albert Black lavished love and affection on my mother and my sister Louisa.

When Father met a premature death in a drowning accident, we clung to one another in our shared devastation and grief. Mother found herself unable to cope with her grief and often turned to me for solace and comfort. I saw nothing amiss in her need to feel my arms around her, for I was her reminder of the man she had loved and lost.

When, one night, she came to my bedroom and crept into my bed, whispering, "Hold me close, please, Severus," I still saw no harm in the coming together of mother and child. However, when her fingers traced their way across my chest and then down to my stomach, I began to tremble. Then her fingers touched that which I knew they should not. I tried to pull away but she shushed me.

"Be quiet, my son, my beautiful Severus. You are the mirror image of your dear father. Do you not imagine he would want you to take care of me, to service the needs of your dear mother in her desperate need?"

I said not one word as I lay rigid, Mother's fingers coaxing me to a state of expectation I had never previously experienced. She shrugged off her chemise and climbed atop my trembling body. I felt her heat as she lowered herself onto my throbbing manhood.

"Mother..." I tried to protest, but she placed a finger on my lips. I fell silent as she rocked back and forth on me. I felt her shudder and in my shame, I gave way to my own animal instincts. She fell into a deep sleep and I lay still, not wanting her to wake and force herself upon me again.

As wrong as I knew it to be, she began to visit my bed twice, often thrice a week. Once, she screamed her passion so loud that Louisa called out from the landing hallway to ask if all was well. Mother brazenly rose from my bed, still wet from our spending, pulled on her chemise, went to the bedroom door and opened it. She told Louisa she had visited me upon hearing my screams, brought on by nightmares of Father's drowning. Whether Louisa believed this outright lie, I knew Mother neither knew nor cared. I never, ever spoke of the matter with my sister.

I knew this liaison to be sinfully wrong. As time went by, I became determined to end her hold upon me. But she would have none of my pleas to end our licentious incest, and demanded even more as time dragged on.

One night, much to the surprise and shock of the villagers, Grantly House, our family home for four generations, burnt to the ground in a mysterious fire. I lay next to Mother one last time, my final escape from her aberrant clutches now almost complete. As my hands closed round her throat, I shivered with a new excitement, a sense of arousal I never before experienced. As she gasped, her last breath accompanying the final seconds of life, an unseen force possessed my soul. Within seconds my second self found life and purpose.

The following morning, constables discovered her charred remains in the ruins of the house. My sister Louisa was found in her own bedroom huddled in a corner, the victim of smoke inhalation, her body spared from the all-engulfing flames. The constables encountered me wandering the grounds incoherently. I behaved as if deep in shock. They accepted my story of being unable to reach my mother and sister despite my best efforts.

After inheriting a small fortune, I went to London for an education under the leading practitioners at St. Bartholomew's Hospital. My chosen profession was a far cry from what my loving father mapped out for me.

Chapter Sixteen

Eliza

To-night I am too tired to write much, with Angelica ill and Philip whining that the tutors work him like a slave. Alex came home exhausted and retreated to his study. Mrs. Reynolds never replied—an admission of guilt, mayhap? Many of our government's men craved seeing Alex crash, before he had a chance to even contemplate a bid for the presidency. I still considered it a nasty ploy and did not mention this second letter to him.

But later that eve, when I entered his study to discuss purchasing new furnishings, he was not there. The open ledger lay upon his desk. I approached it to take a look. The sum of $600 in the withdrawal column astonished me. I looked closer. Had I read it wrong? No, $600 had come out. He always kept meticulous records of our personal finances. I sank into his leather chair, staring at the entry. *Please be an error*, I begged. It should only be $6 or $60. But Alex did not err when it came to finances.

This was not my place, but I needed speak to him. I searched all over the house and the yard. No sign of him.

Maria

James came home with five bottles of whisky, a dozen lampreys and a mysterious smile. Then he whisked a box from his pocket and presented it to me. "For my beautiful and talented wife." I opened the box to a gleaming pearl necklace.

"Heaven above, where did you get this? Marie Antoinette's personal armoire?" I stared at the gems, too shocked to even thank him.

"At Burque Jewelers if you must know." He uncorked a bottle.

"I mean where did you get the money?" Then it came to me. "Oh, God. Did Alex..."

Without another word, he pulled wads of notes from both britches pockets. They kept coming and coming, like a magic trick.

"Aye, lass, the secretary of our treasured treasury, the wizened wizard of the fiscal world himself, gave in and remitted the first installment of my modest demand." He brandished a smug smirk.

"The first installment?" I swept the notes off the table, not wanting to see them. "How much is here?"

"Six hundred, with the other four to follow. I made it easy on him, gave him a fortnight." He took a sip of wine and wiped his mouth with one of the bank notes. "Any more of this comes in, I shall wipe t'other end with it. Haar!" He guffawed like a pirate.

So I was worth a thousand dollars... for now. If this was treasury money, Mrs. Hamilton, if not the entire Congress, would hear about this. God help me, I couldn't end our liaison. My love for Alex grew stronger each day. Now I longed for him even more.

Eliza

As Christmas approached, I hoped to replace a few items around the house. Our aging furnishings looked shabby and unstylish, our tables scratched and nicked, our rugs frayed at the edges. Loath as I was to broach the subject with my husband, I needed to discuss the gravity of this huge withdrawal from our account.

With supper eaten, the dishes cleared and the children abed, I approached him in his study. Engrossed in some documents, his reading specs perched on his nose, he appeared older, from years of laboring late into the night.

"Alex, may I have a moment, please?" I never sat in his presence until invited.

He gestured to the chair across from him. With gratitude I sank into the worn leather. "As we do a fair amount of entertaining, some new rugs and furnishings would more appropriately reflect our status. Are we able to make some purchases, to the sum of, say… six hundred dollars?" I watched for his reaction. He blanched at the amount and avoided looking me in the eye.

"That is excessive." He pulled off his specs and rubbed the graying hair at his temples. "We're not entertaining royalty. Mayhap I can spare a hundred or so, but nowhere near your request."

My anger rising, I clenched my jaw. "The Treasury Secretary of the United States, unable to afford furnishing his own house?" I itched to reveal what I'd seen in the ledger. "We have substantial savings. Your salary more than covers our expenses. We hardly live beyond our means. Why is this such a hardship?"

He reached for his wine goblet, and finding it empty, put it back. As he ran his palm over his forehead, I noticed his hairline was beginning to recede. "I'll give you some funds with my next pay. Friday. But I wish you had asked me earlier."

How much earlier? I wondered. Before he'd made that enormous withdrawal? "I would have, but I have duties as well. Running a household, raising children…"

"Enough, Betsey." He held up his hand, a signal the conversation was over. "I said I'd give you some money, now let me return to work so I can pay for all these flub-dubs you want."

"Yes, sir." I left him alone. If it were a small amount, I wouldn't have cared. But this withdrawal nearly bankrupted us. How I hoped he hadn't fallen into the speculating trap with the likes of James Reynolds. But my husband wasn't about to tell me why he'd withdrawn this large sum, and this greatly disturbed me. I'd never kept aught from Alex. But he never shared all with me. I'd have to find another way to trace the path of our missing funds. He wasn't the only person with connections in the bank system. He might be the Treasury Secretary, but I was Mrs. Secretary!

Maria

With Christmas three days away, we planned to visit my mother and brother in Newburgh. James had paid debts with some of the money Alex had given him. If naught else, James was honorable. He might duck out of a duel, but never a debt. He'd starve before he'd owe anyone, and he'd proved it by letting us starve a few times.

We moved into posher lodgings in High Street across from the market. Our three-story brick house, twenty-four by thirty-four feet, was the largest we'd ever lived in. We had a separate kitchen, washhouse and stable.

I now taught three violin pupils. But my income went on lessons for myself. My instructor, Mrs. Platz, a Vienna native, had taken a violin lesson from Wolfgang Mozart ten years ago. Apparently in as dire straits as we were, Mr. Mozart took on pupils to supplement his income. But Mrs. Platz told me a Viennese friend had written her that he'd died on December fifth.

My heart went out to his poor widow, with small fatherless children. I talked about it with Mrs. Platz, but really wanted to share my feelings with Alex. He hadn't written me a word in weeks. I felt as if half my soul had been torn from me. I missed him so badly, I considered going to his place of work, or even the treasury office, for a brief exchange with him. I still hadn't raised the courage to call on Mrs. Hamilton.

James burst in that eve loaded down with parcels. "There's more where that come from." As he dumped his booty onto the table, a blast of winter air and a shower of snow blew through the open door. I shivered, peering into the street. An elegant carriage sat under the flickering streetlamp. Its stately draft horse let out a whinny and a puff of steam.

"What is going on, James?" I hugged my arms to my sides. "What is that—"

"Mind out the way." He brushed past me and back out to the carriage, returning with a large box. Glass rattled inside. Two brawny workmen followed, carrying armloads of wood. "Dump it before the hearth," James instructed them. They made five trips, and we now had enough fuel to warm us till spring.

James saw the men to the door. "Cheers, mates! Return on the morn at seven."

"Our new coach and driver and horse—for the month." Rubbing his hands together, he piled some logs into the hearth and lit them with the candle from the wall sconce. Within moments a blazing fire warmed the room. "Now you kin eat yur chestnuts hot all winter."

"Where did you get all this, James? There must be fifteen cords of wood here." I warmed my hands, not too displeased with a roaring fire in the hearth.

"Happy Christmas to you, too." He tossed me some bank notes and uncorked a wine bottle. It looked expensive, the label in French. "Also buy yur kinfolk some gifts."

"I'm pleased we'll be comfortable for the time being, but I have an inkling you haven't earned this the honest way. What happened, you mugged Old Nick?"

"No, I mugged Old Sandy—Hamilton, that is. Haar!" He took a sip and rolled it round his tongue. "Aaah. Absolute ambrosia. Almost beats haggis."

I stood there shaking my head, flabbergasted. "He actually paid you more money?" I would have found it more believable that the sky was falling. Why would Alex do this? Where did he get the money? Was he raiding the treasury? God help him if he was. All because of me! I had to put a stop to this.

I sat across from James, trembling. "When did you see him? What did he say?"

"Didna encounter him personally. He sent me a note this morn, before you were up, and told me to collect a parcel waiting at his law office within the hour. And there twas. The balance of his promise to me, the other four hundred. Grand timing, too. I 'ope I din't cause 'im no 'ardship," he mimicked a Cockney, snickering as he savored his wine.

I looked away, unable to stand the sight of him. "James, for the first time, I'm ashamed of you." I wanted to run to Alex, throw my arms round him, promise he'd get every penny back.

Planning to do just that, I jumped up and grabbed my pelisse and gloves.

"Where in bloody hell'r you going? Tis snowing like the devil." He refilled his goblet. I threw on my pelisse and headed for the door. "For some fresh air," I called over my shoulder. "Tis too stuffy in here."

"Maria, fur the love of Saint Andrew, git back in here!" he shouted after me. "We're flush with cash, we kin have a feast fit for a king tonight, and you're trawling the frozen streets?"

I cut him off with the slam of the door. He didn't chase after me. I trudged down the slippery snow-slicked sidewalk, wet flakes lashing at my cheeks and lips. When I reached 79 South Third Street, I had no idea what to say to Alex. All I knew was that I was desperate to see him. Even if his wife was home.

A row of carriages lined up in front of the elegant townhouse. The horses breathed misty puffs of steam. The windows on the right side of his house blazed with numerous candles from a chandelier. My hand frozen inside my fur-lined glove, I knocked on the door. A manservant answered. Thank God it wasn't Mrs. Hamilton!

"Is Secretary Hamilton in residence?" I asked, my breath emerging in puffs of steam.

"Whom may I say is calling?" He eyed me up and down.

"Mrs. Reynolds."

He let me step inside. Entering the foyer, I pulled off my gloves and breathed on my hands. I should have worn my cloak. The pelisse barely prevented frostbite. I shivered with cold and nervousness. Alex must be in residence, or I would've been turned away.

The servant returned and led me into the sitting room. "Please have a seat here, ma'am." He pointed to a settee. Too restless to sit, I stood. Shadows darkened the cold room. Only two candles glowed, no fire in the hearth. My breath came out as steam before me. "Mr. Hamilton will be out shortly," he stated and backed out.

Voices, laughter and clinking glasses floated across the hall. The Hamiltons were entertaining. Glancing in the party's direction, I wished we'd been invited. But we'd never achieved their social status. James's political connections didn't reach Alex's level.

I watched the clock ticking in the corner for what seemed like ages, but only ten minutes passed. When the latch clicked and the door opened, I jumped, startled.

There he stood, a vision of aristocracy and elegance. He registered neither surprise, pleasure nor displeasure. "Maria, what are you doing here?"

I approached him with hesitant steps. I wanted to take him all in—his midnight blue velvet coat, fitted no doubt by a master tailor, blue satin britches and white silk stockings. A profusion of lace accented the ensemble. His rhinestone shoe buckles gleamed. His hair, pulled back in a queue, shone with threads of silver in the candlelight. As he stepped into the room, a golden glow encircled him.

"Alex—please, I need to talk to you." I didn't mince words, now was not the time to be a coquette. "That money you gave James, I shall pay it back—"

"No need. I felt badly I couldn't provide an opening in the department, but I made him promise not to use it for speculation."

We stood within embracing distance. Our eyes met and held. I detected a faint trace of that sensuous cologne and tried not to throw myself into his arms. "Alex, what happened? Why haven't you called to see me? Oh, how I've missed you." I sounded pathetic. But he had to hear this.

"I've been very busy lately, Maria. If I had some time, I would. Now I really must return to my guests. I've got Mrs. Van Rensselaer, three senators and two congressmen in there—" He began to turn his back on me.

I grabbed his arm. "Please, not yet! Do you ever think about me? I never stop thinking about you, how much we relish being together. I—I read that on the fifteenth, Virginia ratified the Bill of Rights and ten amendments became part of the Constitution," I rambled, wanting him to know he could still discuss current events with me. "I also just finished *History of America,* I know tis one of your favorites. I heard poor Mozart died. And I'm taking violin lessons!" I would have babbled on, but he continued walking out. I followed. We now stood in the hall.

"Very well, now I must get back to my guests. I shall call on you." He waved me off.

"Alex, one kiss, please, come back in here and kiss me—" I grasped his sleeve, but the fine velvet slipped from my fingers. He backed away.

"This is neither the time nor the place." He steered me to the door, glancing over his shoulder. "I said I'd call on you. As for now, adieu." His stern tone dismissed me.

But I would not give up. "I'm ashamed of James and I'll pay you back." I found a more dignified voice as he nudged me outside.

"No need. Good night!" He gave a gentlemanly bow and shut the door.

Tears stung my cheeks as I trudged away, head down, my bonnet growing heavy with falling snow. How foolish I'd been to think he'd want to leave his soirée for me. If only he didn't have those blasted guests, we could have visited in that sitting room for hours. His wife wouldn't have interfered. I'd have had him all to myself!

Now I not only detested James, I detested myself. I never would have done something this foolish were I thinking straight. I now admitted it to myself—I was deeply in love with Alexander Hamilton.

Only as I arrived at my door did I remember Alex's entreaty to avoid unnecessary walks in the hours of darkness. But I'd felt it necessary—and he hadn't mentioned the danger again tonight. Did he care for me at all?

Chapter Seventeen

Eliza

The Sabbath, New Year's Day 1792

True to his word, Alex gave me 400 dollars the day after he received his bi-monthly pay. I dared not ask him from whence it came, and he omitted to tell me. But I needed to see the ledger balance and if he'd entered any more debits. During a New Year's reception in our parlour, I stole away to his study. By stealth, as if he could hear me across the hall, I slid the ledger out of his desk drawer and opened it. The debit column showed the 600 dollars he'd already withdrawn, and no more deposits. He hadn't deposited his entire pay—only half. Then, to my astonishment, I saw he'd withdrawn another 200 dollars. That was why he could only give me 400 instead of the 600 I'd asked for. He'd given it to someone else.

Just as I closed the book, a stream of warm water rushed down my legs. I buckled over with pain. I grabbed onto the edge of the desk and slid to the floor. Going into labor, I screamed, "Alex! Someone, help! Help!" One of the servants, I knew not which, rushed in and helped me onto the fainting couch across the room.

"We'll get you abed, Mizzus Hamilton—Nettie! Fetch the midwife, send for Dr. Black! The Mizzus is birthin' her babe!"

Somehow I hung on, heaving deep breaths as the room filled with people. Alex knelt beside me, swept me into his arms and carried me up the stairs. "You will be fine, Betsey," he repeated. He lay me on the bed. Then he asked what I'd expected to hear: "What in God's name were you doing in my study?"

"I was looking for—" The midwife appeared, ordering me to push—hard! My son was born.

We lavished our time, attention and love on John Church Hamilton, the newest addition to our growing family.

Maria

"Hamilton sired another lad. John Church. Named after someone, I reckon." James tossed the papers aside and helped himself to another oyster. We now lived quite well since he'd collected this money from Alex. His gold smithing employment also remained steady. We'd brought Christmas gifts of silver and crystal for my family. James bought logs for their hearths, and we dined as if holding court at Hampton Palace. Lampreys, oysters, caviar—every day, James ordered delicacies and the best French wines. But knowing the source of these riches, I couldn't relish it. I needed pay Alex back somehow.

January dragged on...one snowstorm after another kept us inside and in each other's way. I played my violin, read my books and the daily papers, worked on needlepoint. But Alex occupied my every thought. I even dreamed of him. *His work and new son take all his time*, I convinced myself.

I wanted no more hush money changing hands, no further using me for bait. When James told me he was composing yet another letter to Alex, I left the room in disgust. But he followed me up the stairs reading it aloud, to ensure I missed nary a word.

"It is Mrs. R. who wishes to see you, and for my own happiness and hers. I have not the least objections to your calling, as a friend to both of us. I rely on your befriending me if there should be anything to offer that would be to my advantage, as you express a wish to befriend me..."

I turned on the stair and faced him. "I've heard quite enough, James." But secretly I delighted in his wording it this way. Yes, it was I who wished to see him, and James would save me the trouble of more imploring. That night on my knees I prayed, "Please, God, let Alex call after receiving this. He'll realize we haven't been together since last year, he'll take a recess from work and babies, and escape into my arms."

But I heard nothing. The cold dark weeks passed. By January's end I could stand it no longer. I wrote him. Mayhap I overdid the play for sympathy. But I couldn't help it. I longed for him and let him know it.

My Dearest Alex,

Oh my God I feel more for you than myself and wish I had never been born to give you so mutch unhappiness. I have been sick almost ever since I saw you. I solicit a favor... for the last time. Yes Sir rest assured I will never ask you to call on me again. I have kept my bed these two days and now rise from my pilliow which your neglect has filled with the sharpest thorns. I only do it to ease a heart which is ready burst with Greef. I can neither eat or sleep. I have been on the point of doing the most horrid acts... I feel as if I should not continue long and all the wish I have is to see you once more.

For God sake be not so void of all humanity as to deny me this last request but if you will not call some time this night I know it's late but any time between this and twelve a clock I shall be up. Let me intreat you if you won't come to send me a line of my head I can write no more. Do something to ease my heart. Or els I no not what I shall do for so I cannot live. Commit this to the care of my maid, be not offended I beg.

I was a terrible speller, but it looked all the more sincere, straight from my heart, no drafts, no practice. I folded, sealed it and gave it to Maggie with his address. "Be sure it is delivered into his hands," I instructed her.

With some extra coin in my purse, I went out and purchased more Mozart sheet music. The great maestro was gone, but his music lived everywhere.

When I returned home, James had a visitor, his business partner Jacob Clingman. We'd known Jacob since before we married. He and James had entered several business ventures together. He now worked at the Treasury Department, but merely to fill his time—he had nearly as much money as the treasury itself.

The gentleman he was, he kissed my hand and held out a chair for me. As I inhaled his spicy cologne, a familiar rush flooded me. Lord help me, it was Tricorn, the cologne Alex wore! Jacob's eyes resembled the violet of Alex's, his hair that same burnished red, but a shade darker. I considered him one of James's more savory associates. A widower, he owned a much bigger house than Alex, living off the legacy of his older and wealthy wife Jane. Because he'd married into great wealth, he wasn't obsessed with "deals" and overnight riches. He knew James's shortcomings, but admired him for his zeal. I hoped their partnership would continue and flourish.

I enjoyed Jacob's company and shared his sense of humor, as he did mine.

"Hell's bells, Maria, where did you get off to?" James stood and embraced me, playing the concerned husband because Jacob was there. He bloody well knew where I'd got off to.

"As I'd told you, for a walk. I bought some music." I held up my Mozart scores.

Jacob continued holding out the chair, but of course I couldn't join their meeting. That was no place for me.

"Maria, you could've caught your death of cold!" This came not from my husband, but from Jacob.

"I'll be fine. I'll find a way to get warm. Somehow." I shot a look at James. He nodded, knowing what I meant. As I retreated up the stairs, I decided to visit Mrs. Hamilton, ready to deny that her husband interested me in any way. I tried to think of some way to prove that, though. Now was the true test—in order to keep my lover, I had to be cleverer than my lover's wife.

Eliza

I'd just finished nursing baby John when Alex came into our bedroom with a cup of tea and a plate of cookies. Never in all our years together had he ever served me like this.

"Alex, have you abdicated?" I joked as he took John from my arms and placed him in his cradle next to our bed.

"No, just wanted to talk. Betsey, what were you doing in my study when you went into labor?" He always got to the point, never allowing his victim to prepare a rebuttal, defense, or counterattack. Not that I had aught to say in my defense. I had no business in his study, and we both knew it.

I dared not start lying to my husband now. "I wanted to see our ledger."

"*Our* ledger?" He awaited me to stand corrected.

He was guarded and private about finances. He also ran the treasury as thriftily as it were all his, revealing facts and figures only when necessary. He expected everyone to trust him. And they did. From the president down to every last citizen.

"Very well, *your* ledger. I was curious as to why we were in such straits. You couldn't provide the funds I'd asked for." My stern tone matched my growing ire.

"What else?" he demanded, tapping his foot.

He knew I'd seen what I shouldn't have. But of course, no matter what he said, it was *our* money. "I saw that you'd withdrawn a large sum." I waited for his answer, which he gave without hesitation.

"I borrowed some money from Robert Troup and repaid him." His eyes darted about, not meeting mine.

"What for?" Now *I* demanded. "I deserve to know why, at least."

"Some investments. Naught to concern you while you've five children to raise." He glanced down at the cradle.

"Six children, but who's counting?" My voice rose.

He gave a dismissive shrug. "Oh."

"Alex, if you're investing to the point we cannot afford a parlour carpet," my voice rose, "I should know about it."

"I know a bit about handling finances, dear one." He rarely used this condescending tone, but now he was the Treasury Secretary speaking to common folk, not a husband to his wife.

"I think not, by the looks of our ledger," I countered, struggling to keep my tone respectful.

"Betsey, I had one simple question, and you're making it an inquisition. I answered you. Now I must return to work." He straightened his sleeves and turned to leave.

I clutched his sleeve. "One more thing, sir."

He faced me—stared me down was more like it.

"I also saw a letter addressed to me. Why did you open it and not show it to me?" I inquired.

"Letter? Oh, that." He swept his hand through the air. "Just another one of those vexing things. None of it is true, as I told you last time. Was my word then not sufficient?"

"After one letter, yes. After two, I have my doubts. What exactly is going on with Mrs. Reynolds?" I wasn't sure I even wanted to know. "If some gossip monger is out there trying to spread these vicious rumors, our family might face danger. And if you won't tell me, I'll call on Mrs. Reynolds. But I would rather hear it from my husband."

He narrowed his eyes. "You know how these things float around. Look at the rumors about Jefferson and that Sally Hemings woman."

"Rumors nothing!" I stamped my foot. "Tis all true!"

"Says who?" He cocked a brow. "All I know is that my acquaintance with the Reynoldses is no greater than yours. He's been round to ask me for an appointment, but further to that, nothing. Would you be any more concerned if this rumor were about me and Mrs. Monroe?"

I had to laugh. "If it were true, I'd commit you to an asylum. But Mrs. Reynolds—now, she's exceeding attractive and young. Whoever is making up these rumors certainly took care to make them believable."

"They are not believable," he insisted, folding his arms across his chest. "If you believe them, you are wrong. And that is your problem, dear wife, not mine. There is no truth to any of those letters. And I shall thank you to steer clear of my study in future." He turned on a heel and retreated as I had the last word.

"And I'll thank you to steer clear of my post!"

He gave a slight nod and walked out the door.

Ergo, that was it. He at least admitted he'd borrowed from Robert Troup, his close friend. They'd been roommates at King's College and served in the same militia unit. Robert had tutored Alex in law studies. Now he was a Clerk of the Court in the District of New York. Perhaps he knew why Alex needed 600 dollars. As soon as the snow cleared, I'd take baby John to visit his grandparents, and pay Robert a visit in New York City on the way. Then I'd call on Mrs. Reynolds once more.

Chapter Eighteen

Maria

This morn, as Maggie cleared the dishes and I read the papers with James, a letter arrived by courier. It was from Alex—and addressed to me! Trembling with anticipation and delight, I tore it open.

Jacob Clingman was visiting us, and in the privy when the letter arrived.

"I take it Ham the Ram wants another rendezvous." James nodded in approval. "Tell him to keep his britches on till the morrow. Jacob and I are meeting here with some other investors. I'd like to scout out a prime parcel of land in the southeast quadrant of Northern Virginia. We'll be hobnobbing with old Georgie Washington himself! How 'bout them golden apples!"

"Speculating on some swamp a hundred miles from Mount Vernon hardly qualifies as hobnobbing with the president, James." I dismissed his latest clutch at the aristocracy and held Alex's note to my lips. I inhaled the faint trace of his spicy scent. "It says here Mrs. Hamilton has gone to New York with the younger children. And Philip is away at boarding school. He wants me to sup with him at six this eve." I couldn't keep the shrill glee out of my voice. "So he needs not keep his britches on till the morrow."

"Even better." James poured himself a refill of coffee. "As long as the missus doesna pay another surprise visit and catch her husband with you in friganté dilecto this time."

"It's *flagranté delicto*, you ignorant oaf!" I savored my last mouthful of Viennese coffee he'd bought with the dwindling funds from Alex. "Tis Latin for 'in the progressing misdeed.' And I must admit, the phrase fits."

"Beggin' yur pardon, Madame Aristotle." He bowed his head. "May I put it simply: bloody brilliant!"

Just then Jacob walked in, lips curled in amusement. "Who is quite so brilliant?"

James replied, "Secretary Hamilton, the connoisseur of cash. He and Maria—and I, of course—have bin seeing, er—rather more of each other."

I cringed, wanting to crawl under the floorboards. How could James tell another soul about this, even a close compatriot? If he divulged any details, I'd have to vehemently deny them.

"Are you now?" Jacob's eyes bulged. "Moving in the high circles now, eh, Jimmy?"

"Gittin' there. Right, my sugar mouse?" James turned to me and winked. I worked my foot under the table to his codlings and gave them a meaningful nudge.

"Yow." James rubbed himself, but it didn't faze Jacob. I knew that 'gentlemen' always scratched themselves in socially unacceptable places.

"We have some friends in common and occasionally attend the same events." I swept the letter off the table and under the newspaper. "So, Jacob, when did you last attend the opera?"

I engaged him in lively chatter, for he was an avid opera and theatergoer. James, with no interest in anything musical beyond bawdy tavern tunes, splashed some whisky into his coffee.

As we talked, I could only think: *in seven hours, I'll be back in my lover's arms.* I remained in a constant state of arousal all day.

As James and Jacob prepared for their meeting, Maggie filled our tin tub with hot water. I took a long soak, washed my hair, splashed on some sinfully expensive French perfume, a splurge from my first violin lesson fee, and donned my most suggestive raiment—crimson satin bodice with plunging décolletage and black silk petticoats. The matching satin skirt wrapped round my waist, to be easily *un*wrapped.

At quarter hour to six, I entered our hired carriage. "Please take me to Seventy-Nine South Third," I instructed the driver. I needn't mention who lived there. My heart hammered as the carriage bumped and rolled through the streets. At Alex's row house I alighted and instructed the coachman to return home. I knew Alex would provide my transport back in the morn. Shaking with anticipation and wild desire, I rapped on his door. It opened and there he stood, draped in a black velvet robe *à la française* and carpet slippers, ready for the boudoir.

I fell into his arms and sought his lips. My hands wandered down to stir his arousal. He pushed me away. "Let us wait till after the meal. When I have more—potency."

I nodded. "You're right. We do have all night."

He led me into the sitting room, the scene of that disastrous last encounter. A compleat sett of blue and white table china I surmised was fine French porcelain graced the table. Silver serving dishes gleamed in the candlelit centerpiece. The serving spoons' faceted edges glinted under the candelabra. A salver held sugar and almond paste, a breadbasket, and a bottle slider.

The silver-gilt forks, knives, dessert spoons and crystal goblets added elegance. The finery welcomed me as an honored guest, as opposed to the night I showed up uninvited.

"I commissioned Richard Humphreys to make the silver." He held out my chair.

"Hmm, the best-known silversmith in town. I'm impressed." I admired the craftsmanship. "We own no pieces by him yet. Now I must purchase some."

"Pheasant to your taste, my dear?" He joined me across the table. "I dismissed the last of the servants but a moment ago. Your timing was impeccable."

"I am not hungry. Not for pheasant, anyway." I held my desire at bay.

"Pierre L'Enfant drew up the first plans for diverting the water." He buttered a roll. "He's also drafting plans for the new Federal city. Now he's officially the first general superintendent for the S.U.M. project. Pierre proposes to harness power from the falls by a channel through the rock and an aqueduct."

He bit into his roll. I still hadn't taken a bite or a sip. "But the directors and I feel that he is taking too long and is over budget. However, we shall work it out. Pierre also gave me some news of general interest. From time to time he receives news from various family members and friends in France, Paris in particular. He mentioned that it was strangely coincidental that some time ago, he recalled not exactly when, one of his cousins wrote him of a series of particularly gruesome murders in the capital of the French Republic. The murders, so far as he could remember, appeared to be particularly similar to those that recently occurred here. Four young women were brutally killed."

I lost my appetite.

"Though no suspects were named, the French press were convinced that whoever perpetrated these heinous crimes had fled from the city, mayhap the country in order to escape eventual detection." He finished his roll. "France's greatest detective, according to Pierre, a man named Le Clerc, was hot on the trail of an unnamed suspect if popular rumor was to be believed."

I gaped at him as he delivered this piece of news. Finding my voice once more, I spoke my fears. "Do you think it possible that the killer did leave Paris, found passage to our country and committed those murders here?"

"It is a possibility." But he didn't sound fully convinced by the theory. "There are a large number of Frenchmen residing here, I'm sure there is as much possibility that the killer is a native born American. No theory should be discarded, however. I pressed Pierre to pass his shreds of news to the commissioner. He, after all, is the man best placed to evaluate such things and act on them if he considers it likely."

At that, talk of killers ended between us, for the real matter at hand was not Parisian murders...

All through dinner, my gaze stayed fixed on his eyes, deep violet in the candleglow, and the hands that would soon caress me. At dessert I managed a few bites of mince pye and washed it down with a heady Marsala. "We're truly alone?" I marveled, desire flooding me.

"Yes, but it may be harder for us to rendezvous in future. My wife has received anonymous letters saying I've been seen in your company. I fear she's of the mind that we've been together—" He cleared his throat. "—alone."

Disappointment crushed me. "I'd hoped this wouldn't happen so soon. Tell her it isn't true. Tell her you know both James and me. Tell her I'm related to the New York Livingstons and we meet to discuss politics." Excuse after excuse rushed out in one breath. "Tell her—tell her I have no interest in you, nor you in me!"

"Of course I *told* her there is nothing untoward between us. I need to *prove it.*" Said like a true lawyer.

"We must quell this rumor." My voice trilled. "All right, Alex." I took a breath and calmed. "I shall talk to her myself." I placed my napkin beside my plate and took another sip of wine. It rushed to my head. "She invited me for tea, but I haven't yet responded. I shall accept her kind invitation, and tell her how much in love I am with James, which should convince her how uninterested I am in you."

He tilted his head. "And are you much in love with James?" he challenged.

We'd never discussed intimate details about our marriages, after his first visit to my room, when I'd admitted I still loved James, but couldn't stay with him.

Now, in trying to answer Alex's inquiry, I became flustered. Words clogged my tongue as I tried to formulate a coherent, yet honest, reply. "I still love him, yes. But tis not the same as when we first married. Now you can say I'm—accustomed to him."

"As you become accustomed to a piece of furniture." An understanding nod told me I needn't explain more. "A lumpy sofa."

"No, more like a highboy. But we don't share the same—" My hands fluttered about as I searched for the right word.

"Spark?"

I stammered, taken off guard. The spark between James and me had hardly cooled.

"Devotion?"

This was much easier to answer. "Among other things." We exchanged knowing smiles.

"You need not put on a show for my wife." He sipped his wine. "Frankly, I believe it better not to discuss James. He's not exactly endeared to her."

"I've hesitated because I feel hypocritical, being her guest while—" My gaze dropped as I struggled to find respectable words.

"Fret not, my dear. Sometimes life necessitates keeping up appearances." He swung his goblet twixt thumb and forefinger like a pendulum. "I daresay I find it satisfactory that your devotion to James has waned. Jealousy is a deadly sin, but sometimes rears its ugly head. I only hope if your marriage recaptures its former magic, you'll let me know. That will shed a whole new light on things—between us."

"Worry not about that, Alex." I stood and sauntered round the table to sit on his lap. I ran my fingers through his hair and slid the ribbon from his queue. I wanted him so badly, I burned for him. "You're the only man I'll ever love." Oh, no, had I blurted that four-letter word? "I mean—want." I sputtered, trying to correct myself. But I couldn't un-say what I'd just said.

179

"That's fine with me, Maria. You know why? Because I love you, too. More than you'll ever know."

As I heard those words I desired nothing more than to melt into his arms and drown in his love.

Chapter Nineteen

Eliza

As daylight faded, my carriage pulled up to Robert Troup's brownstone on the outskirts of Greenwich Village. Unseasonable warmth melted the snow, making the roads suitable for travel. A letter I'd sent ahead told Robert to expect me, baby John and his nurse Ruth.

With Ruth carrying baby John, I lifted the brass knocker and rapped on his door. Robert himself appeared. I blinked in surprise. No servants?

"Eliza! As I live and breathe! And this must be John. May I hold the little angel?" He took John from Ruth. Cradling the baby in his arms, he ushered us in.

"You received my letter, I trust?" We exchanged the customary two-cheek kiss and he led us into his parlour. A fire blazed in the hearth. A brandy bottle and two snifters stood on a table next to a chessboard.

"I did indeed, and couldn't be more delighted." He held John up and rubbed noses with him. "He's adorable. He looks just like you!" Of course he was teasing; John was the image of Alex in every way, from the coppery fuzz atop his head to his violet eyes.

"We still have Louisa's cradle. I can bring your nurse—Ruth, is it? I'll show you to your quarters, Ruth." As he led the nurse upstairs, I snooped a bit. I felt right at home here in the cluttered and cozy parlour, the furniture and rug a bit worn. Toys and books lay scattered about, and a colorful patchwork quilt covered the sofa.

Robert came back down and closed the door. "Jennet and the youngsters are visiting kin in Connecticut, expected back tomorrow. Now, what brings you here? A shopping expedition en route to Albany?"

"No, Robert, I fear we haven't the means for a shopping expedition." We sat in the facing wing chairs. "That is what I came to discuss with you. Alex admitted that he borrowed a large sum from you—was it six hundred? Between that and some strange letters I've received, I need to get to the bottom of this."

Robert fingered his queue, leant forward and filled the two snifters with brandy. "Sorry, but my servants are ill, so I'm very much on my own." He looked at me. "Alex didn't divulge what the loan was for. I did ask, but in reply, he told me he was investing in some land speculation. I thought this out of character for him, the Treasury Secretary gambling with his funds like this. He was always so frugal, so careful with his money. As I know he is with the treasury's funds."

"You don't believe him either." My fists clenched in anger. "I understand his not telling me, but why wouldn't he share this with his best friend?"

He sipped his brandy, his eyes shut as he shook his head. "I care not to say I disbelieve him. We've always been candid with each other about everything. I always knew how he felt, and he me. But this time, I find it hard to believe he'd engage in speculation—and resort to borrowing. It didn't ring true."

"Of course it doesn't," I stated. "And I have these letters, which, to my chagrin, are ringing more true every day. I have no proof, of course, and want to believe they're a vicious ploy to cause disaster, but—" I heaved an exasperated sigh. "Alex is a handsome and desirable man, as you know. Well—mayhap you should not know—" I quit stammering and opened my drawstring purse, retrieved the letters and handed them to him. He scanned them and gave them back, his cheeks flushed.

"Who is Mrs. Reynolds?" He refilled his glass.

I told him who the Reynoldses were, and bared my soul to him. I broke down in tears at the end. "I've never told this to anyone before now. Speaking of it makes it all the more distressing."

He handed me a handkerchief from his top pocket. "This cannot be true at all. All the years I've known Alex, I've—" He stopped dead in his tracks and clamped his lips shut.

183

"I know all about Alex and his dalliances before we married. But since—never did I have reason to doubt his faithfulness. When would he have time? He's always working." I scowled. "Neither I nor a willing mistress could keep Alex from his shaping of this nation, assuring his place in history. Work is his mistress. But these letters, and now his spending of large sums—even if it is rumor, someone is out to ruin him." I took a sip. I was not keen on spirits, but lifted it to my lips, trying to hide my grimace. "Of course he has enemies, they all do. Jefferson actually paid the reporter Thomson Callender to print harsh attacks on Washington, Adams, and others. But it never involved the wives. This, I fear, may be a personal vendetta against me. Everyone knows my father is one of Alex's most loyal backers of the bank."

Robert shook his head, and I studied his features: lines around his eyes, strands of gray at his temples, and his face had filled out since I'd seen him last. *We all grow old*, I lamented.

"No one would want to hurt you," he assured me. "I'm sure it's one of his political foes. No level is too low to stoop for some of them. I only wish he'd told me what the loan was for."

"Robert, I must ask you this." I put down the glass and clasped my hands in my lap. "If the loan had been to pay off some blackmailer, would you still have sent it to him?"

He took a deep breath and expelled it. "Probably. I'd give him my shirt, for any reason, as I know he'd do the same. Now you've got my curiosity piqued. I also don't want to see him fall victim to a blackmailer, or worse. If you want to learn the truth, you should hire someone who does private investigations."

I clutched my collar. "You mean—pay someone to follow Alex around and report back to me?"

He held his palms upward and raised his brows in a "what choice do you have?" gesture.

"It seems a sneaky underhanded tactic," I countered.

"Eliza, I can see your fear of danger is eating away at you. You believe his political life may be on the brink of ruin."

I listened, thinking. "Yes, and knowing James Reynolds is a staunch loyalist only adds to my trepidation. Oh, dear." I sighed. "I believe Maria is merely the conduit James used to reach Alex. She's an innocent party in all this. Alex would never give her a second glance." I sat back and nodded. "Mayhap you are right. This involves high stakes. Someone is out to destroy Alex, and it is not Maria Reynolds. She is hardly a seductress."

"There must be someone in Philadelphia whom you can hire." He encouraged me further by topping off my brandy snifter. I much preferred cider. But I drank some more.

A thought hit me like a flash of light. "Robert, I do know someone locally. Her name is Ann Bates. She was a loyalist spy for the British forces, and a very successful one at that. She later taught school in Philadelphia. I even know where she lives—not far from us."

Robert's eyes lit up. "I know Annie. She was in Henry Clinton's espionage during the war and infiltrated General Washington's camp many a time. She was quite successful at her craft. A clever lady indeed. Oh, Annie, what mettle she had." He chuckled. "I have some fond memories of that old gal. Right you are, Eliza, no one will find out what you want to know faster than Annie."

I nodded my agreement, knowing what I must do. "Lord help me, I do not want to hire a former spy—a loyalist spy for the British, no less—to follow my husband around." I took another sip, without a grimace this time. "Politics might be a big game to Alex, his friends and his enemies. But he doesn't realize how a scandal could ruin his reputation forever."

Robert nodded in agreement. "Whether it be true or not, you need to know. His name, his marriage, and your sanity depend upon it."

I decided at that moment to call on "Annie."

Maria

"You love me, Alex? You truly love me? Are you sure?" My breath caught in my throat. My heart danced. His admission rendered me breathless. I melted into a puddle in his lap.

"Maria, I've been awaiting you all my life." He stroked my cheek. "You're everything I've wanted in a woman—allure, intelligence, talent, fun—I've never met a woman who was all those things wrapped in one beautiful package."

I gazed into his eyes, knowing our souls had entwined before this, ages before.

"I wanted you so badly from the moment we first met, at Aaron's soirée," I divulged the risky admission. "Though I knew you were already taken, and your course already laid out for you, I craved your attention, not to simply revere you from afar. I wanted to know you personally, even if only to spend one visit together. Just to be close to you. But I knew it was a fantasy. I was distraught when you left New York to live here. Then, when James made us move here, I knew our paths were destined to meet. It could not have happened any other way."

"Then your initial letter to me had subtext I missed?" His lips curved with mirth.

"Oh, no, not at all," I murmured between kisses on his face, his ears, his lips. "We—I was destitute. James had—" About to blurt it out, I stopped myself. I couldn't bring myself to admit I'd lied to him; I'd been a pawn in James's plot. "All I wanted was to meet you, to be alone with you, for a few stolen moments. That was all I deserved. After all, you are—who you are! I'm—no one."

"Ah, you're far from no one. A pity James doesn't realize that. But I do. I will come clean with you, Maria. I love my wife, but I am not in love with her. As I am with you."

He ran a fingertip over my lips and I tingled all over. I wanted to climb to the roof and sing to the entire world, "The great Alexander Hamilton, my new love, is in love with me!" How could I ever keep this a secret? The best part of being in love was sharing it with others. Oh, how I wanted to tell someone! But who could I trust?

"I am all talked out. Come upstairs." His voice caressed my ears. "Take this candle, for my hands will be busy."

I slid off his lap and grabbed the candle in its holder. He swept me into his arms and up the staircase to a small bedroom. It held one canopy bed with carved bedposts. He set me on my feet. We stood facing each other, our eyes locked. The hunger of a wild wanton gnawing at me, I stripped him naked. I stood back and observed his lean but muscular figure. Shadows from the lone candle played on his hair, his exquisite features. I studied the contours of his cheekbones, the wisdom in his eyes, the curly mat on his chest, his flat stomach, his strong legs.

Our lovemaking seemed different this time, more intense, after admitting our love for each other. It didn't matter to whom we'd promised ourselves at the altar of marriage. Alex and I belonged together. We'd spoken vows that meant more to me than the lines I'd parroted after the minister when I wedded James.

As I'd hoped, he asked me to stay the night. I wanted nothing more than to fall asleep and wake in his arms. I began wishing Mrs. Hamilton would never come home, and we could stay like this forever. But that couldn't happen. We had to keep hiding.

Tonight I got a sample of it when a knock came on the door. Leaving me cold in the bed, he warned me,

"Do not come downstairs." He pulled on his dressing gown and went down to admit his visitor. I crept to the top of the stairs and peeked through the railings in the dark. He lit a candle in the foyer and opened the door. Voices ascended to my ears as I peered down to look.

God's truth, if it wasn't James and Dolley Madison! More people followed, talking and laughing as they crowded round Alex in the foyer. A violinist and a flutist entered, and I nearly fell over when I saw who the violinist was—Mrs. Platz, my instructor! I gasped and choked, trying to suppress the coughing, but I couldn't stop. Mrs. Platz glanced up the stairs. For an instant our eyes met. She turned and rejoined the crowd. I crouched behind the banisters, frozen with shame.

Now with Alex hosting a party, I had to stay up here, hidden. In the cold. In the dark. How I wished to be part of that laughing group! This was how it had to be—with Alex always on stage and me always backstage—hiding.

Chapter Twenty

Maria

"She is beauty in distress." Alexander Hamilton on Maria Reynolds, in his first draft of The Reynolds Pamphlet

Teusd'y eve, Feb'y the 7th, eleven of clock.

I fulfilled my dream this morn—I woke up in his arms. We made love again, but it was urgent and brief. "I have an early appointment, so this has to be a rush tumble." He kept one eye on the clock. It was over before I noticed the movement of either the clock's hands *or* his hands.

As he hustled into his britches, I voiced my wishes for later that day. "Alex, I want to be here when you return, to share supper. I long to be your Mrs., even for one day."

He grabbed his shirt, shaking his head. "Nay, you must return home. Your being seen here will spell trouble—at the very least." He ran his hand over his growth of whiskers. "I need a shave. Be dressed within the quarter hour and I'll have a carriage waiting for you outside."

My heart heavy with dejection, I slid off the bed and plucked up my wrinkled clothing, hardly fit to wear in public. I had to admit he was right. We could not take any more risks. Mrs. Platz already saw me crouched at the top of the stairs.

He sent me home in an old carriage, obviously a spare. Mrs. Hamilton must have taken the fancy one to New York. When I arrived home, James looked up from his pen and parchment. "How went last eve?"

"Fine." I cared not to elaborate, and he didn't ask. He didn't even ask if Alex had given me money. "By the amount of whisky you've already consumed, I can see you have more on your mind." I headed upstairs to change my clothes.

He stopped me. "My cousin Simeon will be here shortly. Maggs is preparing roasted capon and boiled potatoes. You may join us if you wish, but we're meeting with Jacob again, and will be in talks the rest of the day." His way of saying, "I prefer you vacate the premises. We care not to discuss business with a lady present."

Cousin Simeon was a younger, and in honesty, less comely version of James. But any time these two lads bounced their wit and humor off each other, with imitations of everyone from John Adams to Elizabeth Monroe, they had me in stitches.

"Why Simeon?" I asked idly. "I'm not interested in your scheme, just that capon."

"As you know…" He placed the pen in its holder and leant back in his chair. "Last year, Jacob and I bought up claims to back pay of Continental Army veterans. The new government hadn't honored the claims. Because of their dubious value, we got them at a price far lower than the vets were actually entitled to."

I sat across from him. "Yes, I already know about this."

"Sim supplied us with Treasury Department lists," he explained. "He shouldna have, but he was privy to the lists and, desperate for extra income, he took advantage of his position."

As a treasury clerk and another gambler on speculation and dice, Simeon was prone to losing money.

I nodded. "I know all this. They brought you up on charges, and later dropped them."

He sported a smug grin at the mention of the dropped charges. "Now it appears they want to use that minor infraction to press more serious charges against us for something else." He lowered his eyes and continued, "and this time I doubt they'll be dropped." He rubbed his forehead.

"What something else?" I tensed. "Will one of your schemes land you behind bars?"

He looked back up at me. "Jacob and I have an acquaintance, John Delabar. One eve over a few pints, we persuaded him to perjure himself, so that we could pose as executors of the estate of a Massachusetts soldier, Ephraim Goodenough, with outstanding claims against the Federal government."

"How did you know about this Goodenough soldier?" I asked.

"Sim told us about him."

"How does the law know you did this?" I prodded.

He leant forward and clasped his hands twist his knees. "Unfortunately, instead of being dead, as was stated, Ephraim Goodenough is much alive, and decided to bring charges against us. Whilst at work the other day, cousin Sim heard that our generous benefactor Hamilton got wind of this. Hamilton ordered Oliver Wolcott, the Treasury Comptroller, to look into it, question Sim, and write up a report on it. Whether Hamilton's doing this because Sim's surname is Reynolds, and he wants to make life difficult for him and me, I know not. But we're gathering here to discuss a strategy to defend ourselves, because tis likely *Hamilton*, that sod," he hissed, "will take this ball and run with it."

My limbs trembled. My tongue dried up. I licked my lips. "By God, why didn't he ever mention this to me?" Did Alex even know Simeon Reynolds existed? "James, I—I know not why Alex would want to make things difficult for you. He's been giving you money, he's been giving me—" I halted and blushed.

"Aye, we know what he's bin givin' *you*." He smirked, but got dead serious again. "I dinna know if Hamilton knows Sim and I are related, but he may be giving to us with one hand and taking with the other. Ah'm tending not to trust him. However, he could only be playing out his Mr. Righteous role, showing the treasury and President Washington and all his noble peers of the realm how upstanding he is, to clear his path for the kingship—I mean—presidency. All I know is that we need defend ourselves."

"You committed fraud, James. A serious Federal offense," I chided, my tongue so dry I could hardly speak. I didn't dare pause this discussion to fetch a drink.

His gaze now secured to his empty glass, James said, "That's why ah'm hoping you can put in a good word for me to Hamilton. Git him in a weak position, if y'know what I mean. First mention cousin Sim, and how innocent he is of any wrongdoing. Then tell him that Jacob and I meant no harm, it was an error in judgment, and ah'll gladly pay the money back—with interest. Obviously, it's bin spent. But at heart, ah'm a patriot, and ah'll also gladly give back half of my earnings from the Commissary Department."

He blinked when he saw my mouth fall open. "To make amends, Maria. Out of patriotism and concern for our fellow veterans. I shall make this sacrifice. So help me God." He raised his right hand and gave a solemn nod, as if he'd just taken the oath of office. All he needed was a Bible to swear on.

At that gesture I couldn't keep a straight face. "I'll wager Alex will burst into gales of laughter, weak moment or not. James, you're so full of dung, your eyes are brown. You're hardly a patriot, as everyone knows, and you're no veteran. You didn't even lift a musket. I know that Alex respects your father, but Pa and son handing out hard tack and coffee beans in the Commissary Department hardly qualifies as serving in the military. He'll laugh me right out of his b—his house."

James looked me square in the eye. "I ask you one favor. You willna oblige me. Immense. But dinna come crying to me when he ditches you and takes up with some other doxy. You want to keep his interest in more ways than the obvious, this is one way to do it. Tell him you want to help, too, by knitting blankets for soldiers, or volunteering to care for them in the next war." He refilled his glass. "Show him you care about the vets, too. Ask him to raise their pay. Ask him to wield his power to help the vets, instead of wasting his efforts persecuting Sim and Jacob and me. We're innocent citizens who now want to make amends for what I admit was a mistake. I truly believed he had better things to do with his time. Is he not busy enough creating a bank and running the country's coffers? He has spare time to bust my culls?"

"All right, James, somewhere buried beneath all your piles of manure is the truth. It needs be believable," I warned him. "I shall prepare something to say to him. But you'll have to trust me. I shall not memorize and parrot one of your contrived scripts." I would use any excuse to see Alex. "But if he is intent on prosecuting you, Jacob, and possibly Sim, I want to know why he didn't tell me before." After all we'd shared last night, especially our declarations of love, my heart ached over Alex's keeping this from me. I planned to tell him so when we next met.

Cousin Sim arrived, eyes wide in surprise at seeing me.

"It's safe to discuss our strategy in Maria's presence," James assured him. "She already knows all about it." Then he blabbered, "She's even going to speak to Hamilton on our behalf."

Sim gaped at me as if I'd sprouted two more heads. "You—you're on speaking terms with *Secretary Hamilton*?" He said the name with reverence, as in a prayer.

He needn't know we were on loving terms. "Yes, we've exchanged a few pleasantries and—favors, here and there. I may be able to use my influence to get him to reconsider pursuing this case against you."

But before I had a chance to return to Alex's house, and even before the capon was cooked, two burly men delivered a summons. Oliver Wolcott, Comptroller of the Treasury, swore out two warrants for the arrest of James and Jacob, for fraud and subornation of a witness—a serious crime against the Federal government.

"I promise I'll get you out." I grasped my husband's hand as the clerks hauled him off to jail. He did not resist. Sim trembled and burst into tears. I comforted him with whisky and began rehearsing my speech to Alex tonight.

Chapter Twenty-One

Eliza

Albany, Wednsday eve, February 15th, six of clock

As my pen scratched across paper, pouring my heart out to Alex about how much I missed him, I wondered what he was doing. With the children gone, I knew he was lonely in our big house. The servants never provided companionship; they cooked the meals, lit the fires, cleaned up and vanished to their quarters. I hoped Alex was spending his eves engaging in stimulating activities. Anything but working. Work seemed to consume him lately, as he became more vital to the nation's growth.

After urging him to find ways to amuse himself, I kissed the bottom of the paper, folded and sealed it, and left it on the hall table to be posted.

I knew he thought of me, late at night, in bed.

"Please take me to Seventy-Nine South Third," I told the coachman at six of clock, when I knew he'd be in residence. I dashed out of the carriage afore it halted. Candles glowed in Alex's dining room windows. I knocked, and a manservant admitted me.

"Yes, Secretary Hamilton is expecting me," I answered before he finished the question.

Once more I was escorted into the sitting room. I stood, shivering, trembling, waiting.

Alex entered the room in a blue velvet jacket, lace at the throat and cuffs, and matching britches. I almost leapt into his arms.

"Maria, I was just thinking of you! I meant to send you a note to return this eve but got frightfully bogged down with tasks."

"I couldn't stay away, Alex. I counted the minutes till we could be together again." My heart dancing with happiness, I nearly forgot about James sitting in a cold cell. My lover's lips sought mine and I melted in his arms. A ringing dinner bell jolted me to my senses.

"My evening meal awaits." Alex broke the embrace. Obviously his appetite for food won out over his appetite for me.

I clutched his arm as he headed out. "Alex, I must address a most grave matter. James is in jail. And I think you know why."

"He's committed an infamous crime, my dear. But innocent until proven guilty." Vexation toughened his pitch. "Must we discuss this now?"

"Yes, we must," I returned, matching his tone.

He strode towards the dining room. "Do you care to sup with me?" he asked more genially. "Have you dined yet?"

"Yes. No—I'm not hungry." I followed him, my empty stomach churning. "Maggie cooked capons, but I managed not a bite."

Two servants bustled in with serving dishes, set another place for me, and poured wine. "James wants to make amends—re-pay the soldier he'd wronged and re-pay the treasury half his war earnings," I recited my speech and sat.

Contrary to my prediction, Alex didn't die laughing. He nodded, then dived into his roast beef and potatoes. I could not touch a morsel. My plate grew cold. Nor was I interested in wine. "When you ordered Wolcott to investigate this and arrest James, why hadn't you told me about it?" I badgered, as rehearsed, anger rising as I glared at him.

"Why should I have told you?" He glanced at me between bites and sips.

"I believed we were confidantes!" I shouted, though I hadn't meant to. "I tell you all."

He ventured a dramatic eye-roll. "My dear, physical intimacy and tender feelings don't encompass divulging every detail of a man's life."

"Last night it was deep, true love. Now it's tender feelings?" Rage wound me up like a tight spring. "We need discuss our relationship in far more detail. Later. But this involves James."

"And at the time, he'd allegedly left you for another woman. You'd appealed to me, destitute, because he was a swindler, a cad. Why are you so indignant about saving his hide now?" He pointed his knife at my untouched plate. "You should eat. The beef is very savory."

I shook my head, disillusioned and confused, my heart in a muddle. I'd hoped he was taking steps to leave his wife, but I now realized we were miles from that stage. "Alex, I want you to unburden all your problems and cares on me. And I think I was entitled to know you were investigating my husband," I added for emphasis.

"Your husband was already with another woman. Or so you claimed." His narrowed eyes cast doubt upon me. "Any sensible wife would be glad to be rid of him. Especially after committing a fraudulent crime against my—the United States Treasury."

I loathed keeping up the pretense that James had deserted me. But I daren't tell Alex the truth now. I couldn't bear having him throw me out of his house, out of his bed, out of his life. Desperately in love with him, I would die if he left me now.

"Yes, I took James back. Mayhap I shouldn't have. But that arrest came as a shock, and I wish you'd told me about this before." I helped myself to the wine bottle. "Now I can use some of this."

"Maria, you needn't know everything about me. Or what I do to benefit citizens, such as yourself, or the treasury, or aught else. Tis not my nature to have divulged something like this to you. I don't proclaim every good deed and expect rose petals strewn at my feet." He stabbed the air with his fork. "That is Jefferson's style, not mine," he added in a haughty tone.

I now realized if I wanted to continue our affair, I'd have to accept all this.

A server hovered around us with a silver tray and spoon. "More carrots, sir?"

"Yes, please." He certainly did have a hearty appetite. "And another basket of warm rolls. And more butter."

"Jacob Clingman is already free on bail." I bowed my head. I couldn't look him in the eye as I admitted, "but we have no money for James's bail."

The server returned with his carrots, rolls and butter. Appetite still eluded me as he relished his feast.

I twisted my serviette twixt my fingers. "It was a mistake, Alex. You know James, he'll do anything for money, but he meant no harm. He wants to make amends to the government. And so do I. I—I can knit blankets and socks for soldiers. If Lady Washington can do it, so can I." This didn't sound quite as preposterous now. Certainly I could do this. I needed bail money, but I was too proud to ask. Food and rent money was one thing, but this—I just couldn't. Nor did he offer.

Another server entered with an aromatic apple pye and a steaming pot of coffee. "I'll serve this myself. You may leave us till the morn." Alex dismissed her and cut himself a generous slice. "Pye?"

I shook my head.

He poured himself a cup of coffee. "I personally asked Comptroller Wolcott to serve the arrest warrants for your husband and Clingman. Wolcott is Clingman's superior. I cannot let this go by the wayside." He dabbed at his mouth with his serviette and sipped his coffee. "I do not tolerate fraud in the treasury, Maria. I am accountable for everything that happens there. If someone absconds with a penny, I am accountable. That is why I hire men of integrity." He dug into his pye. "Yes, Simeon Reynolds is young and gullible. He should be an accomplice. However, he's not been charged yet. But I preside over the Treasury Department, and whatever happens, tis my burden and my duty to make it right." He projected his voice as if addressing the court.

"I've no more argument in me," I admitted. "No statesman has more integrity than you when it comes to money, especially the treasury's." That was why he wouldn't give me bail money for James. He wouldn't take my word for it. He had to look into it himself. I bristled at what I considered a slight, but I held a great respect for his integrity. He put the treasury before me. I had to accept that. Or leave him. I chose the former, because God help me, I'd fallen too deeply in love with this man to let him go.

"What did you think of *Henry the Eighth*?" He changed the subject.

"I'd read it before." As I pictured the portly king, my stomach churned. "I always liked the play, but loathe the real King Henry. It is sickening how he murdered his wives and destroyed those beautiful monasteries. The self-absorbed tyrant."

That made Alex laugh. "As is the current British monarch, Mad King George. Precisely why we're on this side of the pond."

"My family did not like King James," I said. "They considered him a tyrant as well. He abdicated, did he not?"

"Right you are. A group of His Majesty's subjects opposed both his religion and his absolute power. They deposed him in the Glorious Revolution. Not quite as glorious as ours, mind you." He nodded. "But Parliament did regard him as to have abdicated, and Scotland's Parliament acknowledged that he forfeited his throne. You may remember what I wrote in the Federalist Papers about the authority of the monarch. It was almost unlimited until that revolution, when King James abdicated and William of Orange took over, that English liberty was completely triumphant. I would not want to have lived there before William."

"I do remember reading that." My heart swelled with admiration for him. "I liked the way you delved into English history."

"I always loved to write. Were it not for the good citizens of St. Croix liking my newspaper article, who knows where I would be today?" He scooped up another forkful of pye. "Likely still there, running a sugar plantation, a Caribbean gentleman bean counter."

"That is not possible, Alex." I fiddled with a spoon. "You would have found your way here somehow. This is your destiny. Greatness. To make American history. You never would have been happy to settle for farming on a tropical island."

A wistful smile played upon his lips. "At the time, I had no long-range plans. I went whichever way the wind blew."

"You cannot believe you were blown here—into King's College, General Washington's camp, the Congress, and now the Treasury Department? Surely you must have believed in yourself, in order to seek out Washington's attention, to take those first steps." I sneaked my reflection in a butter knife.

He cut another hunk of pye and slid it onto his plate. "I needn't have sought out his attention. He sought out mine. He was looking for the son he never had, and I was it. I do not know what brought me here—to this pinnacle of my life. I never had a moment to stop and think about it."

"I know why. Because no one else in this nation is capable of your visions." I grasped his hand, wanting to touch this genius. "To merely be in your presence is an honor." And here I was, his lover!

"I'm not sure of that." He glanced at me and looked away again. "I am not sure anyone else would want this job."

"Did not President Washington have others in mind?"

He splayed his fingers. "I have no way of knowing. He never told me if he did. He's not much of a talker.

He gets down to business and doesn't tarry. I'm honored he chose me but doubt I'm the supreme being."

"Alex, you do not think enough of yourself. You must leave your beginnings behind and look to where you are now. You are the most brilliant visionary our nation has. I would be honored to have you as my president." It came out sounding as if I were in a position to give him that appointment. But I meant it.

His lips tightened and his cheeks flushed. He pulled his hand away. "I could never fill Washington's shoes. I don't want to live to see another president. No one could ever replace him."

"Vice-President Adams would make a good president." I knew that would get a rise out of him.

"Anyone but Jefferson." He gave an ironic snicker. "But I haven't considered the presidency. After my public service ends, I prefer to resume my law practice in my old age."

Now that we'd touched on the topic of the future, I dared to be bold. "And does that old age include—us?" I waited for his answer with baited breath.

His eyes softened and he smiled. "God willing."

This was the first time he'd ever mentioned God. I had no idea how religious he was, if at all, or of what faith. But I did not want to press him any further on the subject. If we were to be married someday, it did not have to be in church. We had plenty of time for wedding plans.

The vision of Alex as my husband filled me with warm romantic feelings. My ardent desire for him gave me the urge to initiate our lovemaking, to be the seductress, to render him helpless under my touch. I came right out and propositioned him: "Shall we retire to a bedroom?"

The servants had cleared the table and vanished. The house sat in tomb silence. We were all alone. "Yes, yes, of course," as if he'd forgotten why I was there.

He didn't sweep me into his arms and whisk me up the stairs like last night. "Follow me," he offered politely and led me up to the back bedroom. He lit a fire and turned to me. "Take off your clothes, then." Hardly romantic. But I obeyed. I still wanted him. I would get his mind back in the bedroom where it belonged.

As we slipped naked between the sheets, moonlight streamed through the window. The firelight flickered over his hair and his fine features. I kissed him. Our tongues mingled. His muscles relaxed under my attentive hands. But something else won out.

He flopped onto his back. "It's not going to happen tonight," he murmured. "I'm too done in. What with work, everything on my mind..." His chest rose and fell as he released a deep breath.

"Tis all right, Alex." My voice dragged with the letdown but I couldn't push him. Nothing is less responsive than a tired—and overfed—man. I only hoped my talk of the presidency and God and our future had not turned him away. My hands slid up his body and massaged his neck. "Don't worry, we'll try again in the morning."

But in the morning I woke in an empty bed.

I found a note on his pillow. *Pls remove yourself soon as you awake as not to arouse suspicion.* I obeyed. But of course I planned to come back tonight. First I had to find bail money for James.

Chapter Twenty-Two

Eliza

Feb'y 17th, the Tudor Inn.

Very clean. No bedbugs. Empty chamber pots. We stopped here on the way from Albany. I wished Alex were here with me, as I rocked John in the cradle Robert was kind enough to give me.

I was reluctant to hire Mrs. Bates, but desperate to know if those anonymous letters were authentic. Her services would be expensive, so I'd asked dear Papa for some assistance. I could cut back on household expenses and repay him. Alex need never discover my scheme. But I thought of a safer—rather, *sneakier* way: have Mrs. Bates follow Mrs. Reynolds, not Alex. If her and my husband's paths never crossed, I'd rest easy. But I wondered if Mrs. Bates could find out who wrote those letters to me. That was who I really wanted followed. This heartless instigator intent on ruining our lives. I planned to show the letters

to Mrs. Bates and have her compare the penman-
ship first to Mr. Jefferson, then to Mr. Adams, then to
Mr. Burr, then whoever else I thought of. And prayed
I needn't borrow more money for it.

Maria

I told Mrs. Platz I could not afford violin lessons for
a while. I would put the money towards James's bail
until I raised enough.

At first, she accused me wordlessly, brows drawn,
eyes beady. "Maria, we both know I saw you at the
top of Herr Hamilton's stairs. You did not hide very
well. You're lucky no one else saw you." Her lips
tightened into a thin line, as if chiding a child. And
like a child, I froze.

But I elected to play the innocent. "Herr who?"

Her hostile glare told me she wasn't believing
any of it. So I admitted the truth. "Yes, it was I.
Please—don't tell a soul. It was just that once. Nothing happened. We were simply talking. Mr. Hamilton
has done business with James. But now he's in jail
and I—"

"Stop it right there." She held up a callused hand.
"I admire Herr Hamilton. But I confess I rather mis-
like his wife. She patronizes me, as if she's my better.
She's a Schuyler, we all know that. And I'm a peasant
from Vienna. But in the end, we all rot in the same
dirt. Whatever liaisons you and Herr Hamilton have,
it is none of my business. So I shant tell anyone. As
for your husband, I wish I could help further, but I

haven't the extra funds to advance you for his bail."
She pointed at the chair before her. "Sit down. We'll
have the lesson anyway free of charge."

I wiped away tears of relief.

She brought me a spare violin, and the free lesson
took my mind off my troubles.

Until I went to visit James in jail.

"Did you raise the bail money yet?" came his greeting. "I asked Hamilton for a hundred dolls t'other day.
So far tis no forthcoming."

I recoiled. "He won't give you a lump of coal after
all this," I retorted as the "codlings of an ox" phrase
entered my mind. "You violated what he considers
sacred, the treasury."

"Did you tell him what I told you to say?" He eyed
me questioningly, chewing the bread and cheese I'd
brought him.

"Of course," I huffed. "But he's going to look into it
regardless. He wouldn't trust his own wife with the
treasury, much less me."

James wiped his hands on his shirt. "He guards the
bloody treasury with his life, yet he romps behind his
wife's back. Well, mayhap tis high time she found
out."

I gasped. "No. James, no, don't even think of telling
her. I'll get more money from him, I promise."

"Aye, so will I. With my next letter, mentioning the
possibility of letting Mrs. Hamilton in on this cozy
threesome." He shoved another piece of bread into
his gob and chewed with gusto.

"Please don't, James." I clutched the cold iron bars till my fingers cramped. "I'll see him tonight. One way or another, I'll get you out of here."

"That's my girl." He reached through the bars and we clasped hands. My heart ached for him. He wasn't a hardened criminal. Just someone trying to make a living. But going about it the wrong way at times.

As I scurried out of the jail, my hands and feet frozen, I shivered—from fear of Mrs. Hamilton hearing about me and Alex. Then an idea hit me—I could parade someone in front of her as my lover. This was a desperate act, and an act it would be, but desperate I was. And I knew just the man to play the part of my lover—Jacob Clingman. The reigning king of the theater, David Garrick, couldn't play this role any better!

At nightfall, I dressed, powdered and perfumed myself to spend another night with Alex. I knocked at his door, but the servant told me he wasn't in residence. She knew not when he'd return. I dared not ask where he was. Disappointment dragging my feet, I returned to the carriage. "Take me to number Three Hundred Spruce Street," I instructed the driver.

I hadn't visited Jacob Clingman's stately home since his wife was alive, nigh on two years. It was the largest brick mansion on Spruce Street, three storeys high with a wing on either side. The entire structure measured at least one hundred feet wide. It stood back from the street, a high brick wall surrounding it, ensuring privacy. Behind the house sprawled a garden, orchard, and an assortment of outbuildings.

The carriage rolled to a stop at the entrance. The driver lowered the carriage steps and helped me alight. A female servant with a daring low neckline answered my knock. Before she could escort me to a sitting room, Jacob appeared and greeted me. "I'm so sorry, Maria, I would have helped James with his bail, but I'm low on ready cash." Yet his eyes twinkled as he took my hand and kissed it.

"I shall raise the money somehow." I gave the servant my shawl. "If I skip the rent this month, I'll have enough to bail him out. But there's something else I need discuss."

He led me down the marble-floored hallway into a tastefully furnished parlour. We sat on a French settee with a plush velvet seat and caned back. "Someone is accusing me of having an affair with Alexander Hamilton and sending his wife scandalous letters." Then I blurted, "Mrs. Hamilton invited me for tea, but I haven't yet accepted. I thought it courteous to invite her to call on me. Will you also attend and—" I cleared my throat, cringing with trepidation. "Pretend, just pretend, that we are courting? We can act—cozy, familiar with each other. We'll make it clear to her I have no interest in her husband. This will surely quell her suspicions."

His response came as an amused grin, exactly what I'd expected. I needn't twist his arm. "Pray tell me the time and the place, and I shall be there." Then he excused himself and returned with one hundred dollars in bank notes. "Here. Bail James out with this.

Spend the remainder on yourself. Pay me back when you can."

"Twenty minutes ago you were cash-strapped." I took the proffered notes, folded them, and slid them down the front of my bodice. "But thank you for sharing your golden goose with me." We exchanged smiles.

"My winnings from a card game, which I planned to gamble straight back, but James has helped me in the past. Besides, how else could I repay you for such an enchanting experience as courting you—for Mrs. Hamilton's sake, that is?" His twinkling eyes wouldn't leave me, whether I looked down, up, or across the room.

"You're the one doing me the favor," I corrected him.

"Believe me, the pleasure will be all mine," he countered, with a dazzling smile. I hadn't realized how straight and white his teeth were. They looked like he cleaned them thrice a day. He certainly was meticulous about his appearance. But I couldn't hold him up to Alex. Next to my golden god, everyone else paled as mere mortal.

"Fine. Then I shall write to Mrs. Hamilton and accept her invitation. She's due back from Albany any day now." I tried to keep the lilt in my voice but simply couldn't, not knowing when I'd see Alex again. "I'll return to the jail to post James's bail." I stood. "So I'll be on my way. I need to get him out of there."

Jacob followed me into the hall. "Until such time, good evening, Maria," he said at the door. Then, before I knew what hit me, he swept me into his arms, dipped me, and fixed his lips upon mine. Too surprised to pull away, I was upright again. I should have given him a good what-for. But we both knew what was happening here. He knew my marriage was less than perfect. And I'm sure he suspected my affair with Alex, hence my efforts to quell the rumors. I bustled out of there before he kissed me again—or before I kissed him.

When I arrived at the jail, the guard told me James had been released. I stumbled backwards in surprise. "Do you know where he went?" God above, who had he conned for bail money?

"No, ma'am," the guard replied.

I had to know. "Who posted his bail?"

"No bail, ma'am. Two congressmen called on him, they conversed with him, and ordered his release."

I stumbled out in a daze. Congressmen? Ordered his release? Had he bribed them? My head spun with bafflement. Stunned, I stood on the street, looking both ways. Where on earth had he gone to? I headed for his favorite tavern, The Grog.

As I stepped into the crowded room, the odors of smoke and stale sweat assaulted me. Women weren't allowed in taverns, but James frequented this place so often, I was not confined to the snug.

I found him alone at a side table, quaffing from a tankard. "James! How did you get out of jail?"

He slammed the tankard down, swept the foam from his lips and grinned. "You're looking at a free man, my bonny lass. Care for a spot of mead?" He stood and pulled out a chair for me.

"No, I don't want any mead." I sat. "Tell me how all this leaked out, to senators and congressmen, no less."

In the brightest spirits I'd seen him in for ages, he whistled a sprightly tune. But he smelt rancid.

"You need a bath, James." I wrinkled my nose.

"I need another bevvy." He looked round for a bar maid.

"James, who were these congressmen who ordered your release? Tell me!" I demanded.

"Two congressmen and a senator," he corrected me, still searching for a server. "The congressmen were Fred Muhlenberg and Abe Venable, and the senator was James Monroe."

I pressed my palms on the scarred table and leant forward. "Why on earth did they release you?"

"Because ah'm a charmin' persuasive gent, why else?" He winked and continued, "Because someone, the congressmen wouldn't divulge who—but I know who—told Muhlenberg that I had it in my power to injure treasury members, including Hamilton, also deeply concerned in ventures using public funds for private gain—" He paused and smirked. "He'd frequently advanced money to me—and other insinuations of an improper nature. Unable to keep his gob shut, Muhlenberg repeated the story to his cronies Venable and Monroe, both anti-Federalists and anti-Hamiltons, I maeght add. Then Muhlenberg had the culls to call me a rascal. But I detected a grudging

215

respect in his tone when he called me that." He bran-dished his practiced smirk that always accompanied a swagger.

"Who could've told Muhlenberg about this? I can't come up with anyone. No one knew aught about this." Surely it couldn't have been Mrs. Platz.

"My former friend who seems to have just grown another face, Jacob Clingman." He grabbed a passing bar maid's arm. "Another ale here and a mead for the lady, if you please."

"Jacob?" I slumped against the chair back, stunned. "I left him not an hour ago! Lord above, he gave me your bail money!" I hadn't even a chance to tell James about my plan to parade Jacob as my beau for Mrs. Hamilton. "Why would he do something like this?"

"He once served as Fred Muhlenberg's clerk." James drained his tankard and covered a belch with his hand. "He went to Fred for help in this mess Hamilton got us into. But he no doubt wants to git back at me for dragooning him into our fraudulent scheme. He only wanted to save his own arse. And if he thinks ah'm going to pay back that bail money, he's pissin' up the wrong rope."

I clutched the table edge, too stunned to feel be-trayed. "Lord's sake, what now?"

The maid plunked down my mead and a full tankard, foamy liquid running down the sides. James guzzled nearly half of his in one gulp. I didn't touch mine.

"I didna deny their allegations. I told them, 'Fine. Jacob is correct. I do possess valuable information. Ah'll turn state's evidence. But on one condition. That you order my release. Now.' So release me they did. Twenty minutes ago."

"What is state's evidence?" I circled my fingers round the glass but didn't lift it.

"A legal term invented last year." He took a long pull of his ale. "Meaning an accomplice or a defendant in a crime, who becomes a voluntary witness against other defendants."

"Hell's bells, you should've been a barrister." I couldn't help but smile. "You missed out on several callings. You misuse the brains God gave you. Rather, you do use them, but for the wrong things."

"I abhor bloody barristers—and all lawyers." He took another swig of ale and wiped his mouth on his sleeve. "If I'd gone to trial, I'd have defended myself. Anyhoo, I had the congressmen by the culls. Hence, I told them everything they wanted to know about the Treasury Department speculators, their names, when and where they made their speculative investments, and the amounts involved. And for proof of Hamilton's offenses, I have letters he wrote to me, which I granted the congressmen access to." His lips curled. "Ah'll not let a hoose fall on my head. If Ham wants to play it this way, he's bringin' a butter knife to a gunfight."

"You told them Alex was embezzling public funds?" I stiffened. My heart stilled. "Oh, no, James. This has gone too far."

"Ballocks." He flipped his hand. "Ah'll not let him dick me round. He had me jailed for a minor infraction, for hell's sakes."

"Yes. For committing fraud!" Of course I had no power to stop him. If this became public, and of course it would, I would never see my Alex again.

He drained his tankard and slammed it down. "The congressmen considered it minor enough, or they wouldn't have freed me just on information. Fraud for a soldier's back pay of four hundred dollars is rabbit shite compared to Treasury Department members—and the secretary, no less—using treasury funds for personal profit."

My mind whirred. How could I save Alex from ruin? I had to act fast—before Mrs. Hamilton started believing those blasted letters she'd gotten.

Chapter
Twenty-Three

Eliza

Feb'y 22nd

Ah, home at last! I breathed in the familiar beeswax aroma of my hallway, swept off my shoes and wiggled my toes in the parlour carpet. After bathing myself and the children, I supervised a splendid meal of roast beef and potatoes. When Alex came home, I flirted with him as a young and pretty coquette. But later, in bed, he claimed "I'm limp with fatigue," and I understood.

Tucking the covers round him, I soothed, "You've been working too hard."

I daren't mention my visit to Robert Troup, or the name of Ann Bates. I was still intent on finding out the truth behind those letters. But as Alex fell into slumber, I brimmed with confidence—no other woman could hold his interest.

I'd read in yesterday's papers that James Reynolds had been released from jail. *I suppose his wife is relieved,* I thought next morn as I entered our parlour and halted. Who did I find engaged in lively conversation with Alex? None other than the newly freed fraud himself!

Dressed in tailored velvet finery, his hair shining, Mr. Reynolds stood to greet me with a gentlemanly bow. "Best morn to you, Mrs. Hamilton." I bade him good morn and left them alone.

I called on Mrs. Bates, bringing the cursed letters with me.

Mrs. Bates had earned quite a reputation as a spy during the war. She was famous or infamous, loved or hated, depending on which side one asked. Having read of her brazen spying activities in the papers, I grew to admire her for her bravery and raw spunk.

On this crisp sunny day, I walked to her Mulberry Street house, three doors from Mrs. Betsy Ross. I bowed my head to the American flag hanging above Mrs. Ross's front door.

I approached a plump matron in a pink shawl, sweeping Mrs. Bates's porch. Taking her for a servant, I asked, "Is Mrs. Bates in residence, please?"

To my surprise, she balanced the broom on her shoulder like a musket and held out her right hand to clasp mine. "Mrs. Bates at your service, ma'am. And who may you be?" Her melodic bell-like voice rang out.

"I am Mrs. Alexander Hamilton."

Her eyes, as blue as today's cloudless sky, brightened as she relinquished my hand and dipped in a practiced curtsey. "Lady Hamilton! To what do I owe this honor, ma'am?"

As she regained her erect posture, I placed a hand on her shoulder. "Please, Mrs. Bates, I am not royalty. I am Elizabeth to you. And this bowing and fawning always embarrasses me to the point of cringing." But for some reason Alex enjoyed it.

She leant the broom against the porch rail and swung her door open, ushering me into her house.

"Tea, coffee, brandy, mead, ale, name your poison," she offered as she threw off the shawl, pushed up her sleeves and carried an overstuffed wing chair to the hearth. Her arm muscles bulging, she handled the heavy item as if a feather pillow.

"Cider would be nice if you have it."

As she bustled out, I glanced round her sitting room. Oil paintings and sketches covered three walls. The largest portrait, gilt-framed and centered over the mantel, displayed George Washington—as the Major General of the Continental Army—in military regalia.

On the fourth wall, a collection of muskets and pistols hung in a circle resembling a sunburst. I'd wager she could shoot the beak off a flying duck while standing backwards.

She returned with two crystal goblets on a silver tray and handed one to me.

"I sacked my servants last week." She sat across from me on her settee and hiked up her skirts to mid-calf, revealing mud-stained boots. I surmised she'd worn those storming through Valley Forge. "Caught them pilfering. Nothing major, coin and such, but I tolerate no insubordination."

I nodded my understanding. "We've had to dismiss our share of servants for the same reason."

As I sipped my cider, she downed her drink, throwing back her head. I then realized she hadn't joined me in my spot of cider—her poison had been whisky.

Mrs. Bates smacked her lips and displayed a bright but gap-toothed smile. "Now, Lady Ha…er, Elizabeth, of what service may I be to you?"

I retrieved the letters from my drawstring satchel and handed them to her. "Someone has been writing these anonymous letters. I need to know who. And I shall allow you to employ whatever tactics—er, methods you deem necessary. But I much prefer you follow the female mentioned here, rather than the male, who happens to be my husband."

She slid on a pair of half-specs hanging about her neck on a chain and read each letter. I sat dead silent as not to disturb her concentration.

Mrs. Bates removed the specs and her skirt hem fell back to her ankles as she stood. "'Scuse me a moment, ma'am." She went to her writing desk, dipped a bright red quill pen, and jotted down some notes.

She turned to face me. "You are right, I do not feel comfortable following the Treasury Secretary about town. I can, however, investigate the comings and goings of this Mrs. Reynolds. It would yield the same results, if these letters are true."

"I cannot believe they're true," I insisted, watching her for some reaction, a clue to what her spying mind was thinking. But she showed none. "I cannot believe my husband would step out. What I really need to know is who wrote them, so that I may confront him and sully his name in return. I have a few suspects, and was hoping you could look into that."

"Suspects?" She cocked her head to one side. "Such as?"

"The top three. Thomas Jefferson, John Adams and Aaron Burr, in that order," I declared the obvious.

She cringed. "I couldn't ascertain who wrote these for certain. I could compare handwriting—"

"This was what I was hoping you could do, Mrs. Bates."

"Please. Call me Annie." She flashed another smile but grew serious once more. "I can try, ma'am. But it could be anyone. Some loyalist blacksmith who disagrees with your husband's policies. Some lunatic with nothing better to do. The possibilities are end-less."

"Can you start with Jefferson, Adams and Burr then?" I urged.

She nodded. "But I highly doubt they'd write their own letters."

"They write to newspapers," I countered. "Can you get those letters and compare? If it's their secretaries' penmanship, that will narrow it down."

223

"Very clever, Elizabeth." She nodded. "That would be one of my methods. I also can determine where they purchased the stationery and possibly the ink. I loathe to bring this up at this time, but this might cost a considerable amount, depending on the duration and labor involved."

"Of course." I expected the business part of this. "I know. I'm fully able to compensate you. Do not doubt my ability to pay your fee."

"I wasn't saying that, I—" She cleared her throat and continued. "I require a deposit of half, to cover expenses."

I reached down my bodice and retrieved fifty dollars. "Will this do for now?"

"Tis more than adequate." She slid the money between her own bosoms and held up the letters. "May I keep one of these for the time being?" She folded one and handed me back the other.

"Of course." I took the letter from her and slid it into my satchel. "Tis better if I keep one of them, so they'll be in separate locations. I'll call again to learn of any progress. It wouldn't be wise to call at my residence."

"During the war I was known as The Concealed Crony. And I did my bit for my country, Elizabeth." Pride filled her voice as she glanced up at the portrait of Washington and gave a little salute.

"I know you did. And I applaud you. You're a true patriotess." We bade each other good day. I returned home and tried to put it out of my mind.

I knocked on the door to Alex's study and he admitted me. "I came to ask if you'd like tea. But I need to know something else."

He looked up from his work. "I still can't afford a houseful of new furniture."

"Tis not that," I retorted. "What was James Reynolds doing here?"

"I advised him to leave town," came his reply with no hesitation. "Not out of friendship, but on account of his earlier threat that he could reveal information that in his words 'would make some of the heads of departments tremble.' Congressman Muhlenberg told me that James had information about some Treasury Department members, my having used treasury funds for personal gain, I'd frequently advanced money to James, and other allegations." Alex's voice cracked with fatigue as he massaged his eyes with thumb and forefinger. "James told Muhlenberg and Senator Monroe he'd divulge proof of my offense if they released him. So they did. He drives a hard bargain."

"What proof? Tis not true!" I threw my hands up and they fell to my sides with a slap. "You committed no offense!"

"James Reynolds claims he has letters from me saying I did." A weak smile curved his lips. "But he did me a favor when he exposed those other Treasury Department members. This information, I found useful. Now I have evidence of thieves, thanks to Jacob Clingman and James Reynolds."

The words "advanced money to James" stuck in my mind. Those two huge withdrawals from our account book appeared in my mind's eye. Was Alex paying Mr. Reynolds some kind of blackmail? I wouldn't put it past Mr. Reynolds, the scoundrel.

"I can maintain my innocence," Alex insisted, his tone firm and lawyerly. "I know what to tell those congressmen if they question me."

"What will you tell them?" I asked.

"That I never used public funds for private gain!" His voice boomed throughout the room. "Not a penny. James Reynolds is the thief. His offense was heinous. Fraud—against the treasury!" He scowled. "That was horrid enough. But as for these alleged letters I had written him, claiming I was using public funds for private gain—I politely and gentlemanly told him that if he dares accuse me of this again, I shall face him on the dueling field."

My heart leapt to my throat. "Oh, no, Alex." I staggered backwards and crashed into the wall. "No. I don't want you dueling anyone. Please promise me you won't."

"It is up to him." He glanced out the window. "If he keeps his gob shut hereafter, it won't be necessary. But he's a coward through and through. The only reason he resides here in Philadelphia is because he fled that challenge from Jon Dayton in New York. He's as yellow as bile—and reeks twice as much. The best thing James Reynolds can do for himself is to grow a pair."

"A pair of what?"

His eyes lit up in amusement. "A pair of what every man needs to be a man."

I'd already forgotten what I'd come in here for. All I could think about was James Reynolds trying to wreak revenge on Alex because Alex did what was right and lawful—had the man arrested for a Federal offense. Then I thought of those letters accusing Alex of having an affair with Maria Reynolds. It was all a jumble in my mind. I much feared that all these strands were somehow connected.

Chapter Twenty-Four

Maria

My hand shook as I wrote to Mrs. Hamilton. *I apologise for not accepting your invitation sooner. To make amends, please join me at my home for tea Fryday next.*

Then she would see me and my "lover" Jacob cozy up together.

As I sealed the letter, James slunk in and headed for his whisky bottle atop the cabinet. He looked haggard. Brown smudges hung under his eyes.

"What is it, James?" I readied my pen for my invitation to Jacob. "You're downright surly."

He took a swig straight from the bottle. "I just come from Hamilton's house."

My heart lurched at the sound of his name. Oh, no…

"He told me tis in my best interests, in light of these most recent events, to leave town. Then he brought up the possibility of a duel, if I dare further besmirch his sterling reputation. I think he reads too many o'those Shakespeare melodramas. He fancies himself Richard the bloody Third or something. A duel. Bah!" He loped over to the fire and spat into it. "Sod that."

I almost fell out of the chair. James and Alex dueling? I couldn't imagine it in my wildest nightmares. "No, that cannot happen! Let us end this chapter. I've invited Mrs. Hamilton here as well as Jacob, to make it appear we're lovers, to quell suspicion of me and Alex. Then I expect things will calm down again." I was never calm with Alex; he still made my heart thump and my knees tremble. But I hoped that this incident was over with and we could resume our affair.

"You and Clingman?" He eyed me with a mixture of confusion and mistrust. "Why him, of all people?"

"Because it will be believable." I pressed the seal into the wax on the letter. "Mrs. Hamilton knows his status, as does everyone. He's a wealthy widower, he's handsome, and affable, and—in light of everything that's happened, since I'm supposed to be separated from you, tis natural that I would seek him out for solace. Not that I would..." I fluttered my hands, flustered. "I mean, if we were really separated."

He threw his hands in the air. "But Clingman? That sod bloody well helped get me arrested and shot off his fat gob to a congressman about me, in case it slipped yur mind."

"I know that, but truth be told, James, you really were guilty," I reminded him. "It would have come out in the end. That 'dead' Massachusetts soldier, very alive, pressed charges. You weren't going to come out of this unscathed. Frankly, I can't blame Jacob for trying to save his hide. You were the instigator in that scheme, as usual."

He scowled into his whisky bottle, tipped it back and drained it. "Have fun spooning with Clingman in front of Mrs. Hamilton. Mayhap you can show her how to put a spark into her own philandering husband."

"Another episode you instigated," I couldn't resist throwing out.

"And I dinna see you out-stigating it." He cocked a brow and tilted his head in challenge.

I did not want to discuss Alex with him any further. "James, are you really going to leave town?"

He smirked. "Not a chance. Bugger him. If he wants to duel me, ah'll oblige him. With another hole to his arse. Afore he takes his ten paces and turns! Har!" He finished his whisky, pulled his jacket off the tree stand and shrugged into it. "I've a meetin' at the Bunch of Grapes. I shan't be too late, no moore than an hour past closing. Ah'll fetch supper out."

Murmuring a "good eve" to him, I began my note to Jacob. As I wrote, I tried to keep my mixed emotions at bay. I was disappointed in him for telling that congressman about James's knowledge of treasury embezzlers, which now involved Alex. However, I felt James deserved to get caught this time. He'd dragged Jacob and poor cousin Sim into the fray.

In a way, I felt that justice had been served. James had cooled his heels in a jail cell, and Alex would emerge looking even more the picture of integrity and honor. I couldn't in good conscience stand behind James and condone what he did—using a soldier to defraud the government—although his schemes did keep us out of poverty. I could not support myself giving violin lessons. Financially, I still needed him. I didn't like it, but those were the facts. Did I still love my husband? Yes. But not the same way I loved Alex. If only James hadn't lost that bid for the Continental Congress. Our lives would be so different…

I sealed his note and gave them both to Maggie, with meal money, as these deliveries would keep her out till late. She wasn't gone a minute when the door knocked again. Thinking it was her having forgotten something, I opened it. To my surprise, two well-dressed gentlemen stood there. One of them I recognized as Senator James Monroe.

"Mrs. Reynolds." He removed his hat and gave me a slight nod.

"Y—yes—yes, gentlemen?" I stammered, stepping back, feeling the color drain from my face.

"Is Mr. Reynolds in residence?" Monroe asked.

"No, sir," I was quite relieved to say.

"May we speak with you, then?" The other man asked. About to tell them James had left town, I stepped aside and let them enter.

"I am Senator Monroe, this is Congressman Muhlenberg." Although I'd met Monroe at gatherings and had been formally introduced, he now acted as if he'd never set eyes on me.

"Please, do come in." My head whirred. What could I tell them that they didn't already know? God in heaven, would they ask me about Alex? I shivered despite the blazing fire in the hearth.

I offered them sherry. They refused. They also refused a seat. Thus I hoped they would state their business and depart.

"Mrs. Reynolds, your husband possesses letters Secretary Hamilton wrote to him. Are you aware of the existence of these letters?" Muhlenberg asked, with the trace of an accent I couldn't place.

I certainly was, but did I dare show them to these men? What would happen to Alex if I did? James always stashed them in a slot in his writing-desk. I kept my own cherished letters from Alex, my prized possessions, under the bedroom rug.

I looked Monroe directly in the eye, then Muhlenberg. "I know of no letters from Secretary Hamilton," I avowed. "I do not pry into my husband's personal business."

"We know for a fact that the letters exist," Muhlenberg insisted. "A former clerk of mine, Jacob Clingman, told me about these letters. Your husband verified Clingman's claim when we questioned him. In fact, tis one of the reasons your husband was freed from jail."

"I still know not where he keeps them." I stood my ground. God forbid, if these men found out about Alex's and my affair, it would be all over for us. His wife would find out, then the world. I'd never see him again.

"My husband has left town, on the advice of Secretary Hamilton. As you may well know." I held my head high and stood straight and tall—taller than Monroe.

They glanced at each other, as if they doubted my sincerity. Perhaps it showed in my eyes. "No, we did not *may well know,*" Monroe replied in an acerbic tone.

If James walked in the door this minute, I could claim that he'd lied about leaving. That was hardly out of character for my husband. I just wanted these men out of here.

"Mrs. Reynolds, if you are aware of their whereabouts but fail to reveal them to us, you can be charged as an accessory. You don't want that, do you?" Muhlenberg shook his head as if chiding a child. All he needed do was 'tsk tsk' and wag his finger at me.

I let that sink in but knew I couldn't tarry. I didn't want to spend my best years in jail for something James did. My blood boiled hotter by the minute. How could he do this to me—and to Alex?

"We can order the premises searched, Mrs. Reynolds," Monroe threatened, keeping his tone calm. He began to sound like his wife, with that false French lilt.

"Very well, then search it. I still know not where these alleged letters are." I silently cursed James for letting this happen. With regard to my knowing where the letters were, it was my word against theirs if they found them. But the possible contents of those letters sent shivers down my spine. I trembled with fear.

Monroe turned to his crony. "Frederick, go to Judge Gilbert. I shall wait here for your return with the warrant." Muhlenberg nodded and turned to leave.

"Wait!" I held up my hands as if in surrender.

They regarded me with expectant looks. "I shall look." I sidestepped over to James's writing desk. "He—he sometimes keeps correspondence in there." I did not want a judge ordering a search of my house, which would turn up the letters—including my hidden letters from Alex. Moreover, I hardly wished to entertain James Monroe till then.

I leant over the desk, pretending to rummage through it. I pulled out the paquet, bound with string, and handed it to Muhlenberg. Glancing at the top letter, he nodded at Alex's penmanship. "We commend your cooperation, Mrs. Reynolds. It is wise and prudent of you."

I knew the meaning behind his words: Dread the consequences if you do not cooperate. "Gentlemen, why do you want these letters?" I had to ask. "Is it not enough that James revealed names of treasury embezzlers, whom you can now question and arrest?"

"We have questioned the men whose names your husband gave us." Monroe tucked the letters into his inside coat pocket. "They've confessed to their crimes and they've been arrested. But there is one man we haven't yet questioned. And that is Secretary Hamilton. We doubt evidence exists in the treasury's books or his books. He would not be so careless as to leave a trail that would implicate him, as the others had. Therefore, these letters..." He patted his jacket. "...are the written evidence we need in order to arrest him."

Arrest Alex! "No, that cannot happen," I blurted. "I know for a fact he would never use treasury funds for private gain. And you men, you know him a million times better than I do!" Realizing I'd protested too much, I calmed my tone. "I hardly know him—I've—I've only met him once or twice. But everyone knows how honorable he is." I clenched a fist on my hip. "How dare you accuse the Treasury Secretary of taking treasury money for speculation or—or aught else?"

They exchanged another furtive look. I knew my outburst was a mistake. They fixed their beady eyes on me, filled with suspicion. And with good reason—why would the wife of the man who'd turned state's evidence defend the Treasury Secretary?

As I feared, Monroe asked me just that. "Why are you protecting Secretary Hamilton, Mrs. Reynolds? Shouldn't it be your husband whose name you want to defend?"

I had to think fast. "Because he is our Treasury Secretary. I respect him and I respect President Washington. My husband already confessed to his crime. It was fraud, involving the pay of a dead soldier who inconveniently came to life. James's crime involved a paltry four hundred dollars. But he saved the treasury thousands by revealing the names of those

who'd embezzled. I daresay James is entitled to a reward for exposing thieves who so criminally swindled the treasury." I used the slang term "swindled"'
that I'd learnt from James, who'd learnt it from soldiers during the Revolution.

"Swindled?" Amusement curled Muhlenberg's
thin lips.

"Yes, a term from the war, in reference to the
British imposing those many unfair taxes upon us,"
I informed him. "If you'd served your country as my
husband had, you'd have heard of it." I raised my chin
in defiance. I was an equal match to these two, who
certainly hadn't been elected on their intellects.

Monroe paced the room, head down, hands
clasped behind his back. He stopped and nodded,
looking out the window. "Mayhap a reward is in order." He faced me. "If your husband ever returns. Did
he state his destination?"

That was all James had to hear. Even if he'd sailed
to China, he'd grow wings and fly back if a reward
was involved. "I believe he went to New York." They
had no way of knowing that was where he'd fled
from, ducking out of a duel. Desperate to change the
subject of my having defended Alex so staunchly, I
said, "I trust James will contact me. I shall keep you
gentlemen apprised of the situation. Now if you don't
mind, I've chores to do. My servant is not here at
present to show you out."

Muhlenberg headed for the door—he would probably bolt for the nearest tavern. But Monroe wasn't

quite finished. "How well do you know Secretary Hamilton, Mrs. Reynolds?"

I would not let him trap me. No one knew I possessed any letters from Alex. I'd even told James I'd burnt them.

"Hardly at all. We've only met once or twice, as I said before." I looked him in the eye, unblinking, my voice steady. Even I believed it.

"Where was this?" he probed.

Why all this questioning? He would not trick me to implicate Alex in any wrongdoing. I was not about to mention that Alex had given James money. He'd find out whilst prowling through the letters.

"At parties, gatherings—we occasionally travel in the same social circles." I tried to keep my voice casual, but I quaked inside. I licked my dry lips. I hoped he hadn't noticed.

Monroe cast me a stern eye. "I heard in casual conversation, I recall not when or where, you were seen about his neighborhood—possibly calling at his residence." Was Monroe a lawyer? I tried to remember. This certainly sounded like a cross examination.

"Of course. Mrs. Hamilton and I have had tea together," I defended myself. "Why do you ask?"

"If I recall correctly, you were seen going to tea—" and he drew out the 'eeee' in 'tea' "—when Mrs. Hamilton was in Albany."

"Seen by whom?" I clenched both fists. "If you're about to accuse me of anything untoward, you'd better produce proof."

"I do not recall." He shook his head. "Never mind, Mrs. Reynolds, tis neither here nor there." He headed for the door. "We bid you good day." They saw themselves out. Shivering, I made my way to the fire, knelt and rubbed my frozen hands together.

I wondered—should I add Monroe to the list of suspects in the writing of those anonymous letters to Mrs. Hamilton?

Eliza

To-day I received an invitation from Mrs. Reynolds—tea on Fryday. Her husband must have left town. My heart went out to the lonely woman. I marked the appointment in my date book, unable to blame *her* for what James had done to that poor soldier he'd claimed was dead—and what he'd done to my husband. "You're well rid of him, honey-bun," I spoke aloud. I knew the pretty young thing would find a husband worthy of her.

The thought of Alex in a duel made me tremble with fear. Stumbling to the settee, I called on Ruth, our nurse. "Bring me the smelling salts, please."

"Lord above, Missuz Hamilton, you ain't with child again?" she sputtered, dashing out the door.

"Lord above, I hope not," I prayed out loud. No…I couldn't be!

I tried to dismiss the possibility of Alex dueling as my fear haunted me. Alex would never survive a duel. If he ever did agree to such madness, that would be a fatal decision. *No, it won't happen*, I silently vowed. *We'll both live to our nineties—we'll see our children's children grow up, well into the next century.*

Alex collected foes, as did all statesmen and politicians. It was a miracle Jefferson never met his end on the field of honor.

I hadn't a clue what to talk about with Mrs. Reynolds. I knew she played violin, and we'd briefly discussed books. Why not let her do the talking? I burned with curiosity about her background and lineage. I'd be happy to introduce her to some suitable bachelors—after she divorced that cur, of course. Aaron Burr could file her divorce. I preferred Alex take the case, but I know he couldn't add a divorce suit to his workload. Besides, he liked James Reynolds. He'd be biased in James's favor. So I kept Burr in mind for legal counsel.

Should I show her the anonymous letters I'd gotten? I hadn't received another one, unless Alex was hiding them. Ever since I saw that huge withdrawal in the ledger, I now prowled through his personal files—but didn't see any more letters addressed to me. I chalked it up to a prank, likely old John Adams, bored after harvesting his turnips.

I sniffed the smelling salts and wondered if the arrival of another child would bring Alex and me closer.

Chapter Twenty-Five

Maria

Eager to banter with Alex about *Henry VIII*, I opened my Shakespeare book, but the flowery prose blurred before my eyes. I drifted away in reverie as memories of our last visit filled my mind and my heart...how his blue velvet accented his copper hair, how I begged him to ravish me, his bare body against mine. Now that Alex's business with James was Congress's latest gossip fodder and I got caught at the top of Alex's stairs, I feared he'd end our affair. I put Shakespeare aside and fetched paper and pen.

O, I am distressed more than I can tell. My heart is ready to burst and my tears wich once could flow with ease are now denied me.

I blotted, folded, addressed it, and hid it under my stash of letters from him. They piled up, wrinkled and creased from my reading them, over and over. God forbid if some congressman confiscated them! The thought nauseated me. As darkness crept through the room I slid them back under the rug.

James breezed in next morn as I sat reading the newspaper. The rich aroma of coffee floated from the kitchen as Maggie brewed a pot.

"Greetin's, turtle dove. I need a good scrub more'n I need coffee at present. Maggs!" He called into the kitchen. "Fetch me some scaldin' water, a cake o'soap and a cloth, and ready y'rself to scrub me down."

He turned to me. "Unless you'd rathurr do the honors." He flashed me a wink, hung his keys on the peg and pulled off his boots.

I displayed a sly smile. "I wouldn't give you a bath for twice what you're paying her. How was your eve, James?" I preferred to build up to the news of Monroe's and Muhlenberg's visit rather than dump it on him.

"It was a belter. I scored big at an all-night dice game." He pulled a wad of notes from his britches and tossed them onto the table. A clattering of coins followed as he emptied his pockets.

"Will you take some of your winnings and purchase a haircut?" I reached up and tugged his unruly locks.

"I only just bin to the barber." He pulled the ribbon out of his queue and ran his hand over his chestnut mane.

"Yes, when there were still thirteen states. Have a shave while you're at it." At times I let him skip a few days between shaves because I found the stubble enhanced his sensuality. But his appearance now bordered on untidy.

Whilst he gloated over his booty, I decided to get it over with. "Senator Monroe and Congressman Muhlenberg visited here. They took the letters Alex—Alexander wrote you, under threat of ransacking the house."

He nodded. "Aye, I told them I had those letters, and would furnish them upon my release from jail." He pointed at the cash strewn on the table. "You may have this," he said. "Hamilton gave me some more t'other day, so I dinna need it."

My heart lurched. "He gave you more money? How much?"

"Naught to wet me britches about. Only thirty-five. 'Necessaries of life for my family,' I told 'im. He must'a taken pity on me in the end, for having me jailed. Chewed me out for my 'heinous crime against our government and good citizens'—in the vein of a fogy schoolmarm—then he turned the other cheek and praised me for turning state's evidence. Stood and shook my hand. Cuz of me, four swindlers confessed to embezzling from the treasury and are now behind bars. It pays to know people in high places." He swaggered to the kitchen doorway and peeked in. "Wash water ready yet, Maggs?"

"Coffee'll be ready first, mine master," trilled the singsong voice from the kitchen. "It'll take nigh on all day to heat 'nuff water and a boatload a'soap to scrub you down."

I asked James, "Did he mention a reward? I told Monroe you deserve a reward for turning in those men."

"Nay, dinna expect one. By the sound of Hamilton's high and mighty manner, my freedom is my reward. As if I murdered the president or some such. Tsk." He shook his head. "Ham's never forthcoming with monetary rewards. He deposits that treasury money so far up his arse, he needs reach down his gullet to withdraw it."

Maggie came out with a pot of coffee. James took it and held it up to me. I declined.

"What do you think Monroe and Muhlenberg will do with those letters?" I asked him as he sloshed coffee over the rim of his cup. I didn't want to come out and ask if he'd mentioned me in them. I'd build up to it. James couldn't know that I had any interest in Alex beyond financial. Adulterous women suffered enough in our society. Adulterous women in love with their lovers suffered even more. I needed keep my secret strictly secret.

"He'll likely show them to President Washington. His Excellency will decide what to do with the king of the Feds." James sat and slurped from his cup.

"But James—Alexander never speculated," I insisted. "Why on earth would he tell you he did?"

He chuckled. "Because he did. At one time or anuthurr. It ain't a mortal sin."

I argued, "Tis a mortal sin if he's being accused of using government money."

243

"I never said he used government money." His jumping to Alex's defense made me blink in surprise. "All I said was that he used privileged information as Treasury Secretary to reap huge profits in certificate speculations. And some of that information is in the letters he wrote me." He blew on his coffee and took another sip.

"What do you think will happen to him?" I should have shut up by now, but I needed to know.

He shrugged, frowning. "Who knows? Tis up to Washington. But His Excellency holds Hamilton in such high esteem, he won't git moore'n a slap on the wrist. Hamilton is the son Washington never had. He made Hamilton aide-de-camp during the war. Then his prized pet." James cast a curious sideways glance. "Why are you so concerned about Hamilton's well being? If even he was jailed, which will never happen, prisoners are allowed carnal visits." He brandished a cocky grin.

"I—I was simply concerned," I stammered, taken off guard, "for my own well being. I didn't want them implicating me in this, as your wife. Did Alex—did he ever mention my name in any of those letters to you?" I held my breath awaiting the answer.

He splashed whisky into his coffee. "Hmm…" He looked up in one direction, then the other. "Not that I remember. What would he say? 'Yur wife's a great shag'? Worry not, yur innocence in this is intact. Although I daresay that's the only part a'ye that's intact by now."

I ignored that remark, releasing a long sigh. Relief always made my bladder want to void. So I dashed to the privy and did just that.

Eliza

Would you care to meet a lovely lass? I wrote to the most eligible bachelor in town, and checked my date book: next Friday was tea at Mrs. Reynolds's home. I finished with "This Friday at 2 sharp. RSVP."

As I blotted the letter, Alex knocked on the door frame. "What time are we supping tonight?"

"The usual." I folded and sealed Jacob Clingman's letter.

"I need dine early." He glanced at the clock in the corner. "I have an engagement at seven."

I nodded, adding, "There are clean shirts in the top drawer of your highboy. Oh, and your brown riding boots are back from the cobbler's."

As he turned to leave, he asked, "Whom were you writing to?"

"Jacob Clingman. I invited him for tea." I readied another sheet of paper for my invite to Mrs. Reynolds.

"Clingman—for tea?" His voice boomed. "Whatever for?"

I knew Alex disliked the man. Clingman was a Burr toady and a staunch Republican.

"Naught that would interest you." I dipped my quill in the ink. "I believe he would make a fine match for Maria."

"Maria who?"

"Maria Reynolds." I looked up at him.

He recoiled as if stung.

"Surely you don't begrudge the poor girl some happiness, Alex. You ran James out of town. She's alone now, and well rid of that cad. The least I can do is help her find a suitor." I began writing the salutation. "And I shall recommend Mr. Burr as her divorce lawyer. Unless you'd care to take the case, as a personal favor to her."

"Favor? I don't even know the woman. No, I have enough cases already." He waved his hands, still talking as he walked away, "Don't volunteer my services. I have no interest in..." His voice faded as he clomped down the stairs and out the door.

I resumed my invite to Mrs. Reynolds, but didn't mention that I'd invited someone else. It was enough that Jacob knew. Then I'd let Mother Nature take over!

Maria

Mrs. Hamilton invited me to tea again, before my hosting her. This became confusing. Tea at her residence this Friday, tea at mine Friday next. I wrote it all down.

I hadn't heard a word from Alex. Desperate, I posted that letter I'd written the other night. No reply. I penned him another. Still no reply. I waited at the door for the post delivery and devoured the papers every day.

"Please don't start investigating this mess James started," I implored President Washington from my kitchen table. But not a printed word about that. I did see "Treasury Secretary Alexander Hamilton..." It stopped my heart—but it was only about his Report on Manufactures, which he submitted to the House. The article explained his plan to establish a manufacturing sector through government subsidies and tariffs. I knew this already. I was part of it! A surge of excitement rippled through me, but died a fast death. "No, he doesn't miss you, you silly twit," my better judgment berated me. But, God above, I still loved him and desired him.

I arrived for Mrs. Hamilton's tea at two sharp on Friday. *Is Alex home? Will I see him?* I wondered, trembling. I held my skirts as the coachman helped me out of the carriage. As I rapped on the Hamiltons' door, my last visit here rushed back to me in vivid color...he'd greeted me, draped in midnight blue, arms open and ready for me...all mine. Not a soul disturbed us.

I fought back pangs of longing as the door opened. A clean young manservant showed me in. The entry hall smelt of lemon and wax, polished and fresh. Mrs. Hamilton glided down the hall. "Maria, hello!" She clasped my cold fingers in her warm ones. I looked down at our hands, joined, thinking: these four hands caressed the same man...our two hearts love him...she and I share him. I resented her, envied her, wished I stood in her place. At the same time I hated myself for feeling this way about the kindly mother of six, inviting me into her home to share her table.

"Come in, come in, warm up," she chirped, beaming. "Ah, for adult company!" Children's voices floated down the stairs. Loud little feet pounded on the floor above. Was it always this noisy? I didn't dare ask her.

"I have one other guest coming, if you don't mind." She ushered me into the parlour.

"Of course I don't mind." But when the door knocked again and her "one other guest" stepped inside, I had to hold back gales of laughter.

At the threshold, looking at me as if I'd sprouted a third eye, stood Jacob Clingman!

"Jacob, what on earth—"

"Maria!" He entered and waltzed up to me. I held out my hand, which he kissed, again and again, a serious breach of protocol.

"You know each other?" Mrs. Hamilton clasped her hands together, obviously delighted. That spared her the awkward introductions.

"Oh, yes, quite well. Don't we, Maria? Let us show Mrs. Hamilton exactly how well we know each other." He made a show of running his finger down my cheek and cupped my chin in his hand, eyes pinned to me in an adoring gaze.

He turned to our hostess. "Mrs. Hamilton, Maria and I are—well, to put it delicately, since she and James have separated—courting. And if my dreams come true, she will become Mrs. Clingman ere long." He turned to face me. I struggled to keep the astonishment from my face. It was one thing to parade as lovers, but he was pouring it on so thick, I'd need a hammer and chisel to work it loose. "I was going to wait, but I can wait no longer, my sweet." He dropped to one knee before me and grasped my hand. "Maria, my dearest one, will you give me the honor and privilege of becoming Mrs. Clingman?"

"I—I—" I gulped, too dumbfounded to speak. Why hadn't we rehearsed this? I should have known he'd make a theatrical production out of it. What would he do next, burst into an aria?

"Wait!" Mrs. Hamilton twirled round, her skirts rustling about her. "Stop right there!" She called across the hall. "Alex, come quickly! You must see this!"

Oh, no. My mouth dried up. I swayed, ready to swoon right there. Before I took another breath, Alex stood in the doorway. Our eyes met and locked. We all stood in a frozen tableaux.

"Now, Jacob, repeat what you just said!" Mrs. Hamilton held out her hands to cue him, then turned to her stunned husband at her side.

Jacob, from bended knee, recited, "My dear Maria, I love and adore you with all my heart and soul. Will you give me the honor and privilege of becoming my wife, so I may be proud to call you Mrs. Jacob Clingman?" Now I knew he'd rehearsed this. Again, time stood still.

Three pairs of eyes bored into me. I managed to sputter, "But Jacob, this is so sudden!" I didn't dare look at Alex.

"Please, Maria." He squeezed my hand. "You are the only one I will ever love. Say you'll be my wife and mine forever and ever, till death."

Out the corner of my eye, I saw Mrs. Hamilton wave her hands, urging me on. She stage-whispered, "Say yes, say yes," all but pushing my head forward in a nod.

"Uh—yes?" It came out as a question. Now I dared look up. Alex stood rigidly, mixed emotions playing around his eyes, his lips pulled into an odd jumble of light amusement and raw disbelief.

Mrs. Hamilton applauded. Jacob wrapt his arms round me and planted a hard kiss on my lips, letting go only when I began gasping for air.

Alex didn't budge from his spot but folded his arms across his chest and leant against the door frame.

"Before aught else is said, you need take one step at a time," Mrs. Hamilton spoke, and I dreaded what would come next. Would she offer to hold the wedding here, with Alex walking me down the aisle? Oh, how to back out of this?

But she turned to her husband. "Maria is not yet divorced from James and needs the services of a good lawyer. If Mr. Burr is unavailable, will you handle it, Alex?"

He answered without missing a beat. "You're right, Betsey, let them take it one step at a time. Let her ask Mr. Burr first. If in fact that is whom she wants to hire. Tis really up to her." Now he looked at me, expressionless, as if we'd just met. "Mrs. Reynolds, did your husband leave town as I suggested?"

I couldn't lie to him. "He's planning to. He moved out of our house." My voice small and timid, I wanted to crawl under the sofa.

He nodded, raising his brows, but I couldn't read him at all.

Just then, a maidservant came to the doorway. "Mr. Hamilton, Congressman Laurence is here to see you."

"Of course." He addressed us. "Please excuse me. Good day, Mr. Clingman and Mrs. Reynolds—soon to be Mrs. Clingman. Mrs. Hamilton, I shall see you at supper." Averting my eyes, he stepped out, closing the door.

Jacob stood and clutched my shoulders. "I shall count the moments until we begin our life together, my love." He smiled, showing both rows of gleaming teeth. Sitting across from our beaming hostess, he gave me a "How did I do?" look.

I tried to keep the anguish from showing on my face as we went through the motions of afternoon tea.

Chapter Twenty-Six

Eliza

I had an exceptionally enjoyable afternoon with Maria and Jacob. Over tea and scones we chatted about Shakespeare and Mozart, funned about Jefferson and Monroe. The lovebirds brought an element of joy into my house I hadn't seen in ages. Their gay laughter and tender displays of affection made me realize how Alex and I had grown apart.

Of course he was making history while keeping his law practice alive, buried under work. But for our few hours at supper and abed each night, we breezed past each other on the stairs or in the hall. When we did converse, it was about the children, the house, or money. We hardly exchanged any words of love.

Our last amorous encounter gave us baby John. Since his birth, we hadn't lain together as man and wife. Falling exhausted into bed each night, when he did get to bed, he'd give my hand a gentle pat, and within a moment, fall dead asleep. I could not begrudge him his moments of glory, his fame, or his place in our nation's history. After things calmed down, I knew we'd fall in love all over again.

Showing Maria and Jacob out, I espied a familiar figure across the street, lurking next to the lamppost. My guests now out of sight and earshot, she bounded up to me and curtseyed in greeting. "Good day, Elizabeth, but much better would it be if not quite so cold." She rubbed her gloveless hands together.

"Annie, I told you not to call here. Mr. Hamilton is in residence at present. How would you explain yourself if he saw you? He knows who you are!"

"Simply. I'll tell him I'm from the *Philadelphia Gazette* and request a personal quote about the current state of his new bank. I have an answer for every question, ma'am. Since I was in the neighborhood, I thought it prudent to save you the trouble of a journey to my dwelling."

"A former Revolutionary War spy now a reporter for the *Gazette*?" I shook my head. "Mr. Hamilton is trusting but not gullible. You must stay out of sight." I glanced over my shoulder. "However, if you have an answer for every question, answer this: have you any information for me?"

"The answer brings me here. Alas, I have no information, but have been earning my fee. Whilst following Mrs. Reynolds to what I hoped was her latest rendezvous—uh, sorry—I'm not sayin' I wish this to be true, for your sake, but—" She stumbled over her words.

I expelled an exasperated breath. "Carry on! Where did you follow her to?"

She pointed down at the ground. "Right here. Shortly after, I saw the young man enter, and I hovered about until now. Obviously nothing untoward was taking place. Unless there's something you're not telling me—" She cleared her throat, backing down the top two steps.

"No, Annie, you followed her right here, to tea with me, and the young man I just learnt is her new paramour. I say with glee I'm convinced there is nothing untoward or otherwise between her and my husband. They barely acknowledged each other. She has eyes only for Mr. Clingman." A happy smile spread my lips. "I shall remit you the balance of your fee."

Annie scowled. "Elizabeth, I daresay, that is no proof your husband and Mrs. Reynolds haven't been—" She cleared her throat again. "—untoward. I strongly urge you to let me continue my investigation until I have proof positive, one way or t'other. I planned on following Mrs. Reynolds for several days at least. And I've contacted all the local newspapers, where I compared the handwriting of your anonymous letters to that of letters written by the secretaries and scribes of Mr. Jefferson, Mr. Adams, Mr. Burr, and for good measure, Mr. Monroe. I went to the *Gazette of the United States*, the *Philadelphia Gazette*, the *Pennsylvania Post*, the *Pennsylvania Chronicle*, and *Dunlap's Daily Advertiser*. I also obtained original documents written by these men themselves. I can report to you with solid certainty that no resemblance to your letters appears."

"You've been thorough in this," I complimented her, "but I want this investigation to end." I could not admit to myself why, though. "I am convinced my husband and Mrs. Reynolds are no more than strangers and shall put this matter to rest."

She pulled out a hankie and blew her nose into it. "Elizabeth, if you will forgive my boldness, I'm reading between your lines, and I can discern your reluctance. But you cannot be convinced in a situation as dire as this without proof. I daresay tis because you're afraid of what I might discover, and if I do unearth some proof, you won't want to believe tis true."

"Now listen here—" But I halted myself. Rigid and tense, I gripped the doorknob, my knuckles bloodless, my other hand clenched into a fist. "You're right. I cannot bear to know if my husband is unfaithful." I released a defeated sigh.

She clucked. I took a deep breath and prepared to share my feelings. "I'm needy for someone to confide in. I've given you much intimate information already. Yes. I am afraid of the truth. Please keep hold of the letter I gave you and continue to ascertain who wrote them. I'm sorry I was short with you."

"I understand, ma'am. As you can imagine I've seen folk much more distraught. This is hard for you, I realize. I shall continue to work on your behalf, free of charge. Meanwhile, can you tell me who his other foes may be?"

I shook my head. "Anyone who follows Jefferson, any Republican. I now realize it will be nigh on impossible to finger a suspect, unless you are one of those soothsayers who sees the unseen by reading tea leaves."

She brandished a smug grin. "I need no tea leaves, ma'am. I've dismantled many a haystack and discovered more than my share of needles. Tis why I am one of your husband's largest depositors."

My eyes widened in surprise. "I didn't realize the work was so lucrative."

"Trust me, it is. Quite." Her smugness gave way to a humble nod. "But I cannot discuss particulars, for obvious reasons. Suffice it to say I can afford to work pro bono occasionally, for folk I like. Such as yourself." She tugged on her bonnet strings.

"And I can trust you to keep anything to yourself that you do find," I warned. "Ma'am, never shall I divulge my confidences. Ever. Upon threat of death. You have my word as a God-fearing Christian. And as a patriot, since the war is over and the patriots won." For emphasis, she crossed her heart. I half expected her to pluck a Bible from her satchel and swear on it.

"Tis cold out here." Coatless, I began shivering. "Please, do come in for a spot of tea and warm up a bit, Annie." I turned and held the door open for her. With Maria and Jacob gone, the children napping and Alex busy with his congressman, loneliness engulfed me. I was very much alone and wanting for company. She was an intriguing woman, and I was curious to get to know her better. Also I'd realized how desperate I was for female companionship. I needed a confidante. Annie, with her background, fit the bill perfectly.

"Why, thank you, Elizabeth." Looking grateful, for she looked half frozen, shivering, she followed me inside and warmed up before the fire.

I rang for a servant and settled in to enjoy my guest. Tonight I planned to seduce my husband and recapture that passion and rapture we'd shared in the past. It had been far too long.

Maria

"I hope I didn't overdo it," Jacob said as we walked to his carriage on the corner.

"Jacob, I know you're a bit theatrical at times, but you could have given Shakespeare a run for his money." I pulled on my gloves. "Tell me truthfully, how many hours did you spend at your looking glass rehearsing those lines?"

He helped me into the carriage. Shivering against the blast of wind, I slid inside and gathered my skirts around me. He instructed the driver to take us back to my house and huddled next to me. His right thigh bumped against my left as the carriage lurched into the street. "I never rehearse," he said. "I prefer spontaneity. Anything rehearsed sounds—parroted, insincere."

"Heaven above, you certainly sounded sincere." My eyes landed on his profile and struggled not to linger. "You had Mrs. Hamilton practically crying into her gold-rimmed teacup."

He placed one gloved hand on my cheek, turning me to face him. "I *was* sincere, Maria. When I proposed to you in front of the Hamiltons, we were supposed to be pretending. But truth be told—I meant every word. I do love you. I have for some time now. Making you my wife would make my life complete." He spoke as if reciting a vow.

"Oh, Jacob," I sighed. My eyes darted about as he held my face captive. An awkward pause hung between us. "I'm very flattered. But my interest in you is on the level of a compatriot." I scrambled for the right words, nothing too harsh. I couldn't bear the thought of hurting him. "Of course I find you physically attractive. Our common interests in reading, music, and theater never leave us at a loss for conversation, and you're a true gentleman. But—romantic?"

I inched away as our thighs bumped again. "I'd never imagined you this way, in all the years I've known you. And I'm already married. You shouldn't be saying this at all. James is your friend. This is entirely inappropriate." There, I'd said my piece as gently but firmly as I knew how. As an ear-witness to Alex's silver tongue, it couldn't help but rub off on me.

He slid closer and stroked my earlobe. I fought a forbidden shiver of delight. "Maria, be honest and up front with me. Do you truly love James?"

I met his gaze. "Yes, I do love him. Of course I love him. I love him very much." My familiarity with

Shakespeare told me once again that the lady doth protest too much. But I couldn't help adding, "and he loves me."

"You can love someone and no longer want to be wed to them. Jane and I loved each other, but by the time she died, our marriage was over, in the true sense," he admitted, but he wouldn't win this argument. James and I hardly married for the reason he and Jane did.

"You married Jane for one reason. Money. And the nation, as well as I, knows it. Jane owned half of North Carolina, she was twenty years your senior, and fancied a young colt—plain and simple." I could talk to Jacob in this blunt fashion—well enough acquainted, we'd had shared many a jibe and a confession.

"It evolved," he admitted. "Just as you and James have evolved. I can tell things have changed between you and him." He cast me a sideways look.

The carriage hit a bump and he nearly fell on me. Our gloved hands met, our lips within kissing distance. I turned away. "Things always change between a couple after seven years."

"When was the last time you and he made love?" he prodded. Startled, I blushed to my roots.

I turned to him and glared. "Now you're overstepping your bounds. I care not to discuss intimate details."

He went on in his bold fashion, "I know you're smitten with Hamilton and I wouldn't assume you've

259

liaised with him, but I know you wouldn't refuse him if he pursued you."

No, I wouldn't let Jacob goad me into admitting anything about Alex. Alex was my cherished secret. "You should have been a lawyer, Jacob. You missed your calling. I feel like a defendant under interrogation for adultery. Now I must testify my innocence." As a wry smile twisted my lips, I didn't dare look at him. "But what woman would refuse Alexander Hamilton?" I so longed for him, my loins—and heart—ached.

"None have, from what I've heard," he answered my rhetorical question.

We sat in silence for another moment as the carriage rolled along. With the afternoon winding down, long shadows of trees and lampposts reached across the streets. Candles flickered and glowed in several windows. The air grew bone-chillingly frigid.

"Would you care to sup with me tonight?" he ventured, and I knew my acceptance would have serious implications. But I had nothing else to do. James wouldn't be home, he usually drank his supper at The Grog or the City Tavern. I knew how I'd spend the evening at home—leaning out the window, hoping Alex would visit. Besides, Jacob was such enjoyable company…

"I'll be happy to. However, Jacob, let us forget our conversation took place. I don't think it wise for you to expose your feelings so candidly."

He nodded. "You're absolutely right. I took a chance, hoping you'd return my sentiment. However,

I shan't give up hope. When I see that look in your eye again, I'll revisit the topic."

Puzzled, I turned to him. "What look in my eye?"

"For lack of a better phrase, naked longing." He captured my hand and slipped my glove off. He rubbed my fingers, warming them. "Now that I know the longing is not for me, I shall assume tis for Hamilton. I can only pray your feelings for him will wane as time goes on. When they do, I hope you'll give me the honor of telling me."

I hoped my nod signaled the end of this conversation. "You'll be the first to know, Jacob." Not that it would ever happen. Alex was my grand passion, and I clung to the hope that I'd one day be the second Mrs. Hamilton. "Now—where will we sup tonight?"

"My residence. I imported a Roman chef who prepares the most delectable, exotic dishes." He flashed a proud grin.

"Oysters are exotic enough for me." I laughed. "I never knew anyone who imported a chef. The Washingtons aren't even that extravagant. And Jacob..." I batted my lashes in shameless flirtation. But we'd now passed the point of propriety. "I also know for a bachelor to invite a married woman to sup at his home is against proper protocol."

He lifted my gloveless hand and brushed it with his lips. "Well, you know me. A few centuries ahead of my time, mayhap."

And he knew me, all right. He'd seen through me as if I were made of crystal, detecting my feelings for

Alex. But Alex wouldn't stand in my way tonight. I longed for a man's warm embrace.

But I kept that to myself. Flirting sufficed—for now.

Chapter Twenty-Seven

Severus

I lay in my bath, allowing the water's warmth to permeate and refresh my body. In truth it had been far too long since I'd found true satisfaction, and tonight, my second self grew ravenous within me. I'd done my best to control the urges, that I might not be harried and forced to leave yet another home, another land. And yet, whatever drove me seemed unaware of my need for security and longevity of residence, the need to find a settled life. No, that inner demon held me in its thrall and I could not stop myself.

I'd made a host of new acquaintances since my arrival in the New World, and some referred to me as 'friend' though I felt such a bond with no one. Only the wife of Alexander Hamilton gave me any cause for pleasure. Mrs. Hamilton was the only woman in this town with whom I felt a warm affinity.

Mayhap, as I'd hypothesized, she represented that which I'd been denied by my own mother, for she epitomized in my mind all that a good mother should be. I could never imagine Mrs. Hamilton mistreating or abusing her children in any way.

I dried myself and dressed in readiness for my latest sojourn through the dark streets. After checking and approving of my appearance in the mirror, I added the final touch to my ensemble, my long white silk scarf.

* * *

Daisy May Thomas, seventeen, skipped gaily along the street, happy to be free of work for the night. As lady's maid to Mrs. Clarissa Allyn, her work was hard but not too arduous, though the long hours left her little time for personal enjoyment. Tonight had been her one evening off, Mrs. Allyn kindly telling her to enjoy herself as she left the house.

Daisy May had spent a happy eve, meeting her friend Lucy Kent, who worked in a book shop by day, and then attending a local music hall where tickets were cheap and the entertainment at times raucous but always fun to watch. After kissing Lucy goodnight, the two parted on the corner of Elfreths Alley where Lucy lived. Daisy May enjoyed walking the last half mile to the Allyn home along the quiet streets. The stars illuminated the sky like the moon's tiny cousins. She made the turn to North Front Street and passed the grounds of the Mortimer house next door to the Allyns. As the Mortimers were away, the sound of a groan coming from inside the grounds alerted her.

"Hello," she called out, venturing closer. "Is someone there?"

"Yes, help me, please," a man's distressed voice implored.

"What's wrong?" She stood rooted to the spot, still unsure whether to enter the Mortimer property.

"I have been attacked," said the voice. "I fear I may be grievously hurt."

Daisy May gasped. "Should I fetch help?"

"In a minute, but first, please can you help me to sit up so my head might clear a little?"

Daisy May's charitable nature took over. She stepped through the gateway and nearly stumbled upon the man lying beside the trunk of an oak tree. He was well dressed, obviously a gentleman. More confident now, she stepped closer. His legs lay sprawled at an awkward angle, his tailored britches smeared with dirt. A white scarf fluttered at his neck in the breeze. As she knelt beside him, he groaned again. She placed an arm round his shoulder to assist him to rise.

"You're a good girl." His voice strained, laden with pain.

"Thank you, sir." She leant over to help him. "Now, we'll get you comfortable and then I will run and fetch my mistress and we will send for a doctor."

"That will not be necessary, Daisy May." He pulled himself from her grasp and struggled to his feet, rising to his full height.

"What? How?" She leapt back. A stab of shock and fright halted her breath. "Who are you, sir? How do you know my name?"

"I know all there is to know, Daisy May." He crept closer. "Did your parents or your employer not warn you of the dangers of walking alone at night, or of the danger posed by strange, unknown men?"

"I'm sure I don't know what you mean, sir." Daisy May's voice trembled. Her limbs shook, her insides churned. Her eyes darted about for a suitable escape route.

"Don't worry, child. It will all be over soon." Before she could react or speak, he grabbed her with both hands and spun her round to face away from him. Before a scream could form in her throat, he wrapped something round her neck, pulling it tighter and tighter. Her final kicks and gasps soon abated.

Severus

I dragged her behind the tree, laid her on her back and began to undress her as my excitement and arousal built towards a crescendo. I spent longer with Daisy May than my previous two victims, using her more than once before abandoning her lifeless body. I placed my scarf back round my neck before strolling home, to bed.

Daisy May's body lay undiscovered for two days.

Chapter
Twenty-Eight

Maria

Wensday, March the First

I'd never been in Jacob's company alone, except for that carriage ride. I squealed with joy as I pretended he was my beau. Was I now leading a triple life, an adulterous wife alone with a man who'd professed his love for me? I'd never even read a novel quite like this. I needed not be coy and coquettish with Jacob, having known him so long. But his heartfelt confession put me on guard, lest I further his ardor.

As we reached Jacob's mansion, I gaped in wonder. "Oh, Jacob, this is more magnificent than last time." Candles blazed in the chandeliers visible through the floor-to-ceiling windows.

"Oh, not really." He alighted from the carriage and assisted me out. His hand lingered on mine after my feet touched the ground. This time an older butler, in formal dress and impeccably groomed, greeted us at the door and relieved us of our cloaks. He ushered us into the sitting room, where a young manservant tended the fire in the massive hearth. Both servants bade us good eve and bowed out. Obviously Jacob hadn't reduced his late wife's staff.

"The evening meal is served at six sharp every eve. At ten, the night staff takes over." Jacob tugged on a rope in the corner, escorted me to a wing chair by the fire and sat across from me. A liveried servant appeared. "Two brandies, unless the lady prefers something else?" Jacob regarded me and I shook my head.

"Brandy is fine." I knew it would warm me.

He clasped his hands twixt his knees. "Maria, I apologize for my declaration of before. I am an open and honest man and find it best to speak my mind—and my heart. It always tells me where I stand with anyone. Which gives me great joy, knowing that if I'd scared you away, you would not be here."

"That's true, I must admit. You didn't scare me away. You just unnerved me. If we start—" I caught my breath. "Well, you know what I'm trying to say." My hands fluttered in my lap. "I don't need an additional complication in my life." What I left unsaid was that I already loved two men, in very different ways, and adding a third would cause me to begin a very tricky—and exhausting—juggling act. "But I'm not one to run away, Jacob. Besides, you'd find me, I'm sure."

He didn't return that with a witty comeback, on purpose, I knew. He deliberately left it hanging in the air—for a later date. We shared a knowing look.

The manservant entered with a tray holding a crystal decanter and two brandy snifters. He placed it on the table between us and bowed out. Jacob laid his snifter on its side. The liquid reached the edge of the rim but did not spill out. "Perfect." He held it upright and offered it to me. "To a long life. With whomever you are destined to share it."

I drank to that, barely sipping, only letting the warm liquid warm my lips and tongue. I did not need a column of fire burning my insides. He reclined in his chair, his tight britches outlining his manly endowments—but not quite as generous as Alex, I concluded with a secret smile.

For the first time, I scanned Jacob head to toe, as a woman sees a man. He carried a firm and athletic physique, his equestrian's muscles well developed. I'd never seen him don a wig over his own abundant hair, brown with an auburn sheen. His hair hadn't Alex's gray streaks, nor had his hairline begun its ascent up his forehead. The firelight danced in his eyes. I fought the temptation to compare his appearance to Alex's, and lost. At least five years Alex's junior, he indulged in the wealth and comfort Jane had provided him. No worry or fatigue lines creased his features. His skin was smoother than Alex's, due to youth and freedom from care.

"I'm far too young to ponder my destiny." I raised a brow.

His smile etched a parenthesis around his lips. I compared his smile to Alex's, then halted myself right there. I refused to let any fantasies enter my mind. I harbored no desire for a friend whom I'd regarded as a cousin all these years. Although he *was* handsome. And desirable. And a superb kisser...

"What are you thinking of, Maria?" He jarred me from my reverie. "Or should I say whom?" He tilted his head and rotated his snifter, the amber liquid coating the inside.

"No one special." I tried to change the subject. "So, what about the price of tea these days?"

"What is truly bothering you?" he badgered. "You can tell me. You're not yourself. You haven't mentioned a book or play title or sonata since last we met. Your mind is elsewhere. But I am here for you. Spill it at my feet. I shall pick up the pieces and give you the perspective you need."

Oh, how I wished Alex had said that to me! How I wanted his to be the shoulder to cry on, as I offered him mine. But no, Alex was intent on guarding his innermost thoughts. Now here sat Jacob, offering to be everything Alex could not and would not be.

"My circumstances have been fraught lately." I cupped the glass with my fingers, wishing I liked brandy. "Mostly about our finances. James's speculating, his other schemes, his coming home loaded down with cash, and then after tossing me a tidy sum, squandering the remainder, leaving us bereft. Not an easy way to live." I ventured a sip and swallowed as I sought out my words. "You are fortunate in that you have a sizable reserve—and no desire to gamble more than you can lose. James draws on the well till it's nearly dry—every time."

He drank his brandy and the tip of his tongue skimmed his lips, back and forth, more than once. Why did I notice this?

"Many times I've offered James assistance, but he always refused," Jacob said. "His pride gets in the way, I realize, but a small exchange between friends is nothing. He's never asked. I even offered him employment at the end of the war. At war's end, he felt like a lost soul with no direction."

"Yea, that was the nadir of his existence." I lowered my head as James's pathetic image evoked a pitiful memory. "I remember his drunken bouts. I could never comfort him when he droned on about his failures, how useless he felt." The memory evoked a sob I couldn't hide. "Poor James. His luck never turned." My heart ached, but still swelled with love for my husband.

"You seem to be better off financially as of late," Jacob remarked, but I needed to change the subject. I searched my mind for the most compelling play I'd attended or book I'd read to date. Should I bring up politics? I knew he was a Jeffersonian, so we couldn't discuss politics without mentioning the inevitable: Alex. He went on, "I see you're both wearing tailored new raiment, popping corks on vintage wines, riding in luxurious carriages—and James had a larger bundle than usual at the last several card games. Did one of his 'schemes' as you call them pay off recently?"

Our recent good fortune, of course, was all due to Alex's generous payments to James, which now would end. But I wasn't about to discuss this with Jacob. "He may have made good on a deal. He doesn't discuss the particulars with me."

"Well, if the funds run low, please come to me," he offered. "I'm more than happy to help."

"I appreciate that, Jacob," I gave my sincere thanks. "You have a heart of gold. Mayhap I will. It's comforting to know I have a benefactor if I need one. For now we seem to be on even footing."

"Then why do you still look so miserable?" He sat forward.

I sensed his eyes penetrating me as I focused on my snifter. "Jacob, are you one of those spiritualists, and you haven't told me?" My eyes met his. He stroked my hand. Sudden desire stirred within me.

I pulled away and settled my gaze on the dancing flames in the hearth.

"I know that Hamilton has been helping you financially," he said. "'Tis all right, that's nothing to be ashamed of."

My eyes flew back to meet his. "What—how did you know that?" I hadn't meant to sound so accusatory. But this hit me like lightning.

He lowered his eyelids. "My former superior at the Treasury Department, Oliver Wolcott. It seemed to have come out when James gave those congressmen the information they wanted, in exchange for his release from jail."

I took a sharp breath and sat up straight. "Very well, Jacob. James did borrow some money from Secretary Hamilton to pay our debts. He also told James he made thirty thousand in speculation. But I'm telling you this in the strictest of confidence."

He placed his glass on the table and took my free hand in both of his. "My dear, I would never betray a confidence, you know that. But I know James didn't simply borrow money from Hamilton. It started out as a blackmail scheme. James got you to seduce Hamilton in exchange for hush money. Tis no secret anymore. I was hoping you'd share this with me, so I could comfort you. But I must inform you: now these congressmen know about it. Being Republicans and political foes of his, tis a matter of time before it becomes public."

"Oh, no." That sickened me. Sweat beaded on my forehead. The sip I'd taken now came rushing back and I had to swallow several times to force it back down. "No, tis not true. That's a fabrication of Secretary Hamilton. James had joined in it, he told me so, and he had given Secretary Hamilton receipts for money and written letters, so as to give countenance to the pretense." Dizzy and faint, I gasped for air. Jacob stood and tugged on the service rope.

The servant bustled in. "Fetch the lady a glass of water," Jacob ordered, turned and knelt beside me, as he had in his bogus marriage proposal.

"All right, I believe you." He held the water glass to my lips. I took a refreshing gulp. "Even if it were true, I wouldn't think any less of you. You were simply a

273

pawn in one of James's schemes to extort money, and so was Hamilton. But it's over now. Put it behind you, and look to the future."

"Oh, Jacob." Emotionally and physically drained, I couldn't tell him how I felt. What had transpired between me and Alex wasn't a casual affair, we loved each other deeply. But I had to keep up the pretense. No one could ever know about my secret life with Alex—not till we divorced our spouses, free to proclaim our love to the world.

I leant into Jacob and wound my arms round his sturdy shoulders. "Jacob, please never mention any of this to anyone. I pray those congressmen will keep quiet about it, and Mrs. Hamilton will continue to think you and I are marrying, just as we pretended."

He brought my head to his chest and stroked my hair, loose from the jeweled combs I'd so carefully arranged. They slipped from my hair and fell to the rug. He gathered my hair in bunches and planted kisses on my neck, my cheeks, and finally, my lips. I responded, for Jacob was my rock, my savior, rescuing me from all that blighted me.

"Not to worry, my darling." As he whispered, his nearness made me shiver with a mixture of desire and trepidation, for I knew not what I truly felt and wanted to keep it at bay. "But now I am not pretending." Once again his lips found mine. Our tongues mingled in an exquisite rhythm, his technique flawless. A better kisser than Alex? I couldn't compare at the moment, my head too cloudy, my thoughts a jumble of emotions that rendered me senseless. I still cannot say whether I'd have followed him upstairs if he'd beckoned me.

The door opened. A servant rang the dinner bell, then backed out and shut the door.

Jacob broke our kiss, cupped my face in his hands and slanted his lips over mine once more for a light peck. "Supper is served. You must eat."

"You're right, of course. I haven't eaten more than a morsel all day." My stomach rumbled with hunger. Savory cooking aromas wafted into the room. My mouth watered.

Jacob led me into the dining room and we feasted on a sumptuous Italian meal of *trucha frita*, "trout seasoned with lemon pepper on a bed of onion and tomato slices drizzled with olive oil," he told me as he cut off a piece and fed it to me. I found that so sensual. Dessert was a luscious custard-like mixture of vanilla, cream, figs and Frangelico liqueur. "It's called *panna cotta con ficci*." The Italian rolled off his tongue as I savored the rich sweetness. "It's made by monks in Canale, Italy. Every woman should see Canale in her lifetime—with a lover."

During the meal we emptied two bottles of a fancy Italian wine I'd never heard of, "Brunello di Montalcino, Tuscany's rarest and longest-lived wine," he informed me. To me, this meant the most expensive.

I remembered telling Alex that we should share an Italian meal someday—how I hoped that someday would come before we grew too old.

After that satisfying meal, my waistband bit into my engorged tummy. Not only was I full, I could barely keep my eyes open. I stifled a yawn, then another. "I'm so sorry, Jacob…" I covered my mouth, cringing in embarrassment.

"We'll talk more tomorrow if you care to." He helped me into his carriage, slid into the seat next to me, and I dozed all the way back to my house.

"It's not you, you're fascinating company, I'm just so sleepy…" I apologized over and over to the dismissive wave of his hand.

After a light kiss goodnight, he saw me in. Without removing my clothes, I fell asleep on the sofa, cradling the pillow Alex and I had lain on.

Chapter
Twenty-Nine

Maria

Next morn as I washed and dressed, I pushed it all from my mind. I stayed busy and did not think about it till I absolutely needed to.

As Maggie brewed coffee, I settled in at the table to read the *Gazette*. James took the cup Maggie poured for him and went to fetch the post. "Look at this. A newspaper in Britain, the *Observer*, has begun publishing on Sundays," I read from a column on the front page.

"Bah! Blasphemy. Leave it to Mad George to let them get away with it." He bent down to retrieve a letter fallen through the mail slot. "As I live and breathe, a missive from king of the Feds himself."

My heart thrashed about. James approached the table and slit the letter open with a knife. I tried not to appear anxious, but held my breath as he took his time reading it.

He finished it, tossed it onto the table, and grabbed a piece of the newspaper. "Ah'm gooin' to the readin' room." He headed for the back door.

"James, what did he say in the letter?"

"Read it yourself. If he's as rotten a bluffer as he is at whist, no wonder I cleaned out the poor sod's pockets that night," he called over his shoulder as the door opened and shut.

James thinks Alex is bluffing? What about? I nearly tore the paper to shreds in my haste to snatch it up and read it.

Dear Mr. Reynolds, The recent course of events has led Congressman Muhlenberg and Senator Monroe to take this a step further, that is, to bring it to Pres. Washington's attention. As our arrangement will soon be public, I see no further reason to provide you with payments as I have been giving you, and deem to terminate our association. I hold receipts for sums remitted to you, and shall retain them as proof of payment should the occasion arise that you plan to inquire of the sums in question...

I skimmed the rest, searching for my name, but it all read like a legal document. This was Mr. Hamilton, Esq. the attorney writing this, not my lover. Shattered, I cradled my head in my hands. It was bad enough Jacob had heard about it through the loose-lipped Wolcott, but now it was on its way to President Washington. I longed for Alex at this moment, to comfort him, for him to comfort me, as Jacob had last night. But a flurry of relief tickled at me. His arrangement with James was over.

What did this mean for Alex and me? Would a similar letter fall through the slot onto the floor, carrying words to end our affaire that had bloomed into passionate love?

No! I must get to him first.

Where would he be now? A glance at the clock told me he'd arrive at his place of work an hour or so from now. I would be waiting when he got there.

James came back in and washed his hands in the basin, flicking drops all over the floor. "I should'a brung more paper with me. At least leave some out there for me, willye? Men like to wipe theirselves, too, you know."

"James, this letter." I held it up and waved it under his nose. "This means it is all going public now that President Washington will know about it."

He gave a one-shoulder shrug. "Tisn't grounds for deportation. Washington's no doubt the biggest speculator of all. He's got naught on me."

"Those letters that Alex—that Secretary Hamilton wrote you. Why would he ever tell you he'd been speculating?" On pins and needles, I had to know.

"He didna use the exact term." James sat at the table. "He said he had information that netted him great sums. Of course he had. He's Treasury Secretary. If he hadn't used inside knowledge to profiteer from, he'd be a bigger fool than I give him credit fur."

"But—incriminate himself in writing?" I shook my head, unable to believe Alex would do such a thing.

"He wrote that he had information, not where he'd obtained it." He poured sugar into his coffee. "'Tis up to Washington, Monroe, Jefferson, and their cohorts to interpret as they see fit and jump to whichever conclusions they care to."

"But Secretary Hamilton is President Washington's pet. He'd never let his pet's reputation suffer, would he?" I fervently prayed that Washington would never betray Alex. But this was politics.

James cocked a brow. "Washington's only one man, compared to how many of Hamilton's enemies chomping at the bit to take him down?"

"Secretary Hamilton obviously trusted you," I stated.

"Why should he not? He knows my father." James slurped his coffee. "When he had Wolcott arrest me, he didna think the whole thing throo. I'd be a pillick not to show those letters to assure my release. I reckon when he was devising this plot, not all the blood was in his brain—if you know what I mean." He gave me a wink.

"Now you'll have to find another way to make pin money." I took Alex's letter at face value, mentally counting how much cash I'd stashed away. Would it outlast the length of James's next scheme?

"Twas good whilst it lasted." He left the table and began cleaning his teeth with a small cloth. I cringed... it was a piece I'd torn off Alex's shirt when we stripped each other in our last frenzy. Shakespeare would have reveled in the irony.

"He hasn't written me off, James," I reminded him. "Only you."

"Hmmf. Why would he continue seeing you? Our arrangement has ended. There's no need." He spat into the basin.

Oh, there's need, I wanted to blurt out. Of course I couldn't tell James that Alex's and my "arrangement" originally to keep James and me from starvation, had evolved into the great love of my life, and I felt half alive without him near me. But of course I daren't tell James this. From now on, I had to see him behind James's back.

"If you want to write him a fare-thee-well letter, ah'll hand deliver it for you." His tone suggested mirth, but I found nothing humorous about it.

Not replying, I went upstairs and began dressing for my next meeting with my lover. And I'd make dead certain it wouldn't be "fare-thee-well."

On the way, I stopped at the general store and purchased some blue ribbons for my hair, knowing Alex favored blue.

I reached his office doorway, walked to the corner and looked up the street, but he was nowhere in sight. I strolled up and down the street three or four times before I finally saw his black carriage and groomed gelding halt at his door. I clasped my hands to stop the trembling, quivering with excitement at the sight of him. As he turned the key in the lock I strode up to him.

His back to me, I tapped him on the shoulder. "Alex, may we talk?" He turned to face me, startled.

Yes, I was bold and daring, but how could he not understand how crucial this meeting was?

"I'm very busy, Maria, perhaps another time—"

I wedged myself twixt him and the doorway. "Please, Alex. We need to talk. I cannot wait another minute. I've been ill, waiting to hear from you and—" I stopped there, knowing I sounded like one of my letters. "Just for one minute. I know you're busy. Please, then I'll go away."

He heaved an impatient breath. Looking anything but pleased to see me, he swung the door open and gestured up the stairs.

I almost floated to the second floor.

He led me down the hall to his private office, which I'd never seen before. One window overlooked the street. A fireplace and mantel held a brass lantern and some pewter goblets. Papers, pens and inkwells covered his mahogany desk. Thick law books stocked the shelves lining the walls. I hugged my arms against the biting chill.

"I haven't had time to order more wood—" He bustled about, tied back the drapes, removed a stack of papers from a chair. "Here, you can sit." He remained standing. "Now, what do you care to discuss?"

I reckoned he was warmer to clients. "Alex, I—I just wanted to tell you that I still love you as much as ever, and just because your arrangement with James has ended, that changes naught between us," I blurted in one breath and gulped, my mouth so dry, my lips felt adhered together.

"Naught has changed, except you are betrothed to Jacob Clingman." He folded his arms across his chest, his features becalmed, almost with indifference.

"No!" I waved my hands about. "That was a ruse to show Mrs. Hamilton I'm not interested in you. He's a great dramatic actor, I have no interest in him, you must believe that."

"I know not what to believe any more, Maria. At first you were destitute…your husband had left you for another woman. Then you took him back. Now you love me. I can hardly keep up with you." His eyes wandered about and out the window, as if he cared nothing about this—or us. His voice carried no intonations.

"Alex—" I approached him, dying to throw my arms around him and beg him to take me. He took a step back.

"This is the truth. I had Jacob pose as my lover so Mrs. Hamilton would think there is naught between you and me. But I didn't expect that mock-marriage proposal! It was an act, is all, an act…" I breathed in his cologne. Desire flooded me.

"If I didn't know any better—" He hesitated, no doubt for effect, "I'd say he is quite smitten."

"Mayhap he is. But I am not. As long as Mrs. Hamilton believes it. I'm in love with you, Alex, you must know that!" I now fought my impulse to grab his sleeve and drag him home. I looked him straight in the eye. "I am in love with you and no one else. And to prove it to you, yes, I'll divorce James."

He regarded me with that detached look. "Do you truly want to divorce James, or is that an act, too?"

"Not at all." I shook my head. "I can never love him the way I love you."

He held up his hands. "I have too much on my mind now to deal with this. Monroe and Muhlenberg visited me the other night. They told me they'd called on you and confiscated my letters to James."

I clasped my hands round his. "I'm so sorry, Alex. I had to give them the letters. They threatened to arrest me and ransack my house. I couldn't let them find your letters to me!"

"It wouldn't have mattered if you had. I told them the truth, so they'll know I did not embezzle. I have a reputation to defend." He eased his hands away and thrust them into his pockets.

"So you really did tell them—about us?" I leant back against the desk or I would've collapsed.

"Yes, I had to. I'd rather be accused of adultery than of public corruption. They didn't want to hear it all, but I made them sit and listen until the entire story was out. My name means too much to me."

"And they believed it?" My voice weakened.

"They left me under the impression that their suspicions were removed. But I do not trust them. They're all Republicans. If they're intent on destroying me, this is the way to do it. And if Jefferson gets wind of it—" He heaved a sigh and rubbed his temples as if he had a pounding headache. "I had to protect my innocence of corruption by admitting to our affair. I can only hope they'll keep their word, and naught more will be said about it. When I revealed the details about us, they blushed like schoolgirls, so I'm hoping that as men of honor, they sealed up the documents and will show them to no one."

I winced, mortified. "Now those men know all the details of our lovemaking!" I paused and asked the dreaded question, "Are you going to tell Mrs. Hamilton?"

He glared at me. "Of course not. Why upset her?"

"Alex—" I pushed myself off the desk and clung to him as if drowning. "Don't be so naïve as to believe these Republicans will keep their words. When it does come out, Mrs. Hamilton will hear of it. So why not tell her now? Tell her all of the truth, that we're deeply in love. Tell her you want a divorce. Now is the time. Mayhap this is an omen that we belong together. I'm so in love with you, Alex, you are the love of my entire life," I rambled on and on. I can't even remember taking a breath.

"And I love you, Maria." He groaned. "God help me, but I do love you."

I pleaded, "Will you divorce your wife?"

He shook his head. "That is impossible at this time."

The torrent of tears I'd been holding back since we'd met downstairs flooded forth. "But I cannot live without you," I sobbed. Through the blur I could see my tears staining his velvet jacket.

He wrapt his arms round me and I pressed my desperate, wanting body to his.

He breathed harder. "Come with me." He led me up a narrow stairway to a garret that held a cot and a small table with a washstand.

He lay me down on the cot and I opened my arms to welcome him.

As he lay on top of me, I wound my arms round his neck. Our lips met. A soft moan escaped from deep within my throat as he stroked my cheek with feathery touches. I parted my lips and he followed my lead. Before another thought about divorce or scandal haunted me, he began removing my clothing. I lay back as he untied his britches and pulled them down to his knees. "This must be a rush tumble," he breathed as he positioned himself between my legs.

We mated in a frenzy of need and urgency. It was over in less than a minute. "Sorry, uh…" he stammered an apology. "Not quite *that* rushed."

"Tis all right, hold me, I want you to hold me like this." My arms held him fast.

He unwrapt my arms from around his neck. "I can't, Maria. I've mountains of work, and clients arriving within the hour." He slid off me and pulled his britches back up. Without another word, he left me alone in the dark windowless garret. I lay there for another few moments, savoring his touch, our mingled wetness between my legs. I dressed and stole down the stairs to his closed office door. Muffled voices sounded from inside. At least he now knew Jacob and I weren't entangled.

As I walked home, I asked myself if I truly wanted to divorce James. With Alex refusing to leave his wife, I had no reason to.

Until that evening when James gave me a reason.

"Congressmen Venable and Muhlenberg were struck with so much conviction... that they delicately urged me to discontinue as it unnecessary. I insisted upon going through the whole, and did so. The result was a full and unequivocal acknowledgment on the part of the three gentlemen of perfect satisfaction with the explanation, and expressions of regret at the trouble and embarrassment which had been occasioned to me. Mr. Monroe was more cold but entirely explicit.

"One of the gentlemen, I think, expressed a hope that I also was satisfied with their conduct in conducting the inquiry. I answered that... I was satisfied... and considered myself as having been treated with candor or with fairness and liberality." – Alexander Hamilton

Chapter Thirty

Eliza

Fryday, March 3rd

Whilst nursing John and rocking him to sleep, the post dropped through the slot. Ada, my parlour maid, brought it to me and asked if I wanted tea.

"No, thank you, I shall wait for Mr. Hamilton. He promised to be home for the midday meal."

But before I had the chance to open and read it, a knock sounded on the front door, and a minute later, Ada showed Dr. Black into the room.

"Doctor, this is a pleasant surprise." I greeted him in a sprightly tone, pleased to see our friendly medical specialist. "It has been too long since you have called upon us."

He doffed his hat and gave a little bow. Such a gentleman! "Good day, Mrs. Hamilton..." He cleared his throat. "Elizabeth if I may?" he posed it as a question.

"I believe Elizabeth more than appropriate considering the services you have provided me." I smiled and he rewarded me with the same. Again, I became aware of that certain something that his smile lacked. As if by instinct, this time I knew the reason why.

"You honor me, dear lady." Dr. Black crossed the room, held the curtain aside and gazed out the window with a desolate sigh. "I thought it an opportune moment to call and see how mother and child are faring, as my house calls necessitated me being in the vicinity this morn." His gaze still fixed on the outside world, he traced his fingers along the torso of our Goddess Aurora statue, a gift from my sister.

I sensed the doctor was nursing a great sorrow, a sadness that had touched his heart and turned part of it an icy fortress. Could I help him? I hoped to try.

"We are fine, Doctor, as you can see. A spot of tea, mayhap?"

"No, thanks just the same, I'm full right now." He approached the cradle and bent to look at baby John. As he reached out to touch his cheek, I noticed, for the first time, what appeared to be scarring on his right wrist, visible for a split second as his sleeve rode up.

"Oh, my dear man, you have been hurt." I couldn't let the moment slip away, as it could be my only way to discover the meaning behind his unsmiling eyes.

He turned to face me. "Ah, you saw the scars. I do not talk of it often, but many years ago I was the victim of a great tragedy. After losing my dear father to a drowning accident, some time later both my mother and my sister were lost to me when our home was burnt to the ground one terrible night." His voice cracked as he appeared to swipe away tears.

My heart went out to him. I searched for fitting words of comfort. But what could I say to comfort him? I perceived he would reveal little more. "You poor man... or boy as you must have been at the time. You have all my sympathy." A lame platitude, I know, hardly a comfort, when I really wanted to go over to him and wrap my arms about him, bring his head to rest on my breast and soothe him by rocking him back and forth.

He nodded, saying nothing.

"And the scars you bear?" I gestured at his wrist. "Were you also burned in the conflagration?"

"I was." He pulled his sleeve over his damaged wrist. "I was unable to save them and my clothes caught fire as I reached out unsuccessfully to my mother. I had no choice but to turn from the flames and try to save myself."

"And you have felt a weight of guilt, have you not, since surviving whilst they did not? Is this why you carry a burden within you, and please, do not deny it, for I have seen it in your eyes, my friend. You cannot hide such things from a woman, you know."

"You are correct, of course." He approached me, and just as I thought he'd reach for my hand in an attempt at human contact, he turned away and gazed into John's cradle again, his eyes forlorn, his shoulders slumped. "Your intuition is quite accurate, but I would prevail upon you not to make this information public knowledge. It was a tragic and terrible time for me as I entered early manhood. It is not a matter I am comfortable discussing with anyone, even you. I only do so now in light of the facts you have cleverly discerned."

Unable to bear watching him relive this horrific memory, I placed my hand on his shoulder. "It shall be our secret, Doctor. You, after all, maintain my confidence as part of your oath as a medical man, and I shall do no less now that you have shared your grief with me. But, please try to understand that you were not to blame for their deaths, and must not be consumed with guilt in the matter."

He thanked me for my concern, but to my surprise took it upon himself to make a hasty exit. "I shall return soon," he called over his shoulder as he saw himself out. Had my intuitions embarrassed him? I hoped not.

Alone with the baby once more, my attention focused on the stack of mail where Ada had deposited it. A letter from Mrs. Bates sat atop the pile. I laid John in his cradle and rocked it with my foot as I slit the letter open with my monogrammed opener. This must be important if she put it in writing.

I saw Mrs. Reynolds waiting outside your husband's law office yestermorn, she wrote in her neat penmanship. *I then saw Mr. Hamilton arrive. They both went inside. After thirty minutes, two other men entered. Ten minutes later, Mrs. Reynolds came out, looking disheveled, I daresay, and dashed down the street.*

*I am still searching out who authored those anony-
mous letters. I shan't let you down, Elizabeth. Every one
of my missions have been successful, and I do not intend
to leave any stone unturned into making this endeavor
a success. Your obedient servant, Annie Bates.*

I folded it and glanced through at the other post: a
letter from my sister in England, addressed to Alex.
She must be bored. I held it aside, with no desire to
open it. Another one from my cousin Henry, trying to
make a living as a poet. I opened the envelope to two
of his poems, but frankly, poetry did not move me.

I assured myself Mrs. Reynolds had found
Mr. Burr's legal fee too dear and called on Alex
to file divorce. I looked forward to attending Maria's
and Jacob's wedding. If our country home was built
by then, I would invite her to hold the ceremony
and reception there.

I decided to tell Annie to stop following
Mrs. Reynolds. All I now wanted was to find the
coward who'd written those letters to me.

I brought the baby to the room he shared with
Alexander, Jr. At the top of the landing, I glanced at
the floor and noticed a shiny object. I picked it up and
inspected it—a gold ear bob circled with diamonds. It
was not paste. I knew what genuine diamonds looked
like. None of our female servers could possibly afford
something like this. Mayhap one of them inherited it.
I questioned each of them, but none claimed it. After I placed it in my jewel box and dismissed it from
my mind, I wrote a letter to Annie. *Please cease following Mrs. Reynolds. I am convinced she's only hiring*

*my husband to handle her divorce. But please continue
trying to find out who wrote me those awful letters.*

I almost wished I'd receive another anonymous
missive, for the more Annie had to work with, the
better. But nothing came. Neither did Alex for our
midday meal.

*A well adjusted person is one who makes the same
mistake twice without getting nervous.- Alexander
Hamilton*

Maria

I drug myself home from Alex's office, alone and
dejected, knowing not when I'd see him again. He
hadn't even said "good day" when he hiked up his
britches and left me sprawled on the cot. I felt—loath
to say the word—used. But he was ever so busy.
Grateful he took the time to make love with me, I
knew he still cared.

I fetched the post and opened a letter from my sister Susannah. With her twins due in February, she
wanted me to come to Poughkeepsie posthaste. Her
husband Gilbert Livingston, a prominent lawyer, had
a caseload as heavy as Alex's. He also traveled often,
trying cases throughout New York. I let out a girly
giggle. Oh, to see Susannah again, to reminisce about
our childhood, to play with my beloved nephews.

I settled at James's desk and penned her an acceptance. Whilst sealing her letter, I glanced at the only
pigeon hole that held a piece of paper. I know I'd
cleaned out the compartments when I'd given Alex's

letters to that odious Monroe. I slid it out and read it. I recoiled in horror that James had written this, but heaved a relieved sigh. Thank the Lord he hadn't sent it.

It was an undated letter to Alex, forbidding him to see me again. *I am putting a finell end to it. You insulted me by stealing into my house by the back door... am I a person of Such a bad Carector that you would not wish to be seen Coming in from my house in the front way?*

I concluded that the intent was to make Alex use the front door, where he might be seen. I folded and shoved it down my bodice, intent on burning it later. I hoped he'd forgotten about it by now.

Yet did it matter? Alex had literally walked out on me, with no sign as to when he'd return.

I tried to busy myself with *The History of the Life and Reigne of Richard the Third,* then needlepoint, then my violin. But I could not concentrate on any activities. Grabbing my cloak and bonnet, I headed out the door and into the cold air. I walked—and walked—and walked, aimlessly, until I realized I was in Jacob's neighborhood.

The same butler who'd greeted us at the door yesterday saw me in, took my coat and bonnet, and ushered me into the sitting room. "Mr. Clingman will be out presently, Mrs. Reynolds." He offered me sherry, but I refused. He bowed out, closing the door.

I warmed my hands by the fire, my nerves jangly, anticipating Jacob's arrival. Everything had changed between us since our embrace and kiss, which I now admit, had aroused me. Naught was wrong with enjoying a dear friend's company, and if it led to a physical expression of affection, then so be it. I saw no harm to anyone, present or not.

"Maria, what a wonderful surprise!" He entered the room and I met him halfway, rushing into his open arms. He smelt like hair powder and that same Tricorn cologne Alex wore. Inhaling the mingled fragrances, I imagined Alex holding me like this.

"You're freezing!" He warmed my hands in his.

"I walked," I admitted, eyes coyly downcast.

"All the way here? Why did you not send me a note? I'd have dispatched my carriage." He cupped my frozen cheeks. They warmed instantly.

"It was spur of the moment." Of course I couldn't tell him why I had to see him, how distraught I was at Alex leaving me cold on his cot. But that wasn't the only reason. I was truly happy to see Jacob. He made me feel—the word was *desirable.* Something Alex hadn't done lately.

We sat on his sofa by the fire as he offered me cakes and tea, but I refused refreshments. "I simply need to talk."

So talk we did. We made plans to attend *As You Like It* at the Philadelphia Playhouse, and a Bach performance by a local chamber orchestra. Events I longed to attend with Alex. But of course Alex and I could never be seen together in public. Not until he took that final step and left his wife.

"And in the spring we will take my canoe upcountry and go rowing on the Hudson—" Jacob planned for the far future, as if I were a maiden. Or was it wishful thinking on his part?

"Let us wait till the ice melts before we make spring plans," I deterred him.

His smile vanished and he cleared his throat. "Maria," he began, his tone stern, "do you plan to stay married to James? From what I saw of you yesterday, it seemed you were bursting to tell me, but held back."

"Held back what?" Now I wanted a drink, but more than that, I wanted to know what he meant.

"That you're not happy with him and are contemplating a divorce."

I tried to suppress a laugh in deference to the gravity of the moment, but couldn't. "I was never aware you read minds."

"Is that what you think I'm doing? Reading your mind? I don't believe I need to, Maria. All I am reading are your words—and your heart." His voice lowered to a rumble.

My sigh relieved me as if a massive weight had lifted from my shoulders. Hands unclenched, limbs relaxed, I knew I could trust Jacob with anything. Almost.

"Very well, Jacob, I have no reason to hold this in any longer. James has been rather, uh—" I searched for the most delicate words. "—inattentive lately. We each have—" My hands fluttered before me. "—other diversions keeping us apart. Not that I don't love him—" I added that qualifier.

"I understand, my darling." Now *he* fidgeted, obviously holding something back.

"What is it?" I braced myself, clutching the chair arms, dreading the answer—he knew about me and Alex, he knew I'd been lying yesterday, and news of our liaison had spread like yellow fever. But what he told me came as even more of a shock.

"Maria, I do believe James blackmailed Hamilton. But there is something else going on with James. Has he told you?" Jacob's voice wavered.

"Told me what?" My first thought was, *who is James trying to swindle now?*

"So he hasn't." His voice dropped and he leant closer though we were alone. "Maria, James has a mistress. Has had for quite some time now. I wanted you to know, so that—if you do begin divorce proceedings, you'll have a much easier time of it. You can charge him with alienation of affection—and adultery. The most basic grounds for divorce."

I shook my head, unsure this could be true. "I know James has had dalliances with tavern wenches. I even heard, through tavern gossip, he'd been about to engage the services of the streetwalker Biddy Cummings, when the night watchman apprehended her and released James with a warning."

Jacob's expression remained blank. This talk about streetwalkers was as foreign to him as my speaking Arabic.

"Pay heed, Jacob, I am not naïve enough to think his all-night activities begin and end in dice games." But the question still plagued me: "Only one mistress?" was all I could think to ask. One sounded exclusive, long term, emotional involvement. Like me and Alex.

"One that I know of. I've seen her with him, at a gathering at Patrick Bevin's home, or coming out of taverns." He stroked his chin. His ring caught the firelight and threw sparks. "I've never seen him with her when he was sober, and I daresay neither was she."

"Has he introduced you?"

He shook his head. "No."

"Do you know her name?"

No again.

"Is she pretty?" Why I wanted to know this, I could not say. Mayhap to give me a reason to resent her if she was pretty, or to deride him if she wasn't.

"Not at all." A sneer curled his lips. "She couldn't hold a candle to you if the candle had twenty wicks. And I believe she's on in years. She certainly looks it."

He sat back and raised his brows, awaiting my reaction. But I had naught to react to. "Tisn't exactly a punch to the stomach, Jacob." The words "so be it" sat on my tongue. Of course this changed the upshot of our marriage. James knew about my liaison with Alex, but my knowing about James's affair made it fair game on both sides. "He never told me," was a lame reply, but I had nothing more forceful to say.

"Why would he?" came Jacob's obvious answer. "But now that you know, you can—" He shrugged to suffice for the obvious words.

"Use it against him in a divorce?" I shook my head. "That is not my nature."

"Why are you so forgiving?" He sat forward, raised his hands and let them fall into his lap. "A wife who's been betrayed would fetch the cleaver and hack off his nether parts."

"I don't know why I'm so forgiving." Would I have been as forgiving hadn't I fallen in love with Alex? "I still love James, but not enough to be jealous. I no longer love him the way I once did. We've grown apart, and only live under the same roof because we're accustomed to each other. But I don't seek out his company, nor does he mine. That is the truth."

"Is it over then?" he asked, a bit too eagerly.

I looked him in the eye. "What if I said yes?"

His gaze intensified. "Then I'd ask you to divorce him so that you can marry me."

I looked away. "I cannot marry you, Jacob."

"Why not?"

Because I'm in love with Alexander Hamilton and want him to marry me, was the answer, of course. "I'm not ready to marry again. I shall let you know if ever I am. But please, do not wait for me." I couldn't do to him what Alex was doing to me, declaring his love whilst unable to leave his wife "at this time."

"But do you love me?" His voice shook, as if dreading my answer.

"Yes, Jacob, but not—I'm not—" I faltered, at a loss for words.

"Not ready." He rescued me before I sputtered any more. "I understand that, and respect your wishes. No more on the subject." He stood and held my hands as if dancing a minuet. "But I want to make you forget both these men."

He needn't say another word. He already knew I loved Alex. But make me forget him? Never.

Chapter Thirty-One

Severus

I sat alone at my small but functional dining table, head in hands. I shook, my teeth chattered, my head ached. My thoughts, usually so clear, assaulted me, a jumble of unfamiliar patterns and sensations.

How, I asked myself, *have I allowed that woman to inveigle herself so far and so deep into my mind?*

In truth, no one had ever been able to 'read' me as Elizabeth Hamilton could. In her presence, my mind became an open book, as though she only need look at me to read my innermost thoughts. Could she see even deeper, into the darkest recesses of my soul, where my most fearful and basest thoughts lay dormant until the need arose for satisfaction? If she ever found that deep dark place within my private self, what would I do? Kill her? No. I'd come to care for her in a way previously alien to me. If she ever confronted me with those thoughts, even though it would cost me dear, I would have only one option, and that I didn't dare contemplate.

A bottle of brandy stood upon the table, a single glass beside it. By the time I slumped forward, my head uncomfortably resting on my hands, the bottle stood empty...

Chapter Thirty-Two

Maria

Jacob and I savored a midday meal of roast duck-ling, red potatoes and asparagus tips. We lingered over chocolate pudding topped with whipped cream, and a savory blend of Colombian and Brazilian coffee beans. He then insisted I play some of our favorite Bach and Mozart pieces on his wife's Stradivari vi-olin. An intense chess match followed, with some lively discourse about who President Washington's successor should be. We settled on John Adams, the most likely candidate anyway. We got along so well, I wished we'd find something to disagree about.

At dusk, Jacob helped me into one of his carriages with two matched grays. As I pulled my heavy wool skirts inside after me, he offered use of the con-veyance for as long as I wished. Too embarrassed to tell him we could ill afford the feed, I promised I'd send the carriage straight back. Whilst holding the door, he gave me a heartfelt kiss—as heartfelt as the freezing day allowed us—and saw me off.

When I arrived home, candles glowed in our front windows and all our wall torches blazed. James sat at his desk adding up a column of numbers with his Stanhope adding machine, a block of wood with several dials built into it.

He looked up and rubbed his eyes. "Where you bin to?"

I dragged one of the Chippendale chairs over to him and sat rigidly, too shaky to relax. I knew this moment had to come but hadn't prepared myself emotionally. I fought back tears as our eyes met. "James..."

He leant forward and squeezed my hand, as if telling me it was all right to say it. "It is time for the truth. I was with Jacob. I was lonely, hence I went to him. We played chess, talked, had a meal."

"Then why the tears? He didna like yur perfume?"

"No, tis not about him." I shook my head. "He told me you have a mistress."

James huffed and tossed his head. "He must'a had a good reason to tell you that. I canna see it popping up in conversation about where to buy girdles."

"He told me because—because I told him—oh, James..." My voice quivered as tears spilled from my eyes. "I confided in him about you and me, how I feel. We both know our marriage hasn't been thriving. We have separate lives, separate lov—" I halted before I rambled farther about that. "What we had is no longer there. You know that."

304

"It ain't?" He truly had no idea how I felt or how things had changed. I considered forgetting the entire thing, especially when he wiped the tears from my cheeks with his most gentle touch ever. "Why are you crying, love?"

"I was going to tell you—" I took in a ragged breath. "Since I became involved with Alex and learnt you have a mistress, things haven't been the same. You don't love me any more, do you? Could you, after what's happened?"

He gathered me in his arms. "Of course I still love you. I wouldna be here if I didn't. I know we havena bin—ye know—together in a while."

As he held me I let the familiar warmth of his embrace stir me as it always did. Next thing I knew, my mouth claimed his and we pressed the lengths of our bodies together. A surge of desire went through me. We broke our kiss and I whispered, "But we always—" I looked at him. As our eyes met, I felt that familiar spark rush through me.

"Always could git our bed rockin'." He cocked his brow and I began to burn from the undeniable fire that still simmered between us.

"Despite all your shortcomings, you can always get me where you want me, you cad." I sought his lips again and we shared a warm kiss that sent another surge of arousal through me.

"There's naught comin' up short here." He guided my hand down to his crotch. "How 'bout giving this button-popper a ride."

Within three panting breaths we reached the sofa, shucking off our clothes. As we coupled, my cries of ecstasy, lust, and yes—love—the kind that no mistress of his could give him—sounded in concert with the chimes of his new case clock.

By the time he'd poured each of us a glass of wine, he looked at me as if expecting me to continue talking. "Now, you were saying before you had yur way with me—" He forced a smile. "Say it."

I took a deep breath. "James, I cannot let another minute go by. I need to get this into the open. I've developed strong romantic feelings for Alexander Hamilton. You have a mistress and—"

"And?" He urged me on, leaving it all up to me.

I wet my lips. "And I believe the best thing would be to divorce. Adultery is the most common charge, and we both committed it. We've broken our vows. They mean naught anymore."

He leant back and crossed his ankle over his knee. At least one of us was relaxed. "Never mind you charging me or me charging you. Looks like we're even, lass. I dinna care to fill lawyers' pockets hurling charges at each other."

"All I'm saying is we've both been unfaithful." I tugged at my sleeves.

He searched the kitchen and I knew he was looking for something to drink. "I expect you'll hire yur Hamilton to lawyer this?"

The sound of his name stabbed my heart. "No." I shook my head. "I cannot do business with him. I know not if we'll even see each other again."

"Why not?" He grabbed the whisky bottle on the table. Though money stayed out of his reach at times, a bottle never was.

I twisted my bottom button blouse till it hung by a thread. "I believe he's lost interest. Since the congressmen now know about me and him, he doesn't seem to want to associate with me any further."

He took a swig from the bottle and wiped his mouth. "Well, if tis sympathy you want, you're crying inna the wrong grog. He's bin a prat to me. Having me arrested, getting those politicians involved. I dinna need that aggravation. I never liked him anyway. Puffed-up superficial mimic. And a chump to boot. Paying me all that money. He's thick as two short planks." Head tilted back, he emptied the bottle down his gullet.

"Then tis settled." I'd calmed enough. The worst of it was over. "I shan't contest it, or whatever you call it."

"Not that I have a fortune you can take me for." With his slight grin came the dimple in his left cheek—the dimple I once loved to kiss.

"I don't want your money, James."

We sat in silence for a moment, the words we'd spoken hanging in the air between us. Emotions clogged me like a stopped drain: relief, sadness, longing for Alex, fondness for Jacob, lingering love for James.

One of us needed to say something about where to go from here. "I'm going to New York to visit Susannah. She's birthing her twins soon," I said.

"Have a grand time." He stared into the distance, and I reckoned he was calculating how much this divorce would cost him. The adding machine would be busy afore long.

Our eyes met once again. "I don't want to know her name, but what is she like? Is she pretty?" I hadn't put much stock in what Jacob had said. "I want to hear it from you."

"Not unless she tarts herself up. She's a good tumble and kin drink me under any table in Philly. We share the same ribald humour. Tis fun, naught moore. A bit of fun." He tossed his head in a "so what?" gesture, but didn't smile.

"Do you love her?" I probed, dreading the answer, but my curiosity got the best of me.

He shook his head and a strange gladness washed over me. "Nay, canna say I do. Never thought about it till you asked."

"Are you going to marry her now?" Why did I need to know all this? Because I still cared about James and always would. "I no longer want to be your wife, but I want you to be happy—with whoever."

"Nay. We have huge rows when we're pissed, then make amends when we're sober. Many's the eve I quit her bed and dinna want to see her for nigh on anutherr fortnight." He toyed with a spoon on the table.

I still wanted Alex to leave his empty marriage and propose to me, but James would always be my husband in a certain way. I stood with wobbly knees. "I'm physically and emotionally drained. Very well then, I shall hire Mr. Burr for the divorce. I'll write and arrange an appointment."

He stood and opened his arms to me. "C'mere, love." I stepped into his embrace. He brought my lips to his and kissed me lovingly and thoroughly.

Exhausted from our lovemaking and our decision, we ended the kiss and relaxed our embrace.

"I wouldn'a set Hamilton up had I known you'd fall for him that hard," he said.

I did not want to think about Alex now. "Tis too late now, James. But I must move on. Going to New York will help. I need a change of scenery."

"Has he given you any more compensation?" His question lacked his past enthusiasm about Alex giving me money.

"No. I never asked and he stopped offering." I'd considered that a leap in our bond together, but I didn't tell James this.

"Just as well." He scowled. "I shite on his stinking money."

"But not enough to give it back," I countered.

"We earned it. Now tis over and we must move on." He gave a dismissive wave.

"I'm glad you see it that way." I needed share my feelings with him. "I've felt lost for some time now, James. I might feel like I belong in New York once again, back home where I came from. I may even stay there."

"Mayhap you're better that way, lass." He ran his fingers through my hair and kissed the top of my head, as if he knew he'd never touch me like this again. "And of coorse Hamilton will return to New York when he finishes his treasury term. He'll have a go at the Senate, I expect, in preparation for a bid for the presidency."

"Alex said he does not aspire to the presidency. He'd be happy as a lawyer and running his manufacturing towns." A profound loss trounced, knowing I'd never share that part of his life.

James glanced at the clock. "I need go out for a while. But I'll be home in time fur supper."

My heart lightened. "That will be so nice. We haven't supped together in ages. I look forward to sharing a meal. Mayhap we can even have a few laughs over some of those Republican boot lickers."

"Tell Maggs to make a roast or—something nice. Ah'll fetch some wine and sweets." Then he did something he hadn't done since we were first married—he kissed me goodbye at the door and tweaked my nose. "See ya, love."

I sat down to write to Aaron Burr. When I finished, I wrote to Alex and poured my heart out.

I posted the letter to Burr and tore the letter to Alex into pieces.

Chapter Thirty-Three

Eliza

Monday eve, March 6th

To-day I called on Maria Reynolds to offer my assistance with wedding preparations. I knew she was not yet divorced, but she hadn't many lady friends. I wanted to help her any way I could.

I knocked on their door. Maria did not answer. Her husband did.

"Why, Mrs. Hamilton!" His brown eyes lit up to a golden hazel. His smile brightened the entire entryway. "To what end do you bestow the honor of yur beauteous presence upon me? I canna trot the wife out, as she's currently not in residence. But please do enter our humble abode nonetheless." He held out his arm, stepping aside, bowing to me as if royalty.

"No, I can call another time…" I couldn't help it, but his undeniable charm and politeness drew me in.

Besides, I was curious to see how Maria had decorated their latest dwelling.

"Be still my heart, as you grace my doorstep." He dressed ever so fashionable: fine linen shirt, velvet fawn britches tailored to his solid physique, polished shoes. He smelt clean and freshly washed...and behaved even more gentlemanly than my Dr. Black.

He summoned his servant, "Maggs," a pale Irish girl. She fussed about, curtseying and fluffing my chair cushion. She served me whisky in a cut crystal glass the likes I'd seen only at the Washingtons.

"Thank you kindly, Maggs. You may take the remainder of the day and eve free," James addressed his servant as politely and respectfully as he did me.

He clinked his glass to mine and remained standing till I was comfortably seated. Impressed with Maria's talent for décor, I calculated the cost of the elegant furnishings and draperies.

"The lady of the castle is out gift shopping fur her family in New York, where she plans to travel," James said. "Her sister is birthing twins within the fortnight."

"Oh, how nice. I have several nieces and nephews as well." Anxious to dispense with the small talk, yet not knowing what we'd discuss afterward, I noticed how neatly the queue captured his thick chestnut hair. I surmised he shunned wigs. But unlike Alex, his abundant crown needn't be covered in one.

I now knew what had attracted Maria to his essence, his person. He exuded utter charm, if naught else. The word 'charisma', new to our language, came to me. If he could bottle and sell it, he'd never need engage in another scheme.

"Then she's off to see Attorney Burr." He left it at that.

I muttered "Oh," as I took a too-big sip. What to say? I was sorry? Congratulations?

But he saved the moment. "I suppose you've heard."

"Yes, and I did ask Alex to offer his legal services, but I suppose his workload proved too heavy…" I noticed his lips curl at the mention of Alex's name. Mayhap they were closer friends than Alex had let on. "I came to see if Maria needed my help in wedding preparation."

"Wedding?" His thick brows knitted, a crease forming twixt them. Noticing all this, I knew I was sitting way too close. I leant back.

"Uh—yes, I—" I stammered. "She and Jacob Clingman, he proposed to her in my parlour. I'm so sorry, James, I thought you knew—" I hid behind the glass and took another gulp.

"Oh, that!" He slapped his knee with a hearty guffaw. He cleared his throat and shook his head. "That was no true proposal. She has no interest in Jake, nor he in her. I thought she'd have told you by now. Twas only a ruse so you wouldn't know about the affair."

My body stiffened. My heart stopped. The blood drained from my face. I cringed, beyond mortification. I began to sweat profusely. Desperate to wipe my brow, I kept my hands delicately circled round the glass. "W—what affair?"

313

James leant forward and set his glass on the table. His eyes bored into me as he bit his lip. I guessed this was the first time in his life that words eluded him. "Mrs. Hamilton—Elizabeth—do you not know by now? Yur husband and my wife. For the love of God, if you dinna know by now, you should."

Dizziness made me lightheaded. The glass slipt from my fingers. He caught it inches from the floor, whisky spilling all over the braided wool rug. I nearly gagged on the fumes.

"What makes you suspect them?" I yet refused to acknowledge it as fact.

"There's naught to suspect." He placed my emptied glass on the table and held my gaze. "Hamilton was here often—very often. I practically caught them in friganté dilecto one eve."

"In *what*?"

"You know—" He waved his hands about and cast his gaze downward. "Ah'm tryin' to be delicate here—"

"Oh." I burned with embarrassment, wanting to crawl under the floorboards.

"But they didna hide it from me," he continued. "Twas no secret in this house. I thought you knew, after all this time."

I did not want to know how long "all this time" was. Annie Bates had been right. Following Maria around, directly to Alex. And I'd refused to believe her. I'd dreamed up every excuse why they'd been together. But should I believe the likes of James Reynolds?

My pride still held me back from believing either of them. But something else haunted me, and it was not eyewitness accounts—it was in writing. "I received some letters," fell out of my mouth, but I needed to tell him. "I believed they came from a political enemy, using me to torment my husband. All I wanted to know was who wrote them. If I could find out, that would tell me if they spoke the truth. Because some sources are reliable, as you know, and some are not."

He nodded, urging me on.

"I could use another drink, Mr. Reynolds." I tried to wet my lips, my tongue dry and gritty.

He stood to fetch the bottle. "Yur wish is my command, dear lady. And I'm James to you. Or Jimmy if you like." He poured me another drink which I gulped too quickly. "Care for some haggis? Twill soothe what ails you."

Knowing what haggis was, from Alex's Scottish background, I fought back disgust. "God, no."

"Then what said these letters?" He sat back down.

"They said Alex was seen with Maria, several times. At your house, at our house, here and there..." I drained the last drop of my drink.

"I canna say they're false, Elizabeth." He pulled his chair forward, closer to me. "Whoever wrote them either has it in for yur husband and hoped you'd leave him, so the ensuing scandal would sell a heap of broadsheets. But obviously that didna happen."

"No. Because I wanted to find out who wrote them first." I stared into the empty glass. "That would tell me if they were true."

"Tell you what. You show them to me, and mayhap I kin tell you who wrote them," he offered.

"How would you know?" I looked into those deep brown eyes. "I've hired the best spy in the business to find out, and she hasn't a clue yet."

"Spy? She? Annie Bates I take it?" he asked.

I nodded. "Yes."

His lips tightened into a thin line as he shook his head. "Her specialty was espionage, sneaking into enemy camps, deciphering code. I doubt she kin do that kinda digging. You need the constabulary fur a probe of that sort."

"Well, she's followed your wife right to my husband. More than once. But I—" A pang of sorrow engulfed me. "Oh, God help me, but I couldn't bring myself to believe her."

"Mayhap you really didna want to know," he spoke the truth.

"You're right." Yes, the moment of truth. Something inside told me James had nothing to gain by lying to me about this. But part of me, that stubborn Dutch streak that reared its ugly head at the worst times, still refused to believe my husband had kissed, embraced, caressed and bedded Maria Reynolds.

"But I need to know now." I gave a resolute nod. "If my husband is finding pleasure in another woman's bed, yes, I want to know. Then I shall act accordingly."

"Then dinna take my word for it." James spoke in an authoritative tone. "Let me see the letters. The authorship will furnish yur proof, since you won't take my word or Annie's word, which you paid fur."

316

Could he dig up what a seasoned spy couldn't? I extracted the letter I kept back from Annie, in case the other got lost. I'd never taken it from my satchel since that day. I handed it to him. He unfolded it, his sharp eyes sweeping back and forth over each line.

I trembled, drained, a wreck by now. What to believe, what not to believe? Did the truth stare me in the eye and I still refused to accept it? My Alex—doing all the things we did in the intimacy of our marriage bed, with another woman? My mind showed me a scene—Alex embracing Maria, his lips capturing hers, his growing arousal, her legs wrapt round his back, whispering endearments—I shuddered to expel these sickening thoughts.

He handed the letter back to me before I could register any more emotions. "I'll tell you who wrote this, and not charge you a groat. Thom Callender, the reporter fur the *Gazette*, is the author, sure as the day is long."

"Callender!" The letter slipt from my fingers and fluttered to the floor. "How do you know?"

"I know him since Glasgow days. I know him like a book." He strode to his desk, opened a drawer and took a sheet of paper out. Sweeping my fallen letter off the floor, he held them both up to me. The ink color and penmanship matched exactly, down to every loop, curve and slant.

"But why? Why? Who spilt this to Callender?" I babbled, turning away. I couldn't bear to see or hear any more.

"Any of the cohorts. Monroe, Muhlenberg, Venable, they're all Republicans, anti-Federalists, Hamilton's sworn enemies," James said. "I wouldna even put it past old Adams or Jefferson. And they all know about it, from the very lips of yur husband. He admitted it all to them, to protect his innocence of corruption by admitting his guilt of the affair."

"But Callender?" I shook my head in disbelief. "How could he stoop so low as to send me these letters?"

"In hopes he'll create a scandal that will sell newspapers," he explained, his tone calm. "He eyed yur husband cavorting with my wife a few times. He wrote to you about it, hoping you'd confront Hamilton over it and divorce him. That didna happen. But Thom's luck came back in spades when Hamilton admitted the affair to those office-holders. Thom's bin known to solicit information to fill his pages. But fur this, he didna need to seek out a story."

He folded his letter and handed mine back to me. "As soon as Monroe and his sidekicks learnt of the events, one of 'em tipped Thom off in exchange fur a generous sum. Everyone's got his price. But scandal monger that he is, Thom does not make things up. Never has anyone bin able to file a libel suit against him—fur the simple reason, he does not print libel. He prints the truth. The man doesna lie, Elizabeth. And neither do I. The only liar here is yur husband," he stated, another ugly truth. "And I daresay, in the blink of yur eye, this will be on Thom's pages and the talk of the nation. Tis a matter of time. The clock's a'ticking."

My breath caught in my throat. I gulped air. I jumped to my feet, paced in circles, fists clenched. "What can I do, how can I save Alex—me—us—he betrayed me, our vows ..." No longer able to talk, I broke down, racked with sobs.

His arms came round me. "You're strong, Elizabeth, you'll git throo this..." he soothed me with his rumbling burr.

My embrace tightened round his strong body as he let me shed tears all over his tailored shirt.

And so I stood, weeping on the shoulder of James Reynolds, when in walked his wife.

"James? What is this?" I heard her voice grow closer. "Who is—"

I pulled away from her husband and turned to face her. Through my blur of tears I saw her mouth fall open.

"Mrs. Hamilton! My God, what happened?" She rushed up to me and pressed a handkerchief into my palm. I swiped at the streaks of tears running down my face.

James took a step back, as if to let us ladies take over.

"I know all about it, Maria." I steadied my voice as I struggled to breathe evenly. "All is out in the open now. You and Alex needn't hide from me anymore. And within days the entire nation will know. My life as I know it is over." I took a few ragged breaths, but no more tears came. I was all cried out.

Maria turned to her husband. He held up his hands as if in surrender. "James, you told her?"

"Not deliberately. Bloody hell, I couldna believe she didna know this." He faced me and cupped my elbow. "Better you know now than read about it the *Gazette*, when it woulda hit you like a sack o'silver dimes."

Now that the shock had worn off, I could think straight. "You're right, James. I wish I'd known sooner, but—" I faced Maria. She'd gone pale, her hands shook. "Maria, I should have known. All the signs stared me in the face, and I refused to acknowledge them. I turned a blind eye, like the fool I am—"

"No," Maria cut in, "Don't say that. You're no fool. It just happened. It wasn't planned."

"It never is." I took in a long breath that helped calm me. "Part of me knew, but the other part refused to believe it."

Maria stammered and sputtered, her hands fluttering at her throat. I continued, "You need not say more, Maria. I cannot change the past. But I trust you will use discretion in the future. Divorced or not."

I glanced at James. He gave me a brief tight-lipped nod.

"Maggs is off, Maria. Ah'll show Mrs. Hamilton out." He led me to the front door. I exited their house, not turning back to look at Maria, but sensing her discomfort. Wife and mistress both mortified, we needed go our separate ways and plan ahead. I knew what I needed to do.

"Ah'm sorry for all the pain this has caused." James stood in the open doorway as I gathered my shawl about me. "I am truly sorry."

"Why you, James?" I looked into his eyes, now downcast, his shoulders slumped. "You're not the husband who should be apologizing to me."

"Twas my idea to flee here from New York. I ducked out of a duel, the only reason we're here. Twas I who set yur husband up. I had no idea Maria would—that all this would happen. Ah'm ashamed of myself. Now two marriages are over. I made a right ballocks of everything." He ran his hand over his hair, shaking his head.

"You're not to blame, not at all," I assured him. "You did not set my husband up. Fate did. He and Maria were destined to meet. Kindred souls like theirs always are. And nothing can keep them apart. But I daresay we helped them along. Without even knowing it, I drove my husband farther into her arms. Now what Alex and I once had is gone forever. You have a new life ahead of you as a free man. As for me—I have six children to raise." I lifted my hand to bid him adieu and he clasped it.

"God be with you, Elizabeth." He kissed my fingers. "And remember: marriages may die, but love never does."

I descended the steps, back to my home, my hearth, and my children—what remained of my shattered world.

Maria

I stood in the middle of the room, shivering as if I'd been doused with ice water. My biggest fear had been Mrs. Hamilton finding out—because that meant the end of Alex and me. As long as she remained blissfully ignorant, we could blissfully rendezvous. I loved him so much, I cherished what shreds of hope I clung to.

James came back in, avoiding my gaze, giving me wide berth as he headed for his whisky supply.

He poured himself a generous splash and took a long pull before finally facing me. "Care to partake?"

"No." I remained standing, hugging my arms to myself.

I stood and he drank. The silence engulfed us.

"All right, Maria," he finally spoke. "Git it off yur chest. Tell me you hate me fur shooting off my gob to Elizabeth Hamilton about something I was sure she knew fur ages. Hell's bells, I knew she was dumb, but not deaf and blind, too."

I raised my hands and let them fall to my sides as I slumped on the sofa. "Oh, never mind, James. I do not blame you. This was bound to happen. Especially since those congressmen got the letters, confronted us and Alex, and ran to the president—"

"I wouldna even blame them alone." He sat beside me. "Mrs. Hamilton showed me some anonymous letters she received."

The letters. I remembered Alex mentioning that she'd gotten some unsigned letters he'd brushed off as lies, but I knew they bothered him. He abhorred tittle-tattle, even if it was true. "And what about them? The writer reveal himself?"

He shook his head, draining his drink. "Didna need to. Thom Callender wrote them. I knew as soon as I lay my eyes upon the letter she showed me. Proved it to her with a letter I have from his very same pen. Then she fell apart all over me. Then you walked in."

Despair engulfed me. "Callender. That dirty rotten scoundrel." I ground my teeth and clenched my fists. "I could crush Callender's throat."

James leant forward and squeezed my knee. "Maria, dinna fret. There's naught to do but look forward. Looking back is torture."

Sage as his advice was, I refused to take it. I would not give up Alex. We meant too much to each other to throw it all away. I now knew my next mission: I had to convince Alex that our love was stronger than anything or anyone—and that included his wife. In turn, he'd have to make her accept our love—or end their marriage, as I was doing. My heart lightened in the renewed hope of becoming the second Mrs. Hamilton.

At that moment my desire to see Alex drove me stronger than the need to breathe. I stood so fast, I nearly fell over. Dizzy, I clutched the sofa arm. James caught my elbows.

"You need to sit, Maria, or at least eat something. You're gooing nowhere like this."

As he sat me back down I assured myself I'd see Alex today. Even if I had to trawl every street in town to find him. I vowed to spend tonight in his arms.

James fetched me a turkey drumstick and some boiled carrots with a glass of cider. I ate and drank, realizing I'd skipped the midday meal.

"Now calm down. All will be fine," he assured me, over and over.

"How?" I wondered. My special secret, my clandestine love, would soon be headlines blasted all over the nation. I couldn't imagine Alex and me continuing like this. He had to leave his wife and marry me. No other way was possible!

I heard James speaking to me in the distance, but my plotting and planning tuned out his voice. Finally he pinched my arm and I jumped to attention.

"What is it?" I looked up. "I was not listening."

"Not listening?" He walked up to me and leaned into my ear. "You're not even present."

I stood and wandered over to the cabinet that held our wine and spirits. I poured myself a goblet of claret and headed back to him. "I'm sorry, I'm only trying to take your advice and look forward. But that seems as torturous as looking back. Because I know not where it will lead."

"At least we took the first step," he said. "Most couples havena the pluck to get divorced when tis the best thing."

"You have no argument from me there," I conceded. "Staying married would be a step backward."

324

"Which is what I asked when you were lost in space—did you call on Aaron Burr?" he asked.

"Yes." I sipped my claret. "He believes he can finalize the divorce in a few months."

"Grand." He nodded. "I kin wait. If you kin."

"We have no choice." I went over my meeting with Aaron Burr in my mind. "We haven't seen each other since his soirée when I played violin. He greeted me warmly but became all business when discussing the divorce. I couldn't remain as professional as he," I admitted, feeling the need to share this with him. "When Aaron asked me to reconsider our marriage, I burst into tears. He said he's morally obligated to ask a client before proceeding with a divorce. But I told him we're—" I sighed heavily. "We're beyond reconsidering. I told him the truth—we no longer feel about each other as husband and wife should." That was my way of telling James I'd always love him—it simply was not enough to remain husband and wife.

"Did he laugh?" James fiddled with the ribbons of his queue.

"Not at all. I believe he admires us for taking this drastic step. Who dares divorce? Even with affairs or absence of love that grows into disgust and loathing, couples remain married. Out of fear, I dare guess."

"Shows how wise you are, lass." He gave me an admiring smile. "I admit I'd stay married—I'm doin' this cuz you made me see what I couldna see right before me own eyes here. I kin live with yur lover and my lover coming and going—but you are far more wise than I, striving to make the best of this one brief life we have here."

"I appreciate your flattery." Yet it made me wonder—how wise was I really? Leaving my marriage in hopes that my married lover would do the same? Aaron Burr hadn't attempted to talk me out of it after his "moral obligation" to ask me. He simply drafted up a document and quoted me his fee. "My life hasn't been all that bad so far, James. I had a happy childhood. We married for love. But for the future, I believe we'll be happier apart."

"You're right, love." He gave a resolute nod. "The woman always sees far past what the man wants to see. We never look past the length of our willies."

I looked straight into his eyes. "Well, I'm glad to hear one of you finally admit it. If that could go into the Constitution, our nation would advance at least two hundred years."

Chapter Thirty-Four

Eliza

Fryday, March 10th

I did not speak to Alex last eve. He arrived home late, and I pretended to be asleep when he came to bed. At breakfast I busied myself with the little ones. We spoke four words: "Good morning" and "Good-bye."

To-day I called on Annie. Altho I no longer needed her services, I needed another woman to confide in. She gave me a snifter of brandy without asking and I gratefully took it. We sat upon her sofa, a needlework project spread out between us.

"Truth be told, Elizabeth, you look as if you've been run over by a team of oxen." She snapped open a snuff tin and pinched some up with two fingers. She inhaled deeply and whistled out. "Pardon my dippin.' I've been tryin'a surrender the noxious weed, but it beckons me. Now. Do tell what's on your mind before you erupt."

"I didn't realize I looked that distressed." A smile came unbidden. "I know who wrote the letters. Thomson Callender."

"Of the *Gazette*?" She squeezed her nose.

I nodded. "Aye, the infamous one and only."

She tossed the tin onto the table. "I know'd I should'a looked somewhere like there first. If anybody's dirtier than officeholders, tis the journalists what write about them. How'd you find out?"

"James Reynolds showed me a letter from him," I told her. "The writing was identical. No denying it. And his explanation confirmed it. Callender was hoping I'd divorce Alex over it. But Callender doesn't know me. I need proof first. Proof in an admission of guilt from my husband. And I certainly never got that."

"Then why are you so distraught? Callender thrives on scandal. You already knew that." She huffed and sneezed.

I blessed her. "James also told me the truth about my husband and his wife. Whilst I sobbed onto his shoulder, his wife came home and admitted it. The only one who's kept silent is my husband."

She reached over and took my hand. "Oh, I'm sorry. I wish I could find words to say, but nothing would be fitting. I only wish I could have found out who wrote the letters first. But I did tell you I'd followed Mrs. Reynolds, and her path led straight to your husband, every time—'xcept once, when she went into Burque Jewelers. I entered after she'd gone, and asked Burque if she'd purchased any goods. With a grin wide as the Delaware River, he told me she'd purchased a pair of expensive diamond ear bobs. Ain't that a kick in the head. Not pearls. Not citrines. Pure ice. Her husband must be goldsmithing a roof on Mount Vernon."

I nodded, knowing James and his financial fluxes. "Yes, their fortunes rise and fall like the tide. When they're flush with cash, they go on buying sprees and move into posher dwellings. They currently reside in a three-story brick with a garden and outbuildings on High Street. Furnished quite elegantly as well."

As I rambled on, another thought entered my mind and niggled at me. I finally recognized what it was. "Wait. Diamond ear bobs? Why, I found a diamond ear bob at the top of my stairs not long ago. I questioned the entire staff, not that they could afford diamonds, but—dear God, it's hers. She was in my house. Of course. Oh, I am so stupid!" I slapped the side of my head, wishing I could kick my own behind.

"No, you ain't stupid," she assured me. "Just trusting. You didn't want to believe what I was telling you. I followed them enough times to conclude they were, uh…meeting. Alone. Yet you trusted him. Not a vice, a virtue."

"Thank you for the accolades, but it changes nothing about our lives now. I cannot bear the thought of Alex touching me again. I shall give him no more children. He can sire future children with—with her." I'd drained my snifter without realizing it, and got up to help myself to the decanter. But I decided I needed something even more potent. "Have you any malt whisky? Preferably something foreign? And older than ten years?"

"Yes to all three." She dashed to the cabinet in the corner where she poured me a glass. "Straight from Glenlivet in the heart of the western Highlands. This'll sprout hair on your chest. Cheers, my bonny lass."

I sipped as she sat back down and hiked her skirts up to her knees, revealing a pair of bright red stockings. If this whisky didn't sprout hair on my chest, it would sprout a hole in my stomach.

When it finally went down, I said, "I now needs go to Thomson Callender and bribe him not to make this story public. It will cost dearly, if what James Reynolds says is fact. Callender pays for scandalous stories, but only if they're true. I expect he takes payment to retract them."

She shook her head. "Nah, don't waste your time. No amount you can pay him will outweigh what he can make on newspaper sales when this hits the sheets. You will live through it, believe me."

"I cannot show my face ever again. I feel like covering it right there, I'm so ashamed. I'll be the butt of hushed whispers and snickers behind fluttering fans whenever I pass by." I cringed.

"As if you're the only woman who's had a—pardon the expression—philandering husband? Look at history, Elizabeth—in Europe, tis the norm. Tis a scandal if a married man does *not* have a mistress! At the very least a married man without a mistress is branded as one of *them*." She flicked her wrist.

I blinked, befuddled. "One of them what?"

"You know." She waved her hand. "A molly. A pansy. As was King Louis the Thirteenth."

"Oh, God above." I began to laugh, although why I found humor in this, I knew not. "No, my Alex is not one of *them* and never will be. He's always been a flirter and a gallant, and I should have known marriage vows would not alter his behavior."

"Mayhap your telling him you know of his affair will alter his behavior." She cast me a sly grin.

"I haven't been able to bring myself to speak to him." I released a loud sigh and took another sip of the heady whisky. "But I do not expect anything will change him. If anyone changes, it must be me."

Maria

Poughkeepsie, New York, March 14

Susannah was delivered of twin girls this morn, named Frances and Ruth, after our grandmothers. We sat round her bed eating pudding and drinking cider as her other tykes ogled their new siblings. I promised Susannah I'd take the tykes out tomorrow so she can rest.

They each had a pony they were too young to mount. I hadn't forgotten how to ride, so Susannah gave me permission to saddle up White Surrey, her beautiful bay mare. They had three other horses, pigs, chickens, goats and a dairy cow. With plenty to keep me busy, I almost stopped longing for Alex, until a letter from Aaron Burr arrived. I'd given him the address here, not knowing how long I'd be staying. He told me the divorce would be final by the first week of April. It loomed up dead ahead. *Need I be present?* I wrote back, not wanting to be. Another letter, this one from Jacob, announced his visit within a fortnight. I hoped it didn't coincide with the date of my divorce. I wanted to be alone that day, to think of James, and wish him well.

I wrote to Alex nigh on two weeks ago and received no reply. So I wrote again. *Now that our love is known, we have no reason to hide any longer,* I wrote in a fifth attempt, having torn up the previous four. *We can be together always, as I trust you and Mrs. Hamilton will make the same brave move to end your loveless marriage as James and I have.*

It made perfect sense to me. Having seen how James's revelation devastated Mrs. Hamilton, I could not see her wanting Alex in her bed any longer. Not one of the four of us needed remain married. Now Alex and I could start our life together. How could he possibly object? Yet another ten days passed with no word from him.

Jacob arrived on the doorstep the day after I received a letter he'd posted from New York City.

"Seems I travel faster than the post!" He swept me into his arms and twirled me round before my nephews' stunned faces.

Susannah, coming down the stairs after nursing the babies, halted in her tracks. "My, if you are James, you certainly have sobered and cleaned yourself up!"

"Very funny, Susy." I took Jacob's hand and brought him forth. "This is Jacob Clingman. Jacob, my sister Susannah Livingston."

He bowed, took her hand, kissed it, and displayed his dazzling smile. "I am here, Mrs. Livingston, for one reason only. To ask for your beautiful sister's hand in marriage. For real this time."

My jaw hit the floor. I don't know why, but I was more surprised than when he recited that melodramatic proposal in the Hamiltons' parlour. My hand grew cold although his hands enveloped it. "God's truth, I'm not even divorced yet."

"As if that matters." He released my hands and slid from his pocket a stunning diamond band. Susannah descended the remaining steps and leant over the newel post to gawk at it.

"Heaven above, Mr. Clingman, it gives off more light than our chandelier when ablaze with a hundred candles!" She flashed him a grin. "You must really love my sister."

"More than you'll ever know." He gazed at me as if I put the Sistine Chapel's ceiling to shame.

Although afraid to, I looked into his eyes. They sparkled brighter than the ring.

Before I could say yes or no, he slipt it onto my finger. "Marry me, Maria. And if you'll not forget Al Hamilton, so be it. I cannot make you love me, nor make you stop loving him. But I do love you and will give you a life neither he nor James could ever give you."

"Jacob—" I glanced away. Susannah had vanished, leaving us alone. "Please let me think." I pressed my palms to the sides of my head, pounding like a hammer. "Mayhap when I get back home and tend to some details—"

"Home? Where is home, Maria? Philadelphia? That is not your home. This is your home. New York." He gestured at the surroundings.

I hadn't even thought of that. I'd planned to go back to Philadelphia, at least keep a residence there, to be close to Alex until we could work things out. But home? No, it was not home. Home was wherever Alex and I could be together.

He had to know this. "Jacob, please. Give me a respectable amount of time to make up my mind."

Which meant until I heard from Alex, divorced or not.

Eliza

I needed face my husband about this. With the dishes cleared and the children abed, I dismissed the servants. As Alex began his usual retreat to his study, I stopped him at the doorway. "Alex, we must talk."

"You want money again?" he asked over his shoulder as he pulled his reading specs from his shirt pocket.

"No, it is not about money!" I retorted too loudly, my chest tightening in exasperation. "Why do you believe our entire lives consist of matters about money? What about us?" I spilt it before he sat at his desk. "I know about you and Maria Reynolds—your affair."

He sat anyway, releasing his specs onto his blotter. I felt he deserved ample time to reply; after all, I'd shot him between the eyes with this.

"And how did you arrive at this conclusion?" he asked in his lawyerly tone.

Oh, what a lawyer, through and through! Cross-examining his own wife when caught like a stuck pig. "Never mind how I arrived. But I do know that Thomson Callender is the author of those letters to me, and every word of them speaks the truth." I approached his desk and stared him down. His chair creaked and groaned as he reclined.

"Callender. I should have known." He shook his head and combed his fingers through his graying hair.

"And I should have known you were bedding another woman." I flattened my palms on his desktop, strewn with documents. "And I cannot describe how much it hurts. As if you buried a bullet in my spine. And severed my heart at the same time."

He gave me his practiced courtroom eye roll. "Betsey, please, do not overreact."

"No, Alex, don't lie to me any longer. You lied about what the letters said. You lied every time you left this house and told me you were working. I know you love her as you've never loved me, and truth be told, I thank her for it. For I could never love you the way I should—as your equal, your companion, your confidante. I am merely the mother of our brood, the keeper of your house, your security."

I took a sharp breath and continued, "Maria is divorcing her spouse. I know not exactly why, but if tis in hopes that you will do the same, I now give you the chance. I shall grant you your freedom, be that what you desire. I am bigger than all of you, for I am offering you a divorce for the right reasons—putting your needs before my own, rather than the other way round. And that is all I have to say—except that if Callender prints this, and you are a fool if you think he won't, you can forget ever aspiring to the presidency."

He heaved a sigh, his eyes downcast, looking more haggard in the candles' flickering shadows than he did in cold sunlight. "Betsey, I do not want a divorce, nor do I fear Callender. What would destroy my reputation are accusations that I embezzle from the treasury, not an affair. And before I'd let anyone believe I've pilfered the treasury or engaged in speculation with James Reynolds with public funds for private gain, I would publicly admit that my real crime was an amorous connection with his wife."

"Why not admit it publicly now, before Callender blasts it across the pages of the Gazette?" I badgered him.

With a key he kept on a ring in his top pocket, he opened a desk drawer and extracted a pile of papers. He plopped them down between us. "This is one of the documents I've been working on lately. It is titled

The Reynolds Pamphlet. In it, I explain my relationship with James and with Maria as well. I also state
in no uncertain terms that my dealings with the treasury have always been scrupulously honest. When
this is published, Callender nor anyone else will be
able to dispute it."

I swatted at the papers as if shooing a fly. "And you
plan to humiliate me and your entire family so that
your reputation with money remains intact?"

"Betsey, if my 'reputation with money' as you
call it is destroyed, so is my law practice and my
livelihood. Never mind the presidency—I could never
presume to fill George Washington's shoes. Can
you support a family of eight and five servants
with—whatever your skills may be? I sincerely doubt
it." He gathered his "Reynolds Pamphlet" and placed
it back into the drawer, locked it and dropped the
key back into his pocket. "So go back to your domestic fripperies and let me take care of the business at
hand—which right now is earning a living and keeping you in servants and flub-dubs." He then slid his
specs on and dipped his quill in his inkwell, a subtle
move to dismiss me.

I turned my back on him and left him alone.

He'd refused the freedom I'd offered him. Was I
relieved? Yes and no—yes, that he would remain my
husband—and although I was soon to be the object
of public humiliation and ridicule, I would not bear
the stigma of a divorced woman as would Maria
Reynolds. And no, because I knew he had no intention of ending his liaison with her. Whilst lying

337

awake late at night alone in our bed, I would know he was warming hers.

Then I remembered Annie Bates's words. At least he wasn't "one of *them*."

The only thing my husband had in common with King Louis XIII was they both favored monarchy.

Chapter Thirty-Five

Severus

Whilst visiting the home of the Hamiltons this day, I sensed a pall of uneasiness in the room as I sat in conversation with Elizabeth. Alex had greeted me briefly, only to quickly excuse himself. "I must retreat to my study and work on important matters of state." After inquiring of her health, which she assured me was as well as could be expected, *under the circumstances*, I found my curiosity piqued.

"Pray tell me what circumstances you refer to, Elizabeth. What could possibly be amiss that may affect your well being, if not your personal health or that of the children? Is it Secretary Hamilton? Does he hide some illness from the public in case the nation may lose confidence in his capabilities?" I sat and took the steaming teacup from her servant.

"Oh, Severus." She used my Christian name for the first time. She refused tea and paced the floor before collapsing into a wing chair. "Tis naught of the kind. I tell you this in trust, of course. Can I count on your continued discretion?"

Seeing her so upset re-engendered those alien feelings in me, that need to protect this lady, this almost divine example of motherhood, which was how I'd grown to see her.

"Am I not by now your trusted friend as well as occasional physician?" I blew on my tea. "You may speak to me with the same confidence with which you would speak to the face that looks at you from your mirror."

She inhaled deeply. "My husband has been unfaithful to me, Severus. He has been carrying on an affair with Maria Reynolds for some long time now, since before the birth of baby John for sure."

"I am so sorry," was all I could say initially. I sensed the deceit of betrayal on her behalf, as much as I was able to 'feel' any such emotions. "Are you to divorce, then?"

"It appears not," she responded, much to my surprise. "It appears Alex has no interest in divorce, and has very succinctly pointed out to me that I am not financially capable of taking care of my children and this household without the envelope of marriage around me."

"Ergo,, you are entrapped in a loveless marriage." I sipped my tea, a bit weak for my tastes.

"On his part, it would appear so." She lowered her head, her tone flat.

"And it means, perchance, you will not require the services of a physician of my specialty any longer?" I needed to know. Now.

She looked at me, her hands clutching the chair arms. "Severus, you are a friend to both of us, but more so, I think to me because we are also doctor and patient. I do not wish to lose either your friendship or your services because of this. I am still a woman, and prone to the same illnesses and diseases that beset any other woman in this world, so it seems to me I will still have need of your special knowledge from time to time."

"Then you may call upon me at any time in either capacity." I placed a smile upon my lips.

"Thank you. It is good to know there are still some men of honor and integrity in this world."

"I thank you for the compliment and your faith in my abilities to serve you." I stood and placed the teacup on the side table. "Now the time has come for me to take my leave, for I have paying calls to make." After we parted, I hastened down the street to my next appointment, recalling with some irritation the conversation I'd had with Alexander Hamilton just the previous eve. We'd met at the City Tavern quite by chance. We shared a few minutes of polite conversation over a brandy. I hoped to take it a little further, to probe into his sources without alerting any suspicion, but his treasury work had blighted any attempts. I needed wait until another time.

"I'm glad to see you here, Severus," he'd greeted me upon our meeting.

"You are?" I alerted, surprised, as no one was ever glad to see me.

"Indeed, yes." He gave me a warm smile. "There is a matter I wish to consult with you about, concerning your time in Paris."

My hackles instantly raised, I looked blandly into his face, but saw nothing untoward in his eyes, no hint of suspicion.

"Oh, yes? And what can I tell you about Paris?" I asked.

"Well, just this. A friend, more of a professional acquaintance really, told me during a recent conversation of news he'd received in certain letters from his relatives and friends in Paris. I should add that he is from Paris himself by origin, but, having lived here for some time now, he still receives news of events at home, as a matter of interest."

"I see, and how pray, does this affect me, Alex?"

"Oh, it does not affect you, at least not directly," he said, much to my immediate relief. I breathed easy now. "Tis only that he mentioned that a recent letter had informed him that Paris had, until some time ago, been subjected to similar reign of terror by night as has our city. A number of young women had been found horribly murdered, strangled and physically violated in the same way as those poor young women who have so recently lost their lives on our streets. Knowing you'd lived there yourself until recently, I wondered if you might have heard of these attacks in Paris, and whether you think it might be possible that some crazed Frenchman has crossed the ocean in order to perpetuate his murderous schemes upon our shores."

I tried to conceal my relief at that point, and gave him the reply I'd already formulated long before, in case such a question came up: "Ah, Alex, I see why you might think that. First of all, let me say that Paris is a very large place, a city far greater than anything we have here in America at this time, and news, even that of murder, can take time to spread by word of mouth. As for the written word, the press, I must confess I spent only a short time living in that great city, and though I knew enough of the spoken language to survive and prosper, I was never very well versed in the reading of French and never bothered to attempt to read their indecipherable newspapers," I lied without blinking.

In fact, I spoke and read French as a native would, but that knowledge was mine alone.

"I confess, I heard nothing of any such murders during my time in the city," the lies rolled off my tongue like honey. "But as to your second point, I would think it quite possible that if the murders there have ceased, as I presume must have happened for you to suggest such a thing, it would be quite possible that the killer has fled to these shores. Lord knows, there are enough Frenchies here already and more arriving every week so it seems."

"Yes, I think that may be the answer." Alex nodded. "When next I speak to the commissioner, I shall suggest he directs his inquiries in the direction of recent arrivals from France, particularly those of the lower classes, from whence I would think such a bestial killer originates."

I feigned a cough to conceal my amusement at this absurd theory. As if some base and peasant-like French laborer could prowl the city streets by night, in his workmen's garb, attracting and killing pretty young things in affluent neighborhoods! *So ridiculous, but good for me*, I thought.

We parted soon after. I'd intended to speak to Alexander Hamilton again, offering my services and opinions to law enforcement as a consultant, if necessary, inveigling myself into their investigations, the better to ascertain what intelligence, if any, they possessed. Mayhap another time…

Chapter Thirty-Six

Maria

Jacob stayed for two weeks, having a grand time. Lodging at the nearby Poughkeepsie Inn, he arrived at Susannah's every morn at ten, in time for the serving of breakfast. Weather permitting, we rode Susannah's and Gilbert's horses with picnic lunches. He played games with the young ones, lawn bowling, blocks, and spelling bees. Evenings we adults spent in the music room. I played violin with Susannah at the harpsichord. I did not let Alex fill my thoughts. Mayhap the proverb "out of sight, out of mind" held some truth after all.

Jacob never mentioned Alex or my upcoming divorce again. But he threw out subtle hints about my accepting his marriage proposal.

"Ah, what a perfect eve for star-struck lovers to plan a future together." He held my hand under the full moon's pearly glow on Susannah's terrace one night. "I do hope at this moment under this same moon, some lucky man is receiving a breathless 'oh, yes!' to a marriage proposal he just offered his lady love, and they plan their future for a happy and joyous life together."

I pulled my shawl closer round my shoulders. "Jacob, I assure you there is. But as for us, I told you I need wait until my divorce is final. And today I received a letter from Aaron Burr. Due to his heavy caseload, he must delay my divorce until the end of May."

Jacob gave a haughty *hrrumph*. "He knew what his caseload was when he agreed to represent you. There is no reason your divorce should take as long as Burr is taking. Do you believe he is deliberately dragging this out so that you will reconsider and stay married?" He sipped at his port and gave his manicured fingernails a glance.

"Why would he do that?" I shot back. "He is in business to service clients, not turn them away."

"Mayhap he hopes if you stay married, it won't give Hamilton any reason to divorce his wife. He will continue to pursue you, and whatever pretty face and fetching figure catches his roving eye. Then the scandalous story can really blow up and further ruin his reputation. It is well known he and Burr are political adversaries. Burr would do anything to make life unbearable for Hamilton."

I shook my head. "No, Aaron would not do something like that. He doesn't know about Alex and me."

346

Jacob leant forward and lifted my chin with his forefinger. "Maria, it is no secret any longer. Ever since Monroe and those congressmen got wind of your and Hamilton's illicit liaison, the entire congress knows. As well as President Washington. You think these men do not tattle amongst themselves over their grogs in the taverns? The longer your liaison lasts, the better for the scandal mongers. And the worse for Hamilton. And he knows that."

"Then why has not he ended it?" I blurted, the words barely out of my mouth when I realized what I'd just said. For all I knew Alex could have ended it. I hadn't heard a word from him since I arrived here. He ignored my letters. I hung onto my hopes by a thread, but I hung on.

"When was the last time you heard from him?" Jacob prodded.

"I wish not to speak of this any further, Jacob. It is late. You should retire to your room at the inn. I bid you good night." Without looking back, I stood and strode from the balcony, inside and up the stairs to my room, leaving him to see himself out.

From my front-facing room, I watched his carriage depart. If Jacob wasn't bluffing and congress did know about us, yes, it would create a scandal. Until the next senator or cabinet member got caught with a woman not his wife. I could not see Alex shunning our love because James Monroe shot off his big mouth. And Jacob was far wrong about Aaron Burr. He was not dragging out my divorce proceedings, delaying the date of the finalization.

I was.

Eliza

I wanted to give Mrs. Reynolds's diamond ear bob back to her, but was unsure if she'd returned from New York. Her home was not far from ours, and I needed to escape the chaos of the household. So I left instructions with the servants and took myself on a leisurely walk, heading in the direction of the Reynolds house.

The Irish maid answered my knock at the door.

"No, Mrs. Hamilton, Mrs. Reynolds is not retorned from New York yet. I haven't hord word when she will."

"Is Mr. Reynolds in residence?" As soon as I spoke those words, I regretted it. Why I felt the need for James Reynolds's company, I wasn't sure. But I could have sat and chatted with him over his smooth whisky all afternoon, listening to his Scottish burr. I had no immediate desire to return home.

"Nay, ma'am." As she shook her head, instant relief flooded me. Wanting to chat with James Reynolds all afternoon over whisky? What was I thinking?

"I shall return another time. Thank you, Maggie."

"Margaret," she corrected me.

With the warm spring sunshine on my back, I walked from there to Annie Bates's house, stopping at the market for some apples, pears and nuts to bring her.

She greeted me warmly and munched on one of the apples. I accepted a glass of port.

"And what brings the pleasure of your company here, Elizabeth?" She wiped juice from her chin.

"I escaped the asylum for a few hours." We shared a laugh.

"Havin' raised four pups, I know your plight." She took another bite. "Sometimes you want to burrow through a mole hole for some peace and quiet."

"And I've reconsidered, Annie. I wish to engage your services again. I need you to continue following Mrs. Reynolds. I now know of her affair with my husband and need to know if they're still seeing each other. That will determine what I decide to do—ultimately." I sipped the sweet port.

She chomped and slurped at her apple as she nodded. "Of course. I'll start this eve."

"No, she's not back from New York yet. I will let you know when she returns."

"You're paying me, Elizabeth." She gave me her wry grin. "*I'll* let *you* know."

Maria

April 15, Ten of Clock Eve

When Jacob asked me to return to Philadelphia with him, the pleading in his eyes was too much to bear.

Glancing about Susannah's high-ceilinged sitting room adorned with velvet drapes and plush carpets, I knew I could have this and more if I married him.

But I was simply not ready to give him an answer. I'd asked Aaron Burr to delay the divorce proceedings—because I needed to hold Jacob off. I still held my breath awaiting word from Alex. Yes, I clung to my dream. However, my voice of reason berated me. The longer I waited for his letters, the less likely I was to receive any.

Hence I remained in limbo—on Hell's border, as was the literal meaning of 'limbo.'

"I shall go back with you, Jacob," I told him.

His face lit up and he clasped my hands. "Oh, thank you, my dearest! We can stop at Nyack and go rowing on the Hudson, then visit New York City and feast on a superb Italian dinner at Caruso's on the Broad Way—"

"No, Jacob." I held up my hand, palm out. "I really need to return and attend to some business."

"What bus—oh, of course. You need to hustle Burr along. Mayhap you should threaten to hire another lawyer." A cocked brow accompanied his suggestion.

"Like Alex, for instance?" I cast him a sideways glance. "No, I'll not change lawyers. Unlike you, I am not in a particular hurry. Neither is James. I don't believe he's even hired a lawyer yet."

"I'm sorry. I don't mean to rush you. But I love you and want you to be my wife, and if I'm at fault for that, I hope you'll forgive me." He clasped my hands.

"Jacob, you're too good for me." My emotions churned inside. I did love him, but was it enough to marry him? Especially if Alex and I stayed lovers...

My heart took a little leap, as I now knew I'd at least be in close proximity to Alex within days. Soon I'd gaze into those violet eyes and feel those soft lips upon mine. I planned to do everything in my power to recapture what never should have slipt away.

Next morn, I bade farewell to Susannah and the little ones with a promise to be together again soon. "Let me know how the twins fare. I'm sure they'll grow fast." I held Susannah's hands as our tears fell freely.

"And you let me know how you fare with—" We exchanged knowing glances. She needn't finish. With Jacob standing there and surrounded by tykes and servants, it was better left unsaid.

Jacob wore me down with his incessant prattle about rowing, so I let him take me rowing on the Hudson. It delayed the journey home by two days, but the closer I got to the uncertainty awaiting me, I preferred putting it off.

When his carriage pulled up to my front door, the house stood in bleak darkness. Not that I expected James to be in. I'd fully anticipated stumbling around in the dark lighting candles.

I wanted to be alone, so I bade Jacob good night at the door after he helped me light six candles and a fire in the hearth. The driver dropt my trunks on the landing as Jacob invited me to his home one more time.

"No, Jacob, I'm very tired, and I'll be fine here."

"You will let me know your progress with Burr?" His hands clasped my arms and I stepped into his embrace. He held me tight.

"Of course." I hadn't expected his warm kiss. But it was Alex I really wanted. Jacob finally departed and I turned to face my empty house.

Next morn, James hadn't come back, but I found Maggie in the kitchen brewing coffee.

"Welcome home, Mrs. Reynolds," she greeted me as I rifled through the post. Nothing from Alex. I flinged it back down on the table.

"Maggie, have you seen Mr. Reynolds?" Through the long night, I'd hoped James would slip into bed next to me, for I felt so alone.

She shook her head, wiping her hands on her apron. "He's hardly here now. He let me stay on and cook and clean, but I secured anudder position living with a family on Market Street."

"Good for you," I muttered as she placed a cup of coffee, three biscuits and butter before me. James was undoubtedly with his lover. As I should be with mine.

Desperate to see Alex, I grabbed my cloak and walked to his law office. My heart hammering, I knocked on his door. The latch rattled and a young clerk answered. I couldn't stop trembling as I asked for him.

"He's not here today, ma'am, he's at the treasury."

Determined to see him, I turned and walked over there. It was near five of clock, he'd be coming out any minute. Not to appear as a loitering streetwalker, I strolled down the block and back again. Finally, at quarter of six, he exited the doors, but with four other men, engaged in intense discussion. My heart leapt at the sight of him. I flattened myself against the brick wall on the corner. They turned and headed in the opposite direction. I did not want to follow them. But I did—all the way to the City Tavern. Dared I wait there till God knows what time?

Too embarrassed to loiter any longer, I turned and headed home.

Next morn, my need to see him surpassed my hunger. I pushed around the eggs Maggie had scrambled for me, unable to take one bite. My stomach churned, my heart clobbered my ribs. "You hardly touched yur breakfast," she commented as I slid the chair back and stood.

Unable to answer her, I tore down the hall to the outdoor privy and lost what little I'd eaten. I staggered back in and collapsed onto the sofa. Maggie hovered over me, offering me some homemade tincture. "I am so desperate I'll try anything," I groaned.

She returned within the half hour, carrying one of our glasses filled with a liquid that looked too much like urine to be palatable.

"This medicine has been very serviceable to others before, and I would have you try it, Mrs. Reynolds," she urged.

She helped me sit up. "What is it?" I was afraid to ask, but I must.

"Tis a bit o'ginseng steeped in claret. Take it in strength and quantity as you find suits your stomach best," she instructed. "I left some in the kitchen. You

353

may also try stewing it in water if the wine be too harsh. But you had best slice it thin, and bruise it in an iron mortar. And if you still be ill, I will summon yur doctor."

"No, no doctor." Too ill to drink it, I let her spoon feed it to me.

She departed, leaving the glass on the table. I took a brave swig of the pungent elixir and my stomach finally settled. I dragged myself upstairs to pretty up.

I pulled my hair back off my face and secured it with two jeweled combs. Wearing my newest azure satin creation from Mrs. Graisbury with matching cloak trimmed in blue fox, I took one more glance in the looking glass. My face had gone so pale from being sick, my rouge looked blotchy. I grabbed a cloth, dipped it in the now-cold tea water and scrubbed it off.

I headed out the door, determined to meet with Alex even if I had to sit and wait all day.

The outer door of his building was unlatched, so I boldly stepped into the vestibule. Voices floated down the stairs, his and another man's. *Ah, he's here!* I clutched at my chest, as if that could calm my hammering heart. My dry tongue stuck to the roof of my mouth. The hallway had no chairs, so I crouched on the bottom step, held my hands to my cramping stomach and doubled over. Trembling, I wiped cold sweat from my forehead and palms.

I hadn't been this nervous that very first night I met him.

I forced myself to breathe deep, and on the third breath, a door closed. As footsteps descended the stairs, I stood and turned. A man I didn't recognize gave me a strange look, passed me and walked out. Now I knew Alex was alone.

I became more dizzy as I climbed each step. *Oh, God, let this be a joyous reunion!* I took one long breath in and out. My hand grasped the knob to his office door.

I turned the knob, pushed the door open, and there he sat behind his desk. He looked up and our eyes met. I nearly fainted. "Oh, Alex…" I grabbed onto the door frame.

He jumped to his feet, rushed up to me and held out his arms. I collapsed into his embrace, weeping with relief and sheer joy.

"Alex, why did you not write back to me?" I blurted out, and realizing this, I added, "Oh, how I missed you!"

He held me at arm's length and his eyes searched my face. I knew how sickly I looked, and hoped he would not comment on it. "I have been very busy."

A mix of relief and disappointment swirled round my heart. I grasped him so tightly, I could feel his arm muscles beneath his shirt. "Then you do not wish to end it?"

He shook his head. "No, but I do confess my work has not given me much, if any, time to think of you in your absence. Every night I fell into bed exhausted. I am aging, I fear."

"No, you are as young and virile as ever..." My voice trailed off. I no longer cared how much I'd suffered in past weeks, agonizing over whether he wanted me any longer. "All that matters is this moment."

His eyes told me all I needed to know. *Dear God, he still loves me!* I sparkled with excitement.

"I'm sorry, my dear, but we cannot talk here and now. I have clients coming in all day and must work late into the eve." He began to nudge me out, with a light swat on the behind.

"Alex, I'm getting divorced. Aaron Burr is handling it," I said over my shoulder as he led me down the hall, towards the back of the building.

"Would you rather I handled it?" We stood at the end of the hall, close enough to kiss, yet he didn't make a move to show any further affection.

I laughed. "Talk about conflict of interest! No, I'm fine with Aaron Burr."

He opened a door and held my arm to usher me out as I babbled, "When will you come see me? James has been with his mistress." I refused to depart until I got a promise from him for our next meeting.

"As soon as I can. Now I must get back to work." He opened the door and a chilly breeze blew stray wisps of hair into my face. "I'm sorry, Maria, but tis best you exit this door and take this back stair. I have Congressman Laurence coming any minute."

"Oh, yes. He knows me." Another acquaintance of James's and mine from his run-for-congress days.

He gave a curt nod. "You simply cannot be seen here at my place of business, with clients and congressmen to'ing and fro'ing."

"Will you come by this eve?" I needled him, desperate for a 'yes' even if it was a lie.

"Mayhap tomorrow eve. But I'm not promising anything."

"Alex, tell me you still love me," I further badgered him, knowing how needy I sounded.

His eyes left mine and darted around, but the alley below was empty.

"Well? Tell me," I insisted.

"I still love you, Maria," he muttered, devoid of any sincerity. Not a heartfelt declaration, but it was better than nothing.

Enough to leave your wife? I bursted to ask, but here at his back door was not the place. I leant forward and planted a kiss on his lips, grabbed my skirts and climbed down the stone steps.

As I trod over the cobblestones, I realized this was why I dreamed of him leaving his wife. So we no longer needed sneak through back doors, and I could travel with him without disguise.

As I walked home, mixed feelings bumped up against each other. My heart now tripped, in tune with my elation. But the uncertainty still hung over me like a shroud. When would I see him again? With this renewed confidence, I headed to Aaron Burr's office to tell him to expedite the divorce proceedings.

Chapter Thirty-Seven

Severus

Whether by bad luck, misjudgment, or because I'd allowed my mind to wander to other things, my luck began to change. From being the ultimate predator, a silent assassin who struck like a ghost in the night, my latest foray into the dark almost resulted in disaster.

For some time, I had lusted after Caroline, daughter of Seamus Carew, butcher, and the purveyor of the finest steaks I'd ever tasted. Once a week, I visited Carew's shop, where I purchased two or three fine lean sirloins, and always passed the time with Carew and Caroline, who regularly assisted her father in the shop. As I discussed the juicy meat that Carew provided for his dinner plate, I imagined Caroline laid out before me, her own soft juicy flesh awaiting my final penetration.

Having followed the girl on a regular basis, I deduced that she visited her grandmother once a week, delivering a supply of fresh meat from the shop, sufficient to serve the old woman's weekly needs.

So, that night, I followed her to the home of her aged grandparent and lurked in wait, my excitement mounting with my anticipation. After two hours in the house, Caroline emerged and began the walk home. I'd already decided upon the perfect spot to waylay her. I duly carried out my plan, first stopping to talk to her as if meeting by chance upon the street, walking beside her a little ways, then pulling her into a darkened alley, a hand over her mouth to silence her screams.

My scarf did its work, but just as I was about to indulge my lust, a voice cried out from behind me.

"What's happening here? What're you doing to that girl?"

I jumped to my feet and whirled round. In the spoonful of light from a streetlamp, I made out the figure of a tall man, his equally tall hat identifying him as a constable. Without time for thought, I took the only available course of action. I charged at the constable, arms extended, hands splayed out before me. I shoved his broad chest, took him by surprise, bowled him over. He fell backwards and landed with a thud. His head made a sickening crack as it hit the ground.

* * *

Constable Fry lay prone for a minute. Head throbbing, he finally gathered himself and stumbled to his feet, staggering out into the street. *Oh, God, where did that horrid figure in black escape to?*

Realizing his quarry was long gone, he turned his attention to the fiend's victim. A brief examination was all it took for Fry to ascertain that he'd stumbled upon the latest murder to hit the city. Fry blew upon his whistle in a call for help, and while he waited for reinforcements, he did his best to look for clues on and around the body. He could scarce believe his luck when he saw that this time, the killer, if it was the fiend who'd been terrorizing the city for months, had made a mistake. There, forgotten in his moment of panicked flight and still tightly wrapped round the woman's neck, was a long, expensive looking white silk scarf...

Chapter Thirty-Eight

Eliza

Mrs. Reynolds has return'd home, Annie informed me in a letter delivered by a courier. *She went to your husband's office yestermorn and was turnd away, waited for him outside the treasury office, and later followd him to the City Tavern, where she tarryed outside a quarter hour and headed home. Then this noontime, she returnd to your husband's office. She did not come out. I stood on the corner, but did not see her. Fourty minutes later, Congressman Laurence arrived. I know him because he served in the War as a commissioned officer. An old frend of your husband, mayhap? Take of that what you will. After one compleat hour, I departed, with no reason to tarry further.*

Ah, yes, Congressman Laurence was a friend of Alex. But why did Maria not come out? Had she spent the remainder of the day at his office? With clients coming and going? Mayhap he'd made her climb from the window as not to be seen. At least he had some discretion left, if she hadn't.

I'm sorry, she continued. *But you payed me for this information.*

Twas kindly of her to apologize, but at least I now knew Maria hadn't lost interest in my husband, nor he in her. Unable to keep my husband from straying, I hoped Jacob Clingman would make her forget him.

Maria

Aaron Burr kept me waiting in his sitting room nearly half an hour, as I had no appointment. But it was worth the wait. He called me in and I sat across from him.

"Why the rapid change of heart, Maria?" He regarded me across his messy desktop, his dark eyes peering at me over a pair of gold wire specs. His receding hairline came to a point above two deep creases in his forehead. His dashing youthfulness had matured into an attractive magnetism. Not as handsome as Alex, he exuded a more virile sexuality. I could see why women petted him, caressed him, swooned at his feet and fought over the chance to let him conquer them. But having met him when I'd just turned fifteen, I believe he still saw me as an innocent ingénue and not conquest material. That was fine with me, for he never sparked interest in me of that sort. We were acquaintances; now he my attorney and I his client, naught more.

"Up till now, I wasn't sure I'd made the right decision in divorcing James," I divulged. "Especially when he told me he'd be happy remaining married and living our separate lives. But I decided it was for the best, as I—I may want to remarry someday." I needn't tell him who I wanted to marry.

He thumbed through a stack of papers, pulled out some documents and placed them atop his ink-stained blotter. "Then I should have everything in order by month's end. I will let you know when you are once again a free woman."

"Thank you, Aaron. I shall look forward to hearing from you." We stood. He grasped my hand but did not kiss it, and escorted me to the door.

"Any suitors requesting your hand in marriage at the moment?" His question took me by surprise as he released the door latch.

"Uh—I—" I sputtered. How much personal detail should I share with him? "One gentleman I've known a long time has been courting me." I looked into his eyes, wider now, more relaxed, framed by raised brows, displaying interest and kindness. "He's a widower, very well off, and I—" I'd said too much already. "I will have to see how things develop. I cannot make any hasty decisions."

"That is smart, Maria. He sounds like he has all the right ingredients. Especially that he's not married. An affair with a married person nearly always ends in someone being badly hurt. Trust me," he added with a knowing nod.

Did he know about Alex and me, and was this his roundabout way of telling me it would end in heartache? I wasn't sure how far word had spread at this point. But he undoubtedly spoke from experience. And I feared because he also knew Alex.

"Good day, Aaron. Please stay in touch." As he let me out the door, I came inches from bumping into a young woman coming in. "Oh, I'm sorry."

"Excuse me." We spoke at the same time.

I stepped aside as she greeted Aaron and he welcomed her with a warm embrace. "So good to see you, my dear one." He planted an affectionate kiss on her lips. She looked almost young enough to be his daughter, but I knew Theodosia was only eight or nine. This budding beauty certainly dressed fashionably and made no effort to conceal her décolletage.

"Honey, this is Mrs. Reynolds, a client of mine. Maria, I present Miss Eliza Bowen."

He certainly was pursuing younger stock as he aged. "Good day, Miss Bowen." I gave Aaron a smile and a nod. "I shall leave you to it."

"Thank you, Mrs. Reynolds," and I noticed a grateful undertone in her voice. The door closed before I turned to descend the steps.

The following morn, I sat at the breakfast table after refusing Maggie's offer of eggs again. For some reason the thought of runny eggs spreading across a plate made me want to retch.

I asked her for a biscuit and tea, knowing my stomach would not handle coffee. Relief calmed me, knowing Alex and I weren't over. My heart tripped

364

in giddy anticipation of possibly seeing him this eve. The thought of his lips ravishing mine sent delightful shivers through me, warming me to my most feminine core. Oh, how I wanted him!

I unfolded the newspaper and began to read the headlines as Maggie entered and knocked on the doorframe. "You've a visitor, Mrs. Reynolds. Tis Mrs. Hamilton. She were here t'other day as well."

Dread washed over me. Had she heard about my visit to Alex?

No, I refused to jump to conclusions. I thanked Maggie, dismissed her and entered the sitting room. Mrs. Hamilton stood at the window.

"Mrs. Hamilton, what a pleasant surprise."

"Good morn, Maria. I trust you are well." As we approached each other she reached out and we grasped hands. Twas a warm greeting for a woman facing her husband's lover.

"How did you know I was back from New York?" I asked, really wanting to know.

"Someone I know saw you yesterday and told me." Her features gave no indication of her inner feelings. Her tone betrayed no emotion.

God above, I hoped no one had seen me going to Alex's office! I let it drop right there. "Yes, I came back with Jacob." I was glad that was the truth.

Without any chitchat about my trip, my family, or how Jacob fared, she took a folded velvet cloth from her satchel and handed it to me. "I believe this is yours. I found it in my house—upstairs—at the top of the landing—outside the spare bedroom, to be exact."

I unwrapt it. Oh, no…dear heaven. I cringed, mortified, and blushed to my roots. Glittering up at me was the diamond ear bob I'd lost. It must have fallen off when I crouched behind the banister that night Mrs. Platz saw me. I considered denying it was mine. But to what purpose? I'd lied enough already—all I wanted now was to live the truth. "Thank you," was all I could say, my voice cracked and dry.

"Maria, my husband promised me he's ended his affair with you," she said.

Her words struck me like a bolt of lightning. *When was this?* I wanted to ask. It must have been after I saw him yesterday. But of course it was not my place to ask her. There was only one way to verify it—to ask Alex.

Stunned speechless, I simply stood and nodded. "I—Mr. Burr told me my divorce shouldn't take more than a few weeks," I blabbed, not knowing what else to say, hoping this would appease her.

She nodded, giving me a hint of a smile. "What about Jacob?"

Now the initial shock subsided, and I eased into the conversation. "He followed me to New York and proposed to me again. He gave me a beautiful ring."

She glanced at my ring finger and raised her brows. "Why are you not wearing it?"

"Oh, I—" I held up my ringless hands, having taken off my wedding band the day James and I decided to divorce. "I care not to wear it outside. Tis rather valuable, and I fear being robbed of it."

She fiddled with her gold wedding band and I surmised she'd want to be buried in it. "Listen to me, Maria. Jacob truly loves you."

"But I'm not sure I love him—enough to marry him. Not yet anyway." And that was the truth.

"Take this advice, my dear." She lowered her voice as if someone were eavesdropping. "When you find a man as good as him, never let him go."

"What do you mean by good?" I needed her to clarify that. "Because he is wealthy?"

She shook her head and took a step closer to me. For the first time I noticed her gray hairline. Lines creased her forehead and the corners of her eyes. She looked older than Alex, although they were the same age. "No, not just that. He is devoted to you. He will not leave you alone for nights on end, claiming work or—some other excuse to get away. He will not hide things from you or lock his study door or his drawers. He won't even look at another woman once you exchange your vows. He will make a most faithful husband. And a loyal family man, should you wish to have children."

Her mention of children struck a chord with me. "Yes, through my marriage to James, we took precautions to prevent it—our nomadic and economically volatile life together hadn't been favorable for raising children," I admitted. He wore lamb bladder condoms which we'd made part of our loveplay, tying the ribbon round the base of his member. But she needn't know all that.

Alex simply withdrew before climaxing. And she certainly needn't know *that*.

"I would like to have children. Mayhap, someday in the future, with some future husband..." I trailed off with a sigh.

"Then do not reject Jacob because at this moment you do not believe you love him enough to marry him. You're a fool to let him slip away. In the name of all the saints, young lady, you can learn to love him." She spoke with what almost sounded like envy.

I appreciated her advice, for if what she'd told me about Alex was true, I'd lost him forever. And knowing someone else loved me that much helped to ease my brokenhearted despair—but a little.

"Thank you, Mrs. Hamilton. You are a kind, forgiving woman."

"Tis easier than being a vindictive shrew, my dear. And God above knows, I carry enough burdens, I have no strength to carry grudges. I shall see myself out." She held up a hand. "Goodbye, Maria."

Had she said this goodbye for herself and for Alex? I wondered as she swept out the door.

Alex did not come to me that eve or the eve after that. Mrs. Hamilton must have told me the truth—he'd chosen her over me, and renewed his vow to forsake all others.

I still licked my wounds over her words about Alex promising to end our affair. I dragged myself around as if I'd been whipped, knocked to the ground and kicked whilst down. I could not see him promising anyone anything, but the proof was plain enough to see—he was not here.

Mayhap he still believed I was planning to marry Jacob! Our reunion at his office had been so brief, I hadn't the chance to convince him that Jacob's proposal in the parlour had been an act—I loved only him, and not Jacob. I needed to set things straight and change his mind. I could not let a silly misunderstanding ruin both our lives forever.

I sat down and penned a letter so quickly I could barely read my own writing. I forced myself to calm down and write another.

I am not marrying anyone but the only man I will ever love—you, my dear Alex. If my dear freend has the Least Esteeme for the unhappy Maria whos greatest fault is Loveing him he will come as soon as he shall get this...P.S. If you cannot come this Evening to stay just come only for one moment as I shal be Lone.

I had Maggie deliver it to his law office.

But another day and night passed, with no reply. I dragged a chair to the window and sat reading, one eye on the street, awaiting the mail carriage. I dashed out to greet the postman, ransacked our post—nothing from him. I collapsed on the doorstep and moaned in despair.

My only contact with the world outside was the newspaper, and on Wednsday, the election results appeared with surprising news—Aaron Burr had defeated Philip Schuyler to take over his Senate seat.

Philip Schuyler was Mrs. Hamilton's father. I knew the Schuylers could not be happy about this. And I was sure Alex seethed with fury.

I finally forced myself to accept the reality: Mrs. Hamilton had not been lying. I would never hear from Alex nor see him again. It was over. All I had left were memories—and his letters to me. I unfolded and read them, over and over, till I'd memorized near every word, kissed them, pressed them to my breast, as they'd come from his heart to mine. The pain of seeing him at gatherings or passing on the street would be too much to bear. I knew I must leave here, and return to my true home, New York.

Just then the post fell through the door slot. I nearly broke my neck getting there, with the last shred of hope for a letter from him. I threw each letter to the floor, my heart in my throat, as my despair further tortured me. The last letter bore a return address I recognized. It was from Jacob.

I walked back to the sofa, sliced it open with a knife and unfolded it. I could not finish reading it for my eyes blurred with tears.

Maria, I love you more than words can convey. Please forget the men who have hurt you and let me show you what a true loving husband can give you. Plus the most delicious Italian meal you have never seen, by a Tuscan chef I imported only for us. I promise I will not attempt to kiss you after consuming all the garlic he plans to add to our meal. Naught but the Stinky Rose, garlic, will keep us apart! Shall we meet this eve?

All my love, Jacob

"Oh, Jacob," I said out loud as I wiped away tears. "How could any woman be fool enough not to love you?"

Chapter Thirty-Nine

Severus

I lounged in my small but comfortable sitting room, the embers of a log fire dying in the grate. The room grew chilled, but so preoccupied was I by the recent turn of events, I didn't bother to rekindle the flame. My head swirled with thoughts of what lay ahead. Had the constable seen enough of my face to identify me if brought to a confrontation? How could I have been so lax, so careless? My planning had let me down, and I considered myself at fault, as thoughts of dear Mrs. Hamilton and her unhappiness overcame me.

The question that now burned in my mind was a simple one: stay or go, the only two options left open. I wallowed in a quandary of my own making, fired by circumstances and feelings previously alien to my mind.

Much to my personal chagrin, I actually cared for another human being. Elizabeth Hamilton had found a tiny niche somewhere in my mind, or in my soul, and I was perplexed by the revelation. Yes, she was all I'd lacked in terms of a mother, though I did not see her as a mother figure. Goodness, no! So for what reason had I allowed my thoughts and mission in life to become so distracted that I now again faced the possibility of capture? As hard as I put my mind to delivering a solution, I failed to arrive at a satisfactory conclusion.

I had to weigh up the risks if I decided to stay, to hope the constable had not seen my face well enough in that brief encounter in the alley... but... the scarf! If made public knowledge, the presence of my scarf, so foolishly left behind in my haste to escape, might lead to someone associating such an item with none other than myself. I felt confident enough to bluff my way out of such an eventuality, for didn't many folk wear such a scarf? I could easily purchase a new one, and deny the one round the girl's neck was mine, but it still constituted a large and potentially unnecessary risk.

Although too soon to have made the newspapers, I picked up the latest offering from the press, delivered that morning and lying where I'd dropped it on the dining table.

The headline that screamed from the front page shocked me to the core. My body stiffened, rigid, as if shot point blank. FAMOUS FRENCH DETECTIVE TO ASSIST IN SEARCH FOR KILLER.

The city fathers, through the commissioner, had invited that damned fool Le Clerc to visit in hopes he could bring his expertise to bear in their hunt for the killer. The article went on to report that Le Clerc had accepted their invitation and was now en route to America on board a fast sailing vessel, the *Marie Claire* that had sailed some three days ago from Cherbourg, France. If Le Clerc saw me, or heard my name mentioned in the course of his inquiries—and the constable from the alley gave the Frenchie even the barest description of the man he'd glimpsed in the alley—and if he'd seen and then mentioned my most defining feature, my eyes, then the game would be up. The bloodhounds would be on me in no time.

The realization dawned upon me. Clenching my tongue between my teeth, I alternately raged and shook. The decision regarding my future had been snatched away from me. I had but one remaining option.

Chapter Forty

Eliza

Alex came home, pale as death.

"What's wrong?" I rushed up to him and grasped his sleeves.

"Aaron Burr defeated your father in the senate election." His voice dragged as if the loss were his own.

I felt as if I'd been shot in the gut. "Aaron Burr pushed my father out of his beloved senate seat?" Father had been the very first senator from New York, and now this upstart defeated him. "Dear God, Father must be crushed." John wailed at the top of his lungs in his cradle. Philip yelled down the stairs, "Make him hush, I need to study!"

"Please rock the baby, Alex. I must write to Father immediately." I bolted to the writing desk.

"Where are the servants?" Alex made not a move towards the cradle but remained standing in the doorway, peering down the corridor.

"I do not know. Go find one if you care not to tend to your own son." I took a deep breath and met my husband's glaring eyes. "I regret snapping like that, but naught seems to be going right lately. Two of the little ones have raging fevers and my father just lost his seat to a man he despises." I didn't add *and my husband still cavorts with his lover.*

"I'm thrice as crushed as your father is," Alex argued back, finally approaching the cradle and rocking it with his foot as the baby continued to wail. "Burr is for or against nothing, but as it suits his interest or ambition." He added in a louder voice, over the baby's cries, "I feel it a religious duty to oppose his career!"

I flattened my palms to my ears. "Oh, Alex, please! Go romp with your mistress and leave me to console my father and my children!" I then pressed too hard on the paper and broke the quill tip. "Damn it!"

"What did you say?"

"Go tell Maria Reynolds how much you loathe Aaron Burr. I only hope he finds time to file her divorce before he kicks my father out of his senate seat." I dipped a new quill into the inkwell. Shutting out my squalling baby and my wayward husband, I began a heartfelt letter to my father, promising I'd go to him soon as the roads cleared.

The room now quiet, I glanced over my shoulder. The baby slept peacefully and Alex was gone.

Breathing a sigh of relief and exasperation, I returned to my writing.

However, peace was not to be my companion, as a knocking on the front door caused me to rise and answer the incessant tap, tap, tap. Standing on my front step was none other than Dr. Black, looking severely disheveled and distressed. He clearly had not shaved, and his clothes looked like he'd slept in them.

"Severus!" I stepped back. "Are you well? You look...well...not yourself."

I almost pulled him across the threshold before he could reply, but instead of following me us usual into the parlour, he stood stock still, as if some barrier stood before him, making it impossible for him to pass.

"Elizabeth, my friend," he said at last, his voice breaking.

"Yes, Severus? Please, tell me what ails you."

At that moment he looked at me. Those sharp cobalt blue eyes appeared as dead pools. Gone was their enigmatic spark.

The fire that burned them, within his very soul mayhap, appeared extinguished, whether temporarily or permanently I couldn't guess.

"I am so very sorry to appear unannounced in this way," he croaked, "but due to certain...shall we say...circumstances of an extreme personal nature, I find I must leave town for awhile."

"I see." Though in truth I did not see at all. "And what, pray, are these circumstances, that they take you away from your friends and those who have come to know and respect you?"

"I must keep close counsel on some things. I called here in the hope that you would at least show me a friendly face before I take my leave. It has been such a pleasure and a privilege to have made your acquaintance, to have counted you as a friend and as a much favored patient."

Now he really worried me. These were not the words of someone planning a short stay away from home. I instinctively felt that Severus in his own way and for whatever reasons, was saying a long-winded and extremely convoluted goodbye. I took hold of both his hands in mine. They felt like blocks of ice. Trying to warm them with my body heat, I shivered.

"Severus, I am not so stupid as to believe you will return soon, and will not pry into the privacy of your leaving, but I too have been privileged, for you have at all times shown me not only the very best professional care, but you quickly became a dear friend to both me and my husband."

"Ah, yes, the good Alex." He almost smiled with shaky lips. "I am so sorry for the way life has treated you and your marriage, and wish I could have helped you in some small way."

"You have always helped me." Tears wetted the corners of my eyes.

He reached out and with the back of one finger, dabbed the tears away, then just as quickly withdrew his hand.

"Severus…I…" but before I could say more, he turned on his heel, walked briskly to the door and opened it. Turning back to look at me once again, he said, "I shall always remember you, to my dying day." He shut the door behind him, leaving me standing there.

Maria

I sent Maggie to Jacob's house with my acceptance of to-night's meal, complete with Stinky Rose. With the newspaper spread before me, I read the senate election results over and over. Aaron Burr had soundly defeated Philip Schuyler, New York's first senator. I knew this was Aaron's first step towards the presidency. I was happy for Aaron, for I did like him personally—I just did not agree with the Democratic-Republicans' beliefs. Truth be told, if I'd been allowed to vote, I'd have voted for Mr. Schuyler. But the state's governing body elected our senators, not the people.

My thoughts centered on Alex, and I longed for him more than ever. How I missed our political discussions. I knew he was consoling his wife right now. The Schuylers were a close-knit family, and even though they belonged to different parties, Alex idolized his father-in-law.

I closed the newspaper, deciding what to wear this eve. Anticipating a lively discussion about our nation's future, I wondered what Jacob thought of these election results. Eager to see him, I now asked myself more seriously than ever if I loved him. My answer:

yes. I even loved him enough to become Mrs. Clingman.

A sharp pain in my middle stabbed me like a knife. Dizzy, I doubled over and grabbed the chair back. It passed after a moment, but a wave of nausea overtook me. I staggered to the sofa and lay down.

Clutching my middle, I tried to reach the bottle of Madeira on the table but could not. I had not the energy to lift myself up. At that moment, a knock sounded at the back door. Only servants and deliveries came in that way. *Sod it*, I thought. I hadn't the energy to answer that, either. Let them leave the delivery on the doorstep. But the knocking persisted. I finally rose and stumbled to the door, expecting a delivery of dry goods, or Maggie...

I yanked the door open and gasped at the sight before me. "Alex!" I blinked, not believing my eyes.

"You look awful, Maria. Have you been ill?" He stepped in and I drowned in his violet gaze.

"Not any more. Oh, Alex, I missed you so much." My hand still clutching my middle, I wrapt my free arm round his shoulders and drew him to me. "I never thought I would see you again!"

"I told you I'd be here when I could. My, you must sit. You do look ill." He removed his hat and smoothed down his hair.

"But your wife told me." I led him into the sitting room. "You'd promised her to never see me again." I held my breath awaiting his answer, as a criminal about to hang waits for the trap to fall.

"I never said that."

I nearly fell over. "So she did lie!"

He swept his eyes across the room as trial lawyers do whilst performing. "She did ask me to promise to end our affair. But not to never *see* you again. There is a difference—a rather big difference."

Tears of joy sprang to my eyes. Thank God he was a lawyer and took every definition literally. "But we do not need to end anything. My divorce is nearly final. I shall be free afore long. If Aaron Burr is true to his word, that is. Now that he's a politician, I know not how honest he is."

His lips spread in a sneer. "Burr is a lawyer first, and a wily one at that. You'll have your divorce. But you do look ill."

I wished he would stop bringing that up. Oh, if only he'd arrived twenty minutes hence; I would have been draped in finery, bathed and perfumed and combed and rouged, on my way out to see Jacob. Instead he saw me like this, in an old linen frock, sleeves rolled up, my hair pinned up in a mess, my face pale. "I'm fine. Just something I ate." I guided him to the sofa and we sat.

I clung to him. "Alex, I am about to be free. I need to know—do you now plan to free yourself as well? Tis our fate to spend the rest of our lives together, surely you know that." I stroked his hair, twirled his queue twixt my fingers, my arousal increasing with every breath. "I do not want to sneak around like this, in and out of back doors."

As he looked away, an invisible barrier rose twixt us. "I cannot do that, Maria. My reputation has suffered enough. I cannot add a divorce to my list of offenses."

"Divorcing a wife you don't love for a woman you do love, an offense? Jefferson's reputation hasn't suffered," I reminded him of his rival's fate.

He looked back at me, tilting his head. "He never divorced. His wife died."

"But he fathered all those children with Sally Hemings," I persisted.

"He never divorced," he repeated, louder this time.

I had no more argument in me. He would never leave his wife, and I had to accept that. "But we will still see each other, of course," I stated. I would not give him the chance to say no.

"I told you, I didn't promise her I would never *see* you again. Only that I would…" His eyes raked over me with naked longing. "Oh, God, Maria…" His lips claimed mine. We wound our arms round each other as our kiss intensified. Raw desire filled me as my hands wandered down his body. As I was about to fondle his surging manhood, a sudden wave of sickness overtook me. I pulled away and held my head in my hands, willing it to pass.

"What is wrong?" He clutched my shoulders. "You are ill, aren't you?"

"No, I'm…yes, I've been ill since I returned from New York. I know not what it is, some horrible disease…" I doubled over again.

He pushed my hair from my forehead, rocking me gently. "What are your symptoms?"

I swallowed to force the rising sickness down. "I've been retching in the mornings, my stomach has been cramping, I have nausea—"

"Maria, I've heard all this before," he said.

"What?" I looked up at him.

"This is no horrible disease. You are going to have a baby."

Chapter Forty-One

Eliza

"Mrs. Bates to see you, Mrs. Hamilton." Our servant Maura stood in the parlour doorway.

"Thank you, please see her in." I put my pen down and greeted Annie. "I can ring for a drink. Tea? Wine? Brandy?" I hadn't even thought to offer anything to eat. My mind still reeled from those disastrous election results.

"Nay, I'm only popping in for a moment." She slipt her shawl off. "Your husband went to the Reynolds residence. I daresay he is still there. If you care to go there and confront him—"

"No." I cut her off. "I am beyond confronting. I am nearly beyond caring at this point. You needn't follow either of them any longer, Annie. I know what is going on and tis not going to end."

"Is there aught else I can do, Elizabeth?" Concern softening her tone, she took a step closer.

I rubbed my ink-stained hands together. "Yes, Annie. Be my friend. Please. Just be my friend."

Severus

Knowing the great French detective Le Clerc would soon apply his bloodhound-like skills to the case, I made haste with my departure. Citing a need to visit an ailing private patient who required a permanent physician, I left a letter of notice at my landlord's office, with two months' rent in lieu of such notice. I had few personal possessions, and packed only necessities into a portmanteau. I brought this to my friend Silas Brunt, the chemist who'd supplied me with medicines and medical equipment during my stay in the city.

"Why the hurry to depart, Severus?" He help me push the portmanteau down his hallway.

"I need to leave for personal reasons...I'll tell you about it another time." The portmanteau now settled in the nook under his stairs, I stood upright and brushed my hands together. "Oh, one more thing..." I hastened back to the door and retrieved my medical bag. "If you can mind this while I go make travel arrangements and bid farewell to some acquaintances, I'll be much obliged."

I offered Silas a hearty handshake with a promise that I'd return the following morn.

"I've no doubt you intend to spend the night in the bed of some lady friend, indulging in some innocent lust before taking your unfortunate leave of her and your practice," he surmised with a chuckle, as we regularly shared jests and traded suggestive innuendos.

"You know me too well, old chap." I chuckled right along with him.

I navigated the tree-lined streets that led me close to the home of my last real friend on earth, or so I hoped—Mrs. Hamilton. Darkness hung like a pall over the city, perfectly matching my mood. As my footsteps echoed in the empty darkness, the air felt heavy, almost as though mother nature sensed what was about to transpire and held her breath. The moon played hide and seek with the earth as thick cumulus clouds scudded across its face, cutting off its baleful glow, then illuminating all once again as whatever drove them across the sky swept them away. A faint mist appeared out of nowhere, rose directly from the ground beneath my feet, and muffled my footsteps.

I drew my new white silk scarf closer round my neck, seeking extra warmth from the increasing chill of the night air. I encountered not another living soul as I stalked the darkened streets...until...

Less than a block from the Hamilton residence, I spotted a lone female figure hurrying almost recklessly around a corner, mere yards ahead of me. I licked my lips. My mouth watered.

Perfect.

I fell back against the cushion, stunned. "No, how—how—how can that be, Alex? We—were so careful."

"We were," he assured me. "If you refer to you and myself. How careful have you been with James?"

"James and I only—" My mind raced back to the last few times we'd coupled. He hadn't had his condoms on hand. We took our chances. I tried to remember my most recent monthly course. I could not. "I could be two months along already. Two months ago, when we made love so intensely, you forgot to—you did not—" I flushed, too embarrassed to say it—he'd spilt his seed inside of me.

Now he looked as dumbfounded as I. He sat still, his eyes fixed on mine, at a loss for words for the first time since I'd met him.

I licked my dry lips. "It—it could also be James's."

He heaved a deep breath. His shoulders rose and fell in what looked like relief. "Then will you raise the child as your husband's and give it his name?"

"Of course, I must. As long as I have any doubt as to the paternity, I will not hold you accountable in any way. It would be terribly unfair to you." I already knew our liaison had ruined his chance for the presidency. His fathering an illegitimate child would destroy him.

The wave of nausea passed. My appetite even returned, my stomach growling with hunger.

"Thank you, Maria. If you come upon hard times, I shall contribute anything I can to the child's up-bringing, education—I only beg that you do not give him—or her the name of Hamilton."

"You needn't beg." I touched my fingertips to his face. A shadow of stubble dusted his chin. "You needn't even ask."

"Now I believe I'd best leave you alone to get some rest."

I nodded my thanks but could say nothing. He stood, but made no move to leave.

I glanced at the clock. It was going on six, and Jacob expected me at seven. "I cannot rest yet. Jacob is waiting for me."

"Oh, yes. Jacob." He nodded and broke his gaze.

"'Tis not like that. Please, Alex, I never loved any-one the way I love you. The marriage proposal in your parlour was a ruse, please believe me." I reached up and grasped his hands. He clasped my fingers in turn. But he made no move to embrace me. "You must believe me!"

"I do believe you, Maria. But we met too late, when fate had set our paths, and we could not undo what fate had already done. Had that been you instead of Elizabeth Schuyler at that soirée at her aunt's house in Morristown, you would be Mrs. Hamilton right now."

"I know." Oh, fate could be so cruel! "What year was that anyway?"

"Oh, it had to be…" He squeezed his eyes shut as he counted back the years. "Seventy-nine mayhap?"

I shook my head. "Then it could never have been. You would not have wanted to court a miss of but twelve years old."

He widened his eyes and blinked. "God above, I hadn't realized you were that young."

"Well, I was," I confessed. "I do not feel so young anymore."

"You have your whole life ahead of you, Maria. I am middle-aged. When my term at the treasury department ends, I shall move back to New York, resume my law practice and hope to enjoy my golden years hearing cases, gardening, seeing my children grow up—" He halted when he realized what he'd said.

"That's all right, Alex, because I was planning to move back to New York also. Not to follow you there. But because there is no longer anything for me here." I felt queasy again but did not tell him. "I must get ready for Jacob."

"Of course." Then he asked me the same question I'd asked him numerous times: "When will I see you again?"

Now it was my turn to say, "I do not know."

* * *

I could not disappoint Jacob and refuse this sumptuous feast because I felt ill. His Tuscan chef had created a fabulous meal consisting of what he called '*in-salata belissima*,' Italian' bread, veal Florentine with the Stinky Rose—garlic—and ricotta sauce, risotto with pureed strawberries, and macaroni pudding for dessert. I ate as much as I could, which was not much.

We sat in his parlour afterwards, dipping spoons into the rich pudding that shamed our ordinary fruit ice. Somehow the dessert—or mayhap it was the garlic—calmed my roiling stomach.

When we finished, he settled next to me on the settee, our thighs touching. *Tis now or never,* I mentally gave myself a shove. "Jacob, I need tell you a few things." Still searching for the precise way to phrase this, I moved silent lips, prompting him to tilt my chin upwards with his other hand.

"What do you want to tell me? Is it good or bad? Then mayhap we can work through it together."

"Tis all good," I assured him. "I think so anyway," I had to qualify it. "Jacob, I'm—I believe I am ready to accept your marriage proposal."

Before I took another breath, his arms clasped me, his legs pumping in excitement. "Oh, Maria, how I've longed to hear those words! My love, we will—"

"Rein in your spur, I have more," I announced.

He leant back, his hands now cupping my cheeks. "Carry on, my love."

"I will be brutally honest. I made the decision to marry you but two hours afore arriving here." I fidgeted with the lace around my sleeve. "Then, within minutes after I made that decision, I realized that I'm—I'm going to have a baby. And I cannot tell you with absolute certainty if James is the father."

His gaze fell like a rock from a cliff as he gave me a knowing nod. "I take it Hamilton will not leave his wife over this."

"No. And he will not let me give the child his name. I do not want to halt my divorce from James. I—" I took a deep breath and rubbed my sweating palms on my satin skirt. The nausea began to rise. I swallowed to force it down. "I do really want to be with you. But—will you still have me now, knowing this?"

He stroked tendrils from my moist forehead. "Maria, I said I loved you, and I meant it. Unconditionally. I will be happy to raise the child as mine. And he or she will be happy growing up with his or her half-brothers and sisters, as I hope we will have many more."

"Thank you, Jacob." My voice broke with relief. "You are a candidate for the sainthood."

"Ah, wait till you relish my boudoir performances, my dear. I hardly conduct myself as a saint twixt the sheets." As he brandished a rakish grin and cocked a brow, he ceased to resemble the same proper Jacob I'd known all these years.

I instantly felt well. "Do you care to give me a sneak preview?"

He reclined and focused a sultry gaze upon me. "Nay, I do not. I wish to wait until we are lawfully wedded and in our marriage bed."

"My goodness, Jacob, you are far ahead of your time." I gave him a saucy smile.

He leant forward and kissed me. My arms wound round his neck as our lips met, warmly and comfortably. *Learning to love Jacob is easier than I ever thought possible*, I silently affirmed to the long-suffering Mrs. Hamilton.

Severus

The young woman narrowly avoided colliding with me as I appeared like a phantom in the night and blocked her path. "Oh...sorry, sir..." She sidestepped out of the way. I shot out a hand and laid it ever so gently on her shoulder.

"Careful, my dear, do not tread so quickly upon these uneven streets. And what brings you out alone at such a late hour? Don't you know how dangerous it is? Especially these days? You're lucky you haven't been accosted...or worse...as yet," I warned her in a chilling tone.

"I was hurrying to my employer's home. I just enjoyed my half day off by visiting my parents." She straightened her cap as the moonglow illuminated her smile. "I'm so relieved, sir!"

We resumed walking. "Are you indeed? And why is that?" I inquired, excitement building within me, from my watering mouth down to my burning loins.

"I thought at first you might be that fiend we've read about in the papers, going about at night, killing young women." She covered her lips with her hand and tittered.

The mention of the word "fiend" helped to accentuate my rage. I now sought only an ending, a release of the fire that burned a column down my body—and within my soul.

"And what makes you think this killer is a fiend?" I quizzed her.

She waved her hands about. "Oh, sir, surely you must agree, for no normal man could surely perpetrate such atrocities, and, well…I've heard things, you see."

"What things, girl?" My voice gathered volume as my rage mounted. "What have you heard? And from whom?"

"Well, sir, the papers say the monster kills the women first and then he…he…well, he does *things* to them." Her voice weakened as she glanced about, as if expecting this "monster" to leap out from behind a tree and slaughter us both.

As I sensed her fear, a cruel grin spread my lips, baring my teeth. "Come now, you speak riddles. To what *things* do you refer?"

"Rumor has it, sir, that the madman violates them, after throttling the life from them, not before. He's a morbid ghoul." She shuddered.

I ignored that hyperbole. We walked a few more steps and she halted before a Tudor-style house. "Thank you for seeing me safely home, Dr. Black."

"You know me?" I turned and faced her, standing toe to toe, blocking her way to the entrance.

"Oh yes, sir. I've seen you visiting the house, and Mrs. Parr, the Hamiltons' cook, told me what a good friend you are to Mrs. Hamilton. I'm a personal maid to Prudence Fisher, a near neighbor of the Hamiltons. Mary Ann's my name."

Those few words were sufficient to seal the girl's fate. No one could know that I prowled these neighborhood streets late at night. "Come, I'll see you safely inside." I cupped her elbow. As we crossed the gravel driveway, the street lamps' glow faded. The staff entrance lay at the end of a narrow passage that ran along one windowless side of the house. She led the way towards the door...and with my rage fully fuelled, I struck.

I threw the scarf round her neck, pulling the ends tight. She began to choke and gag, kicking backwards at my legs. Prepared for such a move, I easily avoided her efforts. Within seconds, she slumped in my arms. I lowered her, almost reverently, to the ground.

Now the time had come for me to crown my stay in the Colonies with my most sensational 'love affair' to date. Quickly checking for any sign of another soul, I yanked her skirts up around her waist. Removing her undergarments, I took a few rapid breaths, pondering my special predilection. I then removed a long slim knife from a pocket sewn into the inner lining of my jacket. I set to work with a manic vengeance, slicing and hacking until all that remained was a bloody pulp of flesh. My knife glinted in a sudden shaft of moonlight as I cut away the bodice. I took a moment to savor the silent, unmoving breasts, before once again succumbing to the red mist of rage controlling me. I used a slicing motion until, sated with my efforts, I placed the dead girl's severed breasts down on the cold ground, one on either side of her head.

As quickly as the frenzied attack had begun, it ended. I rose to my full height and surveyed my latest handiwork. A bystander, had there been one, might have been surprised to witness tears falling from my eyes. An unbearable grief crushed me as my mind cognized this sadness and tragedy. Dabbing at my eyes with my still-pristine scarf, I fell to my knees and, muttering a prayer, gently placed a kiss on the forehead of poor innocent Mary Ann. She hadn't deserved this.

With time slipping away, I needed to depart the scene of my final statement to the local constabulary and the soon-to-arrive Detective Le Clerc. Looking down, I noticed a dark red spatter of the girl's blood on my attire. My previous killings had not resulted in such blood loss, having been restricted to strangulation, but this time I'd allowed my rage free rein. Under normal circumstances, escape might prove problematical. Not so now. I shucked off my coat, turned it inside out, placed the knife within its specially crafted pocket, and flipped my scarf round my neck. Keeping to the shadows, encountering nary a soul, I approached Silas Brunt's home. The chemist was already abed, so Brunt's manservant admitted me and readily accepted my explanation: "Oh, that...I attended a premature birthing emergency, hence the blood..." I made light brushing motions across my front.

When the servant retired for the night, I penned a note of thanks to Silas, changed into clean clothes from my waiting portmanteau, and crept out. I deposited my bloody clothes, bagged and weighted, in the inky Schuylkill River, knowing the minimal chances of them ever being discovered.

* * *

Nobody would have recognized the bearded man in priest's garb who, later the following morning, boarded a ship bound for Brazil, where missionaries such as 'Father Michael O'Brien' complete with convincing Irish brogue, were much in demand. To all intents and purposes, Dr. Severus Black simply faded away, leaving nothing but questions behind his sudden disappearance.

Maria

May 10th, 10 of clock

"This arrived by courier, Mrs. Reynolds." Maggie placed a letter next to my breakfast plate.

"Who is it from?" Jacob sat across from me, his fingers laced round a coffee cup.

"From Aaron Burr. He told me he would give me a few days' notice before the divorce is final." I sliced the letter open with my paring knife. "To give us time to finalize our wedding plans."

"I wish you would let me see the dress," he pleaded once again, so many times now I'd lost count.

"No and that is final. Tis bad luck for you to see the dress afore the ceremony and we need none of that." I unfolded Aaron's letter and read what I'd expected. "One of his clerks will deliver the final decree on Tuesday." I met Jacob's adoring gaze. "So we may be married on Wednesday."

"Why wait?" He placed his cup down, stood and rounded the table to lean over behind me. "Let us be married immediately you receive the papers." He began massaging my tense neck muscles.

"Jacob, that is so hasty!" My eyes slid shut as the knots in my neck loosened.

"And ever so romantic." He kissed my ear. "Will you indulge me?"

"Yes, darling." I relaxed under his soothing touch." Before the ink is even dry, if you wish."

"Those men were simple fools to let you go, Maria." He turned my face to his and planted kisses on my lips.

"I learnt some lessons of my own, though," I admitted between kisses. "The biggest is that a marriage should only be between two. Any more than that, it gets rather crowded."

"I'll always respect that," he promised, like a vow.

"Please do."

May 15th
The expected knock at the door made me jump nonetheless. A courier handed me a letter from the office of Aaron Burr, Esquire. I managed to open it without tearing it. Jacob and I read it together.

"You are a free woman, Maria." My husband-to-be smiled down at me and our lips touched lightly. "For the next few minutes or so."

Together we walked down his long marble hallway to the strains of *Jesu, Joy of Man's Desiring* from the beautiful Bach cantata, performed by the string quartet he'd hired. We entered his drawing room and faced the minister.

After we exchanged vows and kissed for the first time as man and wife, I closed my eyes, reveling in this special moment. But I took a few seconds for a small wish—*my dear Alex and my dear James, wherever you are, I hope you are happy.*

Chapter Forty-Two

Maria

July 5, 1804, New York City

Jacob and I had come to the city to see the opera *The Poor Soldier*, which had been President Washington's favorite. He'd seen it right here, at the Park Theatre. We lingered on for a few days, although the streets reeked of rancid garbage and filth in the scorching heat. I longed for our country home and fresh air.

Jacob went to visit some friends whilst I headed for the Battery in hopes of a cool breeze. I joined the stream of clerks and commercial men hurrying down the Broad Way, brows knitted and lips pressed together. It was then I saw those violet eyes. I halted in my tracks.

So did he.

"Alex." We stared at each other for what seemed like an eternity. He finally opened his arms and embraced me, right there on the street. "Maria, how good it is to see you. How have you been?"

"Very well." I couldn't tear my gaze off him. "And you?"

The twelve years we'd been apart had aged him, as I knew they had aged me. His hair nearly all gray, he wore it shorter as in the current fashion. The lines around his eyes had deepened; a crease divided his brows. But he hadn't gained an ounce of weight. In his black jacket with bright buttons, white waistcoat, black britches and white stockings, he looked as trim and toned as the first time I laid my adoring eyes upon him.

"Getting by." He gave a one-shoulder shrug. "We located here in 'ninety-five and I resumed my law practice."

"I know." One would have to be living in another world not to know what former Treasury Secretary Alexander Hamilton was doing with his life.

Passersby bumped against us and he led me over to the curb. "Would you care to visit my home for a bit? The family are up at The Grange, our estate in Haarlem, and the house will be quiet—and cool. The sitting room gets a nice breeze this time of day."

"I would like that very much, Alex." I could not describe the emotions that hit me with the ferocity of a gale force wind as I gazed into those eyes. The shock of seeing him had knocked the wind out of me.

"I'm at number twenty-six." We continued down the Broad Way, toward the Battery where I'd been headed. I'd have passed right by his house without even knowing it.

We climbed the porch steps and entered his three-story brick townhouse. The silence of the dark hallway engulfed us. The hot noisy world vanished as he shut the door.

He slid off his jacket as he led me into a sitting room appointed with elegant French-style furnishings. A pianoforte stood against the facing wall. My feet sank into the plush rug. He gestured to a sofa covered with a rich gold embroidered cloth. Without asking he poured two glasses of wine and handed one to me.

"Madeira?" But I knew as soon as I sipped.

"Of course." He always knew that was my favorite.

"Alex, I was so very, very sorry to hear of Philip's death. I did send you a note of condolence and hope you received it." I needed to get this out of the way before we spoke of anything else.

His eyes saddened and looked away. "Thank you. Of all my sons, he was the one most like me in every way, poised to follow in my footsteps. Only when the shock wore off did I realize he could have died no other way but on the field of honor."

"But—dueling, Alex? God, it should be illegal!" I shuddered at that barbaric custom: gentlemen shooting each other at point blank range.

"It is illegal here. That is why they go to New Jersey. But twas Philip's destiny. If only he'd lived he *would* have followed in my footsteps. But it was not to be." He bowed his head and continued softly, "His birthday was eleven days after mine. We always celebrated them together. He would have been twenty-three this past January." His voice broke with emotion.

Twenty-three. The age I'd been when Alex and I began our love affair. I looked at him and for the first time, I saw those beautiful eyes fill with tears. Although my heart broke for his loss, I felt it best to stay quiet and let him speak again.

With a deep sigh and a quick swipe of his eyes, he met my gaze. "So, how is Susan?" Somehow he knew my daughter's name.

My lovely girl brought a smile to my lips. "Very well. She's visiting my sister in Poughkeepsie at present."

"I know she's eleven now," he stated. "Whom does she look like?"

I tried to halt the smile but didn't quite make it. "Me." But with her copper hair and violet eyes, I knew—Alex was Susan's father.

"Good for her." His grin came easily enough.

"I never meant to lose complete touch, Alex." I owed him this explanation. "When Jacob and I left Philadelphia, and I had the baby, our lives just—"

"Tis all right," he saved me from having to expound further.

But there was something I needed to know. "Would you like to meet Susan some time?"

Without hesitation, he said, "Yes, I would." His eyes focused on some faraway point in the distance. My surprise and dumbfoundedness gave way to unspeakable sadness.

As I expected, he moved closer. He put down his glass, took mine, wrapt his arms round me and brought my head to his shoulder.

"It feels as if not a moment passed since we last held each other like this," he whispered into my ear, his lips close enough to ravish me, yet he did not make a move to attempt a kiss.

"I know." Altho he did not look quite the same, now in my arms he felt the same.

"We are alone here, Maria. Say the word and I am yours today, tonight—for as long as you want me." His voice regained the husky rumble that always drove me wild. I even detected a trace of that Tricorn cologne. It brought back vivid memories.

We both knew our love had never died, and we had unfinished business we could continue, here and now. But I knew better than to act on it.

"How old are you, Alex?" I asked.

"Forty-nine."

"And I am thirty-eight," I stated. "Far too old to indulge in any unquenched desires."

"Is that the only reason?" He ran his fingertips over my cheek.

I lifted my head from his shoulder. "No. I am very happy with Jacob. Another liaison together would not be the wise thing to do."

"You are right. It would be downright foolish and reckless. I'm sorry I ever suggested it." He shook his head, regret dragging his voice down. "But I never stopped loving you, Maria."

"Nor I you. And always wondered what if…"

"Never mind what if," he cut me off. "We are here now. We can make the best of this fleeting moment or not."

I closed my eyes and kissed the love of my life. But this time I harbored no fantasies, clung to no dreams of a future together, of leaving spouses, of rising above scandal and ridicule. All we had was now.

When we parted an hour later, as I was to meet Jacob at Fratello's Restaurant, I considered inviting Alex to join us for dinner. But when I realized I still could not tear my gaze from him, I refrained. Sitting through an evening of chitchat about politics and music—all the while pretending—would be too painful to bear.

But oh, how I longed to see him again!

As if he'd read my mind, he asked, "When will you be back in the city?" We stood in his doorway, our hands still clasped, neither of us having the willpower to let go.

"Any time," I answered too eagerly. "I am only in Westchester."

"We can plan a day, say—early next week, I can clear my schedule." He took a breath, "And do bring Susan…" He let the suggestion trail off to float through the air.

"Not unless you are absolutely sure," I said.

"Of course I'm sure," he replied.

With a definite date to meet here next Monday at noon, I tore myself away, hurried down the steps and went to meet my husband.

Westchester, New York

July 12, 1804

I sat in the music room tuning my violin. Jacob entered and rushed up to me. "Maria, did anyone come by?" His voice and hands trembled, crushing the newspaper he held.

"No, what for?" Knowing something terrible had happened, I stood. The violin slid to the rug. "Jacob, what happened?"

He ran his hand over his face. "Maria—Hamilton is dead."

Jacob became a blur before me. I could no longer stand. He caught me as my knees gave way. I sank onto the sofa. "My Hamilton?" I blathered, unable to comprehend exactly what he'd said.

"Yes. He died yesterday."

"You—you sure it wasn't his son?" Oh, please, God...

"No, my dear. Alexander Hamilton, the former Treasury Secretary."

"Oh, God, no. How—what—what happened?" I stammered.

"He and Aaron Burr had a duel in Weehawken. Burr wasn't hurt. But his bullet hit Hamilton and lodged in his spine. He lingered in agony and expired yesterday. I heard some men talking with the tailor just now. I took a newspaper that verified it." He held the paper out hesitantly, as if afraid to hand it to me. "I'm so sorry, Maria. If you want to attend the service alone, I'll understand." When he saw I couldn't move, he placed the paper on the table and left the room.

Struck numb with shock, I could not speak, the devastation so great, I could not even sob. I shut my eyes and his vision came to me, clear as if he were sitting here, his violet eyes, his calm voice...

A duel? How could he be so insane? And with Aaron Burr? Our vice president? It didn't seem real to me. I expected Jacob to run back in and tell me it was all a big joke.

I took the paper and flung it across the room. I could not bear to face it right now, glaring up at me in print. I just wanted a few more moments to believe it couldn't be true.

July 14th

Struck numb with shock, the entire nation mourned, but New York City displayed an outpouring of unspeakable grief. Citizens wore black arm bands, stores and offices closed, forlorn church bells tolled since daybreak. The streets filled with citizens paying their respects to our great Founding Father, statesman, the man I'd never stopped loving.

As I walked to Trinity Church in the early morning mist, ships slumbered in the harbor, their flags at half mast. I arrived at the church early enough to get a seat, long before the funeral procession arrived. Inside, I would be spared the state funeral, for I couldn't bear the sound of the muffled drums, the riderless horse with Alex's empty boots and spurs reversed, pallbearers carrying his casket, the throngs of mourners jamming the streets, windows, rooftops...

The church was already half full when I entered. I slid into a back pew, wanting to blend in with the shadows, unnoticed. As I sat on the hard bench, my wadded handkerchief between my clasped hands, I remembered all the beautiful moments we'd shared. Memories I'd cherish till my final hour.

As the service dragged on, the church became sweltering. I spent at least two hours with the handkerchief pressed to my face, to ward off the smell of unwashed bodies. When I almost fainted from the heat, the service ended. I slipt out and gulped the hot sticky air, but compared to the fetid odors inside, it greatly refreshed me.

Mrs. Hamilton exited the church garbed in a black bombazine dress, de rigueur for widows. On the arm of her oldest son, she walked with her head up, bearing her grief like a brave banner.

I pushed my way through the crowd and approached her. "Mrs. Hamilton—I am so sorry."

I half expected her to slap me square in the face. In her grief, who knew what her reaction would be? But this was something I had to do.

"Maria, I knew you'd be here." She slid her arm from her son's and gestured for him and her other children to stand by. She clasped my hand and led me away from the milling crowd.

"I planned to tell you this someday, Maria, but never thought it would be this soon. You loved him in a way I never could. And he loved you—in a way he never loved me. For that short time, he was truly happy. I knew he had someone else but didn't want to admit it to myself. Finding out he had a mistress wasn't such a shock, but I was surprised it was you."

"No, you are his wife of twenty-four years and gave him six children," I quickly corrected her. "I could never have given him that."

She looked into my eyes and dabbed at tears with a lace hankie. "But you gave him what I never could. Romantic love, companionship, respite from his endless work. For that I will always be grateful, and because I knew you would be here today, I give you this." She reached into her purse and took something out. She pressed it into my palm and closed my fingers around it.

I opened my fingers to see a gold band nestled on my palm. I read the engraving around its outside. 'To my one true love, Christmas 1791.'

"It was meant for you," she said.

Confused, I asked her, "Then why did he never give it to me, if it was meant for me?"

"He found himself strapped for cash and gave it to a goldsmith, in lieu of a payment he owed him. It's made of solid gold. The goldsmith never melted it down or sold it, but kept it and later gave it to me, out of—" She paused. "Pity, I suppose. He had a kind heart."

"He owed payments to a goldsmith? Who was he?" I asked.

Her eyes met mine. "Your former husband, James."

So this gold band, meant as a symbol of Alex's and my love thirteen years ago, now came back to me, through James, and through Mrs. Hamilton, in the most undeniably ironic way. But now it was finally mine, as it was meant to be.

"Why did not James pass it off as his own and give it to me?" I whispered, but James and I both knew the reason: I was not his one true love.

I slipt it onto my finger and never took it off.

I asked my daughter Susan to have me buried in it.

My ring and I shall rest in Saint John the Evangelist Cemetery in Dutchess County. I am grateful to Mrs. Hamilton for her forgiveness, her kindness, and never interfering, for the pitifully short but happiest moments of my life, when we shared Alexander Hamilton.

The End

Epilogue

August 16, 1804

Sitting atop the hill overlooking the small settlement of Queenstown in Natal Province, South Africa, contentedly puffing on a clay pipe, the tall man turned the page in the newspaper that had taken several weeks to reach his semi-isolated corner of the world. As he read of the death of his friend Alexander Hamilton, tears stung his eyes. Oh, poor Mrs. Hamilton, a widow, now nearly destitute, with children to raise on her own.

He shut his eyes and relived the events that led him to his current home. Dr. Solomon Bruckman, general practitioner to the inhabitants of Queenstown, a largely Jewish community some fifty miles from its nearest neighbor, remembered when he'd assumed another identity. The one-time Dr. Severus Black, knowing the law would soon be on his trail once Detective Le Clerc arrived in Philadelphia, choked out a farewell to his friend Mrs. Hamilton, went back out on the streets, and carried out his final killing. In the guise of a Catholic missionary, he hustled to the harbor, finding passage on the barque *Emerald*, bound for Brazil, from where he later sailed on the clipper *Lady Marian* as ship's surgeon. He arrived in South Africa some six weeks later.

Realizing his name might yet lead to his eventual downfall, a change was in order. As a large number of Jewish immigrants arrived in Natal, Dr. Solomon Bruckman was born.

Learning the tenets and customs of the Jewish religion was easy enough and he quickly learned to affect a suitable accent. To all intents and purposes, Dr. Black ceased to exist, and Dr. Bruckman soon engaged in conversation with a group of settlers. The poverty-stricken mob flocked to him, grateful they could trust the good doctor to treat them as they began their new lives in the province.

Although news from around the world rarely reached these parts, Dr. Bruckman was able to obtain occasional copies of American and British newssheets. One day he read that the great Detective Le Clerc had returned to Paris after assisting the Philadelphia authorities in chasing down the killer of several young women. Though no arrest had been made, the authorities commended Le Clerc in succeeding to force the killer to leave town, as they sought out an un-named English-born doctor who 'may be able to help with their inquiries.' However, Le Clerc had asserted that the most recent slaying of twenty-year-old Mary Ann Fowler must have been perpetrated by a different killer due to changes in the perpetrator's methods. Sporting his practiced smug grin, he snickered in amusement. *And still they blunder like fools in the dark...*

The doctor looked up as a beautiful, almost regal looking African hawk-eagle soared high above his hilltop vantage point—another predator, flying free. The one-time Severus Black sighed in appreciation of the spectacular view as a thin column of smoke escaped his pipe in futile pursuit of the unfettered bird.

Dr. Bruckman soon became a valued and popular member of the new community. Most residents found the doctor affable and approachable, if perhaps a bit aloof, as evidenced by his piercing cobalt blue eyes—eyes that never quite matched his warm smile.

Once or twice a year, the doctor would take leave of his patients and neighbors for a week at a time, ostensibly to visit friends in Cape Town. As the years passed, no one ever associated the occasional murder of a young woman in Capetown with the popular and respected doctor from the tiny settlement over a hundred miles away. Why on earth should they?

As the sun began to set over Queenstown, the one-time Severus Black, now Solomon Bruckman, folded his newspaper and prayed for his dear friend Elizabeth, now a distant memory. He descended the hill as evening fell upon his new homeland's quaint and peaceful panorama.

Author's Note from Diana Rubino

SHARING HAMILTON contains only a few fictional characters, but more about that later. I kept as close to the historical record as it would allow.

Maria divorced James Reynolds when she found out he had a mistress. Conflicting sources exist about Maria's wedding to Jacob: Some say she married him twenty minutes after Aaron Burr sent her divorce papers, and others say she married him a half hour *before* her divorce was final.

The servant James Reynolds hired, Maggie "Maggs" McKivan, sailed from Belfast, Ireland in the spring of 1773 on *Friendship*, bound for Philadelphia. She came as an indentured servant because she exchanged seven years of her service to Patrick Bevin of Philadelphia who agreed to pay her passage. To date, that is all we know about Maggie. Her story, though, is similar to the many anonymous people who came to America to create a new life.

All the letters written in the story are authentic and are copied word for word, except the letters between Mrs. Hamilton and Annie Bates. Annie had been a spy during the Revolutionary War and lived in Philadelphia at the same time as the Hamiltons, but there is no evidence Mrs. Hamilton hired her to follow her husband about town.

Hamilton's remark "Burr is for or against nothing, but as it suits his interest or ambition. I feel it a religious duty to oppose his career" may well have been the first of many harsh remarks and affronts that resulted in the famous duel that sent Hamilton to his grave and caused Burr a lifetime of disgrace. Provoked by Burr's defeat of Hamilton's father-in-law Schuyler in the Senate election, Hamilton began making disparaging comments about Burr's character. The public feud reached its peak in 1804 with Hamilton's effort to block Burr's bid for the governorship of New York. When Hamilton subsequently hinted that Burr's relationship with his daughter was incestuous, Burr's challenge to the duel immediately followed.

In 1799, Aaron Burr and Hamilton's brother-in-law John Church faced each other with pistols Church purchased in London. Church shot off one of Burr's coat buttons. No one was hurt.

In 1801, 27-year-old lawyer George Eaker and 20-year-old Philip Hamilton dueled with the same pistols. Eaker's shot felled Philip and he died the next day.

Burr and Hamilton used the same pistols in their 1804 duel.

When John Church moved to upstate New York, he took the pistols with him. They were used by a family member in the Civil War. The Chase Manhattan Bank purchased them in 1930. They are now in the bank's vault under Wall Street.

The seventeen-year-old Eliza Bowen whom Burr greeted on his doorstep became his wife when he was 78 years old. She divorced him two years later, and he died the day she served him the papers. Her divorce lawyer was Alexander Hamilton, Jr.

Although Maria Reynolds Clingman vanished from history, her daughter Susan became the ward of Aaron Burr, as he took in and supported abandoned and orphaned children throughout his life.

Hamilton may have been working on The Reynolds Pamphlet during his affair with Maria, but he did not publish it until 1797, after Thomson Callender made "The Reynolds Affair" public. In the pamphlet, Hamilton admitted his involvement in the affair, so as not to tarnish his reputation lest anyone accuse him of fiscal corruption.

The charge against him, he said, was "a connection with one James Reynolds for purposes of improper pecuniary speculation. My real crime is an amorous connection with his wife for a considerable time...with his connivance...with the design to extort money from me."

James Reynolds, Hamilton said, was "an obscure, unimportant, and profligate man."

To show that his communications to and from Reynolds pertained to blackmail and not to speculation with treasury funds, he printed the twenty Reynolds letters, which had not been available to Callender. He added some thirty other documents: the Muhlenberg-Monroe-Venable memoranda on their 1792 investigation; his correspondence with them in 1797; his fiery exchanges with Monroe; a testimonial to the authenticity of Maria Reynolds's handwriting by a boarding-house keeper who knew her; a statement by Oliver Wolcott; and a denial by Noah Webster, of Callender's charge that his revelations had kept Webster from proposing Hamilton as Washington's successor in the presidency. He said he'd deposited all the original documents with William Bingham in Philadelphia, where any gentleman might inspect them. Bingham said that he never received the papers. All, including the Reynolds letters, have disappeared.

When the work appeared, Hamilton's friends were appalled. "What shall we say ... " Webster wrote, "of a man who has borne some of the highest civil and military employments, who could deliberately ... publish a history of his private intrigues, degrade himself in the estimation of all good men, and scandalize a family, to clear himself of charges which no man believed. ... "

Hamilton's enemies were delighted. They ignored his points of defense and continued their charges of speculation in public funds.

Thomas Jefferson observed that Hamilton's admission of adultery seemed "to have strengthened than weakened the suspicions that he was guilty of the speculations." Some people considered Maria Reynolds "an amiable and virtuous wife, seduced from the affections of her husband by artifice and intrigue." Others called her a fallen woman. Hamilton was condemned either way.

One reviewer said that Hamilton "holds himself out as trotting from one lodging in Philadelphia to another after ... a prostitute!" Another said that he had "rambled for 18 months in this scene of pollution, and squandered ... above $1,200 to conceal the intrigue from his loving spouse." Yet another declared that any man who used his own home as "the rendezvous of his whoredom, taking advantage of the absence of his wife and children to introduce a prostitute to those sacred abodes of conjugal, and filial retirement, to gratify his wicked purposes" could not boast of anything except, possibly, virility.

As the ultimate insult the Antifederalists printed a second edition of Hamilton's pamphlet, without alteration or addition, at their own expense.

Many years later James Monroe paid a nostalgic call on the widow Mrs. Hamilton.

As Allan McLane Hamilton, Alexander's grandson, told the story, Mrs. Hamilton was in her garden talking with a nephew when a servant approached her bearing a card with Monroe's name. On seeing the card, Mrs. Hamilton, "much perturbed," said in a low, angry voice, "What has that man come to see me for?"

Her nephew followed her back to the house. Monroe rose as they entered the parlour. She did not ask him to sit down. He bowed and addressed her formally in a kind of set speech he had prepared—that it was "many years since we had met, that the lapse of time has brought its softening influences, that we are both nearing the grave when past differences could be forgiven and forgotten."

She answered, "Mr. Monroe, if you have come to tell me that you repent, that you are sorry, *very* sorry, for … the slanders … you circulated against my dear husband… I understand it. But otherwise, no lapse of time, no nearness to the grave, makes any difference." Monroe bowed, turned, and left.

–from http://www.AmericanHeritage.com/

Elizabeth Hamilton died on November 9, 1854 at the age of 98. Her daughter found a locket around her neck. She opened it and saw that it contained an early love letter from Alexander. Elizabeth had stitched up the creases many times over the five and a half decades she outlived her dear husband.

Alexander Hamilton started the U.S. Treasury with nothing, and that was the closest our country has ever been to being even. – Will Rogers

Hamilton Wedding Bands

Author's Note from
Brian L. Porter

When I was asked once to create a half-page section either as a preface included as something of a lead-in, to be included or it was decided to space I have known Diana for some years, having at one time been the editor of one of her earliest novels.

The creatures of Seventh Night had in fact been living with in my mind for some time and I had originally intended as a burial of my own novel, but the chance to bring this to life in print at last was simply too tempting to resist.

Although not a natural creation, it is in fact modeled upon on a real story, the celebrated killer who stalked the streets of London both during and after the Second World War. A disturbing man with a penchant for women and a need to convey a certain message to society, that he was probably a psy...

Author's Note from Brian L. Porter

When Diana asked me to create a fictional serial killer who could be included as something of a back story to her latest novel, I was delighted to agree. I have known Diana for some years, having at one time been the editor of one of her excellent novels.

The character of Severus Black had in fact been 'kicking around' in my mind for some time and I had originally intended to use him in one of my own novels, but the chance to bring him to life in Diana's latest book was simply too tempting to resist.

Although he is a fictional creation, he is in fact modeled in a part on a real necrophiliac serial killer who stalked the streets of London both during and after the Second World War. A disturbing man with little to commend him, I have tried to convey a certain 'humanity' to Severus Black's personality, a plea from the heart in some ways for a misguided and misunderstood, tortured mind and soul.

Dear reader,

We hope you enjoyed reading *Sharing Hamilton*. Please take a moment to leave a review, even if it's a short one. Your opinion is important to us.

Discover more books by Diana Rubino at https://www.nextchapter.pub/authors/diana-rubino

Discover more books by Brian L. Porter at https://www.nextchapter.pub/authors/brian-porter-mystery-author-liverpool-united-kingdom

Want to know when one of our books is free or discounted? Join the newsletter at http://eepurl.com/bqqB3H

Best regards,
Diana Rubino, Brian L. Porter and the Next Chapter Team

About Diana Rubino

Diana's passion for history and travel has taken her to every setting of her historicals and paranormals. Diana now writes biographical novels with no fictional characters. She is working on the Sassy Ladies Series, featuring strong brave women in history.

Diana owns an engineering business with her husband Chris and they make their home on Cape Cod. She's a member of Romance Writers of America, the Richard III Society, and the Aaron Burr Association. Visit Diana on her website, dianarubino.com, on Facebook at facebook.com/dianarubinoauthor, and on Twitter @DianaLRubino.

Also by Diana Rubino

The Yorkist Saga
   Thy Name is Love
   The Jewels of Warwick

The New York Saga
 From Here to Fourteenth Street
 Bootleg Broadway
 The End of Camelot
Vampire Romance
 A Bloody Good Cruise
Time Travel Romance
 Traveling Light
 For Love and Loyalty
 Dark Brew
Contemporary Romance
 Faking It
Paranormal Romance
 A Necessary End
Thrillers
 Still Crazy
 Murderous Digs (short story collection)
Cookbook
 Around the World in 80 Meals
Coming Soon
The Sassy Ladies Series
 Oney—My Escape From Slavery
 Eliza Jumel Burr, Vice Queen of America

About Brian L. Porter

Brian is the bestselling author of over twenty published works, including novels, a bestselling short story anthology, and a number of children's and poetry books. Known originally for his Jack the Ripper fictional trilogy, *A Study in Red, the Secret Journal of Jack the Ripper, Legacy of the Ripper* and *Requiem for the Ripper*, his most recent and successful works to date are his new Mersey Mystery series of books, *A Mersey Killing, All Saints, Murder on the Mersey, A Mersey Maiden,* and the newly released, *A Mersey Mariner*, with other books in the series to follow. Twelve of his books have achieved bestseller status.

His most recent success has come from his true-life books *Sasha, A Very Special Dog Tale of a Very Special Epi-Dog,* winner of The Preditors & Editors Readers Poll, Best Nonfiction Book 2016 and now an international bestseller, and *Sheba: From Hell to Happiness,* which became a UK bestseller even before its release, based on advance orders at Amazon. Both books relate to the amazing lives of two of the ten rescue dogs who share the author's life and home.

He has previously won a number of awards, including The P & E Best Author, 2010 Award, and a Best Thriller Award for *A Study in Red,* and Best Mystery Award for *Glastonbury.*

He lives in the UK with his wife and ten rescue dogs.

His website is at http://www.brianlporter.co.uk/

See his author pages at

http://www.amazon.com/Brian-L.-porter/e/B00466KITC/

And as Harry Porter at

http://www.amazon.com/Harry-Porter/e/B00O43IIF8/

Also by Brian L. Porter

The Mersey Mysteries
A Mersey Killing
All Saints, Murder on the Mersey
A Mersey Maiden
A Mersey Mariner
Last Train to Lime Street (Coming soon)
A Very Mersey Murder (Coming soon)
Thrillers
A Study in Red - The Secret Journal of Jack the Ripper
Legacy of the Ripper

Requiem for the Ripper
Pestilence
Purple Death
Behind Closed Doors
Avenue of the Dead
The Nemesis Cell
Kiss of Life

Dog Rescue
Sasha
Sheba: From Hell to Happiness

Short Story Collection
After Armageddon

Remembrance Poetry
Lest We Forget

Children's books as Harry Porter
Wolf
Alistair the Alligator, (Illustrated by Sharon Lewis)
Charlie the Caterpillar (Illustrated by Bonnie Pelton)

As Juan Pablo Jalisco
Of Aztecs and Conquistadors

Select Bibliography

Ambrose, Douglas, *The Many Faces of Alexander Hamilton*, NY University Press, 2007

Atherton, Gertrude, *The Conqueror*, Frederick A. Stokes Co., 1902

Brookhiser, Richard, *Alexander Hamilton: American*, Free Press, 1999

Desmond, Alice, *Alexander Hamilton's Wife*, Dodd, Mead & Co., New York, 1953

Hamilton, Allan McLane, *The Intimate Life of Alexander Hamilton*, 1910

Hamilton, Alexander; Jay, John; Madison, James, *The Federalist Papers*, 1788

Hamilton, John Church, *The Life of Alexander Hamilton by his Son*, D. Appleton & Co., New York, 1841

Hickey, Donald R., and Connie D. Clark, eds., *Citizen Hamilton*, Rowman & Littlefield, Lanham, MD, 2006

Kaminski, John, *The Founders on the Founders*, University of Virginia Press, 2008

Karlsen, Carol and Laurie Crumpacker, eds., *The Journal of Esther Edwards Burr, 1754-1757*, Yale University Press, New Haven, CT, 1984

Langdon, William, *Everyday Things in American Life*, Scribner's Sons, 1951

Larkin, Jack, *The Reshaping of Everyday Life*, 1790-1840, Harper and Row, New York, 1988

Loth, David, *Alexander Hamilton, Portrait of a Prodigy*, Carrick & Evans, New York, 1939

Miller, John, *Alexander Hamilton, Portrait in Paradox*, Harper & Row, New York, 1959

Mitchell, Broadus, *Heritage from Hamilton*, Columbia University Press, New York, 1957

Oliver, Frederick Scott, *Alexander Hamilton, An Essay on American Union*, Macmillan, New York, 1931

Rogow, Arnold, *A Fatal Friendship*, Farrar Straus & Giroux, New York, 1998

Rosenfeld, Richard, *American Aurora*, St. Martin's Press, 1997

Smith, Adam, *The Wealth of Nations*, 1776

Smith, Billy, *The Lower Sort*, Cornell University Press, New York, 1990

Syrett, Harold, ed., *The Papers of Alexander Hamilton*, Columbia University Press, New York, 1965

Weigley, Russell, *Philadelphia, A 300-Year History*, W.W. Norton & Co., New York, 1982

Papers:

Alberts, Robert, *The Notorious Affair of Mrs. Reynolds*

Hamilton, Alexander, *The Reynolds Pamphlet*, Philadelphia, 1797

Websites:

http://www.politbyte.com/, Home of the World's
Best political sex scandals database

http://eliza-hamilton.livejournal.com/profile

http://www.politicalgraveyard.com/

http://www.answers.com/topic/common-year-
starting-on-saturday - Put in any date and year
in history in the Gregorian or Julian calendar, and
this will tell you what day of the week it fell on.

http://nysparks.state.ny.us/sites/info.asp?siteID=27

http://www.sheilaomalley.com/archives/
005683.html

http://www.jeffersonlegacy.org/

Jacob Clingman: http://bit.ly/29VkGG7

Boston Public Library: http://bit.ly/2a6aPfx

Life of Alexander Hamilton by his Son John Church
Hamilton: http://bit.ly/29Tn6Ga

Maps:

http://www.davidrumsey.com/index.html

Internet Photos:

Photo of Hamilton and Eliza's Double Wedding Band:
http://bit.ly/29IA7Pd

Photo of Schuyler-Hamilton House, Morristown, NJ:
http://bit.ly/29H7iqg

Photo of Eliza Hamilton's Grave, Trinity Churchyard, New York City:
http://bit.ly/2aaNGv6

Photo of Alexander Hamilton's Grave, Trinity
Churchyard, New York City:
http://web.uvic.ca/~rutherfo/hamilton.html

Sharing Hamilton
ISBN: 978-4-86751-528-0 (Mass Market)

Published by
Next Chapter
1-60-20 Minami-Otsuka
170-0005 Toshima-Ku, Tokyo
+818035793528
5th July 2021

CPSIA information can be obtained
at www.ICGtesting.com
Printed in the USA
LVHW041753200721
693166LV00006B/709